A Dream of Democracy

Aftab Shirazi

Order this book online at www.trafford.com
or email orders@trafford.com

Most Trafford titles are also available at major online book retailers.

Printed in Victoria, BC, Canada.

ISBN: 978-1-4269-2182-7 (sc)

ISBN: 978-1-4269-2183-4 (dj)

Library of Congress Control Number: 2009912297

Our mission is to efficiently provide the world's finest, most comprehensive book publishing service, enabling every author to experience success. To find out how to publish your book, your way, and have it available worldwide, visit us online at www.trafford.com

Trafford rev. 01/25/2010

www.trafford.com

North America & international
toll-free: 1 888 232 4444 (USA & Canada)
phone: 250 383 6864 • fax: 812 355 4082

To my wife, without whom I am nothing.

ACKNOWLEDGEMENT

My father was a brilliant scholar and linguist. He used to sit me on his lap as he narrated the history of the world with the foibles of past leaders.

He thus awakened in me a curiosity which has forever been alive. Thank you father.

CHAPTER 1.

"May I speak to Mr. Damania please" the caller said in a very thick Middle Eastern accent.

"Who is calling?" I enquired.

My name is Haroon Bashir, I am an employee of the Iranian Embassy in Ottawa sir, and I have been asked to contact you."

"Excuse me sir, I can't imagine what the Iranian Embassy could have to say to me on a Sunday morning at 7 a.m." I replied.

"Mr. Damania, I would rather not tell you over the telephone. I would prefer to meet you for lunch and have a discussion."

"Mr. Bashir, I am a retired chartered accountant living in Canada who has never been to Iran, nor had any business connection with your country, so I would appreciate if you could give me some idea as to what we're talking about."

"Mr. Damania, please believe me, this is very urgent and you with your considerable business experience will quite understand my reluctance to speak on a public telephone line. We will of course be happy to pay your fees if you would be kind enough to join us for this luncheon meeting".

So I went for lunch with Mr. Bashir. He was a man of about sixty-five years, slightly balding, about six feet tall with a tanned complexion, a bit overweight, immaculately dressed and with a bright smile exposing even teeth. It was his eyes that bothered me. Very deep set and it appeared that they were watching me intently as if my every thought was clearly comprehended by him.

"Mr. Damania, it is a great pleasure to meet you. You have no idea how significant this meeting is. We have waited more than ten years for this day and this occasion." We had a beautiful luncheon, discussed politics in Iran and as I am keenly interested in the history of Iran, particularly as I am a Zoroastrian, I received a lot of interesting information about the history and traditions of Iran.

"So what is all this about, Mr. Bashir?" I asked him

"Mr. Damania, we have a company in Iran which is manufacturing equipment for the purification of oil. With our constant experience with oil production, we feel we are qualified to export this equipment, but there are a large number of problems of a political and economic nature that impedes exportation to Canada, so an experienced chartered accountant like you would be a great asset to this Iranian corporation. We would therefore request you to travel to Iran at our expense and meet certain Iranian businessmen. We are willing to compensate you at the rate of five thousand Canadian dollars a day for the period that you are in Iran. Of course, the compensation amount is negotiable. What do you think?"

As I am now retired, I thought the offer was quite reasonable. And of course I would also have the opportunity to travel in Iran and see the religious sites of Zoroastrianism.

"When would you like me to come to Iran with you?" I asked.

"There is one problem Mr. Damania, time" said Bashir, "Would it be possible for you to join us for a flight this Monday?"

As it was already Wednesday, I was in a bit of a quandary as to how I could have my documentation ready and everything packed in four days. But as the fees offered were so generous, I grudgingly agreed to go.

CHAPTER 2

We traveled first-class on British Airways from Toronto to Tehran via Beirut. Mr. Bashir insisted on ordering champagne and later on a single malt Scotch whiskey, which was my favorite. Fourteen hours later we arrived in Tehran. It was extremely cold and I guessed the temperature to be about 4°C. I had not realized that Iran could be so cold in late January. A limousine took us to the hotel "Bahisht", which I later learned was the Farsi word for heaven.

I was surprised to find female employees at the reception desk, their heads covered by the usual ceremonial Islamic scarf, but their eyes and faces exposed. At least two of the girls were very beautiful and spoke English with a soft lilting accent.

"Welcome to Iran, Mr. Damania," said one lovely girl to me. "I hope you will like our beautiful country and will enjoy the Zoroastrian history that you are so interested in."

I was quite surprised as to how she could possibly know that I was interested in Zoroastrian history or that I was a Zoroastrian. Mr. Bashir must have noticed my surprise because he smiled in his usual perceptive manner.

"The employees of this hotel have been made aware of your importance as our guest and of your interests, Mr. Damania. Be assured that every desire of yours will be looked after immediately."

The leery look that he gave me as he said that was a bit disturbing, but I did not ask for clarification. Mr. Bashir and an employee of the hotel took my luggage to my suite. As I was about to tip the employee, Mr. Bashir held my hand and would not allow me to pay. The baggage handler bowed and left the room without the tip. "Is it against your law or your religious principles to tip an employee?" I asked.

"No sir. It is against our faith and our rules of hospitality to allow a guest to pay for any services rendered. And I mean any services at all."

His leery expressions when he said that, once again left me a little uncomfortable, but I kept that to myself.

My suite was indeed luxurious. There was cable television in English, French, Farsi, Arabic and even German. The view from the window and the balcony was indeed breathtaking. Teheran is located partly on a mountain sloping into a valley. The top of the hill is covered in snow during the winter months but the valley is relatively warm and clear, hence scenically some of the best urban views one could hope to see are available in Teheran. The refrigerator was filled with pop bottles, juices, carbonated water, and some chocolates. Noticeably absent was alcohol, presumably because of the religious laws of an Islamic state.

Mr. Bashir had indicated to me before leaving that four executives of the corporation I was supposed to advise would meet us for dinner. As the discussions were of a very confidential nature, my suite was considered most appropriate for the meeting and discussions.

It was about noon and the long flight and excitement of the day had tired me. Our meeting was scheduled for 6 p.m. and I therefore had plenty of time for a nap. I awoke at 4 p.m., shaved, showered, got dressed and watched television in Farsi for an hour or so. Exactly at 6 p.m. the concierge informed me that five gentlemen were requesting permission to come to my suite. I advised they were welcome.

Mr. Bashir led the group to my suite and made the introductions. "Mr. Damania, this is Mr. Aftab Qureshi. He is a professor of Iranian history at the University of Teheran. I would also like to introduce you sir, to Mr. Yazdegard Malek. Mr. Malek is presently an adviser to the department of defence. He is a retired general of the Iranian army and perhaps the most decorated officer in the Iranian forces."

"Let me also introduce you sir, to Mr. Feruz Kirmani. He was the minister of revenue in Iran prior to his retirement last year."

"This Sir is Mr. Jahanbaksh Mirza, who was until last year, the minister in charge of religious affairs until he had a slight disagreement with the Iranian Cabinet and resigned."

I shook hands with all the gentlemen and invited them into my suite. "May I offer you gentlemen some refreshments? Would you like some juice or mineral water? Unfortunately I cannot offer you anything of an alcoholic nature as I believe that is forbidden in Iran."

Mr. Bashir had a twinkle in his eye and his typical, sardonic smile as he reached into his briefcase and extracted a brown paper bag with a rubber band on top. "Mr. Damania, there are exceptions to every rule, especially when we entertain honoured guests like you. For that reason we have brought you a beverage, which is now temporarily converted into a totally legitimate Islamic drink." He opened the bag, and I saw a full bottle of single malt Scotch.

"Gentlemen," I said, "I am very flattered by your graciousness and hospitality, however I do not want to offend the sensibilities of any of my guests here tonight."

Instead of responding to my statement, Mr. Bashir opened his briefcase again and extracted five crystal glasses. He placed a glass in front of each person which he filled with a healthy quantity of Scotch. From my fridge he took a bottle of soda and some ice cubes and filled the glasses. I was surprised that these Iranian Muslims, well-placed in the Iranian government, would sit and have Scotch with me. But I did not comment. I was also a bit surprised that every individual in the group could speak fluent English. Another point that was also bothering me was why a general, a minister of revenue and a minister of religious affairs would come to a meeting to discuss with me possible exportation of equipment to Canada.

We toasted each other and Mr. Bashir called the restaurant downstairs to order dinner. "We have a special Iranian dish, Mr. Damania, made of rice, meat and saffron, which I have taken the liberty of ordering. I hope you like it. Knowing that you are a Parsi and share the same blood as we do, I would be surprised if you do not like this dish. I believe in India, the Parsees call this dish pilaf, am I not right?"

'Parsees' is a term normally used for Indian Zoroastrians and I was a bit surprised that an Iranian gentleman would use that phrase to describe us. I was also flattered that he had taken pains to find out something about us.

After we had had our drinks and dinner was completed, two of our waiters cleared the dishes and served coffee before leaving my suite.

"Now to business gentlemen," Mr. Bashir said. "Let me begin this way. Mr. Damania, first I want to apologize for telling you a complete lie. We had to misrepresent the facts because If we had spoken the truth, you probably would not have come with us to Iran."

"Well Mr. Bashir, I guessed as much when you introduced these gentlemen as being involved with the Armed Forces, Ministry of Religion and Ministry of Revenue as well as a Professor of History. I would be very surprised that they would be interested in exporting machinery and equipment to Canada. However, you have retained my services, and I am already here so let us proceed."

Bashir went back to where he had left his briefcase and removed a volume and placed it before me. "Mr. Damania, it is not that we do not trust you, but the information we are about to disclose is so critical that we are placing this volume of the "Avesta" before you. May we request you take an oath in the name of "Ahura Mazda", that any thing you hear in this room will remain totally secret, both for our security and your own."

The "Avesta" is the holy book of the Zoroastrians, just as the Bible is to the Christians and "Ahura Mazda" is the Zoroastrian word for God. I was intrigued by all the secrecy, but I wanted to humor these gentlemen, so very solemnly I placed my hand on the "Avesta" and swore to "Ahura Mazda" that anything stated in the room would remain totally private. They all looked at each other and bowed to me.

"Well Mr. Damania, let us begin with a historical reference which is directly connected to why we have brought you to Iran. I am sure your knowledge of Zoroastrian history and the connection of the Parsees to Iran is far superior to mine, but there is a reason for this introduction. In the eighth century A.D. the Arabs conquered Iran. Initially they used some force to convert Zoroastrians to Islam. There were also financial incentives given to the Iranian Zoroastrians to convert to Islam. If a man died leaving several sons, only the sons who had converted to Islam would share his estate. The remaining Zoroastrian children inherited nothing. This became the law."

"Within one hundred years from the date of the Arab conquest the Arabs left Iran in the hands of the newly converted Iranian Muslims. Later, the Shi'ite form of Islam took over, so today a majority of Iranians are Shi'ite Muslims. Poets such as Omar Khayyam could not possibly perform or write their poetry under the Sunni form of Islam, which vigorously forbade any form of art depicting humans as idol worship and romantic poetry as contrary to the dictates of the Koran."

"For several decades thereafter, the newly converted Iranian Muslims were extremely brutal towards the Zoroastrians. In order to obtain employment, money and position, the Zoroastrians pretended to be Muslims. They attended the mosques, they publicly participated in Muslim prayers, but at home they remained Zoroastrians. After some decades, people did not question each other about their faith and several Zoroastrians became prominent in the Iranian government of the time. As you know, Mr. Damania, the last Zoroastrian king of Iran was Yazdegard Shehriyar. His grandson was general Ram Ahuramazd. The people and the rulers of Iran were under the impression that the general was a Muslim, but in fact he was a devout Zoroastrian and protected other Zoroastrians from Muslim fanatics. He was not only respected and loved because of his military successes and bravery, but in their hearts, the Iranians thought of him as their Emperor. For twenty years he enjoyed glory and power. Ironically it was a Zoroastrian antagonist, jealous of his power and position that reported his religious beliefs to the then Shah of Iran. The Shah was absolutely stunned that his most reputed general was not a Muslim. He gave Ram Ahuramazd two options. He could either become a Muslim immediately and keep his position and power, or keep his religion and be beheaded in the market square as a pagan."

"Ram Ahuramazd would not consider giving up his faith to save his life. Nor did he feel that remaining in Iran would be safe for him and his family. You must remember Mr. Damania that by this time a few thousand Zoroastrians had emigrated to India and had been welcomed there by the Hindus. They were well liked and respected and Ram Ahuramazd decided to emigrate to India. His Muslim friends and the remaining Zoroastrians were shocked and in despair that the direct descendent of the last Zoroastrian Shah was about to become a lowly immigrant in a foreign country."

"Ram settled in an Indian town called Surat. There were no armies to lead for a Zoroastrian in India and as he was an `Athornan' or of the priestly class, he decided to become a priest in the latter part of his life."

"Back in Iran, the oppression was so great that after Ram's departure a majority of practicing Zoroastrians emigrated to India."

"As the Zoroastrians had almost disappeared from Iran, there was no one to oppress. Also all the historical structures, the culture, the poetry and architecture were from the Zoroastrian era, hence over the years an admiration for ancient Iranian history and Zoroastrian architecture once again became prevalent. Poets and scholars such as Firdosi lauded the ancient Zoroastrian leaders and kings. Scholars and intellectuals were nostalgic about ancient Iran and once again wanted the descendents of the original Yazdegard Shahriar to rule in Iran."

"Centuries later, the Pahlavi dynasty took over in Iran, and of course you are quite aware of our recent history and the dethronement of the last Shah of Iran."

"At this stage in our history, several of our military leaders you are familiar with such as general Malek and astute politicians like Mr. Kermani, professors and intellectuals such as Mr. Qureshi and even some intellectual Muslim religious leaders like Mr. Mirza, came to the conclusion that religious intolerance, bigotry and persecution of non-Muslims was completely contrary to our culture and history. So we all came together and decided that we needed traditions to bring our country back to civilization. Unfortunately, centuries of oppressive Islamic rule left us with very few cultural options, except to connect ourselves with our ancient history and to continue in the traditions of the ancient Zoroastrian kings and leaders, who permitted freedom of worship and refused to proselytize."

"Over the last decade at least one hundred thousand army officers, important police officers, politicians and professors have joined our group. We call ourselves "The New Order." We have sworn to bring back the ancient Zoroastrian monarchy and are willing to give our lives for this cause, if necessary."

"Now let us discuss how we should resuscitate the old ideals with a traditional link? Our obvious conclusion was that the ancient Iranian monarchy must be replaced on the throne. Mr. Damania, this is not just idle chatter amongst the educated and the intelligentsia, these views were supported by Ram Ahuramazd. He was indeed a very unfortunate man. After the fanatics discovered that he was still a Zoroastrian, they attacked his family and three of his sons were brutally murdered. As far as descendants were concerned, his only heir was his grandson. So he dispatched all the female members of his family and his grandson to India. This grandson came to India with a large number of other Zoroastrians and actually, he was their leader. The story goes that the local Maharaja was approached by the Zoroastrians seeking immigration. The Maharaja allegedly wanted to inform them that his country was too crowded and could not accept newcomers, so he filled a cup with milk and presented it to the leader of the Zoroastrians thereby indicating to him that there was no place for anyone else in India. The story goes that Ram's grandson added sugar to the milk, stirred it to dissolve the sugar, thereby demonstrating to the Maharaja that Zoroastrians will mingle and become part of the Hindu community of India. The Maharaja was very impressed by this gesture and accepted the Zoroastrians. What an irony of fate that the direct descendent of the last Zoroastrian emperor then resided in India. This grandson of Ram, do you know his name Mr. Damania?"

"His name Mr. Damania was Nairyosang Dhaval and he actually proceeded to India and arrived there before his grandfather did.

"No" I said, "I know the story, but not the name of the character that you just mentioned."

"Now as you know Mr. Damania, all the things I have mentioned happened hundreds of years ago. It therefore took us almost ten years both in India and in Iran to authenticate the lineage of Nairyosang Dhaval. We had to look at the records in Surat, Mumbai, Navsari, interview literally thousands of people, including Zoroastrian religious priests, to not only check out, but to finally confirm the last existing male descendent of Nairyosang Dhaval. It was only in December of 2005 that we finally concluded our investigation. Then we had the difficult task of contacting almost each and every member of our organization, not only to inform them about what we had found, but also to obtain their consent to proceed and communicate with that direct descendent and to obtain his cooperation and his agreement to maintain absolute secrecy. Because if there is the slightest leak, his life, as well as our own lives would be in grave jeopardy."

"Are you with us up to this point, Mr. Damania? Can you guess who this direct descendent is?"

By this time I was so intrigued with Bashir's revelations, I was practically dumbfounded and did not know what to say. I did not want to be wrong when I guessed, so I told him I did not know, though I had a good inkling who he was talking about.

"My beloved Sir, you are that descendent. You are the eldest male descendent of Yazdegard Shehriyar. The last and true emperor of Iran."

Bashir and all his companions suddenly stood up. Bashir took my hand in his and reverently took it to his lips. The others suddenly knelt in front of me, their heads almost touching my feet. I was a bit embarrassed, but to be very frank, tickled pink also.

"Your Imperial Majesty, we, your humble servants and subjects bow before you. Please accept our homage and allow us once again to place you on the Peacock Throne. Bring us back the glory of the Sassanian dynasty. Most of us are Muslims, but that has nothing to do with our loyalty. We do not want you as our King because you are a Zoroastrian. We want you as our Shah as you are indeed the authentic Sassanian."

"Please gentlemen," I said, "please stand up and take your seats. Your revelations are so traumatic that I do not know how to react. Now where do we go from here?"

"Your Majesty, now relax for the night. Tomorrow we will contact you and fly you to Yezd. There you will meet with the 'Majlis' and they will acquaint you as to how we will proceed in the future."

They all stood up, bowed and quietly walked out of the room, closing the door behind them.

CHAPTER 3.

This had been such an exciting day. I was unable to sleep so I changed and lay down. To be told suddenly that you are the direct descendant of the last emperor of Iran and that you should be sitting on the Peacock Throne was not something I had expected when I came to Iran. I also suspected that perhaps the intake of Scotch may have suddenly exalted my opinion about my heredity. However, Bashir and his companions did not look like people who would expend all this precious time to play a joke on me. I therefore relaxed in bed to contemplate the day's events. Suddenly there was a knock on my door. I checked the time on the bedside clock and saw it was 1:30 a.m. Who could it be at this time? I opened the door and to my amazement saw an incredibly beautiful Iranian girl standing and smiling at me.

"Can I help you miss?" I asked.

"Mr. Damania, don't you remember me? I was the one you met at the receptionist's desk yesterday. My name is Zainab. May I come in for a minute, sir?"

"What is this all about, Zainab?" I asked.

She closed the door behind her. "I was just wondering whether you were lonely in a foreign country with a foreign language and as I speak English, I thought you might like my company."

To say that I liked her company would indeed be an understatement. She was perhaps one of the most beautiful women I had seen or met since I left Canada. My problem was that she looked about twenty eight years old and I was seventy and it was 1:30 a.m. in the morning. However, as she was already in my room I thought I'd have a little chat with this gorgeous Iranian girl. Not necessarily to ogle her but to hear her beautiful Farsi accent. At least that is what I told myself, fully realizing that I was not being honest. Also my intake of the single malt Scotch that evening was making it easier and easier for me to convince myself that my only interest in her was aesthetic

"Mr. Damania, you may not know, but I also belong to the same group of individuals who met with you this evening. It is my duty therefore to do everything in my power to make your stay not only comfortable, but enjoyable. If I could sing or dance, I would perform for you, but I'm not talented in any of those areas. So all I can offer you is my company."

I was a bit embarrassed, but not totally certain as to what she was hinting at, so I guffawed loudly. "But my dear Zainab, there are a few interesting points involving your very pleasant visit to me. This is an Islamic country and they may not appreciate your visiting me alone in my room. I am seventy years old and you look under thirty and it is 1:30 a.m. in the morning. Don't you think that will cause some problems?"

Zainab laughed and looked up at me with her gorgeous light green eyes. "Mr. Damania, custom, age, sex, are all comparative things. Sometimes a person has to overcome her or his inhibitions. And when history is in the making a girl's personal attributes are trivial. A heart can be taught to want and even desire something that may not be acceptable under other circumstances."

"That is very interesting Zainab," I said. "I am indeed flattered by your attention, but aren't you a little concerned about your visit to me at this hour of the night?"

"Mr. Damania, when I joined our organization I had one aim in mind and that was to do my utmost to re-establish the ancient monarchy of Iran. And in order to do that, my first goal is to make you comfortable and happy in this foreign land with a foreign language and to somehow make you feel that you are part of us and we are part of you."

"I am indeed very flattered Zainab," I said "but I cannot imagine a beautiful girl like you not having a boyfriend or husband. Would this not damage your relationship with him?"

"Mr. Damania, you perhaps do not understand the emotional pattern of Iranian women. You see Sir, basically we are very different from western women. Even as adults, we are owned by our fathers. They decide who we should marry. And once we are married, we are owned by our husbands. We have to obey them, satisfy them in every way. At no time in our lives are we really independent of male domination."

"Mr. Damania, let me explain to you what to me amounts to sexual arousal. It is not money, prestige, physical attributes of the man, or personal gain. I have this innate desire to become part of history and to give my body to the Shahnshah of Iran, the direct descendent of the Sassanians. That to me is far more exciting than any personal gain. . Anything that takes place between us will remain totally secret. You have my word of honor as a true Muslim and a woman of honor."

To say that I was totally enchanted would be an understatement. I carefully looked at the front of my trousers and noticed an elevation that had very little to do with my fascination, which was far stronger than my concern for any consequences of a relationship with beautiful Zainab. "Where do we go from here Zainab"? I asked.

Zainab got up from her seat and walked in my direction. She placed both her hands around my neck and looked deep into my eyes. Her hair smelled like freshly cut lilacs, the pressure of her breasts against me was perhaps one of the most intoxicating feelings I ever had. "Kiss me, my Shahnshah. Possess my flesh, anoint me with your seed. For the rest of my life I will be grateful that I became a part of you for a few minutes of my life." I was already intoxicated with her green eyes but when she placed her lips against mine and kissed me deeply and passionately, I was unable to breathe in the normal fashion.

Her breath was fresh and clean. As she kissed me, she pressed her whole body against mine. My great concern was that a certain specific portion of my body was grossly intruding with her softness. I kissed her back and as I held her against my heart I could hear the thumping of both our hearts.

She slowly moved away from me and looking still into my eyes opened the buttons at the back of her dress; then she slowly pulled it over her head and removed it. In awe I looked at that delightful olive skin. She removed her bra and panties and walked up to me. "Do you like what you see, my Shahnshah?" I gurgled a response, but I am not sure what it was. She opened the buttons on my pyjama shirt and removed it, then she removed my pants. Now we were both standing stark naked, looking at each other. I, an aging man of seventy and she, a goddess of between twenty five and thirty. She gently pushed me on the bed and started caressing me and kissing me from my head towards the middle. Then I felt her mouth further enlarging a portion of me that was already extended. She suddenly turned around and laid down. "Now take me my Shahnshah! Honor my flesh with the seed of Ram Ahuramazd's descendant!"

The musk of this delectable Iranian woman was something that I had never imagined. It was like an opiate to my senses. I entered her and we made love for what felt like an eternity. When we finished and I got up, she smiled at me. "I hope you enjoyed me. I am yours, as long as you want me. You do not have to make any commitments or promises. This will be forever a secret between my Shahnshah and his Zainab. I have taken precautions so you do not have to worry about any unwanted pregnancy. But if you ever want me to bear your child, I will be honored."

"Tell me, my beautiful Zainab," I said, "what can you possibly like in a man of seventy? You can have any man you wish with your beauty and your charms. Why me?"

"My Shahnshah," she said, "as you are aware, I was not a virgin. I have already told you that once I had a lover. Since then, I have realized that the history of Iran makes me incredibly erotic. My passion for you is because you are my Shah. Your age, your wealth and even my own future are insignificant considerations. I love who you are not what you are. And I have just realized that you are also a very kind man." With a wicked smile in her eyes she added, rubbing my belly. "Even your considerable girth is attractive to me. This way I can have a little more of my Shahnshah."

"Naughty girl," I said and took her in my arms and kissed her passionately on her mouth. She responded with equal passion. With a twinkle in her eye she asked. "Do you want me again?"

"I think I will wait till the morning," I said. She came into my arms, wrapped hers around my neck, pressed her body against mine and promptly fell asleep.

I had a smile on my face and decided that I was going to enjoy my stay in Iran.

CHAPTER 4.

The telephone rang in the morning. Zainab woke up startled. "Oh my God. I wonder who that is?" she asked. "I'd better get out of here before somebody comes to the door."

"Zainab don't forget, I decide when to open the door. You don't have to worry, I will not let anyone in until you are dressed and out of the room."

I picked up the phone as Zainab went to the washroom. "Hello,"? I said.

"Salaam alaikum Mr. Damania," said Bashir at the other end of the line. "We have serious business to complete today. Do you think you will be ready to fly out to Yezd today? There are several important people waiting to meet with you."

"Why in Yezd?" I asked.

"Mr. Damania. May I explain all this to you on the way to the airport as we are running short of time? As you will require assistance to remember the names of all the people you will meet today, I will take notes for you as to what transpires."

Zainab walked into the room from the bathroom at this point. I could see the question that she had in her eyes. I winked at her.

"Mr. Bashir, as you have indicated, I would need to comprehend all that transpires today, so I think I should bring my own secretary Zainab, who is fluent in English and who can directly communicate with me so that I do not miss anything. I was fortunate to meet this young lady who works at the reception desk and is totally fluent in the English language. I would like to hire her as my secretary. After the meetings are over it would be greatly beneficial if she could privately translate and explain to me what each one has said. With your busy schedule, you may possibly not be able to afford the time to sit with me for considerable periods of time and explain what was said and the nuances of the Farsi language."

There was a noticeable pause in our conversation and I imagined that Bashir was contemplating what I had suggested. Fortunately, he had no idea about the relationship that Zainab and I had recently developed.

"This Zainab, what is her surname?" he asked. I suddenly realized that I did not know but smart little Zainab grabbed a piece of paper and wrote her surname on it. I acted as if I already knew and read it out to Bashir. "Her name is Zainab Haroon."

Bashir seemed a bit taken aback. "Give me a minute, Mr. Damania, I want to check something." He came back a minute later and said, "This is an amazing coincidence. The woman you mentioned is a member of our group. Where did you meet her?"

"Oh, there was a notice in my room, written in Farsi and I wanted it translated. So I went down to the reception desk and this lady not only translated it for me, but spoke to me and offered her help. That is when I realized how fluent she was in English." I lied. Zainab could hardly control her laughter. Bashir hesitated, but it appeared to me that he had bought my story.

"You are indeed a very resourceful man Mr. Damania. Here we go, within a twenty-four-hour period, you have found yourself a bilingual secretary."

I was not quite sure whether he was being complimentary or suspicious, but frankly I did not care.

"No problem at all, Mr. Damania, we will be happy to pay a reasonable salary to her and of course all her travel expenses. But are you sure she is willing to travel with us?"

"I will discuss that with her."

"Will she have the permission of her parents, or her husband, if she's married?"

"Mr. Bashir, the lady has informed me that she is not married and is living independently in her own apartment. I am sure she will be able to go with us wherever and whenever we go."

"All right sir, we must leave for Yezd by noon. Of course, if that is acceptable to you.." Zainab vehemently nodded her assent about the time of departure. I thanked Bashir and disconnected the line.

Zainab ran into my arms, hugged and kissed me. "My Shahnshah, you are a genius. Now I can be with you all the time. I promise you I shall do a lot more for you than just be your secretary," she said with a twinkle in her eye.

"Zainab," I said, Bashir and his friends will arrive very shortly at our hotel to pick us up. I would suggest that you go home, pack your things and meet us in the lobby. I will introduce you to them as my new secretary."

"Oh my Shahnshah, does that mean that they should not find out that I was working all night for you?" She asked with a mischievous smile.

"A couple of things my darling," I said. "First of all we have to be very careful that they do not have the slightest inkling of our relationship. Secondly, I think we are close enough now for you to call me Sharuq rather than Mr. Damania or Shahnshah when we are alone. In public, of course, I will call you Miss Haroon and you can call me Mr. Damania. Okay my love?" She nodded and soon left my room.

Approximately an hour later, Bashir and the other men picked us up. I introduced Zainab to them and we all drove to the airport. I was surprised to notice that we were not taking a scheduled flight. The limousine took us by a circuitous route to the rear of the airport and a spacious private aircraft was waiting for us. Bashir then introduced me to a new gentleman.

"Mr. Damania, this is Mr. Abbas Rouhani. Mr. Rouhani is the sole owner of Multi Mining Inc. This corporation is the largest manufacturer of mining and oil drilling machinery in the whole of Iran. Mr. Rouhani is kind enough to provide us with his aircraft for transportation to Yezd. He is also a respected member of our organization and our greatest donor."

"It is a pleasure meeting you Mr. Damania," Mr. Rouhani said. I noticed he had a cultured American accent and his English was perfect.

It was clear he was a well educated man. I shook his hand and advised I was delighted to meet him.

"Mr. Damania, would you do me the honor of joining me in my personal cabin in the aircraft? We have several matters to discuss privately."

"I would be delighted, sir" I said. I then introduced him to Zainab and he bowed to her. I noticed that he could not get his eyes away from her. But then, no normal male could keep his eyes away from Zainab.

We adjourned to Mr. Rouhani's private cabin. It was beautifully appointed with real paintings of the Elbruz Mountains and what I thought were views of the Caspian Sea.

"This is a beautiful cabin Mr. Rouhani, you indeed have excellent tastes" I said.

"Mr. Damania, I am presently dealing with perhaps the most significant guest and visitor to Iran. We are hoping that the description of guest and visitor is only temporary. If our plans succeed, you will be the most important human being in the nation of Iran. Forgive me if I have not started addressing you as Your Majesty."

Looking at Mr. Rouhani I realized that I not only liked him, but I also instinctively felt his innate intelligence and acumen. I had no doubts whatsoever that this wealthy man had made every single penny of his wealth by himself. I also came to the conclusion that it had not gone to his head. That he was a highly educated, sophisticated and brilliant man, who was also good-natured, organized and kind. Indeed, a very unusual combination. I instinctively felt that this man was a powerful ally and would protect me if it was necessary. After all, I was in a dangerous dictatorship where some individuals wanted to destroy the existing religious theocracy and substitute me as the emperor. Was there a better reason needed by the religious regime to eliminate me?

The plane took off smoothly and once we were airborne Mr. Rouhani said with a twinkle in his eye. "Mr. Damania, as we are in the air and not on Iranian soil, for purely medical reasons and to avoid air sickness, perhaps we should provide you with a large dose of Scotch? Of course only to avoid the ill effects of altitude."

I noticed that the Scotch he poured was Johnnie Walker Blue label. "Mr. Rouhani," I said," your taste in Scotch is as excellent as your taste in art."

Rouhani just smiled and bowed in my direction. "So where did you get your education. Mr. Rouhani?"

"My parents sent me to do my MBA at Columbia University in the United States. All told I have spent some ten years in America."

"As we are going to spend considerable time together, perhaps we should cut down on the formalities. Please call me Sharuq and I will call you Abbas," I said.

"I am honored Mr. Damania, but I can only call you by your first name when we are alone. It would be improper in the eyes of my companions to be so familiar with you. On the other hand, I would be honored if you use my first name, both publicly and privately."

"Now Sharuq, may I discuss our agenda for today? We are flying you to Yezd to meet with a very important military figure in Iran. This must remain totally confidential. His position and his life will be in grave danger if the Iranian authorities find out that he has met with us. His name is General Hashmat Osmani. He is second in command of the Iranian armed forces. He is also a member of our organization. He resides in Tehran but like all other important officials is under constant scrutiny. That is why we are all flying to Yezd, where the Islamic Republic's Secret Service is almost nonexistent."

"Let me bring you up-to-date regarding Mr. Osmani. The General is an educated and sophisticated man. He is a Muslim, but not a fanatic. He resents the ideals of the Islamic Republic's fundamentalists, the oppression of women and the oppression of other religions in Iran. We all may be Muslims, but we believe that religion is a person's private affair and the state has no business to interfere. A religious state is perforce an uncivilized and undemocratic entity, because it forces its beliefs on all citizens without any consideration of their individual ideals. Believe it or not, some of us are very ardent practicing Muslims and yet we believe that an Islamic state is in itself contrary to the dictates of liberal Islam and Shi'ite Islam was itself created to avoid the oppression of fundamentalism that came with the original Arab conquest of Iran. Under General Osmani, there are literally thousands of Iranian soldiers who feel that the Islamic Republic is dragging us back into the Middle Ages. So the annihilation of the Mullahs and the establishment of a secular Iranian state is totally essential for our well-being. General Osmani is in touch with fourteen commanding officers at different military bases in Iran and we intend to remove the present government, if necessary with military force."

"Are you suggesting that you are going to attempt a coup?" I asked.

"Our plan is to assassinate all the ruling religious leaders at the same time so that they do not have the opportunity to coordinate their forces. Once they are leaderless, the army, which is generally controlled by important officers who are our members, will take over the government. Every single religious fanatic will be exterminated. A secular state will be established. We will introduce a democratic constitution and then the direct descendent of the ancient Sassanians, namely Sharuq Damania, would be placed on the Peacock Throne of Iran."

"Abbas," I said, "what if we fail? Thousands of innocent lives would be destroyed."

"You are absolutely right Sharuq and that is why absolute secrecy is essential. I do not believe we will fail. But if we do and no one knows who is responsible for the coup, there can be no arrests or charges. In case of that eventuality, I have made arrangements for all fourteen leaders of the Army, who are our members, together with myself, the four gentlemen you have met, you, your secretary and General Osmani to be flown out of Iran to Switzerland. As you know, this plane belongs to me and will be with us wherever we go. I also have excellent contacts in the Iranian security service, police departments, immigration and customs, so our departure will not be a problem. However, I am very optimistic about our prospects. One other important thing Sharuq, I sincerely believe that any person who has deep faith in religion has to be ignorant and mentally unsophisticated. Belief without evidence is ignorance on stilts. So in fact, the present government and its main administrators are burdened with their religion and incapable of scientific thinking. This is our advantage and we shall use it to manipulate them. All we have to do is constantly tell them how we deeply respect their ardour. Inevitably, this will lead us to comprehend every single move they are about to make."

The plane had landed on what appeared to me to be a rather deserted landing strip overgrown in areas with grass and some debris. "You understand Sharuq that we cannot land at the regular airport as that would draw the attention of the government officials. This landing strip is on my own personal property, officially to be used for aircraft spraying weed killers. We are also approximately ten kilometres from Yezd."

An old Plymouth van picked us up and drove us to an old stone mansion, completely surrounded by sand hills and not visible from the surrounding area. Abbas explained to me that this house was owned by his family for several generations. A servant took my suitcase upstairs to a beautifully furnished room with an antique bed, dresser and two upholstered chairs. The view from the window consisted of sandy hills and some trees in the distance. There was no question in my mind that we were in a remote area, distant and unvisited by the locals.

"Sharuq, why don't you rest for a while. In the meantime I will arrange a meeting between our group and general Hashmat Osmani." I nodded and Abbas left the room. I changed my clothes and got into bed to get a badly needed nap. About an hour and a half later there was a knock on my door. I opened and saw Zainab standing there with a smile on her face. "Your Majesty and my darling, you would be amazed how brilliant your Zainab is. I have convinced Abbas that Your Majesty may require my services as your secretary at any time and therefore I should always be available to take dictation. So the next bedroom has been allotted to me. I am sure you will be dictating your memoirs all night, won't you?"

I pulled her into the room, closed the door and kissed her hard and long on her mouth. She responded passionately and kissed me back pressing her beautiful breasts hard against me. " You have a strange way of dictating your memoirs my Shahnshah, I thought people dictated with their mouths? Maybe it's different in Canada."

I pulled her to myself and kissed her hard again. "That is to teach you not to be a smart aleck." I said.

"After your business has been completed with your visitors and you are back in your bedroom, just knock on this wall and your Zainab will sneak in to take your dictation and perhaps also reduce your tension, because I just realized that a certain portion of you is out of control and pushing hard against me. That is very bad for an Emperor's health."

She slipped out of my arms, went out and closed the door behind her.

At approximately 7:30 p.m. we met in the living room downstairs. Abbas stood up as soon as I arrived. Next to him stood an extremely tall man. I would estimate his height to be about six.

"Mr. Damania," he said, "let me introduce you to General Hashmat Osmani, thc most decorated military officer in the Iranian Armed Forces."

General Osmani smiled modestly, waving his hand. "Mr. Damania, Mr. Rouhani is not just one of the most brilliant men in Iran, but also possesses the sweetest tongue in the Middle East. So please don't believe him."

I shook the General's hand. His palm completely engulfed mine and the grip was strong enough to eliminate any thoughts of aggression that a smaller man could ever dream of.

"General, I am honored to meet you! Your reputation sir, precedes your arrival. I have read about your brilliant career, but above all I have read about your incredible integrity. Am I not correct that you were ordered during the Iran/ Iraq war to shoot one hundred and fifty prisoners of war who were allegedly responsible for war crimes and you insisted that they should be given a fair trial before they were punished? I understand your government was quite upset with you for disobeying a direct order to execute those prisoners."

"Mr. Damania, I was only doing my duty as an officer and a gentleman. If a man in power misuses his power then he's no better than a common terrorist and I will certainly accept the compliment that I am not a terrorist or a coward".

"Men with your character are a rare breed, General, my compliments to you." I said.

"Now Mr. Damania, with your permission, we would like to inform you of our concerns. You do realize sir that absolute trust amongst us is of paramount importance. One single traitor or an indiscriminate statement could be extremely perilous to our existence and to the future of Iran itself. That is why we have entrusted you with the knowledge of our lives, achievements and foibles. With your permission, I would like to acquaint you with what we know of your achievements. Please correct me whenever I am a wrong. You were born in the East Africa, you qualified as a chartered accountant in England and worked there for several years before moving to Canada. In Canada, you rose to be a partner in a very reputed accounts firm, being totally responsible for establishing a very lucrative Japanese clientele. Your retirement was viewed by the other partners as a considerable loss to the firm itself. You seem to have a bit of a dislike for Muslims, but it is our belief that the dislike is not for Muslims in general, but for fanatics and terrorists. How am I doing so far?"

I was totally amazed at the complete information they had about me. I also realized two other things. I knew so little about them and the significant danger that all of us faced if we had a traitor in our group, or our secrets were somehow revealed to the Iranian government. I therefore appreciated the care and secrecy exhibited by the members of the organization.

"General, I am indeed impressed at your knowledge of my past and your efforts to keep our organization safe from the theocracy and the government. Please tell me, where do we go from here?"

"All right Mr. Damania, now I will reveal to you the intricate pattern of our next move. Notice that presently the Iranian government and theocracy are totally obsessed with the desire to defeat and exterminate Israel. To all relatively intelligent and experienced military officers that does not only amount to a pipe dream, but an unfair ambition. Remember that we Iranians are Shi'ites, who have had difficulties with the Sunnis for centuries. Even today, organizations such as Hezbollah are not acceptable to the Sunni majority in Lebanon. In Syria, Saudi Arabia, Jordan and Egypt the, Shi'ites are normally treated pretty shabbily. The Palestinians are basically Sunnis and the actual territorial fight is between the Palestinians and the Israelis. The fight is between the Jews and the Sunnis. Why should we get so excited to eliminate Israel, which basically is trying to put down a people who do not like us. So from a military point of view, if the Jews and the Sunnis keep fighting, the Sunnis will have no opportunity to harass us. Also please keep in mind that for centuries Jews and Muslims lived in relative peace. It was the Christians and the Jews that had recurrent problems, culminating in the atrocities of Hitler. Under Islam, the Christians and the Jews are considered ' Kitabis,' which, when translated into English, means people of the book. The Torah and the Bible are considered holy books, and the predecessors of the Koran. Under Islam therefore, Jews and Christians must be respected and protected. Now let us look at our recent history. Who attacked us? Saddam Hussein a Sunni despot who not only killed millions of our people in the Iran/ Iraq war, but also a very large number of Shi'ites, who are the majority in Iraq. Have we ever been attacked by Israel? Have they ever dropped a bomb on Iran? So as a matter-of-fact, a strong Israel at war with our Sunni neighbours would be an asset. Not only that, if they had been our allies, they probably would have helped us during the Iran/Iraq war. So why on earth are we talking of dropping bombs and eliminating Israel when its existence is beneficial to our interests? I envy Turkey. They make certain pro-Islamic statements occasionally, but basically maintain a neutral stance, if not a friendly relationship with Israel. They are smarter than us."

" Lastly, and as a military officer, one must first determine how plausible victory is before attacking an enemy. And I, as an experienced military officer can tell you candidly that we do not have a hope in hell of winning a war against Israel. Even if we did, America is not going to sit back and let us get away with it. America's Jewish population will never permit it. And no American president would be foolish enough to provoke Jewish interests in the United States."

I was quite impressed with the General's clear comprehension and analysis of the political situation in the Middle East. "So what are you going to do about the situation General?" I asked.

"Well Mr. Damania, it is not enough that we merely criticize the present Iranian government and theocracy for their prejudices. We have to analyze the reason for that prejudice. The intellectually elite of Iran are totally disgusted with the theocracy, but they have no choice in the matter. The government is strongly supported by the uneducated classes and feeding them verbiage of the greatness of Islam and convincing them that Islam is threatened, is the only way the government can stay in power. The hatred between the Shi'ites and Sunnis is purposely downplayed and the hatred against Israel is deliberately cultivated. This unfortunately necessitates the strengthening of the Iranian armed forces, the creation of atomic weapons and coincidentally, the suppression of women. And what are the consequences? Millions of dollars that could be spent on education, health and well-being of the people are wasted. As women form half the population of the nation and cannot get adequate education, industry and progress are greatly reduced. We cannot continue to live in this antiquated lifestyle for very long without ruining both our cultural heritage and our standard of living. Which is the enemy that should be immediately destroyed? Is it Israel or the religious theocracy of Iran? The answer is very simple. The Islamic government of Iran must be replaced by a secular government composed of intellectuals with education and rationality instead of faith."

"But General, how do you expect to achieve that without inordinate bloodshed of innocent Iranians and basically a civil war?" I asked.

"Mr. Damania, I realize that the price is high but to delay would be to face a total annihilation of our industry, music, culture and history, the prosperity of our country and our population. A military strike at all the seats of power simultaneously could achieve the results I am aiming for."

"And what use am I to you in that military situation?" I asked.

"As far as the military situation is concerned indeed you are of no use to us, but once we succeed we will need a symbol to unite the people. And I want to be sure that that symbol is not a religious one but a historical one. Iranians are deeply informed and involved with their history. To this day and even under Islamic rule you will hear the lore of the ancient king "Jamshid" who allegedly lived thousands of years ago and maybe belonged to the Zoroastrian faith. Yet the Muslims will fondly relate his achievements to you, both in prose and poetry. Now, to present them with the symbol of the last Sassanian King's descendent as the ruler would immensely impress them. They will live and die for you."

"But isn't that the exact situation that you want to avoid. Create a new superstition to substitute an old one?" I asked.

"I've considered that very carefully, Mr. Damania, but there are two factors which make it safe for us to do so. As you know, we have studied your background. You are an educated man, rational and reasonable, devoid of the desire for self glorification and inordinate power. You are extremely capable of dealing with and influencing people. That very capacity would be invaluable once the revolution is successful. Moreover, from a practical point of view, we are not afraid of your turning out to be a Hitler or a Stalin. You will be a constitutional Monarch like the King of England and we are absolutely certain that your endeavour will be to preserve democracy and not to let anyone assume power without legal authority. I am equally certain that you will use the same temperament that you used in your career to prevent yourself from assuming unlimited power."

"Now let me explain to you how we will proceed with the military portion of this campaign. There are eighteen army, navy and air force bases in Iran. I am not going to bore you with their locations and secondly, as a military officer, I think it will be a derogation of my duty to give out military locations to non military personnel. Suffice it to say that sixteen of these bases have commanding officers who are members of our organization. No army personnel will ever disobey their commanding officer unless there are exceptional circumstances. These officers are very well-liked by their men and we are certain that the men will comply without hesitation with the orders given by them. The remaining two bases will either have to be occupied by us or the personnel will surrender when challenged by the rest of the Army."

"Well Mr. Damania, this has been a long day for you, so let me wish you a good night and sleep well. Please avoid leaving this house on your own. Kindly remember that the Iranian government must be kept under the illusion that you have come here to give us advice on accounting and industry. This area is certainly not known for its industry. Good night, sir." The General bowed and left.

I walked back to my room and changed into my pyjamas. Then I poured myself a large Scotch. I felt tired and had decided to go to sleep after consuming my drink when suddenly I had a thought. I knocked on the wall of my room and waited. In a couple of minutes there was a knock on my door and I opened it to see Zainab standing dressed in a long red dress with a twinkle in her eyes and a smile that literally melted my heart.

"Does my Shahnshah desire me?" She asked with a mischievous smile in her eyes, one eyebrow rising.

"It is impossible not to desire someone as beautiful and well endowed as you, Zainab. I am but a mortal, not accustomed to being in the presence of a goddess." I said.

"My Shahnshah, goddesses also have desires and affections and merely looking at them is not enough." She put her arms around my neck and kissed me deeply and passionately, inserting her tongue into my mouth. She smelled like roses and the scent from her long black tresses was more intoxicating than the drink I had consumed.

"Does my lord and master want to make love to me?" she asked mischievously. For a minute I thought I was dreaming. Was it possible that suddenly I was offered the kingdom of Iran and the love and body of the most beautiful woman I had ever seen?

The cleavage in front of her dress was something I could not keep my eyes away from. She saw me looking at her and smiled. "Does my beloved Emperor want to see more of his goddess?" She asked.

"I want to see the whole of my Goddess. Worship is impossible when impeded by mortal clothing," I said.

With the same smile on her face she undid her dress and it fell to the ground. She removed her bra and panties and stood before me naked. I felt so intoxicated I was wordless.

"Sharuq, you may be the direct descendent of the Sassanians, but merely standing and looking at me will not help your Majesty's slightly extended state," she said, giggling and looking at me.

She slowly undid and removed my pyjama top and bottom and then clung to me. Skin to skin. The ecstasy I felt was indescribable. We kissed again and again, deeply and passionately.

"Zainab," I said, "If I request you to do something specific for me, would you be offended?"

"Not at all my love, what do you want me to do?"

"My love, I don't like nose rings, would you remove it for me?"

Zainab giggled. "My lord and master, if I can take off my panties for you, I can remove my nose ring too. No offense taken." She took off her nose ring and kissed me again. We both slowly moved towards the bed. She took me into her arms and we kissed each other passionately. I started kissing her from her mouth down towards the feet and as I reached her belly button I could smell the musk of her womanhood. Indeed it was one of the most exciting smells I had ever encountered. As I played with her she got excited. "Enter my darling, make me a part of you. Let us become one." At age seventy I normally did not act like a stud, but the beauty and musk of Zainab seemed to have brought me back to my teenage days as I possessed her. She kept on saying "Allah! Allah!" repeatedly. I did know that Allah was the Arabic and Farsi word for God. After we were finished, I tried to get up but she would not let me and held me inside her with her arms and her legs. "What is your hurry? Stay a little longer inside me, I want to bear your weight."

After a few minutes I got up and gently kissed her. "You are absolutely gorgeous my love. Tell me something. Why were you calling Allah when I was making love to you?"

"I don't know, but at your age, I did not expect you to go so deep inside me. So it must be Allah who helped you." She laughed mischievously.

"Well, if this kind of lovemaking is going to continue, I'd better have Allah on my side," I said.

She just laughed and hugged me. "Did you enjoy me my man?" She asked.

"Enjoyment is a trivial word my darling, what I felt was ecstasy." I said.

"My Shahnshah is not only big, but also very big with his words," She said. I just responded with a long kiss.

"Tell me Zainab, how can you, such a beautiful woman, talented, intelligent, educated and young, want to make love to me with so much passion?" I asked.

"I have already explained this to you before. Some of us women are intoxicated by things other than youth. Our excitement comes from association with the man's background and history. Let me give you an example. Suppose you were in a position where you had a choice of making love to two equally beautiful girls, one is just an ordinary girl, but the other was say, Cleopatra, which one would you choose?"

"Of course the other girl. Cleopatra, at the age of about two thousand would be old even for me."

"Now you're not being fair my love. Wouldn't the thought of having the great Queen Cleopatra in your bed, in your arms, be more exciting? When I first came to you, I wanted you because you were the direct descendent of the Sassanians. I would become connected to the history of my land and to take into my flesh the seed of the Emperor of Iran. To me there was nothing more erotic than that. Then once I came to know you, I found out two other things. That you are a very intelligent man and also surprisingly, a very kind man. That, from my perspective, is very unusual. So now I have fallen in love with you."

"But my love I am seventy years old and you are but a child."

She started giggling again. "As to my being a child, you didn't really treat me like a child a few minutes ago. If I was indeed a child and you did what you did to me you would be in jail, wouldn't you? Secondly, you underestimate your age. From my point of view when we first met, you would have been thirteen hundred years old. The last Emperor of Iran."

I did not know what to say to her. It was a shock to me that a young beautiful woman who could almost have any man, would be so excited with a remotely plausible connection with history. But then who knows all the intricacies of a human heart's feelings and eroticism. I suppose for millennia, women have been treated like property owned by the father before marriage and by the husband after marriage. History has taught them to enjoy things other than the choice of the men they marry. They never had that choice so they learnt over the centuries to create their own illusions and eroticism. If the man was forced upon them, then the next best thing to do was to use one's body and sex to manipulate and control him and in the process win his affection. Naturally, in those oppressive centuries, the only sex she was going to get was from that man . And if the sex was good she could use it to make life liveable and perhaps even enjoyable. In these circumstances, what better recipe than eroticism based on say family of the man, his ancestry and history? I now realized that my lovely Zainab was the product of that civilization or lack thereof.

Zainab rose from the bed and in the attached kitchenette she made some tea and boiled eggs and we ate them together. "I sure would like to get out of here and get some fresh air," I said. "I am also very fond of Persian carpets, would you know where to look for them?"

"Sharuq, every bazaar in an Iranian city has carpet malls. Why don't we go and have a look in the mall." She called the chauffeur on the intercom and arranged for us to be picked up in an hour. As the weather was cool we both dressed casually and got into the car left for us by my host. We were driven to the bazaar and the driver took us to the carpet mall.

After shopping for approximately an hour, we returned to the car and to our surprise found two police officers talking to our chauffeur. "What do they want."? Zainab asked him.

"The officers would like to speak to our guest, Mr. Damania," the chauffeur responded.

The officer bowed slightly in my direction and tartly demanded "Your passport please!" I handed my passport and he looked at my photograph carefully and then deep into my eyes.

"You are both coming to the police station with us," he said, very abruptly.

"May I ask the reason officer?" I asked in English and Zainab translated that into Farsi.

"You have a Canadian passport. You are not a Mussalman. What are you doing in Zahidan?"

"I am a guest of Mr. Abbas Rouhani. I'm sure you have heard that name?" I asked sarcastically and Zainab translated.

"And what is this woman doing alone in your company without a "parda"?

"Officer, this lady is my secretary and she has kindly accompanied me to shop for carpets. Is that against the law?" I asked.

"First of all, I would like to investigate what you are doing in Zahidan. There are no significant historical sites here. There is no significant industry or business here and to complicate matters, you are out in public in the company of a young Iranian woman who is not your relative and who is walking around with her face exposed. That is contrary to the dictates of the Islamic Republic. Do you not realize that both of you are suspect?"

I felt a deep dread inside me but realized that the slightest show of consternation to an uneducated man would give him the impetus he needed to harass us. Zainab also appeared to be petrified, so I thought the best course was to accompany him to the police station and hope that there was an educated superior of his who would see reason after hearing my explanation.

They drove us silently to the police station the officer tunelessly whistling some sort of song that seemed to be completely devoid of rhythm.

At the police station we were taken into the office of what appeared to be the equivalent of a sergeant. The sergeant had a large curling moustache, was in uniform, which was only slightly dishevelled. The chairs and table in the room had seen better days and the odour of cigarette smoke permeated the air.

"Sergeant," I said, "I have always had great admiration for the hospitality and politeness of Muslims, particularly Iranians. We are guests in Iran. We have not come here to create any trouble, on the contrary, I have come here as a guest of Mr. Abbas Rouhani, a prominent citizen of your city, to advise him and others about the possibility of increasing trade between Iran and Canada. Your officers have insulted me and my secretary who very kindly agreed to help me shop for some carpets."

I rattled all this out with great pretended equanimity though inside my heart I was quaking.

The sergeant looked up and stared into my eyes. He had green powerful eyes that appeared to be searching deep into my soul. With a beating heart I stared back at him and he lowered them.

"You are not a Muslim, you are an accountant who has come to give advice on foreign trade all based in Teheran. You were walking around Zahidan in the company of a young woman who is not your wife, nor your daughter, without a parda and all alone with you in your car. Does that sound normal to you?" Mr. Damania, you and this lady are under arrest until a security service representative has clarified your position."

Zainab started to cry. I was even afraid to put my arm around her to console her because that might be taken as something unIslamic. Then I suddenly realized that the best way to control the thought process of uneducated filth is to cater to their own trivial concepts of good and bad. With a very straight face I looked at the sergeant and said, "Sergeant, look at me! I am seventy years old, this young lady is not even thirty, she is like my daughter. Do daughters wear parda in the company of their uncles? Even in Iran?" I slightly turned my head to look at Zainab, hoping desperately that she would not make some gesture which would jeopardize my lie about my possible uncle hood. Fortunately for both of us, Zainab was too preoccupied with her fear and her crying to object.

We were both placed in separate cells.

Suddenly we heard some yelling and screaming. Initially I could not recognize what the noise was about. But then I listened carefully and realized that the voice belonged to General Osmani. Later Zainab translated his words for me from Farsi into English. The General was addressing both police officers and the purport of his tirade could be summarized as follows. "You filthy dirty uneducated bastards. Your mothers were whores, your grandmothers were whores and your great grandmothers were whores and your fathers, grandfathers and great-grandfathers were pimps! How dare you insult an honored guest of Iran. You have brought shame to me and the people of Iran by your ignorant behavior."

In the background I could hear a much softer and conciliatory voice. Abbas Rouhani was trying to arbitrate between the General and the police officers. "Gentlemen, the General is rightfully annoyed at your unnecessarily harsh treatment of Mr. Damania and his secretary. Don't you realize that the young lady is young enough to be his daughter?" Let them go immediately and we will forget the whole incident."

I heard footsteps coming down towards our cells. The sergeant and his subordinate seemed to be quaking in their shoes as they opened our cell door. "Apologize to them, now" the General ordered. The two officers bowed in my direction, but did not say a word. I could distinctly observe the emotions in their eyes, abject fear and uncompromising hatred.

The General himself bowed to me and to Zainab. "Mr. Damania," he said, hugging me. "Please accept my abject apology. This should never have happened. And I promise you one thing, it will never happen again." He looked threateningly at the two policemen.

"General," I said, after we left the police station, "I cannot thank you enough. You have proven to be a good friend and I am going to ask you a favor. I would be honored if now onwards you would call me Sharuq."

The General gave me his warm smile. "I will be honored my friend, but there is a condition. You call me Hashmat. Agreed?"

All four of us walked back to the car, "Mr. Rouhani that includes you too. We are friends now and formalities should be dropped." I said.

"Only one thing Sharuq," Rouhani said. "In public let us still be formal, but in private we will be honored to abide by your wishes."

Zainab too had a smile on her face now. We all got into the General's car and started driving towards the Rouhani mansion.

"Sharuq, my friend, please listen to me. You do not understand the people you're dealing with. Next time you want to go carpet shopping please do me the honor of going in my military vehicle with my chauffeur and Madame Zainab, would you please take your face cover with you and pretend you are using it. You both do not know the kind of animals we are dealing with."

"Hashmat," I said with a smile. "I am extremely impressed with your knowledge of the morality of the mothers and grandmothers of these officers. When Zainab translated what you said to them, I suddenly realized that my lack of the Farsi language was a great handicap. You just proved to me what a colorful language Farsi can be when spoken by an Iranian General." Abbas and the General both roared with laughter. Zainab modestly smiled in my direction. Rouhani watched for a moment, until Zainab's attention was diverted and whispered in my year. "How did you enjoy my description of Zainab being like your daughter?"

"You dirty old man," I said and both of them laughed uproariously. Zainab looked at us but did not seem to understand what the joke was. I of course realized that these two old codgers were onto my relationship with Zainab. For a moment it caused me some anguish, but soon I realized that these were my friends and their loyalty was absolute. More significantly, hurting me in any way would be quite contrary to their own interests.

As soon as we arrived home, Abbas went into the basement and came up with a drink and the rest of the day passed very joyfully. At my request Zainab stayed with us and had some wine. The General mischievously told her. "Our Zainab firmly believes that alcohol is against Islam only when the alcohol content is over twelve percent. So wine is acceptable but Scotch is not." "Very funny General," said Zainab. "Your sense of humor never leaves you. It was evident when you dealt with the police officers. I guess it is my turn now." We all laughed and I suddenly realized that a bond had been created between the four of us.

My instinct told me that these were my friends and it was unnecessary to be wary of these men or keep secrets from them. Abbas and Hashmat were the kind of men who would die for a friend and kill an enemy without batting an eye.

CHAPTER 5.

This particular day was very tiring so as soon as we returned to our residence I retired to my room and changed into my pyjamas. The effort to appear brave and to pretend to take the events of the day in my stride had proven to be too exacting. I was tired and just rested. The day's events and their severity started to pale when I thought once again of the General's colorful tirade against the police officers. I even felt slightly amused. However the danger of living in this environment was quite clear to me. I decided that henceforth, I would not venture out without due precautions and always in a vehicle provided by the General.

There was a knock on the door. I opened the door and found Zainab, standing there. She appeared very agitated and her eyes were red from crying. "That was my mistake. I shouldn't have taken you shopping without first checking with the General. I did not realize there would be any problem," she said.

"My darling," I replied, "I'm not blaming you for anything. It was I who suggested going out shopping for carpets. And in any case, how would you know that two crazy police officers would be on the prowl at the same time?"

"You are so kind and always so protective of me," she said. When I looked into her eyes, I saw that incredible expression which my experience and age have taught me could not mean anything else except love. It was unbelievable that this beautiful Iranian girl was possibly in love with me. I could accept her earlier pronouncements about the attraction of my alleged heritage, even her statement that she found me kind and therefore liked me, but the thought that she could be in love with me was not only flattering but also a little intimidating. From a selfish point of view this was very enchanting and enjoyable, but I did not want to be in a situation where I could hurt her.

She came and hugged me. "Sharuq, make love to me. I want to be held, kissed and possessed by you. I want my man inside me." She kissed me passionately, her body tightly pressed against me. Needless to say I did not need much persuasion. She took her clothes off and lay down on my bed and before I knew it I was inside her. We made love and when it was over we lay there, spent.

When we woke up, I noticed that she was no longer nervous, but had a big smile on her face. With some panic, I suddenly realized the enormous tenderness I felt for this woman. Our passion was satisfied and all that was left was this incredible love I felt for her. Looking into her eyes I knew she felt the same. Where would all this end?

She slept in my arms all night. In the morning she got up early and made us some tea. "I must go now Sharuq, somebody might come knocking." she said. She kissed me and quietly left my room.

Later that morning, both Abbas and Hashmat invited me for breakfast. "Sharuq", said Hashmat, "yesterday's debacle with the police has caused us grave concern. It is clear to us now that you are being watched and that the government and the religious authorities are suspicious as to what you are doing in Zahidan. We both think that we must get you involved socially with the significant citizens of this area. Of course we will always tell them that you are our financial adviser and we want to increase our trade with Canada. I would however caution you to be very careful when you discuss this topic with your new associates. Also, they will probe you on your religious views, especially regarding Islam and that is where I would request you to be extremely careful and tell them what they want to hear. If somehow Sharuq you make a few friends in this area and they are satisfied that you are a businessman and not antagonistic to the Islamic government or Islamic fundamentalism, then they will leave you alone and we may even be able to use them for our own purposes. One particular person I am going to introduce you to is Ayatollah Tabrizi. This man is probably the most powerful religious figure in this area. Let me warn you that he is a fundamentalist and a fanatic. Unfortunately, he is also very intelligent and perceptive and has the ear of the Islamic government. It is therefore imperative that you win him over. Convince him that you are not only not antagonistic to Islam, but are a great admirer of the Islamic government in this country. My friend, use all the charm that you used on your Japanese clients and win this fellow over. If he is on our side and informs the Iranian government that you are harmless, they will leave you and us alone and stop spying on us. So Sharuq, your job is cut out for you for today. I have taken the liberty of inviting the Ayatollah for lunch. Of course with the agreement and consent of our host, Abbas." Abbas nodded politely.

"I will do my best my friends," I said. "What you are doing or intending to do for this country of my ancestors and yours is far more important than any of us. And I will not let you down. Any suggestions as to how I should dress? Formally or casually?"

"Sharuq, do not forget that the Ayatollah may be an intelligent man, but he is not an educated man. So formal clothing will impress him. We will also dress formally. Deeply religious people are invariably ignorant so they pretend to dislike western clothing and western behavior but secretly, they are impressed and awed by it."

After getting dressed, 1 went down to the conference room. Several guests were already seated, volubly conversing in Farsi. I had requested Zainab to join me so that she could translate our conversation into English for me. As soon as I arrived, Abbas introduced me to all his guests. The last person I was introduced to was Ayatollah Tabrizi. "Mr. Damania, let me introduce you to one of the leading lights of Islam in our area. Ayatollah Tabrizi is renowned for his wisdom and knowledge of Islam and its correct practice. Ayatollah, this is our friend and guest, Mr. Sharuq Damania. A distinguished financial adviser, who has kindly accepted our hospitality in order to help us improve our trade with Canada."

I noticed that when he was paying compliments to the Ayatollah, Abbas had a twinkle in his eye and I almost felt that he winked at me. I kept a straight face and bowed in the direction of the Ayatollah. "It is my pleasure to meet you sir," I said. Zainab immediately translated this into Farsi.

"There is no need for a translation Madam", said the Ayatollah. "I understand the English language adequately." When I was looking at the Ayatollah I could actually visualize his dislike for me. I could not imagine how an utter stranger would dislike me at first sight. Then I noticed that he was glaring at Zainab. "My daughter, you should not appear in public in the company of a stranger and a foreigner without covering your face." Zainab was totally taken aback and her shock was apparent to me. However, she dutifully translated that statement made in Farsi into English. My first impulse was to tell the Ayatollah to go to hell. As a matter of fact I would have really enjoyed expediting his departure with a good solid kick in his religious ass, however, the warnings earlier given to me to be tactful made me keep my mouth shut.

In order to change the subject, I looked at him nonchalantly and said, "So Sir, do you live here in Zahidan or in Teheran?"

"Mr. Damania, I reside in Iran and travel to every location where I suspect any treachery against our Islamic faith or our Islamic nation."

"And what makes you think Sir, that there is any threat to either Islam or Iran here at this party?"

"You North Americans come into our country, encourage familiarity with our women, do not respect our sentiments, humiliate us with your arrogance and then expect friendship from us."

"If you are referring to me, I cannot imagine how I could do any of those things. First of all, I have tremendous respect for Iran and its culture. Secondly, I have had the pleasure of meeting such nice gentlemen, such as Mr. Rouhani, and General Osmani. And of course, I respect everyone's right to practice his faith as he wishes. So to put it mildly, your allegations are totally baseless."

"Trusting white men has always been the bane of Iran. We definitely believe that non-Muslims are on a crusade to destroy our culture and to steal our oil. You yourself for example, claim that you have come to Iran as a business adviser. Tell me sir, what kind of business advice is needed in a remote part of Iran, such as Zahidan? You claim to be a Zoroastrian! A faith that our ancestors destroyed and substituted with Islam. We do not need any Zoroastrians in this country. We do not want our Islam to be adulterated by other infidel faiths. We want to make Iran a pure Islamic nation."

My immediate reaction was again an incredible desire to kick the Ayatollah in his rear thereby expediting his departure to an Islamic heaven. However, remembering the words of my hosts about keeping him palliated, I took a deep breath and contemplated my next sentence. "Ayatollah, you amaze me with your unIslamic statements! Am I not correct that the Prophet himself has categorically stated 'even if a pagan visits you in your tent, you must welcome and protect him'? Your dislike and disrespect for non-Muslims and whites is totally contrary to what your Prophet has preached. But I suppose you, like all of us, are a mere mortal and therefore cannot adequately abide by the dictates of the Koran."

If eyes were daggers I am sure he would have used his to stab me. But he looked into my eyes and realized the contempt I felt for him. And also the possibility of violence on my part. Especially as I was protected by powerful men such as Abbas Rouhani and General Osmani.

He mellowed a bit, smiled for the first time and said, "Ah Mr. Damania, I see that you have been doing some reading of the Koran. Why this sudden interest?"

"Ayatollah, in civilized western countries such as Canada, where I come from, we respect all religions. To be informed of the faith of others and to admire their good points and to be able to discard the bad ones, is imperative for civilized living. Also, to generalize and accept all Muslims as good or bad is in my opinion uncivilized thinking. Don't you agree Sir?"

"You intrigue me Mr. Damania. You know my views on non-Muslims visiting our country and trying to influence us; however, I must say, I admire your guts."

"That is indeed a pity Ayatollah. I would have very much wished that you had appreciated my interest in your faith, your history and your people and my respect for them, rather than respecting my guts. All animals have guts."

He went completely red. "Are you calling me an animal Sir?"

"Absolutely not. And for two reasons. I just mentioned animals, so, if I call you an animal I would also be calling myself an animal, right? Secondly, such derogatory description of an educated man like yourself would indeed make my behaviour equivalent to that of uneducated filth."

Surprisingly he smiled. "You never run short of words do you, Mr. Damania."

"Again wrong Ayatollah. I like to pay respect to my hosts and their friends. This is something we Zoroastrians always practice."

"We do not have any resentment towards Zoroastrians or Zoroastrianism. However, we believe that our prophet Mohamed took all the good things from several religions, including Judaism and Christianity and then created the most perfect faith, which is our Islam."

"Ayatollah, to believe that anything presently in existence is perfect is to eliminate the possibility of improvement for the future. I am sure the great prophet of Islam would not agree with you on this point."

What I could see was a blank expression in his eyes, indicating to me that further arguments on the subject were futile.

We bowed to each other and parted without further acrimony.

A few hours later when we were home, Abbas smiled as he approached me. "Sharuq, you seem to have had quite a chat with the Ayatollah, and it appeared quite interesting from a distance."

"Abbas," I said, "the Ayatollah has the illusion of being an intellectual and well-informed. Unfortunately both of these are indeed his illusions. The truth is that the man is an ignoramus, who believes vehemently stating a stupid thing several times makes it the truth."

Abbas laughed, "I hope you did not tell him that?"

"If I were to tell him that then I would be reducing myself to his level. No Abbas, you do not participate in arguments with the uneducated, you just undignify them with your sarcasm and contempt."

"Well, my dear friend, you are the first one I have ever met who has not only put the Ayatollah in his place, but has convinced him that he is not infallible. That is quite an achievement and therefore a celebration is absolutely imperative."

"Abbas," I said, "I cannot successfully argue against such a brilliant suggestion."

After a few drinks I returned to my room in a considerably more relaxed and exultant frame of mind. I changed into my pyjamas and eagerly awaited a tap on the door from Zainab. Within a few minutes, the welcome sound came and I opened the door. Zainab hugged me but I could feel that she seemed edgy so I asked her why.

"Sharuq, I am worried about that Ayatollah when he chided me about being alone with you and not covering my face. He is not just giving advice, I could feel the malice and anger in his voice. I think he suspects something between us and he can cause both of us a lot of harm if he so wishes. We must be very careful in the future."

"Don't worry my darling," I said, "we are under the protection of General Osmani and Rouhani and the Ayatollah cannot touch us." As I said this I felt a strange dread inside me. I did not quite believe myself. I was more concerned about Zainab's safety than my own. After all, I was an old man who had seen and lived in the world, whereas this lovely young woman was risking a lot to give me the affection that she felt for me.

I decided therefore to ask the help of the General. Perhaps even confide in him.

She hugged me and we went to bed but we did not make love. She slept in my arms like a little baby. When I heard her breathing comfortably in my arms, I felt a tenderness that was indeed unique.

There was a meeting scheduled by the General and Rouhani the following morning and I arrived in the lobby feeling comfortably rested and relatively at peace. The two men were already there and I noticed that there were four military officers, formally dressed in their respective uniforms. I wondered why they were not introduced to me. The General explained that for security purposes, it was better that we did not know each other's names. The men appeared to be friendly and nodded in my direction.

"Mr. Damania," said the General, "the time for action has now arrived. We will provide you with the basic idea as to how we are going to proceed with our military operations. These men represent different military zones in the Islamic Republic. Basically there are eighteen military bases in Iran and when I say military bases, I mean army, navy, and air force. The nuclear installations are not involved, because their deployment would necessitate the use of one of the three branches of the Armed Forces. Our present criterion is to control these Armed Forces in all the eighteen locations. These four officers are either second or third in command in the Army, Navy and Air Force of Iran. They have a loyal following and can control all the dissidents in their respective troops."

"Now here is the plan. In four days, a segment from each of the eighteen bases will suddenly rise up against the others. It will all occur simultaneously. The remaining troops will be asked to stay at the base and naturally they will not be armed. The Plan for a new Iran will be explained to them. We want democracy, a free country devoid of any influence by the Mullahs, with religious freedom for the entire population of Iran. We will promise equal opportunity to Sunnis, Shiites', Kurds, Christians, Jews and Zoroastrians. There must be no official religion recognized by the State. We will guarantee freedom to practice any religion. With our oil wealth we will promise free education for both men and women. Total equality of opportunity will be guaranteed to all citizens irrespective of their beliefs. Most significantly, though there is religious freedom, interference from anyone in the governance of the nation will be brutally suppressed and eliminated. Mr. Damania, Iran will attain its rightful place as a civilized and wealthy nation, equal to any western nation in the world."

The men at the table all clapped their hands and so did I. Suddenly I had this feeling that I had become a part of history and that perhaps I could contribute to making this country of my ancestors a stable, sophisticated and prosperous land.

"Where do I come in and what do you want me to do?" I asked the General.

"One of the reasons we introduced you to the Ayatollah was to see how you could control and manipulate him. We wanted to observe his interaction with you. What surprised us was that you seemed to have successfully put him on guard. Actually, you have even succeeded in making him feel rather ignorant and bigoted. That, my dear Sharuq, is not a minor achievement. We would like you to meet with him. Get invited to his place. Meet the other religious leaders of the area. Convince them that just because you do not believe in Islam and are not a Muslim does not mean that you are against Islam or are in any manner disrespectful towards the faith of the majority of Iranians. As a matter-of-fact, try to convince them that their faith can be enhanced if they respect the other minorities of Iran and give them the equal rights that they deserve. I have somehow come to the conclusion that you will be able to achieve this. As a matter-of-fact, use the Ayatollah himself as your spokesman. If we can somehow eliminate opposition from the religious leaders and convince them that they are not our enemies, but our allies, we will be able to save literally thousands of lives when the military action takes place."

CHAPTER 6.

"Salaam alaikum, Ayatollah," I said over the telephone. "Do you know who this is?"

"Of course I do! How can I forget the voice of a Canadian visitor who claims he has come to Iran on business and is presently staying in Zahidan, where there is no international business venture and who does not hesitate to correct me on the teachings of the Koran." His sarcasm shocked me for a moment. Suddenly he started laughing and I was intrigued as to what was intended by those sarcastic words.

"Ayatollah, your sense of humor is as deep and meaningful as your religious acumen and knowledge. I am therefore seeking an opportunity to communicate with you and to understand the concepts and ideas of a learned man like yourself. I would therefore like to invite you to have dinner with me, at a place convenient to you. Is that acceptable?"

"Mr. Damania, it would be my pleasure to invite you to my home for dinner any day you wish, though the lack of scotch may make this invitation less palatable to you than to me.

"Alas Ayatollah, you underestimate yourself. How can one think of an alcoholic beverage in the presence of a learned man like yourself, whose conversation can be more intoxicating than any spirit or alcohol?"

He guffawed loudly. "Are all Canadian Zoroastrians as wily and sweet tongued as you, Mr. Damania?"

This time I guffawed to ease the tension of our conversation.

"Why don't we meet tomorrow at say, 7 p.m. for dinner? I will look forward to the evening."

"I will be honored, Ayatollah." I said.

The next day I arrived at the Ayatollah's home promptly at 7 p.m. My driver rang the bell and the Ayatollah himself appeared. "Welcome to my humble home, Mr. Damania. It may not be as luxurious as you are accustomed to, but please be assured that our hospitality and warmth will partially compensate for that."

"Ayatollah, as usual, your modesty and piety compete with each other. The purpose of my visit is to meet with you not to inspect your home." I said these words with a chuckle. Basically an imitation of the sarcastic jollity of the Ayatollah himself. He merely laughed his acceptance of my remark.

Interestingly his home was not as modest as he had indicated. There were several beautiful inscriptions from the Koran with ornate frames hanging on the wall. Surprisingly there were several small Chugtai frames with human figures, which is normally unusual in a Muslim household. Very beautiful, and probably centuries old. He saw me admiring them and walked up to me. "I suppose you're wondering two things. One, how can a Muslim Ayatollah have human pictures in his home. And two, how could I afford to own such ancient art."

"You are right only about one of those issues, namely human pictures in a Muslim home," I said.

"Well, you must delve a little deeper into our history. The Arab conquerors who brought Islam to Iran were Sunnis and conservative. They took a very serious view of human portrayal. The Iranians, who were far more sophisticated and highly developed in art, music and poetry did not feel that the arts were contrary to the Koran. Islam tolerated small pictures of artistic value later described as Chugtai paintings. Hence, I have kept some of these paintings and I really enjoy them."

"Don't you think Ayatollah that it is the sophistication of the Zoroastrian culture that was responsible for the highly evolved state of the arts in Iran at that time?" I asked.

"Oh, I have nothing against the Zoroastrian culture and art of that period. However I firmly believe that the true faith, namely Islam, was the answer for the people of Iran."

"With the utmost respect Ayatollah, I disagree with you. I certainly believe that Islam has contributed considerably to the progress of our civilization. But it is not the only answer, nor the only way for mankind. My own faith in my opinion has also greatly contributed to civilization".

He merely smiled. A smile that could be interpreted as the tolerance of an intellectual to the ranting of a lesser mortal. To his credit he did not proceed further with this argument.

Behind me I heard the rustle of a dress and turned around. A woman in parda walked up to us. "Mr. Damania, this is my wife Mariam." I bowed to her.

"Enchanted to meet you Madam," I said. "Your husband and I are having a heated discussion about religion."

"Mr. Damania, Mariam does not speak any English, but she has come to welcome you in our humble abode." He said something to her and she removed her veil. "I asked her to remove her veil in your presence. Because as of now, you are not only just an honored guest, but also a respected member of our family."

This was an amazing gesture from a man who had just told me that his was the only real faith. This combination of fanaticism and extreme warmth and hospitality was difficult for me to comprehend.

The food served was excellent. Lamb pilaf heavily scented with saffron. Initially Mariam only placed the plates in front of us. There was no cutlery. My face must have indicated my abhorrence to eating with my hands, for the Ayatollah said something and two sets of knives and forks were brought to the table by Mariam. She merely hovered in the background serving us, but not joining us at the table. I requested the Ayatollah to ask her to join us for dinner and he translated it into Farsi.

"Madam, will you not honor us by joining us for dinner? In Canada, we always prefer to have our spouses join us for meals. When the meal is as exquisite as it is today, it would be rude of us to eat without the company of such a talented hostess."

With a smile on his face the Ayatollah translated this to his wife and she joined us. I could detect a delighted smile on her face, which indicated her thanks for my courtesy and words. I suddenly realized that behind that modest face was a woman oppressed by decades of chauvinism. After the meal, she left us to clean the dishes and put them away. But I could notice a spring in her step and a twinkle in her eyes.

"You amaze me Mr. Damania. Every single thought, idea and belief that you have is contrary to my principles. I believe in the supremacy of Islam to the exclusion of all other faiths. I believe that our principles and ideals would ultimately conquer the world. That noncompliance with the Koran and its ideals should be severely punished. If you were before me accused of any of the beliefs that you claim to have and if you were under my jurisdiction, I would have no hesitation in sending you to prison as a criminal who has insulted our faith and beliefs. Yet I'm fascinated by you and actually feel a sense of warmth and friendship towards you. This is inexplicable." He said this as he lit his hookah and I lit my cigar.

"Ayatollah, with the utmost respect, I must tell you that you underestimate yourself. I have come to the conclusion that deep down in your heart you are a very reasonable and rational person. You question your faith and your beliefs which your background prevents you from discarding. Again with the utmost respect, I would like to state that unquestioned faith and belief are not possible for an intelligent and well read man like yourself. Because I come from another world, you can easily tolerate me as an alien who cannot do any harm to your beliefs and your faith. Yet, you are deeply interested in my disagreement with your principles."

His mouth fell open in shock. "I don't believe I'm hearing this. Nobody has ever spoken to me in this fashion and the fascinating part is that instead of being offended, I'm intrigued by you. Can two people so different from each other be friends?"

"That Ayatollah is the unfortunate thing about faith. It does not permit you to be friends and appreciate the viewpoint of others who have different ideals and a different faith. I will be honest with you, I respect Islam but I do not believe in it. I am not at all offended in the least that you do not believe in Zoroastrianism. The capacity to accept diversity of opinion is the sign of civilized man. You do not know me and yet you have offered me your friendship."

"Do you trust me, Mr. Damania? You have just told me that I cannot tolerate any difference of opinion. You also told me that I do not know you. How would you feel if I gave you details about your behavior and actions which normally would be totally unacceptable to me? And yet, I like and accept you as a friend! Would you give me your word of honor that you will not reveal the information I am about to provide to you to anybody, under any circumstances, if I give you my word of honor on the Koran that that information will never be used to the detriment of yourself or any of your friends in Iran?"

His words literally made me sit up. I found it extremely difficult not to express my shock, but I successfully controlled my expressions. "Of course I agree Ayatollah. Your word is your bond," I said with a false smile on my face.

"Then let me tell you all I know about you in Iran. You, your friends and your host every evening, consume copious quantities of Scotch whiskey, preferably single malt. You are having an affair with a lady called Zainab, who is allegedly your secretary. Very many evenings, you have meetings with several important Iranian political figures not necessarily involved with business or industry. Your purported reason for coming to Iran is business and yet you are presently in a part of Iran which has no significant commerce or industry. Tell me, my friend, are you involved in any kind of smuggling or other financial racket?"

To say that I was shocked and scared was to put it mildly. I came to the conclusion that there were spies in the home of my host. The moral issues and legal consequences of a foreign infidel having an affair with an Iranian Muslim woman could be very grave indeed. However, there was a silver lining to this information. The Ayatollah may have found out about my affair with Zainab and my love for whiskey, which were basically modest crimes compared to starting a revolution in Iran. So I decided to play on the Ayatollah's sense of decency and what I truly believed was his affection for me. Secondly, politeness is often the best defence. So with a sad expression on my face I said to him. "Ayatollah. You claim to be my friend and you spy on me? As far as the whiskey is concerned, Yes, I did consume some whiskey, which is not against my faith. My friends, who are Muslims, had nothing to do with that. As far as Zainab is concerned, is it a sin to love somebody?"

"My friend, your consumption of alcohol in Iran is a criminal offense as you know but it is not a serious matter. I will ignore it. As far as Zainab is concerned, there is no law in Iran which prevents an older man from desiring a younger woman. I don't blame you, because she's very beautiful." He said this with a warm and indulgent smile which relieved me considerably. "As a matter of fact, I envy you, but don't tell Mariam I said so." Surprisingly, he started laughing.

"But what about the spying, Ayatollah? Do you spy on your friends?"

"Mr. Damania, one of my duties in this area is to keep a tab on possible political unrest and economic crime. We therefore have our own sources to determine what is going on in our area. Now let me ask you a question. Why do you think I told you what I knew if I wanted to hurt you? Would I not have used this information and had you arrested? The only reason I told you all this is to warn you that you are being watched. Not only by myself but by others. So my friend, the purpose of this conversation was to protect you, not to offend you."

In spite of my fear and concern I felt tremendous affection for this man. A man whose principles, ideals, and beliefs I almost detested and whose religion was a matter of indifference to me. There was one thing in him which was far superior to a majority of friends and acquaintances I have. He was indeed a man of honor and I concluded that under no circumstances would he betray me. Nor would I betray him.

I arrived home totally exhausted and immediately decided my discussion with the Ayatollah should never be revealed to my friends and host. Any allusion to Zainab would unnecessarily bring attention to her, especially as no one in our group had the slightest clue about my relationship with her. Secondly, the Ayatollah had obtained my solemn word that the conversation would remain secret. Thirdly, if his suspicions were made public, they might take some drastic action against the Ayatollah, which may cause grave jeopardy to our future plans. If they did succeed, then my friend who had warned me for my own benefit would possibly be severely hurt. So I decided to keep quiet. However, with the fatigue and exhaustion of this evening, I decided to once again embark on my unIslamic remedy to reduce tension. I must have finished the glass in literally minutes, got changed and into bed. As I was about to doze off, I heard a knock and I knew who it was. I opened the door and Zainab walked in with a beautiful smile and sparkling eyes. "My man looks tired. Do you want me to go away and let you rest or should I come into bed and refresh you with my charms." She asked as she laughed mischievously.

"Come into my arms my darling, your soft delicious flesh will take away all my fatigue and worries." She moved into my arms and kissed me on my mouth. Her mouth opened and her soft, delicious tongue slowly slipped into my mouth deeply and passionately and we hugged each other. "What is the matter with you my love, your body tells me that you are in great anguish?"

After obtaining a promise that she would keep my revelations secret, I told her everything that the Ayatollah had mentioned. She was scared. "Oh my God! That religious devil will destroy both of us."

I explained to her the promise given by the Ayatollah and my faith and trust in him. She did not however sound convinced. I also explained to her the very fact that he confided in me was to protect me. There was no other reason for him to confide in me. I also told her of the warmth with which he had treated me. She clung to me, tightly with tears in her eyes. "I don't care if he hurts me. As long as he does not hurt you. If he kills you, he better kill me too. As long as you are with me, you will protect me."

"My Zainab, you are the kind of woman every man dreams of! Your loyalty, beauty, passion, and above all your capacity to give your self to your man so totally and submissively, is the kind of heaven we do not find in the West."

"I want to belong to you. I want to serve you. I want to love you. I want to be a part of you. Fill me with yourself my man." She said this with much emotion and passion as she completely undressed me. I watched her beautiful hands and fingers as she stripped me. Her red nail polish shimmered in the bedroom light with the occasional touch of her fingers on my naked flesh. The feeling was so sexy it would have given an erection to a castrated bull. Then she moved to switch off the light and I stopped her.

"No Zainab, I want to make love to you with all my senses. I want to look at your naked body in the light to appreciate the beauty and texture of every soft recess of your lovely skin. This will satisfy my eyes. I want to touch every millimetre of your silken body and kiss every millimetre of it. This will satisfy my sense of touch. I want to smell the scent of your womanhood; this will satisfy my sense of smell. And last but not least, I want to taste the honey of your flesh and the nectar of your womanhood. So don't switch off the light."

She walked over to me now completely naked and slipped into my arms. "My Shahnshah and my man, you mentioned making love to me with all your five senses, but now I'm holding something in my hand. It seems to be a sixth sense. Surprisingly it is growing at an enormous pace. My love, put him inside me."

I was inside her and was kissing her passionately. She opened her mouth and surrendered her tongue to me. I could feel her delicious breath on my face. She wrapped her legs around me and pulled me deeper into her. She was saying something in Farsi. So I asked her to translate, and she said," take me, take me, fill me with your seed! Make me a part of you."

After we had finished making love, she remained in my arms. She closed her eyes and fell asleep. With every breath I could feel her breasts soft against my chest and I suddenly realized that heaven was not in the sky, nor in the hands of God. It was right here, between the arms of this delicious Iranian goddess. My Goddess.

CHAPTER 7.

The noise of thunder awakened me in the middle of the night. It was a strange phenomenon for this part of the world. There was hardly any rain and certainly no thunder clouds. I was a bit curious as to why I was hearing the sound of thunder and got up to look out of the window. There were neither clouds nor rain. I also noticed that I could see in the distance streaks of what appeared to be lightning which of course was impossible with the climactic conditions of the area. Before I could discover the truth, there was a knock on the door, it was Abbas Rouhani. "Your Majesty, at last the day has arrived. The destiny of Iran is about to change. Our forces have attacked the Islamic Republic in twelve different areas. General Osmani has taken charge and soon Zahidan will be in our hands. My major concern at the moment is not the operation of the war but the duty of protecting you, if necessary with my own life and I am ready to do so. A couple of points need to be cleared. No one knows of your ancestry or what part we expect you to play in the oncoming days. The only person who may have a suspicion is the Ayatollah. Everyone in this area knows that you are residing with me. The first thing to do is to take you to an area where you will be hidden. Next, we will fabricate some evidence to indicate that as soon as you found out about political turmoil, you took off for Canada. With your permission, I will make some derogatory statements about your cowardice and how you abandoned all your business associates here in Iran even though we had promised you security and safety. Please give me permission to do this and dress as quickly as possible so that we can go away from here."

Needless to say I had no difficulty in complying with his requests and got ready at a faster pace than I ever remember doing. You see, at age seventy, I am not particularly anxious to go to war or be involved in any military escapade.

In the darkness of the night Abbas himself drove me away from his home. It was pitch dark as all the lights in the village were out. We skirted the city and took rural roads and dirt tracks to avoid being seen or confronted by anyone. After about an hour's drive, we arrived at what appeared to be a stone warehouse. It seemed like a place where one would store bricks, mortar or cement. There was a steel door and Abbas opened it with a key. Inside the warehouse, I could see several building materials stored. Abbas explained to me that this was the material he used in his construction projects in the area. He then took me to a cabinet and with great effort moved it. There was a hatch and a door imbedded in the flooring, with stairs leading into an underground chamber. We both walked downstairs and to my surprise I found a living room with a television set, tables and chairs, an attached bedroom with an ensuite, all of which looked very clean and comfortable.

"This living area is completely soundproof. No one will be able to hear you from above, even if they are standing right over this area. We have made certain specific provisions so that every single thing that happens above your area will be heard by you but not vice versa. There is a telephone connected to our number. The moment you pick it up we will know that you are in trouble and come to your assistance. Sir, if necessity arises, just pick up that phone. You do not have to dial. Within seconds help will arrive. The only request I have is that you do not try to get out of this area by yourself until we come for you. Remember, if you pick the phone up it will mean two things to us. One, that you are in danger, and two, that you have a query or you need assistance. To keep you from being lonely, we have requested your secretary Zainab, to attend to you at all times." He said this with a leer in his voice, which I did not appreciate. So I just ignored him.

After Abbas left, I looked around the living space. It was relatively comfortable but one could not avoid thinking of a tremendous similarity to a prison. It appeared to me to be rather strange that I had come all the way from Canada, leaving my beautiful home, to sit in an underground chamber in order to avoid being killed by a bunch of religious fanatics. I laughed at myself and the ridiculous thought that a man recently elevated to the rank of His Majesty the Shahnshah of Iran., had to hide in a soundproof underground bunker. Suddenly, my sense of humor prevailed and I started to laugh. About an hour later there was a slight knock and Abbas once again opened the hatch. He and Zainab walked down the stairs. " Your Majesty, I have brought your secretary to look after you. There are enough groceries and cooking utensils, she will keep you comfortable and well fed. With your permission I will leave now." I nodded, Abbas bowed and left, closing the hatch behind him.

"Oh, my love, what have you gotten into? You know they will kill you if they find you. I have heard that the Islamic Republic suspects you of being involved with the rebels and have posted a reward for any person who provides information leading to your arrest."

"My darling," I said, "When trust and responsibility are placed on the shoulders of an ordinary man, when the task of bringing civilization and democracy to a nation sick with religious fanaticism is one's goal, then one's life is an insignificant thing. I do not know whether we will succeed, but if in the attempt I die and Iran becomes free and civilized, then my trivial existence would be a worthwhile sacrifice. My present concern is not me but my beautiful Zainab. I want you to live, be happy, find a nice educated, intelligent man and remember me as a pleasant interlude in your life."

She moved away from me. Her green eyes flashed in my direction and I had never seen such anger flashing in her beautiful eyes. "So you think that you are a pleasant interlude in my romantic life. And that if it ends, I should start anew with a new man in a new location. Is that what you think of me and my love for you? Perhaps you yourself have considered me a toy and so you attribute the same emotions to me. You are my life, my existence, my soul. If you die, I go with you. I do not know where you come from, but a respectable Iranian woman does not forsake her man when he's in danger. So Mr. Shahnshah, next time you get such cheap notions about me in your cold Canadian heart, just manage to remember a cold Canadian phrase, bugger off!"

The intense expression in her face and the extreme anger she felt made her look so beautiful that I could not stop laughing. I realized that I was laughing for two reasons. First, how beautiful she looked when she was angry and next, I was satisfied that indeed she loved me. Those expressions could not have been doctored even by a Hollywood star. With all the respectful language she had been dishing out to me, the words bugger off., sounded so cute that I took her in my arms and kissed her passionately on the mouth. Initially she tried to push me away but a few seconds later she relented, placed both her arms around my neck and kissed me back as passionately.

"Begum Zainab, his imperial majesty the Shahnshah of Iran, humbly asks forgiveness from the most beautiful woman in his realm. Am I forgiven?"

"Yes, yes, you are forgiven my Shahnshah and I will accept any punishment that you dole out to me for the offense of telling the Emperor of Iran to bugger off." She started laughing and hugged me so tightly that I could feel every nook and corner of her body against mine. That hug also had the effect of slightly elevating a certain portion of my alleged royalty.

She must have felt it, for she smiled, looked into my eyes and said "I think you have forgiven me, my Shahnshah. I can actually feel your forgiveness against me."

"Alright now it is my turn to be forgiven. Give me some indication that you have forgiven me."

She smiled at me and very slowly and tantalizingly undressed and lay down on the bed. "My Shahnshah, accept your woman's forgiveness. Take me now and take me always and do not ever insult me or humiliate me by suggesting that there can be any other man in my life."

As you all know I am seventy years old and have enjoyed a fair number of relationships in my youth, but honest to God, this woman took my breath away. Suddenly I was embarrassed beyond measure as not only tears came to my eyes but I could not control my sobs. She had me against her heart, tapped me gently on my back and comforted me as if I was a baby. Surprisingly, the pleasure of the gesture was so great that my embarrassment for behaving like a juvenile disappeared.

We were both fast asleep when the cell phone rang. I responded and it was Abbas. "I have a matter of the utmost urgency to communicate to you Mr. Damania. The area where you are presently stationed is now surrounded by the army of the Islamic Republic. We have reason to believe that they may be suspecting me of being involved with the revolutionary forces, so it is quite likely that they may search all areas where I have recently been. However, at this point in time, there is no reason to believe that they think you may be hidden in the warehouse. If you hear any commotion upstairs, please keep in mind that you can hear them but they can't hear you. So please do not come out, under any circumstances. We cannot come into your area at this time so we cannot rescue you, but within days we are hoping to annihilate the forces of the Islamic Republic in the Zahidan area. Once this is accomplished, you will be completely safe."

I disconnected the telephone and noticed that Zainab was crying and shivering. I took her into my arms and explained to her in detail what Abbas had said and that we would be completely safe if we did not go out of the basement or foolishly expose ourselves.

There was a deck of cards and I asked her to play a game with me to divert her from her anguish. After a couple of games and some silly jokes, she smiled for the first time. Soon we were lying side-by-side relaxing when I almost fell out of bed with an explosion from above and considerable glass shattering. Zainab screamed and I hushed her up. "Quiet my love, don't make any noise." I then remembered what Abbas said, we can hear them but they can't hear us.

She clung to me and we sat quietly. Now we could hear several individuals shouting and moving all over the warehouse. Zainab translated for me. One male voice apparently stated words to the effect, "I want to be sure that that Canadian pagan bastard Damania or any other infidel is not hidden in this area." We could hear them ransack the warehouse above us. Bags of cement, bricks and wooden cabinets were smashed and thrown around. Luckily, they did not pick up the cabinet under which the door to our hideout was located. After about forty minutes the same man shouted to the others. "I don't think any of those bastards are hidden here."

"Should we burn this place down Captain?" One of the men asked.

"No, leave it alone. We might later use this place to house some of our soldiers. No point in destroying property when we can use it later."

They marched out of the area. For a few minutes we could not believe our good luck. When we heard trucks moving away we both relaxed. The remainder of the day and the ensuing night were like a nightmare. We hardly talked or slept. Hours later, we could not tell whether it was morning or night. And of course we could not look out to ascertain this because we were underground. Zainab made some breakfast, basically just bread, butter and jam and we ate hastily. She also made some coffee which we drank. Then the phone rang. I picked it up. It was Abbas. "My dearest friend, my Shahnshah, are you OK? I have just been informed that the government troops had surrounded your area and were looking for you as well as us. I am so relieved to hear your voice. And God. I'm so grateful that you are safe."

"How far are you from here. And what are our chances of escaping?" I asked.

"The resistance of the enemy forces in this area is now totally crushed. A majority of them have been killed. The commanding officer has surrendered. We are two kilometres from the warehouse and should be in your area within the hour. We will first surround the warehouse before coming in. This is to be certain that there are no enemy forces either inside the warehouse or lurking in the area, so please be patient. We will die ourselves before we allow anyone to harm our Shahnshah." His anguish was apparent and his voice was breaking as he said those words. The relief I felt was so great and the end of abject fear so delicious, that I started laughing and hugged Zainab, who was listening to our conversation. I hung up the telephone and sat down. We were both breathing heavily. I could see tears in Zainab's eyes and I hugged her again.

It was about an hour later when we could hear voices and steps above us. "Nothing to worry about Shahnshah. We are here now!" It was Abbas' voice.

I had never heard anything that sounded more melodious to me than that voice, assuring us of our safety. Soon the hatch opened and Abbas came down. "My Shahnshah, allow me the liberty of hugging you. It may be presumptuous on my part but believe me, the relief I feel at seeing you secure is far more important to me than all the protocol in the world."

I hugged him back. Zainab gave him a tantalizing smile and we all went upstairs. There were about eight trucks with heavily armed soldiers. Machine guns drawn. As soon as I came outside they stood at attention and saluted me. "Brave soldiers of Iran, defenders of democracy, bow to your Emperor, the descendent of Yazdegard Shahriar." Abbas commanded and they all got down on their knees and bent their heads.

"Rise my brave soldiers," I said, "the days of bowing and scraping are over. The era of democracy, freedom, particularly religious freedom and the equality of all citizens, has now arrived. You may all rise." I said.

Abbas was smiling at me, a smile of pure adoration and I noticed that there were tears in his eyes.

I suddenly had a strange feeling and realized the unreality of the whole situation. I, a Canadian citizen, born in East Africa of Zoroastrian, Parsi origin, a chartered accountant educated in England, standing on Iranian soil, was being hailed in Farsi, a language which I had no knowledge of, as the Emperor of this alien land. Was I going to wake up soon and realize that this was either a pleasant dream or the fantasy of drinking too much? Was it really my destiny to be the Emperor of Iran? Especially now, that I was about to retire?

A special seat with a velvet cushion was provided for me in the middle truck. Next to me were two other seats, one for Zainab and the other for Abbas. Both in front and at the rear were trucks with troops ready to defend us. We started moving and within the hour we were far north of Zahidan. There was a lake in the distance and we were passing through a hilly area. As the trucks were negotiating a winding road, I suddenly heard an explosion. In total shock I realized that the two front trucks had basically been eliminated. Body parts were flying in all directions. All the soldiers were killed and the trucks totally destroyed. Before I could realize the severity of the situation, the two trucks behind us were also blown up. Abbas grabbed our hands and pulled us out of the truck. He led us into the bushes along the side of the road where we hid. The remaining soldiers were firing but I was not sure at whom or what. Then we heard a few more explosions. I soon realized that all the soldiers were either dead or severely injured. We were still hiding when we heard voices and approximately two hundred men dressed in the uniforms of the Islamic Republic surrounded the area.

With my stay in Iran now, I was able to understand a few words of Farsi. One officer shouted orders. "Catch all the remaining infidel bastards! Do not kill them. We must take them to the authorities and interrogate them so that we know exactly what they are up to."

In minutes we were surrounded and roughly pushed into trucks. "Which one of you pagans calls himself the emperor of Iran?"

"I do Captain!" said Abbas. "Shoot me if you so wish!"

Suddenly I realized that in the presence of such loyalty and bravery my life was a triviality. I was not going to allow this brave man to die for me.

"He is lying Captain," I said. "I saw this man and this lady stranded on the road with their car in a ditch so I gave them a ride. They have nothing to do with us so let them go. Because I gave them a ride and I was kind to them, this brave man is merely trying to defend me. As evidence, you will notice that I do not speak Farsi and I am not an Iranian. I am your man."

The captain looked at me with absolute disbelief." You are admitting to me that you are the impostor we are trying to catch"?

"Yes I am. And if you let these innocent people go, I promise you I will cooperate with you in every way." I said.

"No one is leaving. You are all going to the authorities who will determine your fate."

After an interminably long drive we arrived at a military camp.

The soldiers rudely pushed us out of the truck and led us into a confined area surrounded by armed guards.

"You pagans have tried to endanger the Islamic Republic. Your fate will be decided by our religious leaders. That includes you, you pagan bastard." the captain bellowed at me.

We remained in that area for almost an hour, after which I was separated from my group and led inside the building. "Wait here and do not make any trouble. We will call you when we are ready."

A half hour later I was led to a small room and made to sit on a chair facing a desk behind which was a portrait of Ayatollah Khomeini. Frankly, I was numb with fear but more worried as to what they would do to Zainab and Abbas.

Soon, I heard voices in the background and strangely enough I recognised one of them. "Stand up pagan!" The captain shouted at me. "Your judge, the respected Ayatollah is about to arrive." To my absolute amazement the man who arrived was my friend the Ayatollah. I could see that he was shocked to see me here.

"What the hell is going on"? he shouted. "Why have you arrested this man?"

"Ayatollah, this pagan claims he is the Emperor of Iran and is actively participating in the revolution."

"Nonsense! This man is an honored guest of Iran! He has nothing to do with the rebels! You have made a serious mistake! Leave us alone so we can talk," the Ayatollah demanded. The captain left the room, closing the door behind him.

The Ayatollah walked over to me. "Mr. Damania, what have you gotten yourself into? Do you know what they will do to you?"

"I don't know what they will do to me, that depends on you, isn't it? You are supposed to be the judge." I said.

"You are a strange man Mr. Damania. Your dislike for our faith, and our customs I can understand, but there is one thing you will never understand about us. A friend cannot be abandoned by a good Muslim under any circumstances. I pledged my friendship to you once, and I will support you in your time of need!"

I was so touched by his affection and his loyalty that I embraced him. "Ayatollah, I am not a Muslim and I am not a religious man, but for the first time I have encountered a true Muslim, whose word of honor is beyond personal advantage."

"Thank you, my friend. The only request I have is that you do not let me down. They tell me that you are part of the revolution. I do not believe that, as I cannot understand why a Canadian citizen is interested in our internal affairs, I hope I am right."

I nodded in agreement and felt extremely guilty that I was lying to a man who had just saved my life.

"I will arrange transportation for you and Zainab to return to Zahidan."

"What about Abbas?" I asked.

"I cannot help you when it comes to Abbas. We have evidence that he is involved with the enemy."

"Ayatollah," I said, "that man offered his life to protect me from your troops! Do you believe sincerely that in order to save my life I will sacrifice his? Walk away from here and leave him to die? You are an honorable man, what would you do in my position?"

"You put me in a very difficult position my friend. Do you not realize that I will be in trouble if they find out that I allowed Abbas to leave with you?"

"Ayatollah, you are my friend! I give you my word that if asked, I will tell them that you allowed me to go with Zainab and without your knowledge I helped Abbas and that is how he escaped."

The Ayatollah merely smiled. "You think any one will believe that? Go my friend! You must leave quickly. May Allah protect you." He bowed and walked away.

I knew in my heart that he did not believe me. I also knew he had no idea that the revolutionaries thought of me as their next Emperor. Luckily, my involvement in the revolution seemed unlikely to him, particularly since he did not know that I was the alleged direct descendent of Yazdegard Shahriar.

An Army officer came with me to contact Abbas and let him know that we were allowed to leave. Zainab and the two of us were driven to a nearby village which appeared to be still unoccupied by the revolutionaries or the government forces. "I have to leave you here now, this is neutral territory. You must make your way from here on your own." I could feel the anger and contempt in his voice. I then became concerned that a negative report from him of our release may cause some problems for the Ayatollah but there was nothing I could do about that. The three of us got out and walked away from his car. He watched us for a while and hastily drove off with tires screeching, causing a cloud of dust and confirming my belief that he did not believe in my innocence and if possible he would hurt us. Once again I realized that our life had been protected by a man whose rigid faith and ideals I had no respect for.

Abbas immediately took charge. "That officer is a dangerous man. We have to get out of this village before he can take any action against us."

Abbas talked on his cell phone for a minute and hung up. "I just spoke to one of our units and they are on their way to pick us up."

A military truck arrived within the hour and we were quickly and driven away. Through the rising dust, after a long time, I could see what appeared to be a military camp. This was confirmed when Abbas sighed with relief.

"The Ayatollah told me what you did for me. You were willing to stay behind and risk your life rather than leave me behind. Why my Shahnshah? I am just a businessman. You are the future of our revolution. If anything happens to you, the future of Iran would be jeopardized."

"You want to call me your Shahnshah. You offer your life to protect me and then you expect me to leave you to be tortured to death? Tell me Abbas, if I had done what you suggested, would I be a man worth anything else but your contempt? Would you have wanted such a man to be your Shahnshah?"

He bowed to me, took my hand and pressed it against his eyes. "Now my loyalty to you is not just because you are my Shahnshah, but because I exist thanks to your bravery and honor."

We were welcomed at the military camp like long-lost brothers. Coffee and food were brought to us. The officers would not sit down in my presence. It was strange to eat and drink with about twenty-five officers standing at attention watching me. Oh the joys of monarchy!

General Hashmat Osmani soon came to the camp and greeted me respectfully but with great affection, almost like a long-lost friend. "My Shahnshah, you caused us a lot of anguish. As a matter-of-fact at one point we were afraid that they may have killed you. Please, sir, in future do not go anywhere without an escort. The future of Iran is now on your shoulders. I have arranged a comfortable house for you. You will have your privacy, but must be guarded twenty four hours a day."

The General himself drove us to a very comfortable house and I could see that it was surrounded by a barbed wire fence. There were at least twenty armed men guarding the property. We entered the house and I was delighted to see that there were no servants, so that Zainab and I could once again be alone after the long tense period that we had gone through. The house was well decorated and furnished with all modern amenities. Zainab found the bedroom and just lay down. She seemed totally exhausted. I went and sat near her and held her hand in mine. I smiled and said, "My sweet Zainab, we have gone through a very difficult period. If you weren't associated with me, you would not have gone through this hell. A very famous English poet, William

Shakespeare said, uneasy lies the head that wears a crown." In my case, it seems there is no crown, just an uneasy head and you my dear Zainab have to share that uneasiness with me."

She opened her eyes and looked deep into mine. "My love and my Shahnshah, when I first met you my attraction was your ancestry. I felt intoxicated at the thought that you were the descendent of the original Kings of Iran. But I've already told you that. Then I came to know of your integrity and kindness and I fell in love with you. If the price of this is what we just suffered, then I'm willing to bear that cost. Apart from my love for you, I've come to the conclusion that I do not want to ever live without you. So here, you have my answer."

CHAPTER 8.

It was early the next morning when General Hashmat Osmani came to my new residence. He knocked on my bedroom door and I was glad that Zainab had already gone to the kitchen. As I opened the door, the General bowed in my direction. "My Shahnshah, we have had considerable military success in the Zahidan area. The Islamic Republic's forces have been completely quelled. As a matter-of-fact most of them have escaped to the north. However we have been successful in arresting five top military officers and approximately eleven government and religious bureaucrats. Some of these men have been responsible for atrocities against other citizens, particularly Sunnis and other minority communities. They have to be dealt with legally. The authorities in Teheran are now completely aware of your status with us as our Shahnshah. There is no need to hide you anymore. It is also imperative that you now take on the duties as the supreme Judge and deal out justice to these men. Would you therefore agree to accompany me to the military compound that we have set up?"

"General, I realize that sooner or later I will have to shoulder certain responsibilities and all of them will not necessarily be pleasant. But if I am going to act as a judge, I want your assurance that you or the revolutionary forces will not interfere with my decisions and that I will be free of any military pressure or political necessities. If I'm going to win the hearts and minds of the Iranians, then that can only be done by convincing them that I am not their Shahnshah for the power and glory, but to genuinely bring in justice and equality to all Iranians, including the Shi'ite majority, even though some of their members may have perpetrated atrocities against others. The innocent will be protected and the guilty punished only on the strength of the evidence before me."

"Shahnshah, do you genuinely believe that a mere military officer like myself would dare to challenge your decisions? I only ask for the privilege of informing you of the consequences of your decisions before you pronounce your judgments. I also seek the privilege of advising you of the penalty inflicted on certain individuals, who should be punished harshly in order to set an example to others in the Islamic Republic. They should be careful how they deal with our citizens and any members of our military forces."

"General, I really respect your integrity and will greatly value your advice! However, the final decision will have to be mine and it will be strictly based on the evidence before me and not influenced by any political necessity. Can I have that deal?"

"Yes my Shahnshah, I agree."

The General and I were driven to the military compound. En route we were protected by six military trucks full of armed men who were both ahead and behind us. As soon as we entered the compound, hundreds of soldiers saluted. The national anthem of Iran was played. It was a scintillating tune. As soon as I got out of the vehicle, two soldiers approached me, bowed then stood behind me to drape an embroidered robe over my shoulders. When this was completed, they all bowed reverently and chanted, 'Long live our Shahnshah! Long live the descendent of the Sassanians! Let the glory of ancient Iran rise from the dust and darkness!"

Thanks to Zainab's constant instructions in the Farsi language, I thought I might be able to speak a sentence or two to thank the subjects of my new nation. As these thoughts entered my mind, I noticed that the General was a bit disconcerted. He knew I did not speak Farsi and could not respond to the warm welcome provided to me.

To my surprise, I stood up, directly looked at the men in front of me and said, probably in accented Farsi. "My beloved Iranians, I thank you for your warmth and reverence. I have come here to bring you the freedom and democracy that is your right and of which you have been so cruelly deprived. Raise your hands to Allah and swear that as of today, all Iranians, Sunnis, Shi'ites, Zarthushtis, Jews and Christians will be treated equally. Do you swear that my brothers and sisters?"

"Yes, our Shahnshah, we swear that! We will obey you and follow you even unto death." The sound of all these men pledging their loyalty was not just gratifying but it also made me feel humble. Did I deserve this much devotion and loyalty? Suddenly I realized why power corrupts. I was mature enough to realize that this power which was suddenly given to me was not of my doing but merely a coincidence of birth. How would a young person suddenly invested with such power have reacted? Now I knew how dictatorships and tyrants come into existence. In that moment I swore to myself that I would never allow power and privilege to interfere with my sense of righteousness and compassion.

Zainab, who was standing with the General and Abbas, was looking at me both with shock and utter affection. I imagine the shock was at my adequate delivery and acceptable grammar in the Farsi language.

The General and Abbas came over to me smiling. "You amazed us our Shahnshah. We did not imagine for a minute that you could manage so well in Farsi," Abbas said to me.

"I amazed myself too, Abbas. I still do not know what prompted me to say what I said but I'm glad I did."

Zainab approached me. "Perhaps my Shahnshah, it was your ancestors who gave you the words to address your subjects."

I whispered in her ear. "My dearest, do not believe in the supernatural. There is nothing on earth that cannot be explained by scientific thinking. Any faith and belief without evidence is ignorance. Your Iran has come down to the present level of injustice and barbarity because of faith." I realized that my words appeared to be inordinately harsh, so I smiled at her and said "My dearest, perhaps it was a beautiful Iranian woman whose instructions made me speak that way, so let my poor ancestors rest in peace".

She gave me a bright smile, which seemed to light up my soul.

They had informed me that several accused individuals would be brought before me for their trial the next morning. I was ready by 9 a.m. and was escorted to a large tent erected for the purposes of the trial. Armed guards surrounded the tent and clicked their heels when

I arrived. A man who appeared to be the court clerk announced my arrival as the judge and asked everyone to stand. The robe was placed around my shoulders by two officers. Then an individual I had never met before, bowed to me. "My Shahnshah, my name is Mohamed Sultani and I am the prosecutor. The gentleman to my right is Shamir Kirmani, he is the court-appointed counsel to defend the accused before you. The man behind me is Mustafa Barzani. He is the translator to assist your Majesty in the Farsi language. If your Majesty permits, we will start the first trial." I merely nodded my head, and the trial began.

"Before you, my Shahnshah is Aslam Sharooki. He was the Qazi of the Juma mosque in Zahidan. He is responsible for the brutal assassination of twelve Sunni Muslims who refused to convert to the Shi'ite faith. Your Majesty will be provided with evidence that two men had their tongues cut off in order to prevent them from praying as their beliefs dictated. Four others were beheaded when they refused to convert. Two women were ordered to marry Shi'ite men against their will. When they refused, the Qazi ordered that they should be raped and garrotted. Four relatives of the unfortunate women were stabbed to death for no apparent reason. Our witnesses are ready to testify before your Majesty."

"Before the witnesses are called, I would like to hear from the accused as to how he pleads and whether he wants to say anything. Mr. Aslam Sharooki, how do you plead to these charges?"

"I plead not guilty."

"Mr. Sharooki, do you have anything to say regarding these charges?"

"Yes I do! Those filthy kafirs were given ample opportunity to see the error of their ways and to enter the true Islamic faith. It is untrue that I ordered the women raped. It is true that I ordered them executed, because they did not agree to accept the true faith and marry true Muslims. I have done this for the preservation of Islam and for cleansing Iran of the pestilence that the Sunnis bring to us. One other thing Judge, I do not accept your jurisdiction. No Kufr is going to judge me, a true but humble servant of Islam."

Two soldiers with drawn daggers ran towards the accused. "Shahnshah, allow us to cut off the tongue of this impertinent beast before he insults you any further."

"My soldiers, if we behave in the same manner as this uneducated filth, how will Iran ever reach the democracy and sophistication we hope to work for? The rantings and ravings of uneducated fanatics cannot possibly affect me or any civilized person. When you visit a friend and his dog barks at you, are you offended? I feel the same about this man."

"Mr. Sharooki, have you anything else to say regarding the offenses you are accused of?"

"I have nothing to say to any Kufr who has the audacity to judge me, a true Muslim and a Qazi." He turned his head to the side and spat in the direction of one of the guards who had drawn his dagger earlier, narrowly missing him.

"Mr. Sultani, the accused has admitted that he has committed the offenses for which he is charged, therefore nothing further is required of you. I will now call upon Mr. Shamir Kirmani, the defence counsel, to make any submissions that he desires."

Mr. Kirmani stood up and bowed to me. "My Shahnshah, the accused has made my position extremely difficult. How can I present a defence when the accused not only admits to all the offenses for which he is charged but attacks and insults not only the judge himself, but the new judicial system? I therefore have no submissions, except a plea for leniency on the part of the accused, who seems to be misguided and cannot differentiate between his faith and his fanaticism. Therefore my Shahnshah, I beg of you to give him a lenient sentence of say, a year in jail, together with counselling."

Mr. Sultani stood up immediately. "My Shahnshah, defence counsel's plea of one year in jail is not only absurd but grossly inadequate. This man has murdered several individuals and he admits it. The only thing he denies is encouraging the rape of those innocent women. If he himself were the judge in this case, he would have brutally executed the accused, perhaps after severe torture. Naturally, we do not want to go back to the old days but he deserves to be severely punished under Islamic law. I would suggest that both his hands be cut off, because they were the limbs of the body used by his executioners. Then he should be beheaded!"

"Mr. Sultani, if we amputated the legs and arms of criminals, we will be continuing the same tradition and methods used by our predecessors prior to our revolution. Your offenses Mr. Sharooki, are extremely grave and the penalty that I am giving you is essential to protect the innocent. You are sentenced to death. Officers, take this brute out and shoot him."

"May pigs feast on your flesh. May the offal of pigs sour your mouth as you enter hell!" Sharooki shouted as he was led out of the courtroom.

"With your permission, my Shahnshah, may I now proceed to bring before you the second accused person for trial?"

After I nodded in agreement a man in handcuffs was brought into the court. As I looked up my shock was intense. The man in chains was my friend the Ayatollah.

"What is the meaning of this Mr. Prosecutor?" I asked Mr. Sultani. "A respected member of our society, a gentleman and a scholar is brought before me in chains? Do you know who this man is? During my whole stay in Iran there is not one single man I have respected more than this Ayatollah."

The Ayatollah smiled at me. "Shahnshah, my opinion of you is now proven to be correct. I plead guilty of having doubted your integrity and sincerity. I thought that perhaps with your elevation to the rank of Shahnshah, you would lose your affection and your sense of justice. I plead guilty of such suspicion."

"Mr. Sultani, what are the charges against this man?"

"My Shahnshah, he has preached time and again at several mosques and other meetings that any secular government in this country must be resisted, if necessary, with physical violence. He has stated publicly that only Islam should be permitted in Iran and all other faiths must be banned. I also suspect that this man has some evil scheme in mind, because for the last three or four months he has kept completely silent. This is a matter of grave concern to us."

"Mr. Sultani, has it ever occurred to you that the Ayatollah may have reconsidered his position? Perhaps altered his thinking in that area? I know the Ayatollah. I have vehemently disagreed with him on several subjects, that does not mean that I do not respect his intellect and his sincerity."

The Ayatollah smiled at me. I could not miss the warmth with which he looked at me.

"The prosecutor is absolutely correct. I did preach those things from the pulpit as he claims. Perhaps he should have asked me why I stopped preaching that before arresting and humiliating me in this manner."

"Ayatollah, our revolution was not created to suppress Islam or the freedom to practice any faith. More significantly, it is imperative that we do not crush individuals who oppose our position. On the contrary, we should try to convince them or be convinced ourselves when their logic is better than ours. Also, if we disagree with them and if their opinion does not instigate violence, then that opinion should be permitted and their right to express it protected."

"Tell me Ayatollah, are you currently instigating violence against us?"

"They all address you as Shahnshah. They ordered me to address you as Shahnshah, so I had to comply. But now, of my own free will, I am going to address you as `My Shahnshah." My Emperor, for whom I am willing to lay down my life. My silence in the last few months is in itself the very evidence that I have changed my mind about you and what you are doing for this country. Yes, I still believe that Islam is the only answer but I have also started believing that there is enormous value in your beliefs and perhaps we can live in harmony with different faiths and different ideals."

"My Shahnshah, do not believe a word of what this man says. His speeches in the past have been very aggressive, instigating violence against our regime," Sultani responded.

A flash of anger could be seen in the eyes of the Ayatollah. "Bring me a Koran!"he shouted. It was interesting to note that even the officers guarding him were intimidated and ran to get a Koran to present to him.

"You can accuse me of anything you want, but there is one thing even my worst enemies will not accuse me of and that is lying with a Koran in my hand. With this holy Koran in my hand I now swear total allegiance to my Shahnshah who has convinced me with his wisdom and generosity that my devotion to Islam can coexist with the progressive thinking brought to our country by the descendent of the Sassanians. Let me see which one of my cowardly prosecutors has the guts to tell me that I am lying!"

"Ayatollah Tabrizi," I said, "I have had the honor and pleasure of knowing you as a scholar and a friend. You do not have to prove your innocence, the prosecution has to prove your guilt. Do not forget Sir, that that guilt has to be proven to my satisfaction sitting as your judge. I have absolutely no doubt as to your integrity and the statement you just made. As a matter-of-fact, I am delighted and honored to receive your support. Release the Ayatollah immediately."

Two officers walked over to the Ayatollah and unchained his hands. He bowed to me and gave me an adoring smile so full of gratitude that I will never forget it.

"This court is now adjourned for the day."

"Ayatollah, I would request you to accompany me to my residence and I will be grateful if you will have dinner with me."

"I will be honored. My Shahnshah"

.

We both walked into my quarters. I closed the door behind us. The Ayatollah hugged me. "Thank you, my Shahnshah."

"This is a great day. Not only for Iran transforming itself into a democracy but also for the protection and enlightenment of its citizens, both Muslim and non-Muslim. What better man to help us achieve that goal than my dear friend Ayatollah Tabrizi?" I asked.

"This is a strange day my Shahnshah. In the morning I was in chains a common criminal, in the afternoon the Shahnshah of Iran is asking my assistance to set up a democracy. The ways of Allah are beyond my comprehension." He started laughing.

"Ayatollah, at one point Islam brought civilization and discipline not only to Asia and Africa, but also to Spain and Portugal. It is my humble belief that thereafter the teachings of the Prophet Mohamed were misinterpreted. Selfish, greedy kings and corrupt religious leaders used quotations from the Koran to suppress individual freedom and destroy democracy. I genuinely and honestly believe that we can turn the clock back to revive the sophistication of the Moorish rulers of Spain and Portugal. We can preserve your Islam, as well as permit other faiths to coexist and prosper. I request your help to make that dream come true."

"I am at your service Shahnshah as long as you promise me that nothing you request of me would be contrary to the teachings of my faith."

"I do not believe that anything I request of you would be against Islam. However under no circumstances will I ever tolerate any kind of religious fanaticism, Islamic or other. There are many Muslim Imams and Ayatollahs who desire forceful conversion to Islam and deprive rights to other faiths. This we cannot tolerate. What better man to preach equality of all religions and citizens than an Ayatollah of Iran who has the strength of character to admit to me as well as all Iranians that he was misinterpreting the teachings of Islam and that he has now corrected himself?"

"I will admit to you Shahnshah that this is going to be difficult for me but with your guidance and help I think I will be able to assist you. If I cannot comply with your orders because of my faith, I will tell you but I will never be disloyal to you."

"Ayatollah, you do not have to convince me of that. I already know."

We both got up, shook hands and he left after bowing to me. I felt a strange and deep joy as I thought, I have just converted a fanatic into an educated, moderate thinking human being.

I walked into my residence and went to the bedroom where Zainab officially slept. I knocked on the door, but there was no answer. I gently opened the door and saw my darling fast asleep, curled up like a little baby with knees drawn in to her chin. I kissed her gently on the cheek and she moaned and opened her eyes. She extended her arms inviting me to hug her and I did. "Come to my bed, my beloved. Your man needs you!" With her eyes still sleepy and groggy, she accompanied me to my bedroom. I closed the door. With a smirk on her face and a gleam in her light green eyes she picked up her nightie and took it off over her head. One look at her voluptuous breasts and all of my fatigue disappeared. She looked at me mischievously and said, "I have a special present for you!" I then realized that she had a Brazilian waxing done. She came over to me and kissed me on my mouth passionately. "Tell me how you want to take me."

I did not answer but picked her up and she pushed herself into me, every millimetre of her body as I placed her on the bed. I undressed and pressed myself against her warm, soft body. We remained that way for a while and I suddenly realized that heaven was not something that occasionally comes after death, but can be here on earth, in the arms of a woman who loves you. She was more intoxicating than anything that I had ever imagined in my life. Soon she was moaning and grabbed my head with her delicious thighs. Then I entered her and she grabbed me with her arms and legs until we both came simultaneously. When it was over, she relaxed in my arms and fell asleep. So innocent, so trusting, totally surrendering and completely trustful of being protected by me. The love that I felt at that moment was such that I was afraid of moving, because I did not want to disturb her. I simply did not want this moment of passion to end.

We both must have fallen asleep because the next thing I remembered was waking up in the morning. She was awake too, her eyes dreamy as she smiled revealing a dimple in her cheek. "Good morning my love, did you sleep well?"

"How can I not sleep well in the arms of a woman as beautiful as you?"

"How is the world doing outside our love nest?" She asked.

"Well, our revolutionary forces are doing extremely well and the Army of the Islamic Republic is falling back on almost all fronts. Yesterday, Shiraz fell and is presently being occupied by our forces. Our old friend, the Ayatollah has joined us and has committed himself to supporting us in every way. He has tremendous influence over the devout Muslim population. I am sure that he can bring them to our side."

"Darling, do you trust him? Are you sure he will not betray you?" She asked.

"No my Zainab. He has sworn his loyalty to me on the Koran. I know that I can trust him. The Ayatollah can be aggressive but he has pledged his devotion and I am satisfied that he will not betray me."

"Just be sure my Shahnshah. You are my life. I don't want you to get hurt."

"Now that we have been so intimate, don't you think you should call me Sharuq, at least when we are in bed?"

"Can I really? You don't mind?"

"Silly woman, you have become not just my bed mate but a part of my being. Do you think I would mind you calling me by my name?"

"Alright, I will, but only when we are alone otherwise they will not approve of my being so familiar with you."

"And what should I call you, my life, my love, my woman, my mistress, or my bed sorceress?"

"Any one of those will do except the sorceress. Am I a sorceress?" She asked with a pout.

"With those shining green eyes, that dimple when you smile mischievously and your scent when you're excited, you could easily be classified as a sorceress because you seem to devour my soul with your beauty and charm."

She sat down on the bed next to me. The mischief in her eyes and the playful smile were already causing visible enlargements in portions of my anatomy. "You better not accuse me of devouring your soul. I don't know how to do that but I sure can devour other things which will leave you much smaller than you are now."

We made love again and had just finished when the telephone rang.

"Salaam alaikum Shahnshah. This is Jahanbaksh Mirza. I was a minister of religious affairs when I first met you. I am now your humble servant and work for your revolutionary government. We have a serious religious problem and are seeking your advice. Would it be possible for us to visit your Majesty and discuss it?"

"Yes Mr. Mirza, I remember you and would be delighted to meet with you. When would you like to come?"

"Shahnshah, we are only five minutes away from your residence."

"Then come right now Mr. Mirza," I said.

Within minutes Mr. Mirza came in with three other men who were introduced to me. After some courtesies were exchanged and tea served, I asked the reason for their visit.

"Shahnshah, do not misunderstand me, we respect all religious groups residing in Iran. However the history of our country is causing some acrimony. Because of the serious dispute between the Muslim world and Israel, there is a lot of animosity towards the Jews residing in Iran. The Islamic regime has brutalized them and I certainly do not favor that. However, after the revolution and occupation by your forces of this portion of Iran, the Jews from the north and south have moved into this area and have applied to erect a synagogue in Zahidan. We cannot permit this for two reasons. The first one is that the majority of the population will be offended if the Jews are given any protection by the revolutionary government. More significantly, our revolution is succeeding and this is an Islamic state. Any support of the Jews by this government will be tantamount to supporting the enemies of Islam."

"Are the Jewish applicants here or close by?" I asked.

"They are waiting in their car outside. I asked them to wait while I talked to you."

"Ask them to come in now," I said.

One of the men who had come in with Mr. Mirza went out to summon the Jewish applicants. They arrived and bowed as they approached me.

"Shahnshah, on behalf of the Jewish community of Iran we greet you as the deliverer of freedom and saviour of our oppressed community. We hope that your government and rule will now protect our interests."

"Please sit down gentlemen. May I offer you some tea?"

"No Shahnshah, your welcome is all we need."

"All right then, what can I do for you?" I asked.

"Shahnshah, for decades now we have been restricted from practising our faith. Our synagogues were destroyed and any overt practice of Judaism has been forbidden. We are Iranians and want to be your faithful citizens! We will be loyal to our country if it will give us the privilege to serve it. There are mosques and churches in Iran and even some places of Zoroastrian worship, why should we be deprived of building synagogues? We are seeking your permission to build a synagogue in Zahidan where a large number of Jews have moved after hearing rumors of your benevolence towards the minorities."

"Gentlemen," I said, "our new Iran is not an Islamic country. There is no religious affiliation. Every faith will be protected and your right to practice yours is granted to you. I am granting you permission to erect a synagogue in Zahidan and to compensate you for the actions of the previous fanatical government, I am ordering as the Shahnshah of Iran, that this synagogue will be constructed with public funds and presented to you as a token of our apology for all the oppression of the Jews of Iran."

Mr. Mirza shot up from his chair, "Shahnshah, what are you doing. This act will be deemed totally anti-Islamic by the majority of the population."

"If I cannot protect the freedom and rights of my citizens, then I am not fit to be your Shahnshah. Mr. Mirza, here is my order to you and to the Ministry of Public Affairs. You will immediately make arrangements to build a synagogue in Zahidan. Organize a committee to work with the Jewish community to plan the construction. I am issuing an edict. Any violence against the Jews or their place of worship, any overt demonstration, will be punishable by death. Proclaim this to our citizens right away. There is no discussion on this subject anymore. It is an order. Comply with it."

"Shahnshah, your wish is our command but don't you think this matter should be considered carefully before such a drastic order is given?"

"Mr. Mirza, if we are going to become a civilized nation, then we cannot be afraid of the wrath of fanatics regardless of the idiotic faith they claim to believe in. As a matter-of-fact, I want to let them know that the oppression of any citizen will be brutally crushed. Now my Jewish friends, you may leave my presence with my personal promise and guaranty that the Jews of Iran will be protected by the Shahnshah of Iran."

To my shock and surprise all four men fell to their knees and touched my feet. "Your Majesty, in the name of the Jewish community and as the Rabbi of this group, I pledge our undying loyalty to our Shahnshah Sharuq."

CHAPTER 9.

Mr. Mirza hastily approached me and closed the door. "Shahnshah, I have some sad news for you. You remember the four Jews who came to visit you last week? They were finalizing the plan of the synagogue with our architects when they were attacked by eight men who will be before you today in court. Two of those Jewish gentlemen were murdered. The Rabbi survived. He was injured and has a non-life-threatening wound to his back. He will be the witness in your court regarding the events of the attack"

I was shocked to hear the news. Partly I felt responsible as I had ignored the advice of Mr. Mirza and therefore put the lives of four Iranian citizens in jeopardy. The look in Mirza's eyes seemed to be a statement to the effect, "I told you so." Of course he did not vocalize his feelings to me. "Was this heinous crime the result of religious fanaticism?" I asked.

"Shahnshah, I respectfully mentioned to you at the outset that there is enormous amount of resentment against the Jews in this country. The Islamic fundamentalists are afraid that their power and control are slipping. Their hatred of the Jews because of the closeness of Israel to Iran is like a poisonous fever. Instead of trying to crush them, I think the proper remedy would be to educate them that all children of Allah deserve to be protected and respected."

"We will provide them with the education that you are suggesting. Education will perhaps alter their thinking on this issue, but education is not sufficient as a remedy for murder. Let's go into court and bring those accused individuals before me immediately."

When I entered the courtroom everyone stood up and bowed. Five of the accused also bowed before me. The other three remained seated until the officers guarding them probed them with their batons and made them stand up.

The pubic attorney read out the charges against the accused. They had attacked the four Jewish citizens with daggers when they were in the company of our state architects. Two of them were stabbed, but the Rabbi managed to escape with his companion. The architects fled from the scene in their car before the assailants could attack them.

"How do you men plead to these charges?" I asked.

One of the arrogant three who had remained seated, yelled out, "We, the followers of Allah and the Prophet do not have to plead before a pagan who calls himself the ruler of Iran. We will kill all Jews, Sunnis and every pagan. No one will claim equality or propagate his false faith in Shi'ite Iran. May you rot in hell."

"So have you committed these murders in the name of Allah and your prophet?" I asked.

"I will not answer a pagan dog who has the audacity to sit in judgment over a Shi'ite Muslim, so once again, go rot in hell?"

"As far as going to hell, I will arrange that for you immediately. Unfortunately, I cannot predict if Allah will let you rot there. My jurisdiction ends on this earth! I hereby sentence you to death! You will be executed immediately! Guards, take this dog out and shoot him." The guards jumped to attention and dragged the accused out of my court. His bravado of a few minutes earlier had ebbed considerably and he was shivering and crying.

There was pin drop silence in the courtroom and a few seconds later we heard the gunshots which eliminated this beast from planet Earth. The remaining seven were now genuinely shaken. One of them stood up. "You cannot do this to us! We did this to protect Islam and the message of the Prophet. After all, we only killed Jews."

"Alas, you sick man," I said, "You do not protect Islam by killing innocent men. As a matter-of-fact you disobeyed the command of the Prophet Mohamed. He clearly stated that a `Kitabi' is permitted to follow his faith in an Islamic state. Jews and Christians are Kitabis and the Prophet had ordered that they should be protected. In fact you have not only disobeyed the command of the Prophet, but have misinterpreted his teachings."

The prosecutor asked the second accused, "Have you anything to say in your defence?"

The man fell to his knees. "Forgive me Shahnshah, the man you just had executed was my guide and leader. I obeyed him! I am sorry!"

"I do not think you are as sorry or sad as the wife and children of those two innocent citizens, whose lives you took without justification. You are sentenced to death. Take this animal out and shoot him." A few seconds later, he yelled `Allah', we heard gunfire and then silence.

The remaining six accused also did not deny their part in the murders, but justified their motives as being the preservation of Islam. I ordered them immediately executed. Their bodies were laid out in a row in front of the courthouse and I invited the news media to televise that site to the people of Iran. I provided a statement from the court, which ran as follows. "People of Iran, the descendents of Darius and Cyrus! Look at the fate of fanatical religious filth who have contravened all the dicta of Islam. Take heed that every citizen of Iran, regardless of your beliefs, will be protected under the laws of Iran that has once again returned to its ancient civilization and tolerance of all faiths and beliefs."

Before returning home, I gave strict instructions to Mr. Mirza to arrange for trusted bodyguards to protect the remaining Jewish families from violence. When I got home, Zainab was watching the news and I joined her. It was a television station from Teheran and the speaker was a local Ayatollah. "That infidel usurper has not only intruded upon our holy nation, but has taken the lives of eight Shi'ite martyrs who were protecting our Iranian brethren from Jewish terrorists. Fellow Muslims, it is your religious duty to kill this infidel and all the traitorous Muslims who are now supporting him. Take up your arms and bring glory to Iran!"

Zainab was crying "They will kill you my love. You do not know the extent of their fanaticism."

"My darling Zainab, if I were to worry about the rantings and ravings of these fanatics, then there is no place for me in Iran as the Shahnshah. We are going to conquer them and defeat them with two strategies. Rational justice and a regime that will protect every citizen of Iran. It will take time, but we will succeed, because we are superior to them mentally morally and spiritually."

I dialled the number of General Yazdegard Malek. His immediate answer indicated that he had noticed the name of the caller. "My Shahnshah, it is an honor to receive your call. How can I be of service to you?"

"General, have you been watching the news from Teheran?"

"Your Majesty, do not pay attention to those ignorant bigots! We have already taken steps to silence that animal. Needless to say, sir, he is fully supported and encouraged by the Islamic government in Teheran".

"What are you going to do about it?" I asked.

"Shahnshah, it is better that you do not get involved. It is the duty of the military to protect you. Leave everything to your humble servants."

"Thank you for your loyalty General, but I choose to be involved. Let it be known that I ordered the extermination of those animals. The people of Iran must be convinced that we are here to protect every citizen, including the Shi'ite Muslims. The protection of Islam is as dear to my heart, as is every other faith. The same punishment will be given to any one who dares to attack or defile a mosque."

"Your Majesty's request is my command and you will be obeyed to the last detail."

"Good night General, may Allah protect you. I congratulate Iran for having an army officer not only with your military talents, but your conscience and integrity."

I went to bed and held Zainab to my heart. She started crying, I consoled her and after a while I could hear her breathing evenly. She fell asleep clinging to me.

I slept restlessly and woke up at about eight in the morning. The first thing I wanted to do was to see the news which was on the Teheran TV station. They were showing a demonstration in the streets of Teheran. There was a mob shouting, "Our martyr has been murdered by the infidel and his mob. We must take revenge." I changed the channel until I found a station airing what had actually happened. The man who had recommended my demise to his followers had been shot dead in the streets of Teheran. I realized that General Maleki was a man of his word. I could not help smiling silently. I am ashamed to say that it is the first time in my life I felt satisfaction and joy that a man was killed. The next thought that occurred to me was that the man who was killed, was not a human but just a dirty religious fanatic. I was satisfied that history will later vindicate me for my feelings of satisfaction.

I immediately summoned the director of our local television station and asked him to broadcast a message from me to the people of Iran. I said, "My fellow Iranians, we have just heard the news that Kerman has now fallen to our revolutionary forces. Another Iranian city is now safe and free of the oppression of religious fanatics. Celebrate with me our progress as we move towards Teheran. Be assured that our troops will treat you with respect. They will never touch your women or children. We will protect and offer you education! We will provide you with hospitals. We will eliminate from the soil of our nation, the foul odour of fanaticism."

CHAPTER 10.

General Maleki arrived at my house at ten in the morning. He respectfully bowed to me. "My Shahnshah, I'm very sorry to disturb you so early in the morning, but it is urgent that I notify you of a very significant development. I had informed you earlier that Kerman has fallen to our troops. Our army was able to surround a significant portion of the retreating Iranian forces. We were successful in capturing five thousand artillery men. The problem is we do not have any facilities to keep them as prisoners of war and though they are enemy troops, I do not think it is fair to execute them. They are soldiers obeying orders. My other issue is, I cannot be sure how many of these men are religious fanatics who may plan to retaliate against our revolution. Shahnshah, what should I do?"

"General, where are the men presently lodged?"

"Your Majesty, we have created a camp, and there is a contingent of our troops guarding them"

"General, take me to that camp!"

"Shahnshah, it is not safe for you. I have no way of knowing which one of them may be a terrorist, sworn to kill you. How can I take such a risk with the life of my own Emperor?"

"General, surround me with heavily armed men. This sight will deter any enterprising fanatic from taking the law into his hands. Always remember that suicide bombers cannot rationalize their actions. A show of force and the possibility of dying without becoming a martyr is normally not attractive to these inferior human beings."

"Shahnshah, is that your command? Then I would like to respectfully inform you that I cannot possibly be responsible for your safety."

"My dear General, trust me. I am not a military officer but unfortunately in my life I have had to deal with an enormous number of inferior human minds. It is only now that I realize that the experience has been a precious gift."

Our car was surrounded by trucks carrying heavily armed troops. We arrived at the prison camp where I asked for a loud-speaker. I entered the camp. The prisoners were silent. "Who is the superior officer of your group?"

"I am General Siddiq and I am their leader. How can I be of service to you?"

General Maleki lost his cool. "If you claim to be a General and a military officer, then you should have the courtesy to address our Shahnshah, as His Majesty."

"Patience, General Maleki. Perhaps, this officer does not know who I am. Let us show him that we treat our enemy soldiers with respect and may be this will teach them to be respectful in return."

General Siddiq appeared to be totally shocked at my words. "Sir, what is the point of discussing anything with you? We represent the Islamic Republic! You will execute most of us. I am the General and will probably be the first to go."

"General Siddiq," I said, "I think we will have to re-educate you in the behavior patterns of civilized nations. You and your military personnel are under oath to fight for your regime. Your personal opinions and beliefs are irrelevant because you obey orders. We, on the other hand, have not come to Iran to kill or convert people to our way of thinking. We want to bring development and democracy to Iran. Nothing is gained by killing soldiers for obeying their orders?"

"Sir, my life is less important to me than the lives of my men. Spare them and I am willing to die."

"Brave soldiers of Iran, you ought to be proud of your General. If such men had ruled the Islamic Republic, there would be no need for a revolution. First of all, let me assure you, no one will be executed because you are soldiers of Iran. However, if we find evidence that you are terrorists, or have committed atrocities, then those individuals will be immediately dealt with. I have another option open for all of you. You have fought bravely and you lost. You have not surrendered to the enemy but to your own Iranians. No one has asked you to abandon your beliefs, or be disloyal to your country. We are going to give you an opportunity to prove your loyalty to Iran by helping us to bring civilization to this ancient land. Our officers will now present the Koran for you to swear to protect and bring democracy to Iran. We must protect all religions from uncivilized bigots. Give your loyalty to our new Iran, we will give you ours."

A tremendous cheer came from the prisoners. "Our Shahnshah has rescued us from death! Long live the Shahnshah!"

As I was walking back to my quarters, General Siddiq joined me. "Shahnshah, I've never seen anything like this in my life. You literally hypnotized them. You converted five thousand sworn enemy soldiers into loyal troops. I am not a superstitious man, but what I just saw makes me wonder whether your royal genes from the Sassanians have anything to do with it."

I laughed, "General, I have always found that when you are totally genuine and have no selfish interest but a true concern for the people you are speaking to, then your words have an incredible impact on the listeners. You all want me to be your Shahnshah, do you think I could kill five thousand Iranian soldiers who were merely doing their duty? Is there any better alternative to saving them and winning their hearts and loyalty?"

Zainab was peacefully asleep in my arms. I was fascinated, watching her and flattered that someone so young could love and be so totally devoted to me. I was afraid to move so as not to disturb her sleep. Suddenly there was a slight vibration in the floor and then a huge explosion. We were both thrown from our bed. The front window had shattered and a part of the wall collapsed. Zainab screamed. I managed to pull her away from the rubble in case of another explosion. Five armed guards rushed into the room. "Oh my Shahnshah, how did this ever happen? We had completely surrounded your residence, so no one could enter without our knowledge. We do not know how we failed."

I asked them to leave the room so that we could regain our composure and get dressed. By the time we were ready, six truckloads of soldiers led by General Maleki arrived. For the first time, I noticed the General was nervous and perspiring. "Those bastards who have done this will pay with their lives! Shahnshah, I promise you I will personally cut off their testicles and shove them up their throats until they strangle."

My composure was slowly returning. "Indeed, General, that is a very novel and picturesque way of dealing with the enemy. Don't you think you must first find out who ordered this?"

"I will get on it right away, Shahnshah."

"General Maleki, find the culprits and bring them to me. Do you understand?"

"Your Majesty's wishes are my command Shahnshah."

Suddenly I heard a commotion and loud voices in the background. One of my guards entered the room. "Shahnshah, the rebel General Siddiq, whom you released yesterday, wants to urgently speak to you."

"No one enters this room before I search him." General Maleki shouted.

"General Maleki, you're absolutely right, search the General first, but do it respectfully and apologize to him. Tell him it is necessary after what has just happened. Do not antagonize him."

"Yes my Shahnshah!"

After he was duly searched, General Siddiq was brought into the room. He saluted and bowed to me. "My Shahnshah, I know that you and General Maleki are suspicious of me and my men. But you must know that we have found the culprits. We have interrogated them and I'm happy to report that they have confessed to this abominable crime. Would Your Majesty like to meet their leader? He is an arrogant religious fanatic and his words may offend you!"

"General Siddiq, have you ever visited a very close friend, whose affection and loyalty are absolute. However, each time you visit his home, his dog consistently barks and growls at you. Does that affect you? Inferior human beings and religious dogs are so contemptible that I apologise for comparing them to dogs." General Siddiq seemed quite taken aback by my words, but smiled, as he agreed with my views.

Five chained men were brought before me.

"Do you know who I am?" I asked.

"You are the Canadian infidel who claims to be the Shahnshah of Iran! You have come to destroy our religion, culture and way of life."

Before I could say a word, one of the officers hit him on the face with the butt of his gun. His face was smashed, and his nose was bleeding. "You think your brutality is going to scare me, infidel? You can torture and kill me but you cannot take my faith from me!"

"Your faith is very strange! You come into the house of a man you have never seen or met and put a bomb without any concern for women and children who are residing there. The only thing you have succeeded in doing is misinterpreting and degrading your Islam, for which I have so much respect."

"You four culprits, what have you got to say for yourselves?"

The other four did not seem to be as foolhardy as their leader. They kept silent and would not answer. "I am about to sentence you to death. Have you nothing to say in your defence?"

They did not answer. "Shahnshah, these four can be shot, like the dogs they are! But I think shooting this leader is an insult to our justice system. I want your permission to cut off his arms and legs and let him bleed to death for all to see," one of the officers said.

"Officer," I said, "this man is not only evil but also diseased. Brutality is not going to rid him of his incurable disease. In our new Iran we do not want to use brutality. We will not lower ourselves to the level of the brutes we want to eliminate. Unfortunately, the death penalty is necessary for a while. One day, we hope to be at a stage where we can abolish the death penalty. Now, gentlemen, let us find out who organized this heinous crime!"

"My Shahnshah, I have already investigated and have the answers to that question." General Siddiq said. "You see, Your Majesty, I did not have to look for these men. They turned themselves in and confessed to the cowardly act. They expected me to be proud of their achievement. They thought that since we had been freed by you, Your Majesty, we would join them and try to destroy the new regime. They did not realize how grateful we were to you for your generosity in sparing our lives. My Shahnshah, before I am ungrateful to you and forget the debt I owe to you, I would rather eat the testicles of a hundred pigs."

"General Siddiq," I said. "I indeed appreciate your loyalty, but your culinary tastes are a matter of great concern to me!" General Siddiq and all the other officers roared with laughter.

At my command, the five bombers were taken out and executed.

Deep inside me I felt a sudden sadness. The thought that I had the power to order an execution frightened me. I confess though, that I felt a certain consolation that five religious fanatics, their minds warped with their misguided philosophy, were no longer the occupants of my Iran. I was satisfied that slowly and surely we were cleansing the land of my ancestors of its worst malady.

In the evening, I was watching a television broadcast from Teheran. The broadcaster announced that a number of genuine patriots had attacked the sanctuary of the foreign "Kufr" and in that attempt, these great patriots had failed. They were all martyred and were now under the protection of Allah. "Have no doubt," continued the broadcaster, "ultimately, the alien Kufr and all his renegade followers will be eliminated from the soil of Iran!"

Suddenly there was a commotion in the broadcast room and the news was interrupted for a few seconds. When the newscast resumed, the broadcaster raised both his arms up in a gesture of prayer. "There is no limit to the brutality of this infidel and his band of thugs! We have just been informed that Mehdi Rahim, the commissioner of our security services and all twelve members of his committee were just killed by a bomb in their office. We believe that this was done by the followers of the infidel"

Before I could recover from my shock, General Maleki walked into the room accompanied by Jahanbaksh Mirza and my friend Ayatollah Tabrizi. "Salaam alaikum Shahnshah," Ayatollah Tabrizi said, "I have not had the honor or the pleasure of talking to my Emperor for a very long time!"

I stood up and hugged Tabrizi and shook hands with the others.

"Shahnshah, did you hear the good news from Teheran?" Maleki asked. "Our operatives have completed an undercover operation in Teheran and every one of the twelve terrorists responsible for the bomb at your residence has been exterminated. They were the most qualified armaments experts, as well as Secret Service operatives working for the Islamic regime in Teheran."

"Gentlemen, I am ashamed to admit happiness at the news of the death of highly trained Iranian officers, but I will not lie to you. Perhaps their death will bring us to our success in a shorter period of time."

Now gentlemen, I have a duty to perform and I want your total attention. I picked up a Koran, which was nearby and asked Ayatollah Tabrizi to stand up. "Come here Ayatollah! You are one of those rare persons who is not only scholarly and brilliant, but has the capacity to realize his mistakes and to amend his thinking when the evidence is provided. You are a scholar of Islam, a man of great intelligence and surprisingly, you have the capacity to see the error of your ways. Such men are rare and must rule the nation. Therefore, as the Shahnshah of Iran, I am hereby appointing you my Prime Minister. Put your hand on the holy Koran and swear that you will protect every citizen of Iran, regardless of his beliefs. You must not under any circumstances, discriminate against any one."

There were tears in the Ayatollah's eyes. "In the name of Allah, and with my hand on the Koran, I swear that I will protect every citizen of Iran, that I will not discriminate against any person on the grounds of religion or race. Above all, I pledge my total and unending loyalty to my Shahnshah."

"General Maleki, you are not only a distinguished military officer but a man whose integrity and loyalty are enviable! You have proven beyond any doubt your ability to support our revolution and to help establish a democracy in Iran. Take this Koran in your hand and swear in the name of Allah that you will protect the revolution and the rights of the people!"

General Maleki stood up, saluted me, clicked his heels and took the Koran from my hand. "In the name of Allah, I swear that I will protect the rights of every citizen and protect democracy in Iran. Above all, I pledge my life and loyalty to my Shahnshah!"

"General Maleki, I am hereby appointing you, the Commander-in-Chief of our forces and the Acting Minister of Defence. Do you accept?"

"I am honored Shahnshah."

"Now gentlemen, I have some important business to discuss with you."

"Ayatollah Tabrizi. You have been very gracious in accepting your appointment as the Prime Minister. I am particularly honored and grateful that a man of your acumen would in fact change your views to such an extent that even though you are an Ayatollah and a respected leader of the Shi'ites, you are happy and willing to work for a non-Muslim. However, Prime Minister, it would be a great asset to our government that the Iranian people fully appreciate that an Ayatollah is supporting the revolution. Therefore, your appointment as the Prime Minister must be publicized and must reach every single Iranian. Not only will this bring us more Shi'ite followers, but it will convince all other minorities that we respect all faiths and our government is not controlled or dominated by any particular group."

"General Maleki, your appointment as the Commander-in-Chief of our forces should be equally publicized, so that the present Islamic government's propaganda regarding our attack on Islam and desire to destroy the faith, may be successfully negated. Gentlemen, see to it that our radio and television stations broadcast these appointments with your pictures for all of Iran to see. I also want both of you to look into another issue. You know the citizens of this country, the ones who are intelligent and educated and deserve recognition. Find me one person from each faith, but most significantly, a Sunni Muslim you know and respect. We want to make them ministers in our government. The important point is that each one of them should be qualified for the position to which they are appointed. You two must work together to make your selections."

"There is one other very important point that I want to make. You both have pledged your total loyalty to me. I also pledge my total loyalty to you. Our private lives are our own business but as far as our public duties are concerned, there should be no secrets between us. Every decision made in the governance of Iran will be thoroughly discussed by the three of us and later, by the new ministers we will appoint. The main issue is that there should be no surprises, or independent actions! The present Iranian government is inundated with religious bigotry and tangential thinking. If we succeed in eliminating that and if our reasoning and actions are totally based on logic, then the Islamic government will crumble and we will win the war. Do you agree?"

"We agree Shahnshah, but we have to be extremely careful that any action on our part is not misrepresented as an effort to undermine Islam," Maleki said.

"All right, gentlemen! We have a lot of work to do! May Allah be our guide."

.

My two appointees got up, bowed and left my residence. They also left me with a sense of well being and trust that I had not felt before. I had a feeling of great satisfaction and victory at the thought that I had converted a brilliant man who was a religious fanatic into a rational leader of a possible future democracy.

I went to my bedroom and noticed that the reading lamp on the bedside table was on and Zainab was absorbed in her reading. One of the most adorable things about Zainab and that which made her look very cute, was her wearing mummy's glasses, like a little girl when mummy is not watching.

"What are you reading my love?" I asked.

"Well, for the last few months I've been teaching you Farsi and you've picked it up so well that I thought I should improve my English too."

"My darling, you already speak pretty good English! A hell of a lot better than my Farsi! Learn as much as you like but for God`s sake, do not lose your lovely Iranian accent."

"You have been so busy lately that you have not spent any time with me. I miss you so very much and I thought I could use the time to learn something useful, so I'm improving my English!"

The soft manner in which she pronounced the word busy, like "beezy" was so sweet and sexy that I kissed her hard on her mouth and she responded passionately. With mischief in her eyes she said, "Sharuq, now that you are the Shahnshah of Iran, you need some regal ornaments to carry with you at all times."

I did not understand what she meant and needed clarification. "Well, a Shahnshah should have a sceptre. That enhances his dignity. And I have a fascinating way of enlarging the size of the sceptre. Here, let me show you."

She started stroking and indeed my `sceptre' started to grow with every movement of her silken hand. "Zainab, if you continue like this...........!"

She smiled at me mischievously and said, "my man, let's make it grow into a sword. I will provide the scabbard, so that nobody gets hurt."

I felt like a teenager as we started undressing and kissing each other. "My Sharuq, my Shahnshah, make love to me. Fill me with your seed!"

I kissed her from head to her toes, imbibing the aroma of her womanhood and then entered her. It was heaven. She wrapped her legs and arms around me, started moving with me and moaning. When we were through, she clung to me desperately, "Stay with me. I need your passion and your love. Don't neglect me."

I kissed her tenderly, "My darling, the deepest love I feel for you is after making love to you. After my passion is spent, pure love is all that remains."

"Sharuq, do you really love me that much? You are the Shahnshah of Iran and I am just a secretary. You can have any woman you want. Will you always love me like this?"

"Zainab, when you first gave yourself to me, I was not the Shahnshah of Iran. I had no position or power. I was just an old man visiting from Canada, a foreign land with a different culture, so very different from yours."

"You said you were attracted to my history and heredity and then you fell in love with me because I was kind to you." "Why me, when you can have a young handsome stud?"

"I do not want a young stud. I want you, my man. Your heredity and origin may have excited me at the beginning, but today, it is you and you alone, that I love."

"You always ask what is it that I love in you when I could easily have any woman in Iran. I've been thinking of all your endearing qualities. Would you like to hear them?" She nodded in agreement.

"You are the most beautiful woman I have ever met or known. You are very intelligent, loyal and extremely faithful. In spite of my age, I know that you really love me. You have an incredibly rare quality which is not prevalent in the Western world, you are submissive to me. We in the West have learned to live with women who demand equality. This can be difficult when they are unkind, inconsiderate and do not share the same ideals. Equal partners should contribute to each other's well being equally. Above all my Zainab, I feel you are always there for me."

"So now my Zainab, I have presented you with all my reasons for loving you."

She snuggled in my arms and with tears welling in her eyes, said, "You are so sweet and so kind! No one has ever made me feel so precious. I will never forget this moment and the kind words that you have said to me."

I kissed her over and over again. "Yes, my darling, you are indeed precious. I may be the Shahnshah of Iran, but you are a real princess when it comes to your goodness and love. Come into my arms, stop crying and go to sleep. I will protect you and love you until the day I die."

Within a few minutes, still clinging to me, my little angel drifted off to sleep. I could feel her breathing softly against me and I also nodded off to sleep.

CHAPTER 11.

We were listening to the news on a Teheran television station. "The arrogance of this infidel is immense. He has the audacity to appoint some one called Rebanovich as Minister of Home Affairs. The Jew was not even born in Iran. He was born in Poland and came as an immigrant with his father during the days of the Shah. Could there be a more poignant insult to our Muslim state than the selection of a Minister from another religion which is the enemy of Islam itself? The Canadian pagan has appointed a Christian as the Education Minister. What other insult will he direct towards our Iran? Will he next appoint a Sunni Muslim to rule over us? Is our Shi'ite identity to be eliminated at the whim of a foreign Western pagan, who cannot even speak Farsi properly? Fellow Iranians, brothers, destroy this monster! Let us establish a pure Islamic society."

I immediately summoned Ayatollah Tabrizi and requested a meeting of some other Cabinet members. "Gentlemen," I said, "I have been watching the news and they have given me a great idea. No doubt you have been watching too and heard the complimentary description of my activities in Iran. The last statement about the appointment of a Sunni to the government of the revolutionary forces is a brilliant idea. We have Shi'ites, a Jew and a Christian in our government. Why not a Sunni Muslim too? Let us taunt them by telling them that I, the new Shahnshah of Iran, took their advice and created a government totally representative of all sectors of the population. What a belittling situation it would be for the decrepit Teheran administration to be told in front of the whole Iranian population that they gave me the idea to appoint a Sunni to my Cabinet!"

Tabrizi and General Osmani were laughing uncontrollably. "Shahnshah, your capacity to undermine and undignify your enemies is incredible! Thank God we are on your side."

"Ayatollah, a supporting statement coming from a revered Shi'ite religious leader and scholar is very touching. I think with the assistance of all you learned men, we may succeed in establishing an Iran devoid of fanaticism. We want citizens to have the freedom to practise any faith they want. I would therefore request that you air the news that I took the advice of the Teheran television station and have appointed Mohamed Sharuk, who is a professor of economics at the University of Teheran and who is presently taking refuge in Zahidan, as our Minister of Education. He is a Sunni Muslim.

"Sooner or later, we will also introduce monogamy in Iran. Women will be given equal rights. The right to divorce will be the same regardless of which party wants to end the marriage. Property belonging to the couple will be shared, depending upon the earning contribution of each spouse and the length of the marriage."

"So now gentlemen, find me an educated, intelligent woman whom we can appoint the Minister of Women's Affairs."

Both Osmani and Tabrizi stood up and bowed, "Shahnshah, your wish is our command! I can assure you there is no lack of educated women in Iran in spite of the repressive policies of the Islamic regime. We will have no problem finding such a person."

The next morning, Tabrizi walked into my office. I had never seen him so amused. He was laughing uproariously. "Ayatollah, what is so funny?"

"My Shahnshah, you are right about the idiocy of the Teheran regime. As per your suggestion we announced on our news channel the appointment of Professor Mohamed Sharuk as the Minister of Education and specifically mentioned that he was not only a Sunni, but that the suggestion came to mind because of the announcement made on Teheran television. Today, we were informed that the Iranian government was so angry that they fired the announcer, because you took his advice. Can you imagine anything more ridiculous than that?"

I could not resist laughing. "Ayatollah, don't laugh at them, thank them. That irrational behavior is very useful to us. If they run their military as they run their television stations, then our victory will be guaranteed. As a matter-of-fact, let us broadcast that we will offer a job to that announcer if he wants a job with us. Let him swear his loyalty to us, we will welcome him. That will make them look really ridiculous in the eyes of educated Iranians."

"Your Majesty, your intelligence and comprehension of the thinking pattern of your adversaries always amazes me. I will make that announcement right away."

I eagerly awaited the evening news from Teheran. Surprisingly, when the news did come, the new announcer was extremely subdued.

Slowly, and it seemed grudgingly, the news bulletin commenced. "Fellow Iranians, this is a sad day for the Islamic regime and for our glorious Iran. The hordes of the Canadian infidel have successfully occupied the city of Shiraz. The birthplace of our great poet Saadi, who is the soul of Farsi poetry, is in the hands of this accursed infidel. Are we going to sit back and accept this insult? Rise my brothers. Let us kill that infidel! We must protect Iran and our Islam!"

The surrender of Shiraz was a matter of great joy to me and I decided that a celebration drink was imperative. I was mixing my cocktail when General Osmani and Ayatollah Tabrizi entered my office. They smiled at me. "Shahnshah, this is a great day for you and for Iran. The historic city of Shiraz is now ours. Five thousand Islamic troops have surrendered to our forces. If this continues, we will be in Teheran by the end of the year." Osmani said.

I offered both men a drink. The General accepted an alcoholic beverage and the Ayatollah opted for a coffee. "General, I want you to be absolutely certain that these surrendering troops are treated with respect and are housed and fed. Not one single act of cruelty or interference with their religious practices must be tolerated."

"Shahnshah, I was absolutely certain that you would demand this and so the order has already been given."

"There is some bad news to report. During the fighting in Shiraz, the famous Masjid-e-Shirazi was damaged. Surprisingly, the cannon shot that caused the damage came from the enemy forces. It is sad that such a historical structure has been damaged."

"General, as Shahnshah of Iran, it is my duty to protect our subjects and our history. You must immediately make arrangements to have the mosque repaired. Announce on television that the Islamic forces damaged the Mosque, and we, the revolutionary forces are repairing it, because it is the duty of the Iranian Monarchy and regime to protect the historic architecture of Islam. Also announce that I, the Shahnshah, was very distressed at the damage and specifically ordered that reconstruction commence immediately. Hopefully that will convince our Iranian brothers that we are not against Islam. We are only in favor of freedom and democracy."

"I will comply with your order immediately, Your Majesty." General Osmani replied.

That evening, our television broadcast was a matter of great amusement to me. "Our beloved Shahnshah was totally scandalized by the negligence and inefficiency of the retreating Islamic forces in Shiraz. How can good, devout Muslims be so careless as to fire recklessly at one of the most significant historic centers of our country? The Shahnshah has ordered reconstruction to start immediately. As a matter-of-fact, it is the Shahnshah's belief that even prior to this unfortunate damage, the Islamic government had allowed the building to deteriorate considerably. He has therefore ordered that not only will repairs be done but the mosque will be completely refurbished so that faithful Muslims can offer their prayers to Allah in beautiful surroundings. The Shahnshah requests the retreating and defeated Islamic forces to be careful of our historic buildings."

Zainab was sitting next to me as we watched the news. She could not control her laughter. "I bet that announcement was drafted by you. Only you, my darling, know how to reach out to the people. They must be quaking in their shoes at what this announcement will do to your popularity with the remaining Iranians still under their control."

With a straight face I replied, "My sweetheart, you give me too much credit, I don't speak Farsi that well."

"My Sharuq, you're smart enough to tell them what to say and to have a translator translate it into Farsi. Secondly, your Farsi has greatly improved, mostly due to classes I provide in bed. Unfortunately, I do not talk much about mosques and construction. We do go to great lengths in discussing erections."

"You naughty little delicious woman. You just wait until bedtime and I will show you an erection that will put the Eiffel Tower and the Qutib Minar both to shame."

She came and sat down in my lap and passionately kissed me on my mouth. I suddenly realized that Allah must have been very impressed with me for I was feeling a sensation that was far more pleasurable than watching the news.

Your Majesty," my Zainab said, "such religious fervor on your part should not be allowed to go to waste. Allah has given you a weapon, your pious decision to reconstruct the history of Iran has enhanced you considerably. Such a weapon is dangerous, if not sheathed and I'm your sheath."

The erotic expression of her eyes and the tone of her voice were so exciting that I took her in my arms and we headed off to bed.

She began to undress and before removing her panties she turned to switch the light off. I stopped her. "No, my love let me have the pleasure of seeing you undress of your own volition and for the specific purpose of giving yourself to me. The greatest joy in my life is not to make love to you, but for you to desire me. Your body used to be for sex but now it is like a temple where I come to worship. When we make love, we are not two individuals, we become one. There is no Zainab and there is no Sharuq. There is only something called Zaishar, the combination of both of us."

She came to me and gently caressed me, "My man, my love, my Shahnshah, your words are so exciting that I'm afraid to let this moment go. I have never felt this way in my life so enter me and make me yours."

Needless to say, I did not need any further encouragement. We made passionate love. I was surprised that at my age I could still be so virile, but then again I had never made love to a woman as beautiful and as desirable as she was. When we were finished, I whispered to her, "You're absolutely incredible Zainab!" She smiled, raising her eyebrows, "Oh, you think all the passion was for you? I was merely helping you celebrate the fall of Shiraz," she giggled. "There are more than a hundred large cities in Iran, I think this kind of celebration is necessary every time a city falls to our troops. Do you agree?"

"You have given me your love, money, a feeling of security and the indescribable joy of belonging to the Shahnshah of Iran. For the first time in my life I can totally trust a man. Your integrity, your love, your kindness towards me, all this comes from the most brilliant man I've ever met. So what can I give you in return? Only two things. My undying love and my body will always be ready for your pleasure."

At my age, another bout of sex so soon after the first was a bit doubtful, even though I was still a bit excited. I just wanted to hold her and be held by her. We lay there looking into each other's eyes and then she was fast asleep, her sweet breath softly blowing against my chest. This was my description of heaven.

CHAPTER 12.

General Osmani arrived at my office the next morning and after the usual salute said, "Shahnshah, I have a special request from a Brigadier Safdari for an audience with Your Majesty. Safdari was the commanding officer of the Islamic forces that surrendered to us when Shiraz fell. He wants to express his gratitude to your Majesty for the humane and kind of treatment that he and his officers have received at our hands. Naturally, I've already informed him that that treatment was pursuant to your Majesty's specific orders."

"Where is he General?" I asked.

"He's in my car, your Majesty, waiting to be summoned. He has already been searched and thoroughly frisked. We consider him quite safe."

"Bring him in General, I would like to speak to him!"

A man approximately six feet four inches tall and dressed as a Brigadier of the Islamic Forces of Iran walked in and saluted crisply. "Shahnshah-e-Iran, accept the gratitude of your humble servant. I have not been raised in the sophisticated ways of the court and must express my views and respect in the only way I can and that is by being totally honest. We, the officers of the Iranian Forces were constantly told that a foreigner has usurped the government of Iran and has threatened the existence of Islam in this country. Your Majesty, we all believed this rumor. When we were defeated, we all expected to be brutalized and killed and to our shock and surprise, all injured men were taken to a hospital and the rest of us were provided with food, clothing and shelter. The Mullah, who was sent with us, allegedly to provide us with religious instructions, berated us to die to protect Islam. We were informed that we would be forced to renounce our faith and become infidels. We merely surrendered because we had no choice. It was a Friday morning when we surrendered. After we were fed and clothed and had the opportunity to wash ourselves, we were offered a visit to a mosque to pray if we wished. Even this offer I suspected had an ulterior motive but when the Friday prayers were completed, I insisted on talking to the mullah at the mosque. I specifically asked him how Muslims were treated in the new regime. The mullah seemed to be shocked at my question. He responded that the Shahnshah had become the greatest protector of all Muslims, both Shia and Sunni. I was shocked that this pronouncement was coming from a mullah in a mosque. I suddenly realized that our government had been feeding us false information all along. I therefore decided to humbly ask for an audience with your Majesty, to not only express my gratitude but to apologize for the hatred and anger we had for you and the new government. I have since then discussed this matter with a large number of my officers and they agree with everything I've just said."

"Brigadier, I'm very grateful for your warmth and good feelings. To treat an officer or soldier who was defeated and has surrendered with brutality, is to reduce ourselves to the level of the Nazis. I did not come to Iran to crush Islam or any other faith. I came here to protect the rights and beliefs of every citizen. Tell your men that they are safe. I will also send a respected mullah to your camp with the holy Koran and any soldier who swears to relinquish violence will be freed."

"Your Majesty, you must realize that we have sworn our loyalty to the regime in Teheran and some soldiers will not go back on their promise to serve the Teheran regime. But then again, our oath and promises were procured after we were fed false information. So perhaps a large percentage of the soldiers will come to the conclusion that we are not bound by that oath and will willingly join your Majesty's forces. I, personally am ready to commit my life and my services to your Majesty. Please accept me as an officer of the revolutionary forces of Iran."

I walked up to him and placed my hands on his shoulders. As he was presented with a copy of the Koran, I said, "You have made a wise decision. You are not a traitor to your country. As a matter-of-fact you will be remembered as a soldier who helped in the establishment of democracy in Iran. Now swear on the Koran that you will faithfully serve under the new Democratic Regime."

After the swearing was completed, I congratulated the officer and he left after saluting me.

One of the things I had started to enjoy was to listen to both the television stations, ours and the Islamic Republic's. Farsi is a very colorful language, with a lot of hyperbole. Instead of `sit down,' one says, `Grace the seat with yourself.' It took me quite a while to alter my own way of speaking. Repeatedly, I had requested our announcers not to be too dramatic before I realized that this was the language pattern and it could not be altered.

This evening, the recap of the news was of the events of a successful day.

"Brothers and sisters of Iran, the Shahnshah sends you his regards. Five thousand soldiers of the Islamic Republic have now surrendered and joined the Shahnshah's forces against oppression and tyranny! Our people in `free' Iran are overjoyed that these brave soldiers have realized that they were being misled by the Teheran government, and in fact, the Shahnshah is the protector of all religions, including our Islam. The mosque in Shiraz is in the process of being repaired. The Shahnshah has ordered that this structure be an architectural treasure in Shiraz. By glorifying the greatness of Islam, the Shahnshah shows his great affection for our faith. Join us, our brothers, in making our Iran the shining light it used to be."

I smiled at this emotionally charged and proud moment. I then changed channels to the Teheran news.

"Brothers and sisters of Iran! Is there any limit to the arrogance and brutality of this foreign pagan? He has desanctified our holy Mosque in Shiraz and is trying to repair it as if it was some Western Church. The brutality of this man knows no bounds! Hundreds of our captured troops have already been slaughtered and many hundreds are being tortured to make them proclaim that they are now working for him. It is rumored that those who did not join him were castrated and forced to eat pork. May Allah erase this brute from the soil of Iran!"

Certainly these comments were not flattering to me. However, the absurdity of the statement was such that I actually enjoyed it.

Brigadier Safdari must have been watching the news from Teheran and called me. "Shahnshah, I do not know what to say. Such lies from Teheran! It boils my blood! I know you have treated us kindly. I have also seen the drawings for the mosque in Shiraz. There is absolutely nothing unIslamic or western in the design. Permit me Shahnshah to make an announcement on our TV station condemning them for the lies they are propagating."

"Brigadier," I said, "do you have a wife and children or relatives residing in the Teheran area? By making such an announcement you will be putting their lives in danger and I cannot have that on my conscience. No, I will not let you do that! You're young enough to be my son, so listen to me. Iran is a beautiful land and we are both committed to preserving and protecting it. We both have enormous love for our land. The people propagating such false allegations are not representative of the rest of Iran. You must learn to treat the ravings and rantings of uneducated fanatical filth with contempt. Once we have won this war, they will wag their tails like loving pet dogs!"

He agreed with me and said, "As your Majesty commands."

CHAPTER 13.

In spite of the ongoing war, there was no specific border between the Islamic Republic and our new democracy. During the nights people travelled across the frontier quietly and carefully. My Generals were concerned about possible enemy activity in our control zone. They had asked my permission to stop this movement, but I did not find it necessary. I wanted them to freely see what we were doing and take the news back to the Islamic Republic. They would be our best witnesses as to the democracy and freedom that was now prevalent. Soon the lies propagated by the Teheran government would become obvious to all Iranians and that would be their downfall. I was not surprised that an unauthorized radio station had been set up and was broadcasting from the Islamic Republic . It was gratifying to note that they were proving me right. They were reporting that returning Iranians were spreading the news that areas under the revolutionary regime were free of oppression and had complete religious freedom. I had also been in touch with many of my ex-clients and manufactures in the United States, Canada and Japan and they were importing oil, artefacts, carpets and many other locally made commodities from our side of Iran. To support us, they had completely cut off imports from the Teheran regime. In the last six months the standard of living in our part of the country had shot up so dramatically that the people residing in the other part of Iran were crossing by the hundreds to our section of the country. The salaries paid to the workers in our section were at least three times the salaries earned by the others.

Another very flattering development was our relaxed attitude towards the wearing of pardah in our section of the country. This freedom was welcomed by women who had succeeded in convincing their husbands to move south in order to avoid religious persecution so prevalent in the north.

We were constantly in contact with media reports from the United States, Europe and other parts of the Middle East. The US and European media were totally favorable to our government. This was not a surprise to me, since any reduction in Islamic fundamentalism was regarded as a reduction in the terrorist activities propagated by Muslims in their countries. It was also their hope that the availability of oil from our resources would be much more reliable. It was in their interest to support our revolution. I, on the other hand, was keen to develop economic ties with Europe and America so that the trade could enhance our capital, improve our standard of living and give us a purpose to completely defeat the Islamic Republic, without enforcing a system of government, that was not welcome by the people. This was the very reason that the Teheran regime portrayed us as anti-Islamic. I, and my Cabinet members respected and appreciated the positive aspects of Islamic faith and culture. We were only opposed to the fanaticism and violence that was practiced against both Muslims and non-Muslims.

The United States had already offered to help us with manufacturing technology, education, and even defence. I was not naïve, and did not think for a moment that this was all done out of benevolence. It did not require a rocket scientist to realize that one of the most poignant enemies of the United States was the Islamic regime of Iran. So any support of their opponents was in their best interests. Also, if we accepted military and other aid from them, then in case at some point in time we disagreed with them, they could use the same military forces to keep us under control. I had therefore taken them up only as far as the manufacturing industry supplies were concerned. I had also agreed to the establishment of three science and technology institutes in our sector of Iran. The production of oil in the last six months had increased by sixty percent. The cost of production had fallen because of improved technology provided by the United States. Every drop of oil that we produced was sold to Europe and America and thereby the standard of living of the people of Iran in our sector had improved tremendously. I have always strongly believed that however fanatical a person may be, an improvement in the standard of living greatly reduces his religious furor.

Today was the day my Cabinet of newly appointed ministers was meeting with me to discuss the future steps we were going to take to establish the country of our dreams. A country devoid of religious fanaticism, that would protect each and every citizen's faith as long as it did not interfere with the faith of others.

Jahanbaksh Mirza, the Minister of Religious Affairs, Feruz Kermani, the Minister of Revenue, Ayatollah Maleki, the Minister of Home Affairs, Mr. Rabinovich, Ayatollah Tabrizi, General Hashmat Osmani and several other newly appointed ministers arrived at my residence which basically served now as Parliament. I had no illusions about this being a democratic government as yet. Each member was appointed by me and held office at my pleasure. However this was only a temporary situation. Once we had succeeded in completely controlling Iran and the people had been educated in the sophisticated systems of democracy, then I would relegate my power and let the people elect the ones that they wanted to run their government. But, before giving them that power, it was necessary to prove to them that our system of administration would bring them prosperity, education and peace.

My prime minister Ayatollah Tabrizi rose and bowed. "Shahnshah-e-Iran, accept the greetings of your humble ministers!"

I asked them all to sit down. "My beloved friends and ministers of Democratic Iran, today I want to present certain new concepts and ideas to develop our country. Many of you may disagree with what I have to say, please do not hesitate to tell me what you think."

"Yes your Majesty," they said with one voice.

"Now gentlemen, I would request you to listen to me very carefully, particularly you, our beloved Prime Minister Ayatollah Tabrizi. Many of the reforms I am suggesting may initially appear to you as contrary to the dictates of Islam. That is not my intention and should not be misinterpreted. Some dictates of every religion are created for a specific time period when those dictates are necessary. As time and civilization advance, those dictates may become out-dated and sometimes detrimental to the people. In those circumstances a termination of those dictates should not be considered anti religious but may even be considered a religious duty. We are facing such a situation. With the prosperity of our land, we have a 100 percent employment of all qualified engineers. We need more qualified technical ability in the country and that can only come now, from women. We should therefore immediately remove all impediments to the education of women. For them to be successful citizens, they should have equal rights with men, both in employment and education, as well as equal salaries. I am issuing an edict that as of today, all women who are eligible will have equal opportunities to enter universities and obtain jobs."

Tabrizi stood up and bowed "Your Majesty, I personally do not have the slightest disagreement with the concept of educating all our women. My concern is the reaction of the fanatics."

"Mr. Prime Minister, we cannot possibly postpone the development of our country to avoid offending fanatics and retrogrades. Please announce on television and radio that as of today, all women will have access to universities and education on an equal footing with men. I am also ordering that separate schools for girls will not be permitted in Democratic Iran, as this is a subterfuge to keep them repressed."

One of my ministers gingerly stood up and bowed. "Permit me, Your Majesty to express an opinion that may be considered contrary to your wishes."

"Mr. Minister, I have specifically requested that you all feel free to disagree with me so please go ahead."

"With the utmost respect Your Majesty, let us not forget that this is a Muslim state and the dictates of Islam forbid the mixing of males and females in educational establishments. Any such move will rile even the moderate members of Iran's Muslim population. I consider myself a moderate Muslim who definitely believes and supports the rights of women, but to remove the partition between boys and girls in the school environment may lead to severe consequences. If sexual promiscuity becomes a problem in such schools, they will blame Your Majesty. The Islamic government in Iran will be happy to proclaim that you are out to destroy the moral fabric of Islamic society."

"Mr. Minister, have you ever considered why in our Muslim societies promiscuity results when men and women are allowed to associate with each other freely?"

The minister nodded so that I may continue.

"Sexual attraction between males and females is a natural phenomenon. As a matter-of-fact, without it we would be extinct. When you suppress that attraction instead of educating it, you create a whole class of men and women obsessed with sex. With the release of control over them they indulge in promiscuity. It is therefore essential that we create an environment where our boys and girls associate with each other and try to become platonic friends. No doubt some unwanted sexual activity will occur, but after a few years the novelty will begin to fade and hopefully our children will learn to respect each other."

" Living in the West, I noticed a very strange phenomenon. We have freedom to consume alcohol. No doubt there are many alcoholics. However, the majority of people who consume alcohol behave rationally, enjoy their liquor and are not a menace to society."

"Unfortunately, I have noticed that many young people coming to America from Muslim countries where alcohol is forbidden, become addicts. My analysis is that when you outright forbid something and it suddenly becomes available, people do not know how to use it and therefore start misusing it."

The Minister bowed, indicating not his agreement with what I stated, but rather his submission to my decision. I then realized that I had a long way to go before I could convert Iran into an educated rational society.

The Prime Minister rose and bowed, "Your Majesty's edict will be proclaimed immediately."

CHAPTER 14.

Zainab awakened me in the middle of the night. "My love, the Minister of Education is on the line and says it is very urgent, would you like to speak to him?"

"I am sorry to disturb you Your Majesty, but the situation is rather urgent. I am afraid I have some bad news. As per your orders, we have opened up six University and College facilities where women are freely accepted on equal terms with men. One of these facilities is an engineering institution located fifteen kilometres east of Isfahan. In order to avoid any danger to the female students commuting to the University, we had provided them with accommodation on the University premises. As predicted by your Majesty, the harmony and progress of the students was enviable, but last night, we had a terrible tragedy. A whole section of the women's' residence was bombed. Forty-seven promising young undergraduate women were killed and thirteen critically injured. I am at the site, Your Majesty, the grief and despair is terrible. Our police department is actively searching for the culprits. They have left a note which states the following. "A university is not a place for a woman. Such insolence is contrary to the culture of Iran and Islam. Let this be a lesson to the pagan and his followers. We, the genuine protectors of Iran will not permit any intrusion from women. Their place is at home with children. Pagan learn from this."

My initial shock and despair when I heard this cannot be described. Was my philosophy and my rule responsible for the loss of so many young lives? I did not know the answer to this question. Immediately, I called my chauffeur and asked him to arrange an armed escort to the university campus. I arrived at a very chaotic scene, weeping parents, police officers investigating the scene of the crime and doctors attending to the injured. There was shattered glass everywhere and the floor was covered with blood and body parts. Upon my arrival, the guards announced that the Shahnshah has arrived and every one moved away with heads bowed.

"My sisters and brothers of Iran. The fanatical animals that did this will be punished. My sympathy and prayers are with the parents of the innocent children who have perished. Do not despair, the guilty will be caught. Remember, your children did not die in vain. Their memory will strengthen our resolve to provide equal opportunities for all the children of Iran, both male and female. We will not allow these animals to control the progress of the nation."

"Shahnshah, what does that do for me? My daughter is dead, she was eighteen years old. She was the apple of my eye. How will I live without my child. Who will look after me in my old age. I am a widow, I do not have a son, she was my only child!"

I walked over to her and hugged her. "My daughter, I cannot do anything to reduce your grief. I am a father myself and I know the agony that you are suffering. As of today, I will try to compensate you. The state of Iran will provide you with accommodation, food and health care. You will not have to worry about your old age. To preserve the memory of your child, we will build a new wing in her name. In the future, I, as the Shahnshah of Iran, promise each and every bereaved parent that your interests will be looked after by our new Iran."

I then asked one of the guards to get me the co-ordinates of all the parents who had lost their children as a result of this horrific crime.

"Who is the officer in charge here?" I asked.

"I am Your Majesty, my name is Captain Ayub."

"Walk with me to my car, Captain! I want to speak with you privately." The officer saluted me promptly and walked with me to my vehicle. When we arrived there I spoke to him again. "Captain Ayub, do you have any clues as to who these barbarians are?"

"Your Majesty, we believe that we have obtained fingerprints of at least ten individuals. The shape and weight of the bomb would be too obvious not to be noticed. We are compiling a list of all individuals with known fanatical beliefs, who have migrated to our area from the Islamic Republic. They are all under suspicion, so we will start comparing fingerprints. Our new investigating techniques will help us to expedite this process. We are also forming a small group of reliable citizens who will be constantly on the lookout for possible terrorist activity. Your Majesty, give me approximately one week and perhaps I will be able to arrest these individuals and bring them to justice."

I gave the officer my personal phone number. "Captain Ayub, as soon as you have any concrete evidence, give me a call, I would like to deal with this personally."

"Yes, Your Majesty."

Feeling really dejected, I went home. Zainab was waiting up for me. "Oh my God, my love, what kind of people can do this?"

"My darling, as I have repeatedly stated, the greatest and most virulent disease of mankind is not plague, cholera, typhoid, or AIDS. It is faith, and fanaticism. Any belief without scientific evidence is an invitation to create monsters out of human beings!"

"What kind of religious believer would murder teenage girls because they're going to university?"

"The fact that you asked that question indicates rational thinking. These animals have their own interpretation of beliefs and blame it on religious teachings and most of this is total nonsense in the present context of our civilization. On the other hand, most of it is also harmless. Praying has never caused injury to anyone, but unfortunately those who pray so ardently do not have the rationality to discard any portions of the teachings which are not scientifically tenable or have become irrelevant in today's world."

"The great Prophet Mohamed was absolutely justified when he insisted on male circumcision and a ban on consumption of pork. For that era, those steps were absolutely necessary to preserve the health of citizens. Pigs consumed excreta and other substances harmful to humans. Today, in the twenty-first century, the pigs have a better diet than most people in third world countries."

To give another example, "Circumcision prevented diseases. Due to the lack of water, the desert dwellers could not wash themselves as often as we do."

"You see my love, the dictum for that time has become redundant in today's world and should be discarded."

"You and I are capable of thinking in this rational way, but the religious fanatics only want to follow the dictates of the Koran. They have refused to budge from that way of thinking. The pity of it is that if the Prophet Mohamed was alive today, he would probably change several of those dicta to keep up with the times and circumstances."

CHAPTER 15.

Zainab woke me when the telephone rang in the morning. It was Captain Ayub. "Sorry to call you so early Your Majesty. Your instructions were to call you as soon as some information is available. You'll be glad to know sir, that we have succeeded in arresting ten individuals who were involved in the bombing. The fingerprints match, and after some diligent investigation, all of them have admitted to their culpability. They have also informed us of two other individuals in Teheran, who were responsible for financing and organizing this criminal act. We are seeking your permission to bring these beasts before you for their trial. When will Your Majesty have the time to conduct this trial? Would you like this matter to go before the normal judiciary or would Your Majesty like to preside as a judge?"

"Captain Ayub, my compliments to you for solving this matter so quickly. Have they been provided with lawyers?"

"Your Majesty wants me to provide these animals, these monsters, these killers of children, with lawyers paid for by the state?"

"Captain Ayub, in any civilized country, a person who is charged with an offense must be properly represented. He is innocent until proven guilty. Please see to it that all these people are properly represented and when both prosecuting counsel and defence counsel are ready, let me know. I will preside as the judge. Kindly expedite your investigation of the two perpetrators in Teheran so that we can apprehend and bring them to justice here in our courts."

"Yes, Your Majesty, I will get on it right away."

I contacted our authorities involved with propaganda. Television personnel and reporters, both Iranian and international were informed of the trial date. They were specifically informed that the trial would be open to the public and there would be no restrictions or publication bans regarding the proceedings.

It was approximately one month after the last conversation I had with Captain Ayub that all the procedures had been completed. The courtroom was surrounded by handpicked and loyal revolutionary guards. Our authorities had already ascertained their total loyalty to me and the Revolution.

Ten individuals were brought into the courtroom with handcuffs and leg irons. As I arrived in the courtroom, every one including eight of the ten accused bowed. I noticed that the police officers escorting them gave these two a knee kick in the tailbone and pushed their heads down in my direction. Evidence was presented by the state prosecutors. Fingerprint experts proved beyond reasonable doubt that these were the men who had planted and detonated the bomb in the women's residence. Defence counsel tried their best to show the weakness in the Crown's case, but there was the indelible evidence of the fingerprints. Again, none of the accused had alibis which were believable. Six of the ten had migrated from the Islamic Republic without any documentation. The ten individuals had no permanent addresses in revolutionary Iran. They did not have any jobs and were found in possession of the equivalent of two hundred thousand US dollars. They had no explanation as to why they were carrying such a large amount of cash in American currency.

After the trial was completed, I asked the men whether they had any statements to make to the court. Six of them were in shock, two crying and two in a daze. Two of them admitted to their involvement and sought mercy from me, the Judge. Two informed me through their attorneys that they wanted to address the court. I looked at the first man and asked him to speak.

"I realize that whatever I say will have no effect on you. My fate is in your hands. My name is Abdul Aziz. I was a captain in the legitimate Iranian army. I was decorated for bravery in the war against Iraq . All my life I have loved two things, my beloved Iran and my beloved Islam. You have come here as an alien and an enemy to both of them. You are destroying our culture and our faith and you have the audacity to sit in judgment on a proud and decorated soldier of Iran. I have no fear of death. I have faced it several times. Allah will take me into his arms when I arrive in paradise. What about you, my Judge? Are you ready to face the fires of hell and share the company of Shaitan when you arrive in hell?"

"Abdul Aziz you are an interesting man. You claim to be a brave soldier of Iran and Islam. You claim to have been decorated for your bravery in the war with Iraq. Yet you have behaved like a cowardly pig in blowing up a residence for young girls who were merely seeking education and enlightenment. So much for your bravery. As far as your faith in Islam, will you please explain to me how killing young innocent girls will merit you the blessings of Mohamed or Allah? If Allah is welcoming your breed of cowards into heaven then you're welcome to it. For such a heaven is not meant as a residence for decent human beings who have served Allah. As the Judge of this court I am sentencing you to death. You will be executed at dawn. My advisers have suggested to me that you should be tortured, your arms and legs cut off and then burned to death. But then I realized that if I did that, I would be in the same category as you barbarians. After your execution, you will not be buried in a grave. We do not want to contaminate the soil of our Iran. Your body will be cremated and the ashes casually discarded."

I suddenly noticed a sense of shock and alarm in the eyes of Abdul Aziz. A man who was not afraid of dying, was afraid of being cremated. What an irrational thinking pattern. I saw the panic in his eyes and realized that his faith and belief in reaching heaven was being shattered. He would not be able to get to heaven and receive the anticipated luxurious accommodations were he to arrive in the form of ashes. I realized that my ideas and concepts of good and bad were totally alien to his thinking. Murder did not bother him, but being turned into ashes after death was a major issue. When dealing with such fanatics, the threat of death may be less successful than the threat of cremation. I thought that in future cases crimes of this nature should be dealt with thus, the convicted criminal being executed and cremated.

Suddenly, Mr. Aziz bowed to me. "Respected Judge, you have decided to take my life, so be it. But I beg of you, please do not have me cremated. Please let me have a Muslim burial."

"Very interesting, Mr. Aziz. You just sentenced me to rot in hell! How come I have suddenly been promoted to `respected judge'? I want to thank you for opening my eyes and showing me how ignorant and low your beliefs and intelligence are. You are not a soldier of God! You are an enemy of Islam! You have insulted the great Prophet Mohamed and his message of kindness and benevolence. If you are admitted to heaven, then I'd prefer to go to hell. Take this animal out of my courtroom and execute him! Cremate his sinful flesh and throw it in a place where the environment will not be polluted."

Abdul Aziz was taken away from the courtroom.

The next accused who wanted to address the court was asked to rise and speak.

"My name is Ahmed Abbasi, I am a Qazi. All my life I have prayed to Allah to give me the strength to face a day like today. I'm being judged and convicted by a pagan who does not respect our traditions and who is an enemy of Islam. May you rot in hell!"

"Mr. Abbasi, thank you for your good wishes. Needless to say that they do not cause me any anguish. As a matter of fact, if scum like you were to wish me good luck, I would consider it an insult. Talking of faith, I genuinely believe that the great Prophet Mohamed, and Allah himself, are unlikely to seek your advise as to my future or the future of any civilized human being. You're sentenced to death. You will be executed at dawn and your body will be cremated and the ashes discarded in the same way as your fellow culprit. Take this animal out of my sight!"

Two of the accused who had freely admitted to their involvement in this heinous crime were treated more leniently and sentenced to life imprisonment. We gave them the option of informing us of the whereabouts of the two who still remained in the Islamic Republic. If this led to the arrests of these men, then I was willing to consider a reduction in their sentences. To somehow nab them and bring them to justice was my goal. It was our intention to deter any further criminal activities instigated by individuals from the Islamic Republic.

Captain Ayub contacted me and suggested a novel way in which the last two men could be arrested. It was indicated to us that apparently a very large number of people residing in the Islamic Republic had come to the conclusion that the peace, security and economic growth that we had achieved was something they all desired. Many of them wanted to either emigrate to our area or help us take over the whole of the Islamic Republic so that Iran would be united, prosperous and democratic. There was an element, which was strictly interested in dollars and was willing to kidnap these two Iranian culprits and bring them secretly into our zone. Captain Ayub thought that the kidnapping was a good option. I, on the other hand felt that if we used their services, any kidnapper would be equally happy to perform the same services for the Islamic government. The reliability of these men was very doubtful. I also felt that it was morally unjustifiable to get involved with one criminal element to arrest another. I suggested an alternative to Captain Ayub. Why not televise the whole occurrence with graphic pictures of the devastation caused by the bomb, the dead bodies of the children and all the details of the trial. Include the admission of the two witnesses as to the contribution made by the two individuals now residing in the Islamic Republic. We will plead with the people of Iran on the other side of the border, to help us catch those culprits and bring them to justice, both for the sake of Iran and Islam.

Our television announcers were carefully selected and trained both for their articulation and expressive renditions. That evening, when I switched on the news, I heard the following. "Our brothers and sisters of Iran, to what shameful low levels has the Government of the Islamic Republic sunk. Watch this documentary of the atrocity committed by your fanatics on our children, innocent girls trying to become educated." At this point, a television reel showed viewers the dismembered bodies of the female students. "Your fanatics have claimed that this was done to preserve Islam. Killing young women because they sought education is supposed to be against the dictates of Islam! Can we allow such barbarity to go unpunished? Even if you are totally opposed to our rational and democratic system of government, is the deliberate massacre of our daughters, because you disagree with our ideals, acceptable? You claim to be devout Muslims and patriotic Iranians, would you tolerate such barbarity in the name of Islam? You think the prophet Mohamed and Allah himself will condone such actions? There were ten human monsters involved in this particular act. Eight of them were caught right here in our territory. They were given a fair trial with lawyers provided by the State and were not arbitrarily punished. Our Shahnshah will not punish any one unless his guilt has been duly proven. Only after a fair trial and conviction were these animals executed. Our brothers and sisters of Iran, two of them are still in your area under the control and protection of your government. Help us punish them. Do not let these men get away. Either you punish them yourselves or bring them to us." After this announcement the names and photographs of the two Iranian criminals were shown on television. I was really impressed with my announcer. I went to sleep comfortably after having spent several nights of anguish.

It was approximately ten days before I received a call from Captain Ayub. "Your Majesty, I have called to express both my admiration and gratitude for your acumen in ordering that news announcement. My secret sources have informed me that there is an enormous amount of outrage in the Islamic Republic. People have openly condemned the government for supporting such terrorist activities. The government, on the other hand, is trying to convince them that these activities were not pursuant to their suggestions, but were independent acts of terrorism. This has two valuable repercussions. Firstly, it will deter other fanatics encouraged by the Teheran government from any such activities, because they will not be able to depend on them for protection. Secondly, the fact that they have to explain their lack of involvement shows their weakness and evidence of their sinking popularity. Now your Majesty, the best news for the last! This morning four Iranian couples crossed our borders illegally and have sought asylum. They have given us information on the whereabouts of the last two bombers. As per your instructions, we have welcomed the families."

"Captain Ayub, when those two terrorists are apprehended and brought into our territory, as per our usual procedure, you will provide them with counsel of their choice at the expense of the state. When the crown and defence are ready, I shall preside over the matter myself."

The families who had provided information on the prisoners were amply rewarded. Strict instructions were given that their names not be disclosed. Even our own officers and security people were not informed of their identities. As an extra precaution, I instructed that these people be given new identities. After being satisfied that they were totally secure from any retribution, I permitted our propaganda personnel to inform the Iranian public of the arrest and detention of the last two terrorists who were caught in Teheran. Our television and media thanked the Iranian people for their assistance in arresting these two terrorists. We made it very clear that without the intervention of the patriotic and kind people of Teheran, justice would have been impossible. A well-documented and televised trial of these men took place before me and they were sentenced to death and executed. Their last words were the usual ridiculous religious garbage where they tried to state that the murders they had committed were for the purpose of protecting Islam. We received a lot of e-mails from the Islamic Republic and were amazed at the positive response of the average Iranian from the other side of the border. I noticed that not only our economic growth and progress were the main charms for these people, but also a majority of the intelligentsia, as well as ordinary Iranians were agreeing with us in larger numbers. It also appeared that the government in Teheran was now under constant pressure from common citizens who were extremely critical of their fanatical stance against us. All interesting e-mail was brought to my attention. I will never forget one particular e-mail from a man in Teheran, who stated as follows. "I am a devout Muslim. Allah and the Koran are my life. At first, when the so-called Shahnshah took over in the South, I was appalled. He was a foreigner and a pagan and had the audacity to try to rule Iran. I was therefore keeping a careful track of all events for more than a year. I find he has brought education, economic progress, tolerance and sophistication to our people. The enemy that I feared was not the Shahnshah, but my own reluctance to accept change. Accept my apologies Sharuq, my Shahnshah. Last but not least, accept this compliment from a poor and devout Muslim. You are not the pagan! You are not the enemy of Islam. As a matter-of-fact, you have enlightened us to the fact that faith can live in harmony with civilization."

I did realize that such excellent diction could not come from some ordinary person, so I had it investigated and I was surprised to find that the man who wrote that was a professor of Islamic law and theology at the University of Teheran. I personally responded to him, not as the Shahnshah of Iran, but as Sharuq Damania. I stated as follows, "Dear Professor, I am very grateful to you for your kind words and praise for my efforts to improve the lot of our people. What you brought to me is far more enlightening and I want to thank you. You have convinced me that our ancient Iran, with its tradition, history, culture, refinement and justice has not been tarnished by decades of fanaticism. A man who is a professor of Islam, does not see me as the demon they are portraying. Yes, professor, I have the utmost regard and respect for your religion and your prophet Mohamed. One does not have to be a Muslim or Christian to appreciate Mohamed or Jesus. If you ever decide to move to civilization and the South, just let us know. We will welcome you."

I received a response from the professor. "Shahnshah-e-Iran, how does a common man thank a person of your calibre with mere words? Your humble servant will kneel before you in submission and gratitude. Yes Shahnshah, I would love to come and work for you."

CHAPTER 16.

Our relations with Turkey were extremely cordial and friendly. Whenever I needed advice on matters relating to Islam, I would contact several individuals in Turkey who helped me. Turkey was the most progressive Muslim country on earth, their fanaticism had been eliminated by their famous leader Mostafa Kemal Attaturk several decades ago. They had a Western type government where religion was not permitted to interfere with the governance of the country. They also had diplomatic relations with us and the Islamic Republic. Whenever we wanted to get somebody out of Iran, we arranged for them to go to Turkey and then fly directly into Isfahan or Zahidan. At my request the Turks got the professor over into revolutionary Iran.

Our newly arrived Professor was given the position of Professor of Islamic Law and Theory at the University of Isfahan. His loyalty to our regime and his pronouncements added greatly to our repute as a civilized nation. He totally favored the ideology of Islam, as long as it did not interfere with the needs of modern civilization. The professor did not mince his words when he criticized the Islamic government for the chaos and fanaticism that it had brought to the people of Iran. I requested him to broadcast some of his teachings on television, both to our own subjects and the citizens of the Islamic Republic. This had a great effect on the thinking of people because of his existing reputation as a great scholar. One of his famous broadcasts went somewhat like this.

"My fellow Iranians. I have voluntarily moved to the south and now serve the Shahnshah of Iran. I have not come south for dollars or financial rewards of any kind. I have come here because of the conviction I have that the future of Iran can be safeguarded and improved only if left in the hands of our great Shahnshah. Remember, the Shahnshah is not a Muslim. I am a devout Muslim and a humble student of Islam. So why do I respect and adore this man so much? I will tell you. Every religion was created to serve the needs of the people of a specific era. All religious dicta are geared for that purpose whether created by Christ or Mohamed. It is therefore imperative to discard those ideals which have become redundant and to create new ideals which would improve the life of our people. Look at what our Shahnshah has done. He has introduced equality of education for both men and women. This has increased for example, the number of female engineers by almost sixty percent Our factories, plants and technical universities are now far better equipped because of these women engineers and technicians. Our industrial production has shot up by one hundred percent. Are you not surprised that now revolutionary Iran produces motor vehicles, vans, trucks and agricultural equipment in numbers that are more than double those produced by the whole of Iran prior to the revolution?"

These statements made by a person who was once an antagonist were extremely beneficial to our side and of grave concern to the leaders of the Islamic Republic. I decided to get the optimum propaganda value from the Professor's televised speech, so I informed him that I would come to the University of Isfahan and address the students of his class. Of course the Professor was delighted to welcome me and we made arrangements for my flight and accommodation in Isfahan. Relaxed and happy with the day's work, I went home to rest. It had been a very long and busy week and the pressure was making me extremely anxious.

As I lay down to sleep, the telephone rang and Zainab answered it. "The Shahnshah is very tired and has just gone to bed. Is it really that urgent that I should wake him?"

"Yes madam, it is extremely important. I must speak to the Shahnshah right away."

I took the phone from Zainab. "Shahnshah, this is Ayatollah Tabrizi, I have sad news to give you."

"What is it Ayatollah?"

"Your Majesty, our new friend, the professor from the Islamic Republic whom you appointed a professor at the University of Isfahan, has been brutally murdered. Four men broke into his apartment at the University and stabbed him to death. Your Majesty, it was so brutally done. Before killing him, they cut off his tongue. They have left a note which says, `this is a warning to all traitors and supporters of the pagan king. If you have such bad things to say about our Islamic Republic and our faith, then you will not be able to say it because you will not have a tongue to say it with!'

I was so shocked at this barbarity that I did not have any words to respond. My first impulse was to cancel my trip to Isfahan. Then I realized that this is exactly what they wanted. To be affected by their barbarity was to play into their hands. The best course was to go to the University, attend the funeral of the unfortunate professor and show the students that we will not be affected by such acts. We will arrest and punish the culprits after a fair trial. I discussed with Ayatollah Tabrizi my preparations for arrival at the University of Isfahan. I also requested him to join me and condemn the acts of these terrorists. The condemnation coming from a reputed religious leader such as Ayatollah Tabrizi would have a great impact on all Iranians. Tabrizi agreed immediately to join me. But as I hung up the phone, I noticed that Zainab was standing next to me completely shocked with tears in her eyes.

"My darling Shahnshah, you are not seriously thinking of exposing yourself to these murderers are you? Please do not go. Do not risk your life. If something happens to you I will not be able to live without you. The great progress that you have brought to this country will disappear. If you do not have any pity for me at least have some pity for Iran."

"My precious love, we cannot allow such things do go unheeded. It is my duty to face the danger and to crush the enemies of our progress. I cannot just sit back and accept the murder of a friend. The grief I feel must be shared with all Iranians. By punishing the culprits, we will send a very strong message to these barbarians."

Zainab walked away from me crying and I followed her. "My love, every possible precaution will be taken. The most faithful and efficient guards will be with me. They will protect me with their lives, if necessary. You have nothing to worry about. I'm only going for one night. Tomorrow evening I will be back and you better be ready to give your delicious body to me. I promise you, it would be an exciting night for both of us. Just get some sleep before I return, because neither of us is going to do much sleeping when I return tomorrow."

Next morning I flew to Isfahan by helicopter. Surrounding my helicopter were five others containing officers and soldiers known for their loyalty and military skills. Once we took off, I felt quite safe. We landed in Isfahan at the university complex. I was driven to a spacious suite reserved for me in the heart of the University building. My apartment was totally surrounded by the apartments of my bodyguards. My speech was scheduled for one p.m. and every student who wanted to attend was carefully checked for weapons. Our officers had already ascertained that every single student who was permitted to attend was not antagonistic to us. I opened my speech with a greeting.

"My beloved children of Iran. I had intended to come and speak to you about the great Professor who had come to educate you all and show you that civilization and Islam can coexist. Unfortunately my message of joy has now got to be altered to a message of pain and sadness. Tell me, my children, how could we possibly deal with such brutality? Have you heard about the cutting off of the professor's tongue? Well, that act of barbarism not only leaves me with an aching heart, but also the feeling of such immense anger which I promise I will utilize to exterminate these brutes, whatever the cost. Ah beloved Professor! Rest peacefully in heaven! I can promise you one thing, your murderers will never meet you because I will send them to hell."

Almost one thousand students rose from their chairs and there was one loud chant. "Kill the barbarians Shahnshah, kill these enemies of humanity!"

It was difficult for me not to shed tears when I attended the funeral of the Professor. I placed my arms around his wife and two of his children. I humbly apologized for what had happened to her husband and the children's father. I assured them that they would be protected, educated and maintained for the rest of their lives and that my door would always be open to them. The poor widow was inconsolable, but the children being teenagers, felt more anger than grief and my promise of revenge against these beasts was some consolation to them.

After the funeral, I summoned the Commissioner of Police for Isfahan to my quarters. I asked him what progress had been made in arresting the culprits.

"Shahnshah, we have a few leads. We have their fingerprints, and surprisingly, one animal forgot to take his wallet with him. Though they were all masked at the time of their entry into the university campus, their repeated firing of machine guns drew the attention of many students. We got an excellent description of their physical proportions. We were able to identify the man who left his wallet behind and we also found out that one of his companions had a slight limp. We have checked the link between these individuals and I found out that they were four military officers who were close friends. All four are officers in the Army of the Islamic Republic and the man with a limp was one of them. It appears that they have all returned to the Teheran area, but we know exactly where they reside. Subject to your Majesty's approval, I was thinking of sending some of our own qualified experts to the north to exterminate them."

"Commissioner, I would greatly appreciate it if we could abduct and bring them here. Try them in our courts and punish them, when they have been found guilty!"

"Shahnshah, that will be much more difficult to perform but I will do my best to obey your Majesty's command. Please give me one week to set all this up."

My speech to the university students was broadcast live on television. The reaction from our own citizens was very favorable. Surprisingly, the reaction from the authorities in the Islamic Republic was total silence. I was surprised at this and came to the conclusion that their silence was to avoid any allegations of complicity with the criminals who had committed this murder. I therefore instructed our authorities to investigate whether any politicians or government officers of the North, had either instigated or assisted in the commission of this offence.

When I arrived in Zahidan, the airport was filled with my supporters. There were shouts of `Long live the Shahnshah' and` kill those beastly murderers.' I did not address the supporters. I wanted them to realize the truth and what I felt inside. An intelligent, educated and kind man had been brutally murdered for no reason at all, except that he supported our policy of freedom. I just bowed in their direction and got into my limousine to go home.

The welcome I got at home was a different story. As soon as my guards and chauffeur had escorted me into my private quarters and left, Zainab came running to me. "My darling Shahnshah, the love of my life is back safe and sound. My prayers to Allah have been answered. She ran into my arms, hugged me tight and kissed me passionately. To say that this was exciting is to put it very mildly indeed. There were still tears in her eyes but also a mischievous smile on her face. "My Shahnshah has risked his life for his people and has come home safe. He must indeed be very tired and in need of relaxation and love." She slowly unbuttoned her dress and took it off followed by her bra and panties. The mischievous smile was still on her face as she walked up to me. She unbuttoned and took off my shirt and my trousers, placed her hand inside my underwear and looked into my eyes. "The Shahnshah may be very tired, but certain parts of him are rising to the occasion in a very engaging fashion. She knelt down and took me into her mouth. I suddenly forgot the sad demise of the professor and the anger I felt for his murderers. At this moment of time there was no Shahnshah, no Iran, no grief, no vengeance. There was only Zainab, who had bathed and perfumed her body and hair just to please and satisfy me. Apart from the passion, I felt incredible love for this beautiful woman who would give so much to an old man like me and ask for so little in return. I placed her on the bed and kissed her from head to toe. Every kiss was a divine experience of her soft beautiful flesh and the aroma of her feminine scent. We hugged and kissed for quite some time, then she sat up, looked deep into my eyes with lips slightly parted, and said. "Your Majesty, at your age any further extension of your royal body may be detrimental to your health. My man, you better enter me now and fill me with your royal seed." Needless to say I did not need any further encouragement and entered her. As I made love to her, she moaned, wrapped herself around me and kept repeating in my ear. "I'm yours. I'm yours."

Later, I told her exactly what had transpired in Shiraz.

CHAPTER 17.

Rauf Irfani, Behram Sharaf, Abdul Azari and Tehmul Shazad were riding in a Jeep. It was after midnight and they were on a dirt track not frequented by normal travelers. Their nervous tension was obvious from the fact that Rauf and Behram were smoking incessantly and there was total silence in the car. They had reached an unmanned section of the border with the Islamic Republic. The chances of a military patrol being around were existent but remote. However, if they were caught, the consequences would be extremely severe. To enter the Islamic Republic without permission was normally a capital offense except that no court would be involved. The transgressors would be shot on the spot. All four men were dressed in Islamic religious garb with long beards and turbans. They looked like mullahs. Closer scrutiny would have revealed some rather unpriestly qualities in them. They were all in their late twenties. Rauf and Tehmul were both six feet two inches tall and they all had athletic builds and looked like they could be part of an Olympic team rather than priests of Islam. Something that was not visible was the fact that they were trained military officers and crack shots. At the bottom of their suitcases there were machine guns, grenades and other equipment not usually required by religious Muslims on their way to a mosque. The military equipment in their suitcases was wrapped in their clothing and copies of the Koran were neatly laid over the top before the suitcases were closed.

Rauf was busy with the direction finder. After driving for approximately six to seven kilometres he breathed a loud sigh of relief. "Well guys, I think we are in the Islamic Republic. Behram fiddled with the radio until he got a channel from the Islamic Republic which was broadcasting religious music. The direction finder was hidden in a box under the passenger's seat and would not be obvious in a search of the vehicle. They then manoeuvred the Jeep carefully to the main highway connecting to the south of Teheran.

Every one seemed to be less tense and they were trying to talk in a normal fashion even though the tension was still apparent in their voices. Because the radio was being played at a very high pitch, the approach of a police vehicle was not heard and within seconds their Jeep was surrounded by four military vehicles. Soldiers jumped out and pointed machine guns at them.

Rauf, the unquestioned leader of the four and the most articulate in the group gently stepped out of the Jeep with arms raised, bowed in the direction of the officers and approached them. "Allah Akbar my brothers! Why would you point your weapons at servants of Islam who are in the service of Allah?"

The officer in command walked over to him and looked him in the eyes. "What are four alleged servants of Islam doing at 1:30 a.m. seven kilometres from the border of the kingdom of the pagan? I did not see any mosques in the vicinity."

The other three kept absolutely silent, even though they were panic stricken. They knew that if any one could help them get out of the situation, it was Rauf.

"My brother officers of the Islamic Republic, we are so grateful and thankful to Allah that you are here to protect us and help us escape from the tyranny of the pagan. We have survived a whole year in the realm of the infidel unable to practice our faith properly with constant tirades against the Islamic Republic. Our families live in that area and we could not escape without them so we stayed as long as we could. We came to the conclusion that we must escape from the tyranny and return to the Islamic Republic. Is that a crime my brothers?"

"Are you suggesting to me that you got into a Jeep and crossed the border without any one stopping you at the other end?"

"That is precisely what I'm suggesting to you officer. I know that you and your men are protectors of our faith and that same faith and my prayers must have helped us when we escaped into our Iran." Rauf said as he raised his arms and eyes upwards in the alleged direction of Allah in the heavens.

The officer walked up to his other companions and conferred for a while as the four men in the jeep, though pretending to be at peace, were trying hard to contain their panic. After what appeared to be an interminable discussion, the officer walked back to Rauf. "Gentlemen, you are free to go. We are sorry to have doubted the word of a man of the faith. Give me your names and I will give you a document that will provide you with free passage all the way to Teheran."

Without blinking an eye, Rauf responded., "I am Abdul Jabbari. My companions are Rashid Khureshi, Anwar Sultan and Sharuq Arshad. Thank you very much, kind officer, Allah will always protect you."

Rauf waited patiently at the driver's side of the jeep until the officer completed the document and presented it to him. He then got into the driver's seat and nonchalantly drove off as if nothing had happened.

For a few minutes no one spoke. Once they realized they were out of sight of the military, Abdul spoke up. "Rauf, you motherfucker, how shall I thank you for saving our lives? My goodness man, you are so glib! You would probably even succeed in talking to Allah and convincing him to let a sinful rat like you into heaven." Every one roared with laughter at the release of tension.

Tehmul spoke up "My God, how on earth did you think of all the names you attributed to us?"

"I just made them up."

"Thank God, I do not have any sisters." Said Behram.

"What has that got to do with anything?"

"This bastard Rauf visits me and my family almost every week .With his glib talk any woman is in danger. I don't believe there are any women who will keep their panties on in the whole of Iran, when Rauf starts chatting them up."

They all laughed. Suddenly, Rauf became serious. "OK guys! Now listen up. We are dealing with very dangerous people and every step we take could be our last one. So we have no margin for error. Here is how we will proceed. As you know, we have four cell phones in our possession. They must be used only in emergencies. Under no circumstances should any of us mention any of our real names when we are conversing with each other. Behram, Tehmul and I will follow and investigate the four murderers. Once we have found a spot where we can take them and imprison them, we will make arrangements so that the Iranian police will not be able to find their location. We will individually abduct them at the proper time. No investigation or questioning is possible until all four are in our custody. If any one of them is free, they can inform the police of the disappearance of the others and this can lead to intense scrutiny and search by the authorities. Once all four are arrested, our next step is to question them if necessary with the use of force. The goal is to find which ministers of the Iranian government had appointed and coached them to assassinate the professor. Our next step will be to abduct or kidnap the responsible ministers who are involved with these criminals. All of them will somehow have to be taken back to our democratic state, tried and punished. If you're wondering why I have not mentioned Abdul, the reason is as follows. Abdul will be kept totally out of the investigation. In case we are caught, he should be free to get assistance for us. Also I have a plan to use him in the investigation and questioning of the prisoners, which I do not want to reveal at the moment. As far as possible, we should not be seen together anymore. Now I will give you the names of the four assassins."

"The leader of the group is Rashid Arshad, a Major in the Iranian Armed Forces. The second man is Captain Farhang Azhar. The third person involved is Captain Raza Moravid and the last man is Lieutenant Shakil Sajjad. Keep in mind, that all four are extremely well trained military officers with enormous experience in undercover activities. My investigation has revealed that they are trained assassins, skilled in judo, karate and arm to arm combat. Be assured they will not be easy to control. All three of us except Abdul, will now tail the four at different times. The authorities suspect that four religious mullahs have entered the Islamic Republic from the south, they might be watching for some criminal activity by individuals dressed as mullahs. For this reason, we will shave off our beards and dress like young people in Teheran. In order to communicate quickly and easily, I have decided that we should stay in a hotel, each in a separate room. It is imperative that we are not seen together at any time. The only way we will communicate with each other will be on our cell phones. Any questions?"

They all nodded their heads indicating that they understood what was said.

Rauf was a wizard with cell phone and computer technology. He had somehow established contact with all the cell phones operated by the four alleged murderers. Every call that they made or received was recorded on his computer which was kept in his hotel room. All the conversations of the four accused were available to the four investigators. On at least four occasions, the accused had conversed with two of the ministers of the Islamic Republic. Whether these were the true culprits was still unknown to them.

Every day, one or the other of the investigators followed the four individuals to their homes and work so that within approximately ten days the regular movements and activities of these men was known to them. This investigation led to the conclusion that every Thursday evening, the four individuals were seen at the Parliament buildings in Teheran. The next task was to find out who they were meeting there. This was difficult as no one was permitted to enter the Parliament buildings without specific permission. Rauf somehow managed to bribe one of the Parliament employees who served refreshments to the delegates. He convinced him that it had been his dream to see the great Parliament of Iran, the seat of government from where the laws and governance of the state originated. The waiter bought the story and agreed to let Rauf take his place for one night, for a sum equivalent to one hundred U.S. dollars in Iranian currency.

As he served coffee to the delegates, he noticed that the four culprits were in the company of two Iranian ministers. One was Raza Abadi the Iranian Minister of Defence, and the second was Shameel Qureshi, the Minister of Religious Affairs. This made him conclude that perhaps these were the two ministers involved in instigating the crime.

For the next three weeks, the investigators regularly followed the four culprits on Thursdays to and from Parliament.

Rauf had found and rented an abandoned farmer's cabin, ten kilometres from the heart of Teheran. The story he had given the owner was that he had lost his wife to cancer and wanted a quiet place to reflect on the future. Inside the cabin he had established a soundproof room with the necessary tools and recording equipment as well as equipment to restrain and imprison individuals. He had also purchased a van and had it soundproofed. At his insistence, Abdul had been totally kept out of these arrangements. The other two hardly ever saw Abdul and wondered what had happened to him. Next, Rauf obtained three military police uniforms, which would fit Behram, Tehmul and himself. Now, they were ready for the final action. It was the third Thursday of the month. The three investigators followed the four accused to the Parliament and waited for them to finish the conference. It was about 11:30 p.m. when they left the building and entered their vehicle to return home as was their usual practice. Our three investigators were dressed in police uniforms and when the accused's vehicle stopped at a sign to turn right, Rauf drove his van in front of it. Before they could respond or react, Rauf got out of his vehicle, raised his gun and approached the driver who was Lieutenant Shakil Sajjad. At the very same moment, Behram went to the passenger side and pointed his gun at the face of Captain Farhang Azar.

"Gentlemen, you will quietly walk with us to our vehicle unless you want your wives to become widows. No sound or movement without our permission will be permitted. Is that understood?"

The fear on the faces of the four was clearly visible as they nodded their assent and quietly followed Rauf to his van. As soon as they were inside the van, Rauf and Behram handcuffed all of them and placed leg irons on their feet. They then placed tapes on the mouths of the four men. Next, the vehicle which was driven by them was driven away by Tehmul and abandoned in a deserted portion of farmland. He removed the license plates so that the vehicle could not be identified as belonging to the four culprits. Tehmul ran back to the van and they all drove to the deserted cabin where the four accused were to be questioned.

At the cabin Rauf started the questioning right away. "I want you four to listen to me very carefully. We are completely aware of the murder you have committed in Zahidan. And any equivocation or subterfuge on your part will be brutally punished. We know the facts, we want the reasoning. Why did you do it?"

"You filthy dirty criminals, do you think you can intimidate officers of the Islamic Republic of Iran with your ridiculous threats?" Major Rashid Arshad said.

Rauf kicked him hard in his testicles. The major bent over in agony. "Major, this is merely an indication of what is to come. If you do not cooperate, you will not just be kicked in your testicles but we will arrange to sever and feed them to you for breakfast. So you better cooperate and now!"

Rauf then walked up to Captain Raza Moravid. "Well, Captain," he said, "are you going to cooperate, or would you also like a kick in your testicles?"

"I live to serve Iran. Your threats mean nothing to me "

Rauf kicked him very hard in his testicles and the Captain collapsed and moaned in agony.

"Well Captain, has the threat started to mean something to you?"

"Bugger off, you bastard"

Rauf gave similar treatment to the remaining officers without any visible success. Suddenly, Rauf left the room and brought in a man with handcuffs and leg irons. The man had a very long beard and his face was discolored from bruises. The other investigators had never seen or met this man. Tehmul walked up close to Rauf and whispered in his ear, "who the hell is this?"

Quite loudly, so that he was clearly heard by the prisoners, Rauf said, "this is the bastard who arranged for the transportation and facilitated the movements of these four criminals in our part of Iran. Do you bastards know this man? He works directly under Iran's Defence Minister Raza Abadi." Tehmul watched the four prisoners and was surprised to find that they did not seem to have a clue as to who this man was.

"Behram, Tehmul, hang this bastard up on those hooks on the wall and strip him," said Rauf.

Behram and Tehmul were initially shocked at this brutal suggestion made by Rauf but complied. The man was hanged by his arms and his legs were also buckled to the wall hangers. When they stripped him as ordered, they noticed that he had innumerable bruises and cuts on his body. Another strange aspect of the man was his extremely bulbous eyes, which seemed to protrude far beyond his face. One other noticeable factor, was his penis and testicles, which seemed to be extremely large and protruding for a man his size.

"Jamshid," said Rauf. "You will now give us the names of the ministers who arranged for these four animals to go to our part of Iran and commit the murder."

"Go to hell, pagan bastard, I'm not scared of you."

To the shock and dismay of both Behram and Tehmul, Rauf took out a large knife and started cutting off the testicles of the prisoner. The loud cry from the prisoner was shocking to his two colleagues.

"Rauf, you can't do this. We cannot act like animals," said Behram.

Rauf walked up to Behram, aggressively looked into his eyes from an angle, where the other prisoners could not see him and then winked. Both Behram and Tehmul were shocked at this strange behaviour but kept silent.

Very slowly Rauf cut off the testicles of the prisoner and threw them in front of the others. The cry of the prisoner was so loud that every one in the room was in shock.

"Alright, you bastard, are you now ready to give us the names of those ministers?"

"Go to hell you monster, may you rot in hell," said the prisoner.

To the shock and dismay of both Behram and Tehmul, Rauf took his knife and cut open both eyes of the prisoner. The scream from the prisoner and the screams of the shocked men in the room reverberated in the whole room. The prisoner had collapsed. His head was hanging down on his chest. He appeared to have fainted.

Rauf took his knife dripping with blood and wiped it against the shirt of Major Arshad who cringed in shock. "Very shortly gentlemen, your testicles and your eyes are going to meet the same fate. So go to your room and think about it. I will demand an answer from you within four hours. Behram, Tehmul, take the prisoners to their room."

The three investigators took the prisoners to their room, handcuffed them, locked the cell door and returned. Rauf could see the anger in their eyes. "We cannot agree to cooperate with such barbarity. How are we different from the butchers in the Police Department of the Islamic Republic? If you behave in such a fashion we will not accompany you or assist you in any manner," Behram yelled.

"Cool down Behram. Give me a chance to explain everything to you. First, untie this prisoner, Jamshid. I'm not sure if he is dead." The other three did not respond but just kept staring at Rauf.

"Listen to me guys, for once trust me, get this prisoner down and revive him then we will talk."

The other three unhooked the prisoner and placed him on the ground. The blood oozing from him was a revolting sight. Suddenly Rauf walked up to the prisoner still lying on the ground and said to him. "OK bastard, get up and introduce yourself to my friends. To the shock of the three friends, the man got up and pulled out a plastic mask covering his face. He had normal eyes without any signs of injury. Then he wrenched out a plastic skin tight covering from the rest of his body. The three were stunned to realize that the man behind the plastic covering was no other than their colleague Abdul.

"What the fuck is going on here?"

"Well my friends, you must learn a lesson from all this. Nothing is what it appears to be. You must check the evidence before condemning a person."

The relief felt by the three friends was so intense that they all hugged Abdul. "Oh my God, that Rauf is a conniving bastard indeed. So all this was an act to impress the prisoners?"

"Yes my friends. Now let us open the microphones and check the discussion that they are having in our absence. Let us hear their reaction to our so-called act of barbarity. Perhaps this will convince them that their future sexual activities will be seriously curtailed or even become nonexistent, if they do not cooperate."

"But how the hell did you cut out his eyes and draw blood, which we actually saw?." Behram asked.

"Cherry tomatoes, my friend, with a little bit of white paint and a black rounded spot in the middle." He picked up the guck that had fallen on the ground and brought it to Behram. "Would you like to taste it?"

"Fuck you, you moron!" Behram responded. "Eat it yourself"

They activated the microphone and heard the voice of Lieutenant Sajjad. "Major, as a soldier of Iran I am quite prepared to risk my life for my country but these barbarians are not out to kill us. They are ready to maim us and patriotism or no patriotism, I want to die with my testicles intact."

"Don't be a coward lieutenant, that is exactly what they want you to think. They may have done those barbaric things to impress us but I do not think they will have the guts to do the same to officers of the Iranian army." Major Arshad responded.

"Well Major, you may be quite right but with the utmost respect, I do not think it is fair to expect us to take a chance with our very existence."

"Those damned ministers encouraged and ordered us to commit those crimes. As military officers we obeyed their orders. I'm not going to lose my manhood and my life. Especially when I know that they will get off scot-free." Captain Azhar stated.

"What do you suggest we do?" Captain Moravid asked.

"I think we should make a deal with them. Give them the names of the ministers in return for our freedom," Lieutenant Sajjad said.

"And what do you think our Iranian Generals are going to do to us when they find out that we betrayed the ministers, thereby allowing the terrorists to kill them?" Major Arshad asked.

"Over and above our freedom, we should also obtain their agreement not to inform any one as to how they found the names and involvement of the two ministers." Lt. Sajjad said.

"But how can we trust them? What if they promise not to reveal our names and still provide our names anonymously to the Iranian government?" Captain Azhar asked.

"More significantly, has it occurred to any of you that they may be listening to our conversation? Speak softly, for God's sake." Major Arshad said.

"I have an idea. How about requesting them to let three of us go free, then promising them that the fourth person will provide the names of the ministers," Lieutenant Sajjad said.

"They will never agree to that," said the captain.

"No harm in trying, is there?"

Rauf was carefully listening to this conversation. "Listen guys, I think my plan is ready now." He brought a little device which looked like a cell phone and attached it to the listening apparatus that they had used to track the conversation of the prisoners. "Now we will open this device so that they can hear the conversation in this room. The little gadget I've attached to the sound system will completely distort the voices. They will hear what is being said but they will not be able to identify whose voice it is. The CIA and FBI have successfully used this equipment in the past. You Abdul, get ready for some more acting. On this occasion your testicles will not be participating in the show. Now gentlemen, who in your opinion is the most timid of our prisoners?"

Every one unanimously agreed that the Lieutenant seemed to be the softest and the brightest of the bunch.

"Don't worry about his intelligence or his bravery. We do not expect him to do anything for us. He is merely a pawn. The only reason we are selecting him is because they think he wants to save his hide. One more thing Tehmul, bring Lieutenant Sajjad here for questioning. Our conversation with him must remain secret. Disconnect the equipment so the others will not hear us."

Tehmul brought the manacled and chained Sajjad into the room. "Sit down Lieutenant and listen to me carefully. Do you know what happened to the other fellow who refused to answer our questions? His eyes and testicles were removed, he was beheaded and we had his body incinerated. The ashes were not buried in a grave, they were flushed down the toilet. On the Day of Judgment, he will not be able to approach Allah. Now in your case, as you are a cowardly murderer, we think that it is absolutely necessary for you to meet with Allah and receive your punishment. However, you should also be punished on earth for your barbaric behavior. We have decided to do the following. We will cut off your testicles, remove your eyes, then we will cut off your arms and legs. This will all be surgically done so that you do not die from loss of blood. We have no anaesthetic so you will feel the full agony and pain of the torture. We will then leave you in the city centre where everyone will be able to see you. May be they will take you to a hospital and you will probably survive to spend the rest of your life a total cripple begging the good Allah for death. Raza, tie up the prisoner and get the knife ready!"

Sajjad was shivering. Suddenly, his bladder gave way and his pants were drenched. "My God, what kind of brutes are you? Why would you do this to me? I was only following orders."

"That is exactly what Hitler's murderers used to claim after the Second World War. Now Sajjad, are you ready for your surgery"?

"Look! Please! What information do you want from me? Will you let me go if I help you ?"

"My dear fellow, for your crime of brutal murder, you expect me to let you go because you provide me with some information? I will offer you the following. You will provide us with the names of the two ministers who were involved with the murder of the professor. You will come with us, contact them and inform them that they are needed immediately by the Prime Minister, who has a matter of national emergency to discuss with them. Once they are in the vehicle which you will be driving, we will take care of them. You won't have to worry about anything else!"

"If I do all this, will you let me go? Even if you do, where can I go? If those ministers are abducted, the other three officers you are holding will immediately know and inform the military that I was the rat who gave you the information. They will immediately execute me!"

"I've already considered all those possibilities," Rauf responded. "We are questioning all your companions. Once we are through with each person, he will not be allowed contact with the others. No one will know which officer gave us the information. In any case, none of your companions are going to be released. They will either be executed immediately, or if they are compliant, we will take them south to Democratic Iran where they will be tried and punished. One commitment I will make to you. No one will know that it was you who provided us with information. When you go into the parliament to convince the ministers to come with you, you will be fitted with an explosive device which will be controlled remotely by us. We will be able to hear your complete conversation. If you try to double cross us by warning them, the explosive device will be immediately detonated and you'll be meeting Allah much faster than you ever anticipated. You appear to be a relatively rational guy, even though you're a murderer. We do appreciate the fact that the real criminals are those two vicious bastards, the ministers. Their fate has already been sealed but you still have a chance of redeeming yourself and showing your penitence by helping us punish those evil men. In Democratic Iran, you will be tried for murder but we will mention to the judges that you cooperated with us and helped us to bring these animals to justice. I will personally plead with the judges to give you a lenient sentence and on my honor as a soldier of the Shahnshah, I promise you that after you have finished your sentence, I will help you integrate yourself into the population of the civilized part of Iran. I'm relatively certain that my Shahnshah will order leniency in your case at my request."

"What will happen to my companions? I do not want to be the rat who is responsible for the death of my brother officers. Will you promise that you will let them go?"

"The treatment accorded to your companions will depend upon their cooperation. If they help us in arresting and punishing the ministers, then we will request the Shahnshah and his court to give them the same leniency as we will request for you."

"Let me go back to them to discuss this matter. Perhaps we can all come to an agreement to jointly cooperate with you," Sajjad said.

"We cannot permit that. You will be given the opportunity to redeem yourselves individually. We will not permit any of you to know what the other is doing. A part of our strategy will be to protect each of you so that if one of you cooperates with us and the others do not, they cannot take revenge on you after we have left. Once you have made your decision, you will be confined separately and then taken to the Shahnshah's courts as I've promised. Tell me, what is your answer?" asked Rauf.

"I cannot give you my answer right away. I want to think about it for awhile. I'm ready to cooperate with you but am very concerned that every time I look into the mirror, my conscience will bother me." Sajjad responded.

"Listen Sajjad, let us not kid ourselves. After all, you and your companions committed the brutal murder of an innocent professor. That act cannot be easily forgiven. The brutality for which I have promised to torture you does not give me the slightest compunction. If you're worried about looking in the mirror because you're providing us with information, then you are a hypocrite. You should have been ashamed of looking in the mirror because you are a murderer. I'm going to confine you in a separate room for exactly four hours. At the end of that period, if you have not agreed to cooperate, then the torture and execution will begin immediately. Is that clearly understood?" Sajjad nodded his assent.

Rauf then summoned Raza and Tehmul. Sajjad was handcuffed, leg irons were placed on his feet and a mouth guard was inserted to silence him during his captivity. This was necessary for the uninterrupted questioning of the remaining prisoners. He was then escorted out of the room and imprisoned a reasonable distance from the interrogation area. The next person to be brought into the room was Captain Raza Moravid. He was asked to sit down and his leg irons were removed.

"Captain Moravid, I will be direct with you! You have committed the murder of an innocent and enlightened professor in our area. The punishment for such brutality is death. However we are more interested in punishing those two ministers of the Islamic Republic whose orders I presume you had to obey. We want their names, possible locations where they can be arrested and any other information which may help us to arrest and transport them to Southern Iran, where they will be tried by a duly appointed court."

"You expect me, an officer of the Iranian army, to become a traitor?"

"I'm surprised at your concern of being considered a traitor. Shouldn't you be more concerned about being a murderer? Listen Captain, I'm not giving you any choices. This is an order and you must comply without reservation. Those two vicious men who are ministers of the Iranian government ordered you to commit murder! Don't you think all your accomplices should be tried and convicted?"

"Yes I did obey the orders of the ministers. I was told that this Professor was preaching against Islam and against the Islamic Republic. I was informed that it was my duty to exterminate such an individual. I did have some doubts but then, as an army officer one does not question the orders of his superiors however wrong those orders may be. I will not betray my ministers so you can do as you wish!"

"I presume you saw and heard what we did to the first man who disobeyed our orders. I don't care a hoot about your morality or your ideals. If you do not provide us with the information we want, we will as promised, remove your eyes, cut off your limbs and let you die in slow agony."

The Captain was visibly shivering. "Ya Allah, what barbarians you are! How will you face your maker when you die?"

"We do not expect a reprimand on barbarity from an admitted murderer. Be assured that by disobeying our orders you have just signed your own death warrant."

Rauf nodded to his colleagues and they placed handcuffs, leg irons and a muzzle. He was then taken to another room and imprisoned there. The audio system was turned on at Rauf's request. This allowed the investigation to be heard by the prisoners in their cells but they were unable to identify the voices.

"Bring the prisoner here!" Rauf said and Abdul walked up closer to the microphone with a big grin on his face. "Now that you have disobeyed our commands, we are going to chop off your arms." A whooshing sound was heard as if a sword had hit something and Abdul let out a bloodcurdling scream. "That is your right arm you murderer. Now chop off the left arm! A second agonizing scream was heard. "How does it feel to be armless you filthy barbarian!"

"Kill me! Kill me! You bloody beasts! Don't let me bleed to death!".

"Are you ready to cooperate or should we take your eyes now?"

In perfect imitation of someone in immense agony, Abdul replied, "Please do not remove my eyes. I will tell you the names of the ministers and where to find them. Do whatever you wish with them, just kill me, do not leave me in this state to live the life of a blind cripple!" Rauf and his companions had great difficulty in not bursting out into laughter. Abdul's performance and voice modulation could have easily fitted into a Hollywood horror movie.

Rauf turned on the audio system to hear what was being said by the remaining prisoners, fully knowing that Abdul's histrionics must have been clearly heard.

"Well my brother officers, I think the moment has arrived for us to face death. I wish I had a weapon in my possession, I could easily end my life without being degraded by these animals. We are at their total mercy. What about you all? Are you willing to become traitors?"

"We are officers of the Islamic Republic of Iran. We will never surrender or degrade ourselves." They all replied in unison.

Rauf and his companions heard every word. "I think our only chance of success lies with Lieutenant Sajjad, but to be totally certain, we should terrify him a bit more. Our talented actor Abdul is once again required. I've switched on the sound system to the room where Lt. Sajjad is confined. We will now pretend that Major Arshad, Captain Azhar, and Captain Moravid are all being sentenced to death. This will do one of two things, it will put the fear of Allah in Sajjad, probably making him more compliant or if he comes to the conclusion that all of his companions have been executed, he will not be afraid of anyone finding out that he was the informant. Are you ready Abdul?"

Abdul nodded his assent.

Rauf started speaking in the microphone for the benefit of Sajjad. "Now you gentlemen have heard the unequivocal decision of Major Arshad, Captain Azhar and Captain Moravid. They have categorically refused to help us or show the slightest penitence for their crimes. As the chief officer and the representative of the Shahnshah, I have decided to sentence them to death and execute them immediately. The senior most officer should be shot last. First, bring in Captain Moravid!" Rauf waited for about three minutes to give Sajjad the impression that they were bringing Captain Moravid into the room. Behram and Tehmul then pretended to enter the room making sure that their footsteps could be heard by the prisoner in the adjoining cell. Rauf spoke as if he was addressing Captain Moravid. "Captain Moravid, you have indicated your unwillingness to help us but I'm going to give you one more chance. If you decide not to take it, you will be shot immediately. Will you agree to help us?"

Abdul imitated the voice of Captain Moravid, as best as he could. "I will not be a traitor to my country!" Abdul took a loaded gun with blank ammunition and fired it in the direction of the microphone. As soon as he fired he screamed loudly as if he had been shot. A large volume of an English to Farsi dictionary was dropped forcefully to the ground to imitate the thud of a body falling. "Take this filthy bastard's body and dispose it off," Rauf ordered. Two of his companions pretended to drag the body out of the room.

"Now bring Captain Azhar in!" Rauf ordered. Again, a three minute gap was allowed between his statement and the pretended entry of Captain Azhar. The same question was asked of Captain

Azhar and upon his refusal to cooperate, the pretence of shooting him was presented for the benefit of the others. The last performance was to demonstrate the alleged refusal of Major Arshad to cooperate and his immediate execution. A pretence was once again made of dragging his body out of the room.

Rauf switched off the microphone. "Well guys, what do you think? Did we convince Sajjad? Let us give him a couple of hours to absorb the demise of his companions. We will then approach him and I have a strong suspicion that his sense of patriotism and loyalty to his government will be greatly reduced. He may try to convince himself that the ministers and his government committed a sinful act and to palliate his conscience, he will probably attribute the whole fault to the ministers and that he was merely obeying their orders."

Rauf's three companions were genuinely impressed by his acumen and comprehension of human psychology. However, to keep the subject light they started joking. "Rauf you son of a bitch! You are like that Nazi bastard Mengele! I did not know you were so devious!" Abdul said.

"When dealing with fanatics and brutality you have to be devious. Most people are afraid of death, but fanaticism and faith are like drugs. Somehow they dampen the fear of death. We have to use other incentives and threats to make them co-operate." Rauf responded.

Two hours later Lieutenant Sajjad was brought into the investigation room. Rauf observed him very carefully and noticed that the prisoner was extremely nervous and pale. His eyes were constantly darting from side to side and he seemed to have an inadvertent twitch in his left arm.

"Well Lieutenant Sajjad, I'm sorry to inform you that your three fellow officers did not comply with our request and have now been executed. What is your decision?"

Rauf and his companions noticed that Sajjad was shivering uncontrollably. "I hope you will give them a proper Muslim funeral," he said in a whining voice.

"Absolutely not. A murderer who does not repent for his crime does not deserve a proper Muslim funeral. Their bodies will be incinerated and the ashes will be discarded as garbage. A good Muslim hopes to appear before Allah on the Day of Judgment to accept his rewards, an unrepentant murderer does not deserve that privilege! You do realize that ashes from the garbage can cannot appear before Allah on the Day of Judgment to obtain remission from their sins and enter the gates of heaven. Lieutenant Sajjad, if your decision allows you to obtain absolution from Allah be assured that your brother officers will not be there to keep you company. What is your decision? Yes or no!"

"I have thought this over very carefully. Those two ministers gave us false information. They told us that the professor was an anti-Islamic terrorist whose sole aim in life was the destruction of our Republic and Islam. After speaking with you, I've come to the conclusion that I have committed the murder of an innocent man. I therefore seek your forgiveness and also hope that Allah in his mercy will forgive me."

Rauf's companions looked at him with great respect. They realized that he had accurately evaluated Sajjad's thinking and was able to predict how he would react.

"Now listen carefully Sajjad. This is our plan. We are going to wire you with an explosive device which will be controlled by us. You will also be connected to our communications system so that we can monitor your conversations and gestures. You will be dressed in your full military uniform to meet with the two ministers in their office. Inform them that the Prime Minister has sent you to summon them on a matter of significant emergency and he has to consult with them. They must accompany you immediately to his residence. If you try to alert them by words or gestures, we will detonate the device. Once the ministers have agreed to come with you, bring them to the vehicle in which we will be waiting. We will be dressed in the uniforms of the Army of the Islamic Republic and we will pretend to be the guards sent by the Prime Minister to protect them on their journey to his residence. Once you've completed this task, you do not have to worry about a thing. As for yourself, I will keep my word of honor as promised. I will ask the Shahnshah and seek clemency for you. Any questions?"

CHAPTER 15.

They all entered the vehicle and Abdul got into the driver's seat. Sajjad was wired with the explosive device and the microphone. He seemed nervous but fully prepared to complete his assignment. Rauf sat next to him. His companions were fully armed with submachine guns and grenades. "Listen to me carefully Sajjad. You have nothing to worry about if you keep your word and act normally. If you make the slightest effort to alert any one, we will blow you up without hesitation. Is that clearly understood?" Sajjad nodded his assent.

Upon arrival at the gates of Parliament building, Rauf presented perfectly forged papers which the guards accepted as genuine identification of high-ranking military officers of the Islamic Republic. The logo painted on the van also helped convince the guards that they were dealing with their own military officers. Sajjad was let out at the doors of the Parliament building. "Best of luck!" Rauf muttered under his breath.

They were surprised at the confidence with which he walked through the doors. He disappeared inside the building. They could hear every word that he spoke. There were two guards at the entrance to the office of the Minister of Defence, Raza Abadi. Sajjad introduced himself to the guards by showing his identification card. "I have been sent by the Prime Minister to contact the Honorable Raza Abadi. It is an emergency and I have to see him immediately!" Sajjad said.

"I will inform the Minister right away Lieutenant," the guard said and entered the Minister's office. He returned a minute later. "The Honorable Minister will see you Lieutenant." Sajjad was escorted to the Minister.

"Salaam alaikum Mr. Minister. The Prime Minister has asked me to inform you and the Honorable Mr. Shamil Qureshi, the Minister of Religious Affairs, that you are immediately required at his residence. He said that it is a matter of urgency."

"Did he tell you what the urgency was about?" the Minister asked.

"No Sir, I was merely informed that I should bring you both immediately to his residence!"

The Minister picked up his telephone and dialed the number of Shamil Qureshi, whose office was only a few doors away. "Shamil, I have a Lieutenant Sajjad here from the Prime Minister's office. He has come to escort us to the Prime Minister's residence. The Prime Minister says it is very urgent and requires our presence immediately. There is a military escort of four officers waiting to take us there."

"I will be in your office in a minute," Shamil replied and hung up.

Within a very short time he arrived at Raza Abadi's office. Sajjad promptly saluted him and the three men walked out of Parliament towards the waiting vehicle. Rauf and his colleagues saw them approaching, stood to attention and saluted the Ministers. With seeming reverence the two rear doors of the vehicle were opened for the two men and ceremoniously closed when they sat down. Abdul drove out of the compound. The guards at the gate were not interested in the identification of the occupants when they saw the two Ministers in the car. The gate post was lifted and they left without any incident. Unintentionally, Rauf sighed with relief. Abdul drove them outside the city center of Teheran at top speed. The Ministers did notice that they were leaving the city but not driving in the direction of the Prime Minister's palace. Raza Abadi spoke up. "Driver where are you taking us? This is not the direction of the Prime Minister's residence!"

"No Mr. Minister, you're quite right! The Prime Minister is not at his residence. There is a serious security issue and he has convened this meeting outside of the city of Teheran at the residence of his friend Sharif Mohamed" Abdul responded.

"Who is Sharif Mohamed?" the Minister asked.

"I do not know Sir, I was only ordered to bring you to a residence located thirty kilometres outside of Teheran to this address." Abdul handed over a miniature sketch of the area to the Minister. It was done with such cool certainty that if he had any doubts or fears, they were completely allayed and he relaxed into his seat.

Approximately thirty kilometres outside of Teheran, they approached what seemed to be an abandoned farmhouse. Abdul stopped the van and his two companions opened the rear doors of the vehicle.

"Is this ramshackle building the residence of a friend of the Prime Minister?" Raza Abadi asked.

"I do not know what it is Minister. But this is where the Prime Minister wanted us to bring you. Will you please come in with us." Rauf said.

For the first time Rauf noticed the fear and uncertainty on the faces of both men, but they were in a secluded area and if there was any objection or resistance, no one could hear them or come to their assistance. They entered the building and the door was closed. Raza Abadi still seemed extremely concerned but did not say anything.

Once inside and without any warning, Rauf and his companions seized the Ministers and handcuffs and leg irons were placed on them.

"Who are you and why are you doing this to us?" Raza Abadi asked.

"You will be informed when the time is right, so shut up and obey our orders!" Rauf replied.

"You bastards think you can get away with this? Treating Ministers of the Islamic Republic in this fashion? You will pay with your lives for this impertinence!" Shamil Qureshi said. Rauf gave him a solid kick in his tailbone and the Minister collapsed in agony.

"I don't know about paying with our lives Minister, but if you continue with this tirade you will find it extremely difficult to walk again! You will not have a tailbone connected to your ass!"

The Minister was in such agony that he could not respond.

With seething contempt Raza Abadi looked at Lieutenant Sajjad and shouted, "You are an officer of the Islamic Republic! A man we trusted and honoured! You have betrayed us to these infidels? You are a disgrace to Iran and to the Army!"

"You dirty religious bastards! Shamil claims to be a religious man and is the Minister of Religious Affairs and you Raza, accusing us of betrayal? Have you forgotten that you sent me and three other men to Southern Iran to murder an innocent Professor, whose only guilt was that he did not agree with your politics?" Sajjad asked.

It was now apparent to Rauf that for the first time Abadi realized that their abduction was connected to the murder of the Professor. His eyes popped open. "Ya Allah, don't tell me you bastards are all working for that Canadian pagan, the enemy of Islam and Iran?" Raza said.

"The real enemies of Islam and Iran are not the Shahnshah and his men, but you hypocritical bastards who have shamed the name of Islam." Sajjad said.

Rauf could now see abject fear in the eyes of both Raza and Shamil. "What are you going to do with us?" Shamir asked.

"You see Shamir, our first concern at this moment is that filthy hypocritical animals like you should not have children and propagate your inferior genes. The first step is to prevent such propagation and therefore we're going to cut off your testicles. If you like, we will let you keep them as souvenirs. Later of course, we will seriously consider the most painful way to kill you!"

Shamir was now shivering with panic. "What do you want from us? We are only doing our duty in crushing the enemies of our Nation. That professor had embarrassed our government. He was a bad example to others. We wanted to be sure that such a situation does not occur again. Moreover, the idea was not ours, we were instructed to take these steps by the Prime Minister himself. We merely obeyed orders!"

"It amazes me how you all claim to be the representatives of Islam, allegedly protecting it by brutally murdering innocent people only because they disagree with you." Rauf replied. The only decent man in your group is Lieutenant Sajjad, who now repents for his brutality and is willing to atone for his sin. You bastards call him a traitor! Well gentlemen, your days are numbered. We are going to take you to free Iran where you will be tried and punished for your crimes. Your cowardice Shamir was very evident to us when I threatened to amputate the most useless part of your anatomy. To be honest, I would very much enjoy doing what I said, but unlike you animals, we have laws and a judiciary in our Shahnshah's Iran. Take heart. You will not be crippled yet. You will be taken before duly appointed judges who will first put you on trial before they punish you!"

Rauf signalled and the two Ministers were tied up, muzzled and taken to the same vehicle, which still had the signs of the Iranian Armed Forces. Some boards were lifted from the floor of the vehicle and the Ministers, together with Arshad, Azar and Moravid were unceremoniously thrown in. The boards placed over them were so designed that sufficient air would seep through for the prisoners to breathe. Rauf and his companions were still dressed in the uniforms of the Army of the Islamic Republic and they started their long drive in the direction of Southern Iran.

Abdul sighed loudly once they were on their way. He gritted his teeth and softly whispered in Rauf's ear, "To this point, things have gone pretty well. I never thought it would be so easy to nab and imprison these bastards. The problem now is, how we are going to cross the international border without being stopped by their border patrol. How are we going to do that Rauf?"

Very calmly Rauf took a map from his pocket. "We have to drive south for approximately two hundred and fifty kilometres. That is now the border between the Islamic Republic and our territory. There are six military outposts in the region, all very rigidly patrolled by the Islamic Army. Here, you will notice is a very mountainous region. There are tracks used by farmers and these are very difficult to drive on, even for military vehicles. Our vehicle is specifically equipped to drive on that terrain. This area is not normally guarded by the Army, so this is the best option for getting back into our territory."

They drove without incident for approximately two hundred and twenty kilometres. They arrived at a secluded area and Rauf stopped the vehicle.

"What are we stopping for?" Abdul asked. With a mischievous grin on his face, Rauf took out several Army badges. He pinned one on himself. With sarcasm he said, "because of my invaluable service to the Islamic Republic, I've just promoted myself to the rank of a Brigadier of the Iranian Army. You Behram and Abdul are now both Colonels and you Tehmul are a Major. Here are your badges."

"What is the purpose of this ludicrous exercise?" Tehmul asked.

"Gentleman, don't be so naïve! We have just entered the area where we are expecting to be stopped at any moment by the Iranian border guards. We will tell them that we are on a secret mission to track down a possible advance of the Shahnshah's army into our territory. As this information is not confirmed, our Armed Forces have decided that we liaise with our secret agents who are going to cross from Southern Iran into our territory to provide us with current information on their progress. We will then eliminate them on their own side by aerial bombardment. This reduces the possibility of any casualties on our side. The utmost secrecy is required and even the military personnel should not know of our whereabouts. There are spies who have infiltrated our own army, and under no circumstances should they have the opportunity of informing the Shahnshah's infidel regime. What do your think guys? Do I now sound like a genuine Iranian Brigadier?"

All of them stared at Rauf with admiration. "What is the purpose of this instant promotion to Brigadier and Colonels and Major?" Behram asked.

"You naïve little bastard! Don't you realize that we were dressed as junior officers until I just promoted you? Do you think the Iranian border patrol would have believed this exotic story of espionage coming from us Lieutenants? However, they might be too scared to question the orders of a Brigadier, two Colonels and a Major, even if they suspect us. Once we successfully enter our own territory, who cares what they find out. Our military rank will provide us with the precious time needed to cross safely into Democratic Iran."

They continued driving, fully realizing and appreciating Rauf's plan. They entered the winding path that was approximately twenty kilometres from the location where they expected to cross into their own territory. Suddenly, as they turned left, they noticed two tanks blocking their path. "Oh my God!" Tehmul exclaimed.

"Shut up and let me talk to them." Rauf said.

Nonchalantly, Rauf stopped alongside the tanks. Noticing the insignia of a Brigadier of the Iranian Army, the soldiers jumped out of the tanks and saluted him. Rauf looked at them casually and asked, "Soldiers, have you seen any unusual enemy activity in this area?"

"No Brigadier, everything is quiet here. There is no easy passage from this area into the Pagan's realm. We have been carefully scrutinizing this area for several days."

"Who is the Commanding officer here?" Rauf asked.

An officer with the insignia of a Captain jumped out of the tank and saluted Rauf. "Brigadier, I am Captain Abbasi. I'm in charge of this unit."

Rauf got out of his vehicle and approached the Captain. He put his arm around the Captain's shoulder and very confidentially informed him that there was an expected incursion from the Pagan's land and that the utmost secrecy was necessary to eliminate this possible danger without exposing Iranian troops to possible injury and death. He looked into the eyes of the Captain and continued. "Captain, you seem to be a very dedicated officer and I think that I can trust you. Not a syllable of this should be revealed even to your own troops!"

"Absolutely Brigadier. I will not utter a word of this to any one. You have my word of honor."

"Give me your name and your identification number, Captain. If we are successful as we hope to be, I will personally mention your name to the Commander-In-Chief."

The Captain grinned with pride and smartly saluted Rauf. "Thank you Brigadier for your kindness Sir."

Very casually Rauf got back into his vehicle and gestured Abdul to continue driving. They drove on the winding road until the tanks disappeared from their view. With a sigh of relief Rauf exclaimed "I need a cigarette badly!"

"You were absolutely fantastic Rauf!" Behram said. "How the hell did you manage to keep your cool in this situation?"

"It is easy with such dedicated and brave companions like you all," he said with genuine modesty. This was the first sign of relaxation observed in his demeanour. Suddenly they all realized a feeling of extreme warmth and affection for each other. They were now in the area from where they were intending to cross into Southern Iran. It was dark since there was no moonlight. It took a little while for them to find the rugged forest trail they were intending to use. It was almost two hours of incredibly rough driving before Rauf was satisfied that they were once again in the terrain controlled by the Shahnshah's regime.

"Alright guys, it is now time to change into our own uniforms. I'm sure you will agree with me that after such an arduous journey through enemy territory and having succeeded in getting back to Southern Iran, we don't want to be shot at by our own military!" They got out together with Sajjad and changed into their military uniforms, while Sajjad got into civilian clothing. They were now on the highway heading in the direction of Zahidan. After a few miles, they were thrilled to see the first military battalion of the Shahnshah's troops. This not only relieved the incredible tension they felt, but also served as cogent evidence that they were indeed back in Democratic Iran. Rauf greeted the Battalion with great gusto and presented their documents to prove the authenticity of his four companions. The officer examining their papers seemed extremely impressed. "Captain Rauf Irfani! I am honored to meet you, Sir! We have been anticipating your safe return and have instructions directly from the Shahnshah that upon your arrival, we should escort you into his royal presence. Officers, I will be grateful if you follow me to Zahidan." Rauf and his companions could not hide their pride and joy at the special sentiments expressed by the Shahnshah himself.

"A couple of things Officer. There are five prisoners who have to be transported to the Shahnshah's court for trial. I will be very grateful if you take charge of them so they do not escape. Secondly, why do you address me as Captain? I am only a Lieutenant".

"Captain Irfani, where are your prisoners?"

Rauf and his companions slowly removed the floorboards of the vehicle to the utmost astonishment of the Officer. The three Iranian officers, Major Arshad, Captain Azhar and Captain Moravid were unceremoniously dragged from the vehicle. Their sudden exposure to light and removal from a cramped position made them look groggy. Next, the two ministers Abadi and Qureshi were pulled out of the van.

"Who are these men?" the Border Officer asked.

"These three are the ones who brutally murdered the Professor. Those two are Ministers of the Islamic Republic who instigated and authorized the murder."

"This man in the civilian clothing, who is he?"

"That is Lieutenant Shakil Sajjad. He belongs to the Army of the Islamic Republic and initially was with this group of murderers, but when he realized that they had tricked him with their lies, he decided to help us by providing valuable information which led to the arrest of these men. I'm going to personally speak to the Shahnshah to request leniency for him."

"Captain Irfani, I still haven't answered your second question. Why did I call you Captain. The Shahnshah has ordered a promotion for you and all your colleagues. He has specifically commanded us to inform you of his decision when you return safely into our territory. Congratulations Captain Irfani."

The four officers hugged and congratulated each other. Even Shakil Sajjad walked over to them and heartily congratulated them.

"You bastards! You think you have won the war don't you? Wait until the Army of the Islamic Republic catches you and punishes you! You filthy pagan traitors!" Raza Abadi shouted. No sooner was his sentence completed when one of the officers in charge kicked him hard in the testicles and the Minister fell to the ground.

"Raza Abadi, we the pagan traitors as you call us, have one very significant quality. We are quite capable and efficient at kicking the shit out of religious dogs like you. If you would like another one, ask for it. This pagan traitor would be delighted to give your testicles a second dose of treatment."

Minister Abadi was too busy massaging his testicles and moaning in agony to adequately respond to the challenge of the officer. The two Ministers and three Iranian officers were once again thrown into the truck and the door was secured. Sajjad was now treated as a comrade by Rauf and his friends. He was allowed to sit with them in the front seat of the truck. As they passed a little village, Sajjad noticed that almost all the women had not covered their faces with a pardah. Some of the ladies were wearing pantsuits and a few even wore short dresses. Rauf saw his expression and started laughing, "Yes Sajjad, in Democratic Iran, if the girl is over the age of sixteen, no one can force her to wear a pardah. And any physical force or interference by her parents, religious or school authorities or any person of the inferior generation, is severely punished. If the parents force her to wear a pardah against her wishes, she has the option of contacting the Ministry of Education and immediate steps are taken to punish the interfering party. You may not know this, but under the new legislation introduced by the Shahnshah, boys and girls receive the same education in coed schools. They are encouraged to communicate and interact with each other. This prevents them from acting like sex starved maniacs as was the case when they were segregated and prevented from developing normal friendships. Sajjad, did you know that our wise Shahnshah has made it illegal for parents to interfere with mixed marriages? Shi'ites and Sunnis can now marry freely. Zoroastrians, Christians, Muslims and Jews can intermarry. Interference by the parents is a crime unless they can establish before a marital tribunal that the union is only being discouraged because of criminal activity, lack of education or moral turpitude. These are the only issues they are allowed to voice an opinion on. The final decision is not left to the parents, but to the Marital Tribunal."

Rauf noticed Sajjad's shocked expression of disbelief. "What do the mullahs say? Don't they condemn this as being unIslamic?"

"What is your definition of being unIslamic? Do we want to leave control of the lives of our people in the hands of individuals who have never seen the rear end of a University? There are highly educated Islamic scholars in the service of the Shahnshah. These men and women are not only well versed in the dictates of the Koran, but also in creating modern-day interpretations and amendments that would make the lives of all Muslims more progressive and closer to what Allah would want for them. Our Prophet Mohamed was a very brilliant and sophisticated man who created Islam to make life better for its followers. One must always keep in mind that some of his dictates were created for a very backward people who lived in the desert, which was not easily controlled by the state. Since then, several Islamic civilizations have come and disappeared such as the Moors and the Great Mogul Emperor Akbar of India. They brought peace, prosperity and tolerance to the people. Do you think the fanatical rantings and ravings of our present-day mullahs can compete with that sophistication?"

"As children we have been taught in the madrasas that total obedience to the Koran is the only way to reach heaven."

"My dear Sajjad, every single dictum in the Koran, Bible or Avesta was created by highly sophisticated men of that era to solve the problems of that time. To use dicta created in the eighth century to remedy the problems of the twenty-first century would be an insult to both Allah and the Prophet. Our Shahnshah is aware of all this. I can say with the utmost confidence as a Muslim that perhaps the only genuine protector of true Islam and Muslims is this Zoroastrian Emperor, the Shahnshah."

"I will admit one thing Rauf, seeing those women walking alone with uncovered faces was an extremely attractive site."

"Now Sajjad, your appreciation, does it come from your head or your dick?" Rauf asked.

Sajjad laughed merrily. "Is it illegal in your Shahnshah's Iran to express one's appreciation both ways?"

Rauf laughed and patted him on his back. "I'm starting to believe that there is hope for you. We might be able to convert you into a really civilized Muslim."

Tehmul butted in. "No Rauf, that is highly unlikely. You gave this long, convoluted speech about civilization and Islam but our friend's concentration was totally on the pretty girls walking without pardah." They all laughed it off.

They had now entered the city of Zahidan. Sajjad had visited Zahidan three or four years earlier. At that time, Zahidan was an overpopulated and underdeveloped city. He was shocked to see it today. There were wide tree-lined avenues. Enormous growth and construction, new buildings all carefully planned and beautifully landscaped caught his attention. He could not keep his eyes off all the pretty girls walking around. He noticed that there was a new synagogue and a new church, but the most shocking observation was the huge university complex designed by architects to combine Western and Iranian architecture. A couple of kilometres west of the University was a twenty-five storeyed building. On the side of this structure was an inscription in Farsi which read, `Allah created men and women. Messengers of Allah, from time to time, brought the kindness of Islam, Christianity Judaism, and Zoroastrianism. It was an ignorant man who claimed that one message was superior to the other, thus killing the very message sent by Allah.' 'This hospital is for men and women of all faiths and beliefs. We will try to cure your ailments, only you can cure your minds.' Underneath these words was a picture of the Shahnshah and the words `Shahnshah of all Iranians.'

Rauf and his companions had seen these buildings several times but in spite of that their throats became constricted. The love and loyalty they felt for the Shahnshah brought tears to their eyes. They avoided looking in the direction of Sajjad because they felt embarrassed.

"Who is this man, your Shahnshah? How can he change the face of a whole city in such a short time. How can he succeed in changing the thinking pattern of a whole nation?"

"That is not all, my dear Sajjad. This man is a Zoroastrian from Canada. He is a chartered accountant and is seventy years old. He has absolutely no experience of being a politician or running a country. When he arrived here, he did not know one word of Farsi. You can see his achievements by looking at the city. You should hear his speeches. Professors teaching Farsi at Universities have admitted that they cannot equal his diction or fluency."

Sajjad seemed to be listening with total absorption. "Tell me more about the legal changes that the Shahnshah has introduced," he requested.

"The Shahnshah believes and has convinced us that every new generation is mentally superior to the previous generation. They normally have more education, more logic and above all, more scientific information. To bring progress to a people, the first thing you must do is to remove the power of the older generation over the new generation. The so-called experienced elders always claim that they have more wisdom but in reality their beliefs are nothing more than grounded ignorance based on religious concepts and ideals based on unproven superstitions. It is therefore imperative that their control over the younger generation be removed completely. That is precisely why the Shahnshah created the Marital Council to prevent interference with mixed marriages by the parents. Now look at the second aspect of the benefits we are reaping as a result of his dicta. He has introduced a law which necessitates totally equal opportunities for women in education as well as employment. Before the Shahnshah's arrival, approximately twenty percent of the women in our part of Iran were educated and capable of being employed as doctors engineers or lawyers, but they were not permitted to hold these positions. As a result, we lost twenty percent of our intellectual manpower for absolutely no logical reason. Their integration into the working world has suddenly increased the gross national growth rate by about thirty percent. In order to completely eliminate prejudice without interfering with religious beliefs, the Shahnshah has decreed that the State will actively encourage mixed marriages and any interference from the parents or relatives without the involvement of the Marital Council, is severely punished with a seven-year jail sentence. The Shahnshah correctly believes that mixed marriages will eliminate the power of religious fanatics. He has also decreed that it will be illegal for either spouse to insist on the other converting to his or her faith. To encourage this, the following has been decreed. If a Sunni marries a Shia both parties get an income tax exemption of twenty-five percent for the rest of their lives . If a Muslim marries a Jew, Christian or Zoroastrian, each party gets a fifty percent income tax exemption for the entirety of their lives. You know that the school system in our Iran is totally free for all children. There are efforts being made to make university education free as well. That will take a little while because of financial reasons. However, children born of a mixed union will receive free university education immediately. Any public furor against encouragement of mixed marriages is also punishable with a minimum of seven years imprisonment. Let us look at the results, the Jews, Christians and Zoroastrians have become a part of the nation. They have no fear anymore. They contribute exactly as the Muslims do. With so many children marrying outside of their faith, the inferior generation is afraid to point a finger at others and are grudgingly making every effort to become friends with the minority communities because they are concerned that the next child to marry outside may be their own. The reputation of being against mixed marriages and absorption may, at the minimum, lead to loss of employment and income, and at worst, a long jail sentence. Even the ignorant fanatics have decided to stoop to conquer without realizing that they will never rise to a position where they can do any harm to our civilized society. Do you know Sajjad that when the Shahnshah arrived here, this was the poorest part of Iran, contributing just twenty percent to the nation's economy? Today, even though Iran is divided, we are producing two hundred and twenty percent of what the Islamic Republic is producing. What do you think of that?"

"Before the arrival of the Shahnshah, Iran could have used its enormous oil revenue to improve education, hospitalization, development of natural resources and creation of industry and employment. Oil resources, however enormous, do ultimately deplete and even disappear. It is therefore essential that you use the income from oil to develop other industries, agriculture and income producing activities so that when the oil is gone your economy still continues to survive. What did the Islamic Republic do? They built nuclear bombs, expended enormous amounts of money on propagation of religion and oppression of the minorities while actively and financially assisting terrorist groups all over the Middle East. In today's world it is not so difficult to manufacture an atomic bomb. The question is whether you can ever use it. Even if you can, what will the consequences be to your own country when other countries respond? For example, suppose Iran uses a nuclear weapon on Israel, that nation is quite capable of retaliating and causing enormous loss and destruction in Iran. That is not all. Whether you like them or not, the Americans are not going to sit back and take it. To fight a nuclear war against the United States is sheer madness. When a man who is five feet six inches tall and weighs a hundred and twenty pounds attacks a man who is six feet six inches tall and weighs two hundred and twenty pounds, the attacker is not brave, he is insane."

"What do you think are the Shahnshah's views on a negotiated peace with Israel and the reaction of the Islamic world, if he succeeds?" Sajjad asked.

"It is not an issue as to his Majesty's views or the opinion of the Islamic world. It is a question of facing reality. Israel is here to stay because it is a highly sophisticated nation. They do not want to conquer any one, but just want to be left alone. The only two countries in the Muslim world which can successfully attack Israel are the Islamic Republic and Pakistan because of nuclear weapons. Now Pakistan has enough problems of its own and will only give you lip support. If Iran tries on its own it will be exterminated. We should learn from the Turks who have achieved a friendly relationship with the Israelis. Let us look at our pathetic record of Sunni and Shia animosity. We have killed more of each other than the Israelis, so why this inexplicable dislike for the Jews who stayed peacefully with the Muslims for several centuries? The Shahnshah has already made Turkey his best ally. They respect his rationality and democratic views. I have a strong belief that the Turks will support us militarily because they do not trust the Islamic Republic . Imagine a second ally as sophisticated as Israel. Which Arab or Muslim country would have the courage to attack the combined forces of Turkey, Israel and our own Shahnshah's fast developing armed forces?"

"Do you not feel that a union with pagan Jews to fight our own Muslim brothers is totally against the dictates of the Koran?" Sajjad asked.

"Two things are wrong with your logic, Sajjad. If you call the Jews pagans then you are contradicting the teachings of our Prophet Mohammad himself, who considered the Jews and Christians, `Kitabis', or people of the Holy Books. He ordered us not to antagonize them. Next, why do our so called Muslim brothers consistently have Shia, Sunni battles? What kind of brotherhood is that? As a matter of fact there is a false sense of unity which prevails between the Sunnis and the Shias because they perceive the Israelis as the enemies of both. Once the threat of Israel is gone, the Sunnis and Shi'ites will once again start killing each other. Thus in a sense, the existence of Israel is necessary to keep peace in the Middle East."

Sajjad nodded, though he seemed to be only partially convinced.

"I do not want to change the subject abruptly Rauf, but my future has to be determined as soon as possible. What do you think they will do to me. I want you to know that I genuinely regret my behaviour. I participated in the murder of an innocent and sophisticated man. Allah will never forgive me but can you at least guide me as to what I should do to reduce my sentence?"

"I don't know what to say to you Sajjad. I'm not a judge or a lawyer so I am not able to advise you on such legal matters. All I can say is that I'm an officer in the Shahnshah's army and he has been kind enough to promote me, and to proclaim my achievement of bringing those criminals to justice. I will definitely give evidence on your behalf and tell the court of your assistance in arresting them. I'm quite sure that this evidence will be taken into account to determine your sentence. I also have to appear before his Majesty to give him a detailed report of this incident. I will be sure to tell His Majesty of your exceptional cooperation and that I believe you to be sincerely repentant. At the time you committed the crime, you were convinced that the man you were sent to assassinate was a traitor. I will also request the Shahnshah to meet with you and if he agrees, you will have the opportunity to plead for yourself."

"Thank you, my brother. I promise you I will be grateful to you for the rest of my life."

Rauf drove his van into the barracks of the military compound. He led Sajjad to the commanding officer and introduced him by giving a short description as to who he was. A room was allotted and Rauf entered with him. He took out a Koran and placed it before Sajjad.

"Place your hand on the Koran and swear to God that you will be faithful to the Shahnshah and Democratic Iran. I'm not keeping you here as a prisoner, you have freedom to move around, because I trust you. Do not misuse my trust."

Sajjad took the Koran in his hand and swore the oath as was required. Rauf left the room to allow him the privacy that he needed to wash up and compose himself in order to meet the required authorities. Rauf went back to his room and found that there was a message for him. It was from the Royal Palace. "The Shahnshah-e-Iran would like to speak to you at your earliest convenience. Please confirm that you have received this message and communicate to us when you will be able to come to the Palace."

Rauf immediately dialed the number and informed the Palace authorities that he would appear before His Majesty within one hour.

With a grin on his face and glee in his heart, Rauf shaved, bathed and donned a new and perfectly ironed uniform. He borrowed a military motorcycle and rode to the Royal Palace. At the entrance, there was a device to check for weapons and explosives and he had to pass through this. After the officers were certain that he was clear and his credentials were carefully checked, he was taken by two armed guards and presented to a Colonel.

"So you are Captain Rauf Irfani? I have heard good things about you Captain. The Shahnshah is very eager to meet with you. Follow me please."

The construction of the inside of the building was done with the highest quality of black and white marble. The walls were covered with portraits of Iranian kings, poets and other historical figures of Iranian history. The ceiling was of carved marble inlaid with the well known Iranian semi precious stone called Firoza.

As Rauf walked beside the Colonel, he noticed that they were being escorted by two armed men carrying machine guns. They traversed a long corridor until they came to a huge doorway of carved oak. Without having to knock, the door was opened by two soldiers from the inside and Rauf noticed that at the other end of the room was a desk where the Shahnshah was sitting. Rauf felt awed, approaching a man he considered almost immortal. A man who, in his opinion, had changed the destiny of a nation. Upon reaching the desk, the two officers who were his escorts stood on either side of him. The Colonel bowed from his waist, "Your Majesty, I present to you, our brave Iranian soldier, Captain Rauf Irfani."

Rauf saluted smartly and then immediately fell to his knees before the Shahnshah. He could not help noticing that the Shahnshah was wearing a very well tailored suit and a tie. He looked all of his seventy years. One could tell from his eyes that he missed nothing that transpired before him. And yet, a streak of kindness was very clearly visible. The Shahnshah stood up and laid a hand on Rauf's shoulders and asked him to rise. Rauf expected him to be condescending as most superior army officers are but to his surprise the Shahnshah placed both his palms on his cheeks and looked directly into his eyes. Unlike a military General, the Shahnshah said. "Welcome back to Zahidan, my son, you have done a great service to our country by arresting and bringing these criminals to us. This will prevent such occurrences in the future. Would you like to have a coffee or tea or another drink perhaps?"

Rauf had never anticipated the Shahnshah of Iran prosaically offering him coffee or tea as if he was a friend or acquaintance.

"My Shahnshah, it is such an honor for me to be in your presence. To speak with you personally, was beyond my wildest dreams. If I have been successful in performing some trivial duty , I'm very proud to be of service to you. Thank you very much, Your Majesty, for promoting me."

You deserved your promotion Captain. Is there anything else I can do for you?"

Yes, Your Majesty, there is. One of the individuals who was involved in the murder of the Professor is a Lieutenant Shakil Sajjad of the Army of the Islamic Republic. Initially he was uncooperative, but once he realized what a brutal and senseless crime he was forced to commit and how he had been totally brainwashed, he readily admitted his guilt and was instrumental in helping us to arrest his co-accused as well as the two Iranian ministers who organized the killing. Without his help we could not have captured the ministers. I am totally satisfied that he is honest and trustworthy and will be of service to Democratic Iran in the future. On his behalf Your Majesty, I am asking for your leniency in his sentence, if there is to be one."

"How old are you Rauf? How can you be so sure that he is not staging an act to reduce his sentence?"

"Your Majesty, I'm twenty five years old and certainly do not claim to be wise or have any great experiences in life. Your Majesty, we travelled together for seven days through enemy terrain facing the possibility of death. At one point we were stopped by the border army detachment of the Islamic Republic. He had ample opportunity to betray us, if he wanted to, but he stayed steadfast. I trust him completely."

"All right Captain, this is what we will do. You go and bring this Sajjad to me. I want to speak to him personally and I want to judge him for myself. How soon do you think you can bring him here?"

"I will call him immediately on my cell phone and ask him to be ready. I will pick him up on my motorcycle and escort him into your Majesty's presence."

The Shahnshah nodded. Rauf once again bowed from his waist, saluted the King and backed out of the assembly room.

After he made the telephone call to Sajjad, he started thinking of the events of the day. It was an amazing day. It was indeed an amazing week. He had successfully entered the Islamic Republic, captured five murderers and their accomplices. He had succeeded in slipping back into Democratic Iran. More significantly, with the help of his companions, he had converted a believer and soldier of the Islamic Republic into a faithful follower of the Shahnshah of Iran. To top it off, he was promoted and received an incredibly warm reception from the Shahnshah. But most significantly, he had rewarded and protected a new friend and colleague who had assisted him in tracking down the criminals. As Rauf raced through the streets of Zahidan on his motorcycle, he suddenly realized that such wonderful days rarely come in one's lifetime. He parked his motorcycle in front of the dormitory allotted to Sajjad. He knocked on the door which was immediately opened by Sajjad. Rauf was surprised to see that Sajjad appeared quite ill at ease.

"What's the matter Sajjad? You look worried!"

"You are just returning from the Palace of the Shahnshah, aren't you? Has he sent you to arrest me?"

"No, my friend, on the contrary. The Shahnshah has commanded me to bring you to his presence, he wants to talk to you. If he wanted to arrest you, he would have sent the police, wouldn't he? Hop on to my bike."

Rauf rode into the Palace grounds and they were both immediately escorted into the presence of the Shahnshah, who was expecting them.

"Your Majesty, may I present to you Lieutenant Shakil Sajjad, as per your command."

Sajjad fell to his knees before the Shahnshah. "Your Majesty, before you stands a criminal, who is ashamed to be here. I was instrumental partly, in the commission of a heinous offence. My three colleagues and I took the life of an innocent professor. I have no justification for what I did. I'm guilty. The only defence I have is my commanding officers told me that this professor was against Islam and the Islamic Republic. He was encouraging individuals in your domain to cross over into the Islamic Republic to kill politicians and government officers there. They insisted that it was my duty as a military officer to end this carnage. I did not question the integrity of these statements and proceeded to comply with their orders. Since then, I have had the benefit and honor of meeting and becoming a good friend of your honourable officer Rauf Irfani. I'm apologizing not only for my guilt, but also for my stupidity."

Rauf noticed that the Shahnshah was looking at Sajjad, right in the eyes without saying a word. Rauf observed the deep strength in his eyes. Those eyes, they always tried to determine the truth. "All right Lieutenant Sajjad, convince me that you're telling me the truth. How can I be sure that you are not a spy working with the Islamic Republic and that you will not commit other offenses in our domain?"

Slowly Sajjad took a Koran from his pocket. When Sajjad put his hand in his pocket, the guards on either side of him immediately drew their revolvers. The Shahnshah gestured to them upon seeing the Koran and the officers stood at ease.

"In the name of Allah and the Prophet I swear to you that I am not a spy and I will not be unfaithful to you in any manner, my Shahnshah."

The Shahnshah nodded his head. "I have to carefully consider what you have said to me. After the investigations have been completed, you will be informed of what your future will be since you were honest and you confessed. Now, sir, I will request you to step outside, there are some matters I want to discuss with these officers."

Sajjad bowed and left the assembly room. The Shahnshah looked at Rauf, "Lieutenant Rauf Irfani, I am entrusting you with a responsibility. I realize you trust this man. However, I have to be certain that his confession and swearing are not an act. I want you to watch him and inform our Secret Service authorities if there is the slightest doubt in your mind as to his authenticity. Can you do that?"

"Your Majesty's command will be obeyed to the last detail, my Shahnshah."

Rauf was asked to leave the room and the Shahnshah summoned the Chief of the Secret Service.

"Officer, it appears to me that this man, Lieutenant Shakil Sajjad, may be genuinely repentant but we cannot take any chances. I'm requesting you to keep complete surveillance on him. If he sneezes it should be recorded. If there is any suspicious activity on his part, let me know immediately. Is that understood?"

"Absolutely your Majesty."

CHAPTER 16.

Being the Shahnshah of Iran was not a bed of roses. There was the Palace in which I resided. There were thousands of men who were willing to jeopardize their lives for me. There was unlimited political power and enormous wealth and all of this came at a cost. I realized very early in the game the incredible capacity of power to corrupt. More significant was the fact that no one contradicted me. If I was wrong, there was no way of finding my mistakes. For the first time in my life, I was happy to be seventy years old. My age had considerably reduced my vanity. I questioned my own judgments and requested my ministers and other advisers for their advice and their candid opinion about any errors of judgment I was about to make. The economic progress of Democratic Iran was a fact but whether all the decisions I made would be beneficial to the country was an issue I could not decide by myself. Interesting, I thought, the only totally reliable person in my life today was my woman Zainab. There was no question in my mind as to her loyalty and her love for me. But I needed some outside contacts, totally unconnected to Iran.

I received a request from the famous British political writer, Sir Laurence Rogers, for an interview to discuss the changes I had brought about to Democratic Iran. I immediately agreed to meet with him. He had the reputation of being one of the most astute political writers in Britain and the whole Western Hemisphere. He was not judgemental. He was a keen and scientifically minded individual who did not mince his words. He would not hesitate to complement politicians when they deserved it and at the same time, would not tolerate the lack of integrity. One of his greatest qualities was that he was not critical when he disagreed with you. He examined your performance strictly on the evidence before him, without being affected by his own views. I thought that knowing such a man would be beneficial to me.

When he arrived at the palace and was introduced to me, he was extremely respectful and yet not servile. My experience has taught me that if you want to really comprehend the views of a person, questions alone are not adequate. A few drinks and interacting tended to bring out the truth much better than a cross-examination. To my surprise, Sir Lawrence was not just a brilliant writer but also an extremely affable man. I realized that we were both assessing each other and that was fine with me. He requested and was given permission and protection to travel all over Democratic Iran without any restrictions. He was free to visit all industrial, religious, political and educational institutions. He was not a man who came to conclusions upon seeing or hearing things. He thoroughly researched the facts before writing- his articles.

"Would your Majesty like to see the article I have written on the progress you have made in this part of the world? You may have objections to certain things I have to say."

From his tone and the expression in his eyes, I knew that he was trying to determine my reaction. If I insisted on seeing his articles before he published them, that indicated to him my intolerance to take criticism. What he did not realize was that even if I objected to his opinions, I had no control over his writings once he left Iran and I told him exactly that. Sir Lawrence started laughing. "Your Majesty, I must say that I do respect your acumen. I have very many laudable things to say about you and what you have done for this country, but there are areas where I disagree with your views. Are you capable of accepting that criticism?"

"Sir Laurence, I do not believe in controlling the opinions of other individuals. You have provided me with the opportunity of getting a candid view from a completely objective political analyst. If there is going to be any criticism, I'm not worried about it since I cannot control what you will publish after you leave Iran. I do not want to hear about it or attempt to interfere with the free expression of your analysis."

Sir Laurence smiled at me. "Your Majesty, you may already know this, but I'm not very popular with the British Royal family or nobility. They consider me a loud mouth and an upstart, who has the audacity to criticize and humiliate them. I'm surprised that you are not concerned."

"Sir Laurence, does it not occur to you that the very reason I accepted you as my guest and interviewer was because I wanted a completely independent view of what was happening in Iran?. Write whatever you wish, I want to be sure that I have not influenced your decision or judgment in any manner."

Sir Lawrence got up and bowed to me. I wanted him to realize that I was treating him as my equal so, I shook his hand and said "Bon voyage Sir."

Several months had elapsed since Sir Laurence's departure. I was informed that his book had been published but I still had not received a copy. That night, BBC was going to broadcast a one-hour program on Iran and I was extremely keen to watch it.

BBC's famous TV host Peter Jarvis, opened the show by introducing Sir Laurence. He was described as one of the most famous British authors who wrote about political figures throughout the world.

"Sir Lawrence, we have been informed that you have spent approximately four months in what is presently described as Democratic Iran. We are aware that you have met the Shahnshah and have developed a personal relationship with him. Am I correct so far?"

"Mr. Jarvis, that is absolutely correct. The Shahnshah in my opinion, is not only one of the most brilliant men I've ever met, he is a very scholarly and astute gentleman and does not have any illusions of grandeur like some of our own aristocrats in Britain. You have asked me to express an opinion on his achievements and personality. Before I do so, it is necessary for me to draw to your attention the extent of his success in developing the portion of Iran which is normally described as Democratic Iran."

"You must realize that this area of Iran under the control of the Shahnshah was the most backward portion of Iran. There were no oil wells or industries worth mentioning. A large part of this area was basically unsuitable for agriculture since it was semi-desert. This is the area the Shahnshah took charge of when he arrived from Canada. He did not come by himself, he was invited by sophisticated and educated Iranians who were fed up of a fanatical theocracy which was destroying their economy and their culture."

"Millions of educated women were either actively discouraged or prevented from obtaining gainful employment. Hundreds of thousands of Sunni Muslims who were in the minority, together with thousands of Christians, Jews and Zoroastrians, were actively kept out of professional jobs and relegated to labor. The Shahnshah changed all this completely. Equal opportunity for all Iranian citizens became the law. The consequence was that within a period of six months, thousands of significant jobs which were vacant because of lack of available personnel, were filled successfully. This increased the standard of living because of the enhanced production levels. The consequences? The production in Democratic Iran has risen by two hundred and thirty percent. Today, this portion of Iran which used to produce approximately twenty two percent of the gross national product, is producing far more than the remaining sixty percent of Iran."

"The Shahnshah's dictum that the State must protect the rights of every citizen allowing them to follow their religious beliefs has made a tremendous difference in the progress of the country. The law which forbids any interference or discrimination against any of the minority groups, has eliminated the power of the mullahs. Surprisingly, this particular control of the religious theocracy is wholeheartedly supported by the majority of Iranian Shi'ite Muslims, since they have been able to observe at first hand what tremendous progress has been achieved."

"Expert technicians have been summoned from the United States, Britain, Japan, China and other parts of the world to investigate the possibility of oil in this region and they have been successful in finding oil. But that is not all. Investigation into other resources has also been very successful. Southern Iran makes its own automobiles. The quality and price are so competitive that they are expecting to export their motor vehicles to Europe and the United States for the first time next year."

"The Islamic Republic constantly airs propaganda denouncing Democratic Iran, calling it the realm of the pagan and anti-Islamic. However in the last month alone, at least two million people have moved from the Islamic Republic into Democratic Iran. This convinces me that dollars speak louder than propaganda. The Shahnshah's regime does not bother to air any propaganda against the Islamic Republic. They just ignore them with total contempt. This has a strange result. If a statement is aired on Southern Iran's TV network, it is almost always taken as gospel truth by the Iranians regardless of where they reside. Several jokes have become popular in the Islamic Republic. One of them is that whenever the Prime Minister or his Ministers have diarrhoea, it is either because of the evil wishes or the pagan rituals of the Shahnshah and his subjects. This is an indication as to their opinion of the propaganda from the Islamic Republic.

"The Shahnshah has abolished the sharia ritual which demanded that women cover their faces. It is now left to the individual to decide. If a woman is forced to cover her face, she can immediately contact the authorities and the male, even if he is the husband, is severely punished for interfering with the rights of a fellow citizen. Monogamy is now the law. Sharia law has been abolished in all areas including matrimonial and criminal law."

"Would you believe, that almost fifteen million Iranians have now emigrated from the Islamic Republic to the Democratic Republic? The Shahnshah has set up a system to help them enter the Democratic Republic by constantly changing the entry points. This is because the Islamic Republic now acts somewhat like East Germany and does not permit people to either travel to the Democratic Republic or visit their relatives or friends in Southern Iran. They have not yet been able to create anything like the Berlin Wall but I would not be surprised if they try. To eliminate this possibility the Shahnshah has created a website and any Iranian can apply without the authorities of the Islamic republic ever finding out about it. The application must contain his qualifications, experience and record involving any participation in fanatical activities. The web site is so created that the identity of the applicant is completely concealed. After the credentials have been duly checked, and if the candidate is approved, he receives an e-mail telling him where exactly he can cross into the Democratic Republic. This has totally eliminated the control of the Islamic Republic on people moving south. No amount of persecution or propaganda has succeeded in reducing the flow."

"Sir Lawrence, you have given us a very clear picture of the progress achieved by the Shahnshah, but our listeners are also keenly interested in knowing about the man himself. Can you tell us more about his beliefs, ideals etc.?"

"Yes, I certainly can, but per force some of that information has to be my assessment of his views from the conversations I have had with him."

"That's fair."

"Iran has enormous natural resources, over and above it's oil resources. The education level is quite high compared to other areas of the Middle East. The sophistication of the people is also quite high but has been actively suppressed by the religious bureaucracy. With their existing resources, Iran should be economically on par with countries like Italy and Spain. One cannot help but determine that the main reason for its relative backwardness is religion and the fanaticism that prevents the citizens from living happily with each other. The funny part of it is, that the animosity of Iran towards Israel is totally unfounded. For centuries Jews lived relatively peacefully in Iran. The dispute between the Jews and the Muslims is basically a dispute between the Jews and Sunni Muslims. Iran is a Shi'ite country. The Sunnis and Shi'ites have been sworn enemies for centuries. So one would think that the enemy of the enemy is a friend and Iran should be on very cordial terms with Israel and that is where religious fanaticism comes in. In the mind of the fanatical Muslim, it is acceptable to kill a Sunni. On the other hand the Sunni is a Muslim and however much a Shi'ite dislikes him, a pagan is not permitted to attack him. Multiply this concept a thousand fold and you will notice that every aspect of Iranian life is contaminated with fallacious beliefs. The Shahnshah understands this thoroughly, so it is important that we understand his views on religion."

"The Shahnshah once quoted the words of the great English scholar and dictionary writer Samuel Johnson, who described a British university of his time as "ignorance on stilts.". The Shahnshah feels that that is precisely the correct description of religion and faith. He once told me to think about all the religions which have died. Today who believes in Apollo, Jupiter, or any of the Roman or Greek deities? Does any one believe in the idiocy of the ancient Egyptians who built pyramids to house the dead bodies with a hope that some day they would wake up and walk away? Does any one believe in the Mayan ritual where the captain of the winning team laid down willingly to have his heart removed without anaesthetic in the hope of reaching the world above? If all these idiocies have now been discarded by educated people, why should we be arrogant enough to believe that the beliefs and ideals of Christianity, Islam, Zoroastrianism and all other existent faiths will not disappear in time?"

"The Shahnshah's personal philosophy is as follows. Since the beginning of time, the greatest fear of man is death. In order to avoid the fear of death, he has readily believed in a life after. This gives him the illusion that he will not cease to exist once he dies. The second greatest fear of man is the kind of life he is going to have in the hereafter. Naturally, he wants to be sure that it is a good one. To ensure this possibility, he believes in religion. Now as long as his belief consists of babbling in any of the dead languages, no harm is done. Unfortunately every religious fanatic believes that babbling in his dead language is the only successful way to reach the ear of God and somehow therefore, all the other babblers in the other dead languages should be stopped or exterminated. After all, he thinks that they are all pagans and he is the only one with the true religion and belief. This is his philosophy which is responsible for the massacre of millions of people from the beginning of time and continues to this day. One of the easiest ways therefore is to harshly restrict institutionalized religion. The catechizing by religious schools such as the Madrasas in Islamic states and the Christian religious schools in the Christian areas of the world should be banned. Education should be without the involvement of religion and totally secular. Even the private facilities which are financed by parents for the religious education of their children should be controlled or totally banned. We do not want our children to grow up infected with the most virulent and destructive disease that has killed millions."

The Shahnshah believes that every new generation is superior to the previous one. He once said to me, think of people like the Emperor Akbar of India. In his age, he was one of the most brilliant and successful men. He brought in progress and unity between the Hindus and the Muslims. We appreciate all those great deeds but what would happen if that great Emperor miraculously woke up today? He would probably think that the telephone is a fairy tale, the television an impossibility and the computer perhaps an ominous device created to misguide people. On the other hand, can you imagine an intelligent, educated man from today's world going into the world of Akbar? He would completely stun them with his brilliance. If he could create something simple like a typewriter, they would think he was a God descended from heaven to help them."

"The myth of parental wisdom is exactly that, a senseless one. Certainly parents have more experience than their children but they also have less education. Experience without the proper objective thinking pattern does not increase the possibility of making the right decisions. They attribute certain causes for their misfortunes and this attribution is normally the by product of uneducated religious beliefs and therefore the conclusions tend to be wrong. A fanatical uneducated parent will invariably warn his or her son or daughter not to marry outside of their religion. They will tell the child that such marriages are always unsuccessful and that is not all they do. They would interfere with such vehemence that they actually create dissension between the couple. This of course will enhance the possibility of a failed marriage. If the union does in fact fail, they will pat themselves on their backs and claim that they were always right and the child should have listened to them. There is a specific purpose in their claim of wisdom and experience. They want to control their offspring and exercise power over them."

"The Shahnshah therefore believes that a certain amount of disrespect for the parental generation by their children is extremely essential for the progress of the nation. In the Western world, economic independence comes at a much younger age and therefore children have been more assertive in establishing their independence from the inferior generation. A parent should only be respected by their child because of his or her achievement in life and not for just getting into bed and procreating."

"But Sir Lawrence, from your description of the Shahnshah's views, he appears to be totally against all religious beliefs, yet he has helped preserve Jewish, Muslim Zoroastrian and Christian religious organizations and centers. He has actually rebuilt a mosque which was destroyed by religious fanatics. How do you justify that?" Mr. Jarvis, asked.

"Your words `totally against religious beliefs', are exactly what he would be opposed to. Everything should be kept in its own perspective. Religion is like a pain-killer or alcohol. Under certain circumstances and with proper control, it may help reduce human anguish. Think of a very long day at the office with a very miserable boss to work under. Is there anything better thereafter than a glass of scotch? However, is there anything worse thereafter than six glasses of scotch? If you have very severe pain, you take a painkiller, not six of them. As long as religion is kept at the level of that single Scotch or that single prescribed dose of a pain killer it is a tolerable necessity and can be permitted. The moment it interferes with the intellect of important human and scientific decisions then it falls into the same category as the use of drugs such as cocaine and heroin. The Shahnshah has concluded that at the present moment religion should be tolerated. An effort should be made to prevent any form of religion from interfering and controlling others. We should introduce schools which are totally devoid of religious education. They must be completely secular. A new educated generation will grow up and they will slowly discard organized religion. To forcibly ban religion at this point in time, with the lack of education of the masses, makes failure inevitable. You can see evidence of that from the failed efforts made by the Communists to crush religion. The Western world is becoming more irreligious if not anti-religious from day to day. This is strictly the result of more education and more sophistication of the masses. The same procedure will be applied to Iran. Education for both men and women is now not only compulsory but totally free at every level including university."

At this point the interview ended. I turned off the television and very carefully considered the repercussions of what I had heard. There were still several Muslim extremists in our own jurisdiction and there was a possibility of disagreements which could lead to revolts by them. I also believed that there were literally hundreds of thousands of Iranians in our own area who were totally convinced that our departure from traditional Islamic intolerance was extremely beneficial for better earnings and a better life. I knew that I could count on their full support. I therefore decided not to comment publicly on Sir Lawrence's speech. I waited for the next television report from the Islamic Republic in Teheran. To my pleasant surprise, instead of using

Sir Lawrence's description of my beliefs as evidence of my alleged intention to destroy Islam in Iran, they continued with their usual rhetoric of how I as a pagan, was attempting to destroy Islam in Iran. I couldn't help but chuckle at the thought that the lack of rationality in the religious fanatics was extremely helpful in protecting our regime from destruction. I decided to go to bed.

"You have been working continuously since six o'clock this morning. You haven't had any rest and you're seventy years old. Come to bed and lie down in my arms. I will remove all your fatigue." My Zainab said.

I washed, changed into pyjamas and got into bed next to her. She took me into her arms and held me close. Her soft embracing flesh relaxed me immediately and my fatigue was fast abating. She soon began to kiss me all over my face and body. "My Shahnshah, I think your biggest problem is not your fatigue. If I'm not mistaken, I feel something in my hand which should belong to a seventeen year-old and not a seventy year old man." She looked mischievously into my eyes. "What do you think we should do about it?" I slowly pulled her nightie up. Her delicious pink flesh exuded an aroma that could awaken the dead and transport a man from hell back to heaven.

As she undressed, she said in a voice full of passion, "My man, my lover, my Shahnshah, take your woman. Make me part of you. Fill me with your royal seed." Suddenly she started speaking in Farsi. "My man, how I love you, and want to belong to you." I was surprised with my own passion. After the lovemaking was over she just clung to me. "Don't go my Shahnshah. Stay inside me for a little while. I want your weight on me."

Gently I removed her arms from around me and got up. She was so beautiful, soft and kind and at the same time, so deliciously passionate. Once again I could not comprehend how such a lovely young woman could want me when she could have a much younger man. Who could resist a woman like this. I remembered what she had said to me earlier on in our relationship. She had clearly stated that my ancestry and the fact that I was descended from the last Zoroastrian Emperor of Iran was something that excited her beyond comprehension.

I had come to realize that in several Asiatic countries where marriages were arranged, women accepted the fact that the choice of a mate was not in their hands. For centuries the inferior generation had selected spouses for their children. It was acceptable for men to have extramarital affairs. Daughters were primarily transferred from father to husband, almost like slaves. I imagined for that reason they had to live in a world of imaginary sexual pleasure which was not realized by many of them.

Perhaps the thought of sleeping with the descendent of an Emperor was esoteric excitement to Zainab. I guess it was my good luck that I found her. I did believe that she now genuinely and honestly loved me. My heritage may have been a factor in her initial attraction for me but now that she had accepted me as her man and she was willing to become totally mine was sheer ecstasy to me. It made me feel that it was more important for me to be her man than to be the Shahnshah of Iran.

I washed up and came back to bed and took her into my arms and held her against my heart. "Are you satisfied my darling?" She asked. I nodded in assent. She gave me that divine smile of hers and went to sleep in my arms., her breath softly caressing my cheek.

CHAPTER 17.

Manucher Khursheed incessantly toiled with his prayer beads as he contemplated his impending execution. He was placed in the death cells of the Awami prison just outside of Teheran. All appeals of his sentence had been denied. As a last and final step to prevent him from being beheaded, his lawyer had suggested that a plea be presented directly to Prime Minister Shahrukh Mukhtiar of the Islamic Republic. The grounds for the plea seemed rather dubious even to Manucher's lawyer. Manucher's record was indeed unenviable. The only ground on which such a plea could be made was that he was a very devout Muslim. It was rumoured that he had contributed approximately three million dollars of his ill-gotten wealth to the construction of mosques in different areas of the Islamic Republic. He believed that all non-Shi'ites should be exterminated. The Jews, Christians and Zoroastrians were all messengers of Satan. Sunni Muslims were even worse for they had tarnished the purity of Shi'ite Islam. Allah needed their extermination from the universe and he, Manucher Khursheed was going to do exactly that and therefore the brutal and illegal manner in which he had accumulated his wealth was totally justified. The fear of death had been very poignant and distressing for a long period of time. However, since nothing could be done about it, Manucher had decided that he would leave his fate in Allah's hands. If Allah wanted the pagans to live and prosper and he, a devout Muslim to die then the problem was Allah's and not his.

Suddenly he heard the clanging of the cell doors and two prison guards appeared. "Manucher Khursheed the warden wants to see you."

"Fuck the warden, I do not want to see him!"

"Well Manucher, you have two options. You can quietly come with us or we can drag you to the warden's office by your testicles. Which one do you prefer?"

Manucher got up, contemptuously sneering at the guards, but quietly walked with them to the warden's office.

"Sit down," the Warden said.

"I do not need your fucking permission to sit or stand! I am facing death, do you think I'm afraid of a triviality like you?"

The warden completely ignored Manucher's rudeness. "I was looking at your enviable record, Manucher. You were found guilty of six bank robberies and you were only recently caught. In the commission of those robberies, you killed two bank tellers who were innocent and who did not resist you when you placed a gun to their heads. You have three wives. Sorry, two existing wives. You killed one of them together with her two brothers and her father because she refused to fast during Ramadan. They suspect you of being the mastermind behind the bombing of the Sunni mosque in Isfahan. Indeed Manucher, your talents are really varied. You are also an extremely talented forger. Am I correct that in all, you are responsible for defrauding and robbing several institutions and businesses in the amount of approximately six million dollars? What I cannot comprehend is that a man of your brutal nature would contribute half of that stolen money to the building of mosques in the Islamic Republic. Can you explain that?"

"Warden, I do not have to explain anything to you. If I've killed anyone, he deserved to be dead. I do not apologize for doing Allah's work. As to the alleged murder of one of my wives and the so-called bank clerks, I am not admitting anything but if I did those things they were done to pagans working for pagan banks and financial institutions. They bamboozled the money out of our Iran and our Iranian brothers and I'm not sorry for doing that. Let's stop chatting about my alleged crimes and the rest of your senseless philosophy. What do you want from me?"

"You are one arrogant son of a bitch, aren't you Manucher? I believe you have applied to have your death sentence reduced to life in prison. Is that correct?"

"Yes. What difference does it make to you?"

"Some one wants to talk to you about it. He is waiting in the other room. If you want a chance to reduce your sentence, you better talk to him."

Manucher nodded. A man dressed in a well tailored suit and tie walked into the room. He smiled as he extended his hand to Manucher. "I am Behram Marzban, Minister of Communications in the Islamic Republic of Iran."

Manucher ignored his hand completely. He then had second thoughts and extended his hand, looking very curiously at the Minister, which the latter did not miss.

"What do you want with me Minister?"

"Some one very important wants to see you. Please come with me!"

"Who the hell wants to see me Minister?"

"I'm not allowed to reveal that information to you. The guards will escort you to your cell. A suit will be provided to you. You will get dressed and return here and then I will take you to visit that person."

Manucher nodded his assent. The guards led him to his cell and he returned nattily dressed in a blue suit. Minister Marzban could not help noticing that the criminal in his charge was indeed a very large and powerful looking man. Manucher was at least six feet four inches tall and looked like an athlete. He had vicious evil eyes which were capable of scaring off the devil himself. The Minister was extremely happy that he, with his five feet four inch frame, was not going to travel alone with the criminal to the destination they were heading to. There were two armed guards who were going to accompany them in the squad car.

"Now that we are safely in a squad car with two armed guards, would you tell me exactly where you're taking me Minister?"Manucher asked.

"I will, if you promise to behave yourself and not be rude to me or the guards."

"Alright, I promise."

"My dear man, you're going to see the Prime Minister of the Islamic Republic of Iran"

The shock in Manucher's eyes was clearly visible to the Minister.

"Why does the Prime Minister of the Islamic Republic want to see me?"

"That my dear Sir is something you have to ask the Prime Minister when you meet him. I am merely doing the bidding for His Excellency."

The car used its siren to manoeuvre the crowded streets of Teheran until they arrived at the Prime Minister's residence. The gates of the residence were manned by guards with machine guns. As soon as the car stopped, a guard looked into the vehicle. He initially seemed shocked to see a man in leg irons and handcuffs, secured with chains to his seat. He pointed his submachine gun at the driver before he noticed Minister Marzban sitting in the back of the vehicle. He was a bit surprised, until the Minister explained to him that the prisoner was being taken to see the Prime Minister who had requested a meeting with him. The guard bowed, returned to his booth and called the chief security officer regarding the strange visitor, who was supposedly invited by the Prime Minister. The security officer assured him that the Prime Minister had indeed extended such an invitation and that the visitors should be granted permission to enter the palace. The guard then allowed the squad car to proceed through the gates.

On entering the residence, Minister Marzban and the prisoner were passed through an x-ray machine and then escorted to an assembly room. They were asked to sit in front of a desk and two policemen stood in place on either side of the prisoner. A few minutes later, a tall and imposing man dressed in a Western-style suit entered the room. There was no mistaking the strength and harshness of his expressions. The prisoner had seen the picture of the Prime Minister on television and in the newspapers. What he did not realize at that time, was the intense personality of the Prime Minister of Iran. In spite of his accustomed nonchalance, Manucher jumped up from his seat and bowed to the Prime Minister.

Shahrukh Mukhtiar looked directly into the eyes of Manucher. "Sit down gentlemen. Manucher Khursheed, I must say I'm very impressed that you can maintain your calm demeanour in the face of your impending execution. Have you anything to say in justification of your past behaviour?"

"Mr. Prime Minister, if you needed me to voice a justification for my past activities, you would have obtained that information from your guards at the Awami prison. Obviously you have brought me here for another purpose. So, Mr. Prime Minister, why don't you tell me what you really want?"

"The matter I want to discuss with you is of great significance to Iran and to our people. Before I discuss this subject, I have to be absolutely certain that I can trust you. I'm quite aware that you have committed murders and robberies amongst other crimes. I'm also aware that you are a devoted Muslim and would sacrifice your life for Allah and Islam. This belief gives me the confidence that you will loyally serve Iran and perform the specific duties which we request of you. Do you feel any loyalty towards Iran?"

"Mr. Prime Minister, I am loyal only to two causes. The most important one is myself and the second one is Islam. You know my record. Even though I'm not admitting to stealing anything, if I've done so, it is partially for me, and the rest was dedicated to the protection and preservation of Islam. All this you already know, so please tell me what it is you want from me!"

The Prime Minister placed a Koran in front of Manucher. "Place your hand on the Koran and swear in the name of Allah that you will never reveal to any one the information I'm about to provide to you, even to save your own life."

"Why should I provide you with that promise or oath? How does it benefit me?"

"Mr. Khursheed, if you comply with my orders and complete the mission that I'm entrusting to you, I will give you the greatest gift any one can give you. I will give you an official pardon for all your crimes. In other words, I will save your life. I will not lie to you. What I'm asking you to do is dangerous. You may lose your life in the process. However, if you succeed, you will be a free and accepted citizen of the Islamic Republic of Iran. Are you willing to cooperate with us?"

"On the Holy Koran, I swear that I will not reveal to anyone, any information you reveal to me. Before I agree to comply with your request, kindly tell me what exactly this mission is."

"Mr. Khursheed, in spite of your incredible record of brutality, we are quite satisfied that you will do anything necessary for the preservation of Islam, including the annihilation and destruction of the enemies of Islam. We, the Government of the Islamic Republic, have come to the conclusion that certain elements residing in our Islamic land are destroying our faith and our culture. We would like you to help us stop that."

"Mr. Prime Minister. Can you be a little more specific? All true believers want to protect Islam. What specific task do I have to complete."

"Alright Mr. Khursheed, I believe I can trust you. As you're probably aware, the most dangerous and vicious enemy of the Islamic Republic is that Canadian alien pagan who calls himself the Shahnshah of Iran. Half of our beloved Iran is now controlled and ruled by him. The pagan has given equal rights to Sunnis, Christians, Zoroastrians and even Jews. I never thought I would see the day when we would condescend to consider the Jews as Iranians. These very people who have taken the land of our Muslim brothers in Palestine. Would you believe he has now also given total equality to women? They can now have the same jobs as men do. The pardah is not compulsory anymore and they can show their faces in public. All religious schools have been abolished and religious education is only permitted on a private basis if the parents so wish. Manucher Khursheed, all the blessings and sanctity brought to our nation by Ayatollah Khomeini are slowly being eroded by this vicious pagan. This beast must be exterminated. We believe that you have the brains, capacity and above all, the religious furor to accomplish this difficult but holy task. Would you do this for Iran and Islam?"

"Prime Minister, are you asking me to go and kill this Shahnshah of Iran? I have loved very few men in my life and I've hated quite a few. But as far as this monster is concerned, to kill him is not only the duty of every good Muslim, but it will be a matter of the utmost joy for me. Even if you did not offer me any rewards, I will be happy to do it for Iran. The only thing I need is for you to provide me with the necessary weapons and more significantly, the information which would make my task possible."

The Prime Minister smiled triumphantly. In that smile, Manucher saw his sense of jubilation and at the same time he could feel a glint of malicious joy at the possibility of the extermination of the most dangerous enemy of the Islamic Republic.

"Do I have your word of honor Manucher, that the equipment and supplies we are about to provide you with will not be used for any other selfish purpose?"

"In the name of Allah, I promise you Prime Minister, that this equipment and these funds will be solely used for the annihilation of that Canadian pagan."

"Minister Marzban will introduce you to the necessary dealers who will supply you with any equipment you need. We will provide you with one million American dollars. This amount you will use as you see fit. At the end of the operation if you are successful, any remaining funds will be yours. Not only that, we will further compensate you with an additional one million dollars."

"Prime Minister, consider your mission accomplished. Manucher Khursheed does not make promises that he cannot keep. In the name of Allah and the Koran, be assured that within a few weeks, Iran will rejoice and celebrate the demise of the pagan Shahnshah."

The Prime Minister got up and shook his hand. "Go my friend and may Allah be your guide and protect you."

The Prime Minister left the room after which Manucher's leg irons and handcuffs were removed. Minister Marzban placed a hand on his shoulder and escorted him out of the room.

They both got into a military jeep which was escorted by guards and drove to the armoury. Manucher had a long discussion with the military authorities who were in charge. He asked for two submachine guns and two precision long-range rifles which were immediately provided to him. He requested tracking devices, some of them so sophisticated that they could identify individuals and movements inside a building from a great distance. He was also provided with equipment which could trace and amplify sound, thereby indicating to the observer, the number of individuals present and the kind of activity they were involved in. There was also a set of mini rockets and rocket launchers. This was all carefully concealed in large containers of fruit. The amphibious vehicle given to him was equipped with a silencer which would reduce the vibration and sound to the lowest possible limit rendering it untraceable. Radar equipment enabled the occupants to track any movements in their vicinity. Secretly coded transmission equipment would enable the occupier of the vehicle to communicate with specific military authorities in the Islamic Republic and the calls would be untraceable by any other listeners.

"Do you need any other weapon Manucher?" Minister Marzban asked.

"No sir, all I need now is the blessing of Allah and his help in destroying this enemy of Islam."

"Now that you are fully armed and equipped, perhaps you can give me an idea as to how you will deal with this matter. When I return to Teheran, the Prime Minister is definitely going to ask for details of this mission. Naturally, you cannot give exact details but can you give me a general idea of your plan to establish contact with the necessary individuals to help you get close to the Shahnshah." Minister Marzban said.

"That is just the subject I was about to raise and I'm glad you asked that question Minister. The weaponry and the use of weapons to achieve our objective is something I can handle all by myself. The most difficult part of this mission would be to get close to the Shahnshah. We must create a situation whereby access on a constant basis becomes possible. Naturally with my history and record, I cannot approach the Shahnshah or get even close to his residence. Think of it this way. A Minister of the Islamic Republic claims that he is disgusted with the rule of our Prime Minister. He claims that he has come to realize that the policy of the Islamic Republic has become unfeasible and has reduced the quality of the economic and cultural life of Iran. Therefore he has come to the Shahnshah to seek his help and to join forces with him so that Iran can become a prosperous and modern nation. Do you not think Minister, that such a man will be welcomed with open arms by the pagan King?"

Manucher noticed the shock on Marzban's face and smiled.

"Just wait a minute Manucher. Are you by any chance suggesting that I should become a traitor to the Islamic Republic, my faith, my country and my prime minister and go to join that Canadian Pagan in his anti-Islamic activities?"

"No, Minister, you do not have to join or support the Pagan in reality. You must just convince him that you are supporting him. An offer from a Minister of the Islamic Republic to join the government of the Shahnshah would be too attractive a lure for the Shahnshah. Can you imagine the propaganda value this would provide for his government and regime? Such a put down of the Islamic Republic would be too irresistible for the Shahnshah to reject. He will embrace you like a brother. You pretend to accept him as your mentor. Then of course you can appoint me as your bodyguard. You will never visit the Shahnshah without me as your escort. Then one fine day, your trusted guard and driver will go berserk. Maybe he's drunk or maybe he is on drugs. Without warning he fires a bullet into the Pagan's head. I will have a foolproof plan for our escape from the palace and our safe return to the Islamic Republic. Perchance we fail and are captured, you can be the loudest mourner at the Shahnshah's funeral. Proclaim to the people on radio and on television how devastated you are that the man you trusted as your guard and driver turned out to be such a terrible traitor. Your heart is totally shattered that the great Shahnshah has died as a result of your misplaced trust in me. They will believe your story and let you go. Of course if they catch me I will be executed. I give you my permission to celebrate my execution. Just act normally for a month or two and then quietly slip back into the Islamic Republic. The Prime Minister will welcome you back and you'll be considered a hero by the rank-and-file in the Islamic Republic. So my dear Minister, for you, it's a win-win situation."

"What makes you think that the Prime Minister will permit me to act as a traitor? What will the people of Iran think of our Government if one of its Ministers is a puppet of the Shahnshah? More importantly, how do I justify this to my wife and children? If I tell them the truth and the information gets out, the Pagan's followers will kill me in a minute and if the secret remains concealed, my family will disown me completely."

"Minister, the Prime Minister of the Islamic Republic will not oppose your plan. I can guarantee that. Conceded that initially there will be some detrimental publicity for the Islamic Republic, but if we succeed in assassinating the pagan Shahnshah and you return to Teheran victorious, all this hostility would be converted into a complete victory for the Prime Minister and for you. As a matter-of-fact, all Iranians will laud your patriotic zeal and the fact that you risked your life to exterminate the most significant enemy of Iran. We will both convince the Prime Minister that the success of the mission is almost certain and the detrimental propaganda is a temporary phenomenon. Your election to future offices is almost guaranteed thereafter. Keep in mind too that the Prime Minister is getting a little old and may soon depart this world, in which case, who do you think will be best qualified for the new position? The great hero Marzban Behram."

In spite of his own cynicism for Manucher and his integrity, the Minister was quite impressed with this whole concept. There was a great deal of danger involved in this plan, but if they succeeded, the rewards could be enormous. The minister nodded his assent to Manucher.

"The next important point to discuss and successfully arrange is the method by which we will enter the Pagan's area of Iran. Our first effort will be to use an all-terrain vehicle to sneak into Southern Iran in the middle of the night. My tracking equipment will let me know of any activity in the vicinity, so we can easily avoid all southern military and police vehicles. We are also equipped with devices which will make the motor almost soundless. I'm assuming that the southern Iranian forces do not have similar equipment, but in case they do, I will suggest a second precaution just in case we are stopped. Who in your opinion, Minister, would be the least suspect and most likely refugee trying to escape from the Islamic Republic to the south? Think about it."

"I don't know."

"Oh Minister, don't be so naïve! It is the Jew. In today's Islamic Republic these infidels have been crushed. Do you think a single Jew will remain in Iran if he is permitted to go to the South? Especially when that pagan bastard has given them equal rights and made them citizens of the Democratic Republic as he calls Southern Iran? But then Minister, we the genuine patriots will use his own methods against him. You and I will dress like Jews. The hat and the whole bit. As a matter of fact, we will be Orthodox Jews. You with your knowledge and education, better memorize some paragraphs from the Torah so that we can recite them if necessary."

"You expect me, a devout Muslim, to dress and present myself as a Jew?"

"Minister, I am a devout a Muslim like you. I've dedicated my life to the service of Islam and the annihilation of pagans. I've killed pagans. However, when it is necessary to protect Islam, we should not hesitate to do so. Don't you agree?"

Very hesitantly, the Minister, nodded in agreement. They got into their jeep and drove to the Prime Minister's residence. One look at the Minister and the guards quickly escorted them to the Prime Minister. Initially when Marzban mentioned the idea of going into Southern Iran, pretending to be a refugee and seeking the Shahnshah's hospitality, the Prime Minister seemed to be totally appalled. However, when Manucher gave him a detailed explanation of the immense benefits to the Islamic Republic if they were successful, his attitude changed immediately. He started with a long spiel about his great concern for the health and well-being of the Minister if he was caught. Manucher and Marzban saw through this facade and Marzban, deep in his heart was hurt that when it came to a showdown and possible political advantage, the Prime Minister was quite willing to sacrifice him. Later however, he was able to come to terms with the fact that this was one of the principles of politics and personal loyalty and affection for colleagues was superficial. After a good deal of handshaking and hugging, the Prime Minister wished them both good luck and they left the residence.

Marzban went home and had a heart to heart chat with his wife. He did not give any details of the mission but was very specific about the danger. He explained that success would be extremely beneficial to his career and the Islamic Republic of Iran. He asked her to be wary of any snide remarks she may hear about him and failure to keep this a secret would jeopardize his life. Initially, his wife was very concerned and started to cry, but he soon convinced her that he was going to be successful and would return to hold her to his heart for the rest of his life.

They left very early the next morning since they intended to get to the area of the de facto border between the two Irans by nightfall. The documents issued by the Government of the Islamic Republic enabled them to travel freely as long as they were in the northern section of Iran. Once they reached the border, they expected to have some difficulties because it was illegal to cross from one country to the other and the flow of refugees from the Islamic Republic was basically illegal. If they were successful in crossing into Democratic Iran, it did not necessarily mean that they would be accepted. Refugees had to report to the border authorities, were investigated and if it was determined that they were in fact refugees, they were admitted without further ado.

They had gone through four Iranian military checkpoints without any problems. As soon as they saw the documentation presented by the Minister, the officers bowed and beckoned them through. They were now in the border region and so far they had avoided any areas where there was a road connection between the Islamic Republic and Democratic Iran. Manucher drove off the highway and carefully manoeuvred the all-terrain vehicle across arid desert tracks in the direction of Southern Iran.

"Minister, it is now time for us to change into our Jewish attire. Please give me all the documentation that we have obtained from our Government." They both changed into their new attire. Manucher smiled at the Minister. "Rabbi Marzban, greetings from your humble follower and companion, Manucher."

"Manucher, that is not funny. As you have already indicated, we are doing this for Iran and I do not appreciate your humour." Manucher smiled and ignored him.

He took all the documentation to the back of the Jeep, lifted up the seat and pressed a button camouflaged in the floor cover. The compartment slid open and he hid all the documents inside and closed the lid. Without waiting for the Minister to question him he said, "Minister, two Jewish refugees escaping from the Islamic Republic do not arrive with passports and documents issued by the Office of the Prime Minister. We cannot let them see these documents. As a matter-of-fact, arriving without any documentation is the best indication that we are genuine refugees coming to seek asylum in the Shahnshah's realm." Marzban nodded.

The terrain was very rough and rocky and it took them approximately one and a half hours before Manucher took out his compass and after careful deductions concluded that they were definitely in Southern Iran. Smiling, he turned right and drove for another two miles until they arrived at a two lane paved road. There was a victorious look in his eyes. Marzban did not miss the sinister look and the venom that he saw behind the smile. He started to hum a Farsi tune which Marzban recognized and that increased the eerie feeling that he continually felt in Manucher's company. In his mind he interpreted the words. "Oh you mortal, Oh you man, I carry your death in my hand. There is no escape, there is no reprieve, your destiny and death are in my grip." These words coming from a man who was six feet six inches tall with an extensive criminal record! There was also something evil and sinister in his personality and this made Marzban even more uncomfortable. He quietly tried to control his emotions. It was at this moment that Marzban came to the conclusion that he had made a mistake by joining this criminal.

Marzban was a devout Muslim. He had absolutely no hesitation in desiring the elimination of the Shahnshah and his pagan regime. He was doubtful of the authenticity of the information he was given and he had made his own inquiries about the Shahnshah's anti- Islamic views. He was an educated man and could not swallow the propaganda of the Islamic Republic, lock, stock and barrel. He had also received cogent information of the protection the Shahnshah had provided not only to the Jews and Sunnis, but also to the Shi'ites. He had heard of the reconstruction of the mosque which had been destroyed by rebels who were said to have been connected with the Islamic Republic. Having said all that, the Shahnshah was a pagan and a foreigner. Above all he had the temerity to conquer and occupy a portion of his beloved Iran. He had converted that portion of Iran into a secular state, allowing all religions equality, taking away the monopoly that must rightly belong to the one and only true faith of Allah, namely Islam. Whatever his doubts or reservations of the Shahnshah were, this man should not be allowed to live, therefore it was his duty to exterminate him.

They drove for approximately fifteen miles without incident and then as they turned a corner, they noticed two military vehicles blocking their way. "Do not say one word to them, let me do all the talking. Take the Torah out of your pocket and pretend that you are deeply absorbed in your prayers. This will justify your lack of saying anything. I will convince them that we are Jewish refugees and are delighted to find freedom once again in the Shahnshah's territory."

Marzban nodded his agreement. When Manucher got out of the jeep, they both noticed that they were facing two drawn machine guns.

The officers facing them looked ready to fire at the slightest provocation. The moment they noticed Manucher and his Jewish garb, they seemed to relax. Manucher smiled internally. I was right, wasn't I, he thought. The pagan's troops would never think that a Jew would come from the Islamic Republic to attack anything or any one in this part of Iran. He was elated at the thought that the first subterfuge which he had organized turned out to be a complete success.

"Hold your hands above your head and walk over to us!" The two officers ordered. Manucher complied. Upon reaching the officers, he bowed to them. "Officers, let me express my gratitude and thanks to you and your Shahnshah. You have no idea what it feels like to be considered a human being once again. A lot of planning, pain and anguish have been endured to get out of the Islamic Republic, to the serene freedom of your Shahnshah's Iran. My friend the Rabbi is presently thanking God for the deliverance that he has provided to both of us."

"Have you any documentation to identify yourselves?"

"Officers, the Rabbi was sentenced to death in the Islamic Republic. The allegation against him was that in spite of their dictum he was teaching the Torah to Jewish children. He has never made a derogatory statement against the Islamic Republic. He has encouraged children and their parents to become good Iranians, follow the law of the land and to quietly endure discrimination. Nothing has worked. The moment they found out that he was teaching the Torah to children, he was arrested, summarily tried for allegedly anti-Iranian activities and sentenced to death. I'm his cousin. I was successful in bribing some of the guards and we drove south in this Jeep which unfortunately I have to admit, I have stolen from an army officer."

Manucher looked at the expressions of the officers as he presented his well concocted story. He noticed a tiny bit of sympathy in their eyes. He felt deep inside that they were suspicious of him and yet he was quite satisfied with his performance and knew that sooner or later they would believe him completely. His greatest fear was a possible contact between Minister Marzban and the officers. He was not certain that the Minister would be able to lie as beautifully as he had. He was therefore depending on the story about the Rabbi praying to the good Lord for his deliverance and the resulting inability to speak to the officers.

"You have any passports, identification to corroborate your story"? One of the officers again asked.

"Officer, our passports were taken away from us years ago because we are Jews. The Iranian government has this phobia that we will all emigrate to Israel. Officers, I may be a Jew but I'm a patriotic Iranian. In spite of all the prejudice and oppression we have suffered, we still love our country and want to remain here. Now that we are in the free land of our Shahnshah, we're thanking God for our second chance at a new life. Documents like our driver's licenses, health cards, even our credit cards, have been destroyed to avoid being identified if we are caught by the Iranian authorities. Of course we would have been immediately executed, but thereafter they would have gone and brutally persecuted our families. This way, without any identification on our persons, no one will know who our families are in Iran. So the danger was only to us."

"So you have absolutely no evidence as to who you are, or that you are really Jews?"

"Officer, in your years of experience as a military officer, have you ever seen a Muslim pretending to be a Jew in Iran?"

Reluctantly, the officer nodded his assent. He took out two printed forms and wrote down the two assumed Jewish names that Manucher provided to him. He placed a seal on each one of the forms and presented them to Manucher. "Welcome to Democratic Iran. You are now admitted as refugees. May freedom and peace be with you for the rest of your lives."

Manucher bowed deeply from his waist again." May Allah reward you for your kindness, my friend." The officers smiled at him and drove away. Manucher returned to the Jeep. He noticed that the Minister looked extremely nervous and was staring at him. Smiling, he realized that the Minister could not have heard the conversation between himself and the officer. "Rabbi Samuel, welcome to the Democratic Republic of Iran. Now you can call yourself a humble subject of the pagan Shahnshah."

Marzban stared at Manucher as if he was going out of his mind. Manucher roared with laughter. Minister Marzban, I just presented you with your new name. You are admitted as a Jewish refugee in the pagan Kingdom and that is your new name."

Marzban was not impressed with the idea of being described as a Jew. He thought that it was insulting for a good devoted Muslim to pretend to be part of another community or faith. He was also very annoyed by the familiarity with which this uneducated criminal was addressing him. But he had to admit that without the brilliant strategy and acting that Manucher had displayed, the chances of successfully entering Southern Iran would have been very slim. For this reason he decided to save his comments.

After driving for a few more kilometres, Manucher pulled off the highway. "Now Minister, listen to me very carefully! The information that we have entered Southern Iran as Jews should never become known to the public. The Islamic Republic's Prime Minister is going to announce that you are a traitor and that you have escaped into Southern Iran. On purpose, they will tarnish your name and reputation and that will be our best opportunity to get in touch with the Shahnshah. We must also seek to win the confidence of the people of Southern Iran and however much they may pay lip service to the equality of the Jews to the Muslims, they will never respect you if they find out that you pretended to be a Jew, in order to enter Iran. Do not forget Minister, that even the most progressive Iranians are very prejudiced against the Jews. Let us discard these clothes and become good Muslims again. If you are ever asked how you escaped into Southern Iran do not ever mention anything about wearing these Jewish clothes."

They both changed into their regular Muslim clothing. With his usual sarcastic leer Manucher started driving the jeep in the direction of Zahidan. Marzban was deep in thought trying to analyze the thinking pattern of his companion. He had already come to the conclusion that Manucher was a vicious criminal. Kindness, loyalty and even simple qualities like consideration for others were completely missing in his nature. He was the kind of man who would not hesitate to kill you because you were a slight inconvenience to his plans. Being in the company of such a man was abhorrent to Marzban. But he had absolutely no choice. He needed this monster. He was genuinely afraid of doing or saying anything which may suddenly trigger this criminal to attack and kill him. He would have to be handled with kid gloves until Marzban could get away from him and stay away from him as far as possible.

Marzban was a religious fanatic. He did not have the place for any other faith or creed except Islam. What he did not know about himself was that he was basically a very kind and intelligent man. His upbringing and religious education had made him the fanatic he was. The enormous reading and knowledge that he had acquired made him a rational man in every other aspect of life except in his religious beliefs. He may have believed in the inferiority of Christians, Jews and other religious faiths, but he was not the kind of person who would have persecuted or killed them. He believed that ultimately the whole world would embrace Islam. Their conversion must not be accomplished by force but by convincing them that all other faiths were fictitious creations of men and the only true faith that Allah provided for man was outlined in the Koran which Allah directly gave to Mohamed.

It was almost midnight when they arrived in Zahidan. Manucher found a motel and pulled up in front of it. Without asking Marzban, he went in and booked two separate rooms. He picked up his own suitcases and took them to his room. He handed the second set of keys to Marzban without any comment. He did not offer to help Marzban with his suitcases. Marzban was accustomed to being treated with respect. A Minister of the Islamic Republic was not expected to carry his own luggage. Marzban decided not to broach the subject of his impertinence with him. Some day he expected to put this wild animal in his place but that time was not now. He picked up his own suitcases, went to his room and carefully locked the door. He was not particularly anxious to spend any more time in the company of his fellow traveller.

CHAPTER 18.

As was my normal custom, I switched on the news at six p.m. It is funny how the human mind works. There was not a single day when the news from the Islamic Republic did not have something derogatory to say about me or Democratic Iran. Over the last few months, my attitude towards their broadcasts had altered considerably. I had actually started enjoying their fictitious stories about me and our Iran. I think I would have been disappointed if they had said something good about me. I was completely shocked with what I heard this evening. "With utter shock and grief the Prime Minister of the Islamic Republic makes this announcement. A respected member of our cabinet, a man whose love for Islam and Iran was beyond any doubt, has turned out to be a traitor. The Prime Minister had tears in his eyes when he announced that Marzban Behram had escaped with a large amount of cash from the treasury. To the dismay of all Iranians, he is in the company of a convicted murderer and has reached the land of the pagan who calls himself the Shahnshah of Iran. Behram's family have broken all contact with him and are ready to spit on his grave when we arrest and execute him. The whole population of the Islamic Republic is in mourning. Such perfidy from a leader of our land was never anticipated. Oh, all good Muslims who unfortunately reside in the pagan's country, find him and kill him!"

I was in total shock when I heard this news bulletin. I had heard the name of Behram Marzban. I had also heard that he was a bit of a fanatic but also had the reputation of being an intellectual and a decent human being. I immediately decided that two significant steps had to be taken. No doubt there were many spies and agents of the Islamic Republic residing in our territory and they would take the request for his murder rather seriously. Therefore it was imperative that we find him fast and investigate him. It was also necessary to determine whether he was really in our country and the actual reason for his leaving the Islamic Republic. Was he actually a traitor or was there some other reason why he had come as a refugee? I picked up the telephone and asked my secretary to contact my four trusted undercover workers. Rauf Irfani, Behram Sharaf, Abdul Azari and Tehmul Shazad. Their successful entry into the Islamic Republic and the capture of the two ministers who were responsible for the murder of the professor had convinced me that they were reliable and loyal officers and would give their lives for my protection. Also, the rewards and promotions I had given them had made them completely devoted to me. These were therefore the men I could reasonably trust to locate Marzban, investigate him thoroughly and provide me with a detailed analysis as to the exact reasons for him leaving the Islamic Republic. Apart from the reliability and integrity of my men, I also completely trusted their acumen. If Marzban was hiding something, these were the men who would find that secret for me.

Within an hour of my call the four officers were in front of me. Rauf Irfani bowed to me, "We are at your service, Your Majesty."

"Officers, have you watched the television broadcast from Teheran?"

"Yes, Your Majesty. It appears one of their religious fanatics has seen the light."

"Not so fast gentlemen, I believe a lot of what has been stated may be totally inaccurate. We want to be absolutely certain that this Minister is in our territory as a refugee. There can be several other reasons for his deserting the Islamic Republic. It sounds highly improbable that a Minister and respected member of the Cabinet would suddenly turn against the regime that brought him power and money and come to ask for our help. It is difficult for me to accept what appears to be a genuine change of heart when it involves loss of prestige and money. I am suspicious of this story and request you to investigate it thoroughly."

"Consider it done, your Majesty. Until we are absolutely certain of the integrity of this Minister, we will not allow him to get close to you. We will immediately start an investigation on all the newcomers to this area. If this man has come to Zahidan, he must be in the vicinity with a relative or in a motel. I will have that information before Your Majesty, within twenty-four hours." All four of them bowed to me, saluted and left the palace.

After they left I contemplated the situation. Was I being unfair in doubting the integrity of a man, an educated man, on the sole ground that he came from a group of people who disagreed with our thinking pattern? If I was so certain about being right, why should I have the arrogance to believe that there was no other person who could think the same way, merely because at one time he had disagreed with us. Well, let the investigation take its course, I thought.

Exactly as he had promised Rauf appeared before me the next morning. "My Shahnshah, I have news for you which is rather intriguing and causes me some concern. Our investigation reveals that Minister Marzban has successfully entered our territory. Our informants in the Islamic Republic have confirmed that he has been severely reviled and condemned by the Prime Minister and the other Ministers. His family has publicly declared him a traitor and claim that they want absolutely no contact with him. All this could be propaganda by the Iranian government. But surprisingly, there is one statement made by the Iranian government which is entirely authentic. The person who crossed into our territory with the Minister is a man called Manucher Khursheed. The description given by the Iranian television is one hundred percent accurate. This man has been convicted of two murders and is a vicious felon. What I cannot comprehend is, if the Minister is stricken with an attack of his conscience and wants to escape to our territory, why would he come with such a vicious criminal? It does not make any sense. We therefore followed their trail and found that they were residing at a seedy little motel called the Darya Inn. No respectable man would ever stay in a place like that. Especially a man who holds the position of a Minister in the Islamic Republic. Also, your Majesty has heard the rumor that the Minister stole millions of dollars from the treasury. If this is true, why then would he stay in such a dump? This too does not make any sense. With millions of dollars in his possession, why would he sneak into our territory with a convicted criminal as his companion? This is a person who would have no hesitation in killing him and taking all his money. We have taken the following steps and I hope you will approve of them."

"We surrounded the motel and arrested this man Manucher. Our reasons for the arrest were that he was an escaped criminal as per the news reports from the Islamic Republic and as a felon, he was not permitted to enter our territory without express permission from us. We acted as if we did not have an idea who his companion was and arrested the Minister as well, on the grounds that he was accompanied by a criminal. This is when the minister voluntarily provided us with his name and the information that he was a Minister in the Islamic Republic. We pretended to be totally shocked and asked him why he had come to our Iran. His response was that he was tired of living in a religious state where he felt his freedom was restricted. Frankly Your Majesty, I have some doubts as to the veracity of that statement. He deliberately avoided looking into my eyes."

"Where have you kept the prisoners?" I asked.

"At the main police precinct in Zahidan, You're Majesty."

"Just in case the Minister is telling the truth, wouldn't his arrest antagonize him? That will prevent us from using him since he may not cooperate."

"Perhaps the best alternative would be for me to meet with him and judge for myself. What do you think of that?"

"If Your Majesty has decided to meet with him we will bring him over to you after he has been thoroughly checked. With the utmost respect I would recommend that under no circumstances should you meet with that criminal Manucher. He is a very devious and brutal man and I would be very concerned to endanger your Majesty's safety by bringing such a man into your palace."

"I would very much like to meet with Marzban. Perhaps the best thing to do is to speak to him privately. I have heard several stories of his brilliance and education. I have also been informed that he is a fairly good human being on the whole. On the other hand, we are also quite aware that he is a religious fanatic who has no place for any other faith or belief except Islam. The point that you have made about his companion being a vicious criminal and the fact that he has left the

Islamic Republic as a refugee, are also areas which need to be carefully analyzed before we can accept him as a legitimate refugee. Therefore Officer Irfani, I'm now requesting you to bring Marzban into my presence after a thorough check as you have suggested. How soon can you do this?"

"Your Majesty, I can have Marzban brought into your presence within a couple of hours, if your Majesty so desires."

"All right officer. I will wait for you in my office."

As promised, Rauf Irfani returned approximately two hours later. He was accompanied by a man approximately five feet six inches tall. His relatively small build did not in any manner interfere with the intelligent eyes which were alert. I could easily see that he was nervous and concerned. At the same time, he seemed prepared to face whatever came his way. I just wanted to ascertain whether his nervousness was because of his present situation of being uncertain about his future, or was it something else of a more devious nature?

He bowed to me. "Your Majesty, I would like to humbly thank you for permitting me into your presence. For several years I've dreamt of meeting your illustrious self and today my dream has been realized."

"Welcome to Democratic Iran Mr. Marzban. Please do not consider me rude, but before accepting you as a legitimate immigrant it is necessary for me to ask you specific questions to clarify certain areas. I would request you to answer these questions in a forthright manner. Are you ready for that?"

"I am at your disposal, Your Majesty."

Once again, I noticed a shifting of the eyes and a blank look that I could not discern clearly. Was he hiding something? Or was this normal nervousness at being in an alien environment. I could not be sure.

"Mr. Marzban, you're considered one of the leading and brilliant economists in the Islamic Republic. You were solely responsible for bringing up the economy, which had deteriorated to such an extent that Iran, one of the greatest producers of oil in the world had oil shortages. We have a complete record of your academic qualifications. You were always a brilliant student. We are also completely aware of your fanatical concept of Islam and that you consider all other faiths a negation of God's Word and that the only true religion is Islam. I, as the Shahnshah of Iran have the greatest respect for Islam but not to the exclusion of all other faiths. Every faith has been contaminated with man's interpretations and at the same time, every faith has its own good points which must be respected. However, that is my view and I know you disagree with me."

"Having said that, you obtained a Ph.D. from the Harvard University in the United States. I also know that you have attended several seminars at other educational facilities including Oxford and Cambridge in Britain. Your exposure to the Western way of thinking has never been restricted. Tell me Sir, a man of your intelligence and education not only joins the Government of the Islamic Republic, but you became one of the most vocal advocates in encouraging the persecution of other religious minorities. You have succeeded. You are wealthy and you have followers all over Iran. Suddenly, one fine morning, you decide to abandon all your beliefs, concepts and success and come as an immigrant to my part of Iran. Sir, do you not think that this sudden and incredible change in your thinking pattern will not make any reasonable man suspicious?"

Marzban looked at me with his intense eyes. I looked deep into his and I came to the conclusion that combined with nervousness, there was also a possibility of deep-seated hatred. Suddenly, I realized that because of his intelligence, he was able to control his expressions. He looked at me, bowed and said, "Does your Majesty not believe that because of our education and intelligence we are incapable of realizing our mistakes? Should a human being not have the opportunity of changing his thinking to make an effort at remedying the injury that he may have caused in the past?"

"Indeed you have that right Mr. Marzban, but it is difficult for me to comprehend that a man as intelligent and educated as you, a man who has lived and studied in the West and yet for decades believed and condoned fanatical religious beliefs, would one fine morning abandon the lap of luxury and power to correct mistakes."

"Your Majesty is absolutely right about what I believe and the significance I attach to Islam. I do believe that the only religion which should be permitted on earth is Islam. On the other hand there are millions of errant believers who need to be re-educated and not persecuted as we are doing in the Islamic Republic. With the utmost respect, I do disagree with your Majesty's concept and laws which have given total equality to all the religions. However that does not mean that I want these minorities to be persecuted in any way."

"Mr. Marzban, for the sake of argument let us say that you disagreed with the persecution of minorities in the Islamic Republic. How do you justify the concept that instead of staying in Iran and using your immense influence to reduce that discrimination, you abandoned everything and came over to Southern Iran? You had far greater opportunities of undoing the evil by staying there."

"Now let me take you to the second area of my concern. You have not only come to our territory as a refugee but you have come in the company of a convicted murderer, bank robber and a vicious evil man who has been so labelled by your own government and judiciary. Add to that the fact that this man is also a religious fanatic. Now let's come to the third point. Your government has accused you of stealing millions of dollars and escaping. With your intelligence do you expect me to believe that an allegedly reformed religious fanatic would escape from his country with millions of stolen dollars, in the company of a man who could easily kill him and take all the money and on top of that, take refuge in a miserable dingy rooming house?"

This time with complete composure Marzban looked at me. "I can answer each one of your Majesty's questions. Yes, I did enter your territory in the company of a criminal. I think Your Majesty should take a look at this man. In his own way he is a rather brilliant man. He is six feet six inches tall and very well built. No reasonable man would want to accost him in public. He arranged to steal the Jeep from an army compound. In my opinion, I needed him to protect me against any physical attack from the Iranian authorities. He is capable of using any weapon or detection device and can easily track an enemy at any distance, at any time of the day or night. As far as the stolen money is concerned, that is a lie. As a matter-of-fact, I have entered your kingdom without a penny in my pocket. Do you expect the government of the Islamic Republic of Iran to say nice things about me, an ex-Minister, who abandons everything and seeks asylum in an enemy country? Now coming back to this man Manucher. There is absolutely no doubt that he's a criminal and a dangerous man. He was actually on death row, when I intervened on his behalf, falsely claiming that he was doing all this for the preservation of Islam. They bought my story. I had an ulterior motive. I wanted him to obtain the vehicle and provide me with the defence necessary for me to get safely out of the Islamic Republic and enter your territory without any problems. He gave me his word of honor that he would protect me with his life, if necessary. I had my doubts but I had no options. I took his word. I must say Your Majesty that I've come to one conclusion, this man may be a criminal and a vicious person but his word is his bond. You will be amazed at what I'm about to say. In spite of his fanatical beliefs, he is a great admirer of yours and has told me several times that his greatest ambition is to pay homage to you once and thereafter leave both portions of Iran and settle down in some other Islamic country where his criminal record is not known."

"How much did you pay him for his services?" I asked.

"The compensation I agreed to provide consisted of three parts. First, I gave him one hundred thousand American dollars in cash. Secondly, I promised to intervene and speak on his behalf to your Majesty's Government in case you decided to try him in this jurisdiction. And last, I promised him that I would do everything in my power to help him realize his greatest ambition, which was to personally pay homage to Your Majesty."

"Mr. Marzban, are you expecting me to welcome a convicted criminal into my palace?"

"I'm expecting nothing from you Your Majesty. I'm humbly requesting this on his behalf so that I could compensate him for risking his life and getting me safely into Your Majesty's kingdom."

"You can tell your friend that there will be no criminal prosecution against him as the offenses he has committed were not in our jurisdiction. We, as a free and Democratic Nation do not interfere with the judicial processes of other countries. As far as his fear of extradition is concerned, you can assure him that we have so little respect for the administration of justice in the Islamic Republic that I would not permit any one, however guilty, to be extradited to that nation. As to his paying me a visit, I will discuss this matter with my security staff. I want his motives thoroughly analyzed and then I will give you my answer."

Marzban bowed and started to leave. "Mr. Marzban, has it not occurred to you that you are in great danger of being assassinated by the agents of your own government? I have been informed that a reward has been offered by your government to any one who can successfully terminate your life. Whether we agree with you or not, you are now our guest and it is our duty to protect you. I have arranged for a car with a chauffeur. I've also arranged for a safe home where you will be guarded and protected. The only condition is that this man Manucher must not reside with you, but may occasionally visit you after he has been thoroughly checked for weapons by our guards."

I observed him very carefully as I was speaking to him. Any one in his position would have been delighted to hear what I was saying. I looked for signs of relaxation or reduction of anguish in his demeanour. This would have given me the evidence I required to convince me that he was telling the truth. However his expressions denoted to me a feeling of quandary as if he could not decide whether this was good or bad. On the other hand, he did not seem to be at all concerned about the restrictions placed on Manucher's visits to his home. This satisfied me that he was not very comfortable in the company of our latest imported criminal. My conclusion was that a portion of his story was not true, but which portion was it? That was the issue I had to determine. The only way to do this was to somehow be in his company for a longer period of time. Then I thought of an idea. "Mr. Marzban, your knowledge of the law and your acumen in dealing with human behaviour is well known to me. I have an appeal from a trial coming up before me. It deals with the situation that is of utmost concern to me as the Shahnshah of Iran. As you are aware, after a trial, the accused is free to appeal to higher courts but the final appeal comes before me and this is a final appeal. Perhaps you are already aware that in Democratic Iran it is a serious criminal offense for a parent to interfere with his or her child's marriage on the grounds of race, religion or color. We refer to the parental generation as the inferior generation. We have enacted laws that have completely taken away the rights and privileges of parents when they interfere with the lives of their adult children. If they have some serious concerns about their children's behaviour or associations, those concerns must be brought to the state authorities who are highly qualified and educated experts. They alone are permitted to deal with them. I know you may disagree with this, but this is my law, and I will enforce it despite the opinion of any other individual or state. Once the young person complains about parental interference in such matters, the parents are immediately arrested and then experts such as psychologists and jurists converse with them and advise them. They are offered the opportunity of retracting their objections and apologizing to the members of the superior generation. If they comply, they are heavily fined and sent home. For failure to comply, especially in a situation where they are in disagreement with the choice of a partner, the penalty is death. Fortunately for all of us, the prejudices of the inferiors are not as strong as their fear of death, so sooner or later they come to their senses and start pretending that they have made this great sacrifice for their children and have accepted the mixed marriage, all for the happiness of their children. No one of course will believe them, but that leads to less pain in society and tames the inferiors so that they do not interfere any more with the lives of their educated and sophisticated children."

"I have a very interesting case before me tomorrow morning. We have here a Jewish Rabbi. His daughter was studying at the University of Zahidan and met a Shi'ite Muslim student. They fell in love and decided to get married. There was a second problem. The boy's father is a Mullah, a totally uneducated and fanatical individual. His reaction was rather interesting. He was quite happy to accept the girl as his daughter-in-law if she became a Muslim. Both the children brought the matter before the courts, which of course ordered him to butt out. He refused and appealed to the Court of Appeal, which in turn, dismissed his appeal. Now he has come before me with this final appeal. He will have to show me some specific grounds such as lack of education on the part of the bride or moral turpitude before permission is granted for him to interfere. If he fails to show that, he will be ordered to immediately desist from interfering and if he fails to do so, he will be executed. Surprisingly, this is only the second man who is facing the death penalty for the crime of religious interference. If you're interested, please come and join us in court. Afterwards you can give me your opinion."

"Your Majesty, I have heard about these laws that you have proclaimed. I am a devout Muslim. How do you expect me to agree with this kind of law? What purpose is served by making me a witness at a court trial when my conscience says that the whole procedure and justice system are wrong and that the father has every right to interfere under these circumstances."

"Mr. Marzban, we did not invite you to leave your Islamic Republic and come to us. You came for reasons known only to you. You claim that you admire what I've done for Iran. Yet you disagree with the most significant change we brought to this part of our country. How do you justify those contradictions? Think about it. If you're still interested, you will be permitted to enter the courtroom to witness the trial. I'm not interested in your opinion as to whether this is right or wrong. I am only interested in obtaining your opinion as to whether the accused was provided with sufficient opportunity to defend himself."

Marzban bowed to me. "I will abide by your Majesty's orders and will be in court in the morning." He bowed and left in the company of the driver and the guard we had provided for him.

After Marzban left, I summoned Rauf Irfani for a meeting.

"Officer Irfani, I want your advice regarding a certain matter which is causing me some concern. This man Marzban is an enigma. I think he is genuine, however there are a large number of statements he has made which I believe and some where I feel he's equivocating. In short I cannot say that I completely trust him. As you already know, we have provided him with a car, chauffeur and a house. Visits from Manucher will be restricted and he must be thoroughly checked before being allowed into Marzban's home. I have the suspicion that there is a conspiracy afoot. I think we need surveillance, but at the same time, I feel it inhospitable and treacherous to put any bugs in his home or his car. More significantly, my greater concern is not Marzban but Manucher. I have a feeling that they are planning something. How do we check this out?"

Rauf bowed from his waist before me. "Your Majesty's concerns are totally justified and accurate. If Your Majesty had not summoned me, I would have sought your permission to do so because I wanted to impart some information which I consider very crucial to your security. As I have already informed Your Majesty, we were very suspicious of Manucher and Minister Behram. Without your express permission, I could not put any hearing devices into their quarters, however, when Manucher was under arrest and being investigated, I thought it was completely justified to investigate his vehicle. Your Majesty, I was absolutely stunned that the removal of metallic plates in the bottom of the Jeep revealed seven explosive devices. Each one of these could easily blow up a structure as large as your Majesty's palace or even the legislature building. I thought of accosting Manucher or the Minister, but that would alert them immediately and deprive us of the surprise element needed for our investigation. I therefore did the following; we completely disarmed all the explosive devices and then replaced them where we found them. The disarming process is so effective that the rearming of these weapons would require the services of an engineer which will be impossible for them to obtain in our jurisdiction. The reason I replaced the devices in the vehicle was to leave the impression that we were not on to them. We have also planted a tracking device in the vehicle so that we know exactly where the vehicle is at any given moment. Your Majesty, do you not think that we have sufficient evidence now to justify putting a bug in the residence of both Manucher and the Minister?"

"Yes, I think I am satisfied, you may go ahead!"

"Another thing that we have noticed, Your Majesty, is that both Manucher and Marzban repeatedly go out for walks around their residence. Naturally, we have constant surveillance of their property and we were surprised that they would do so even when the weather was very inclement. Then we realized that they may have suspected that their residence was bugged, so conversing as they walked outside of the residence was the safest manner of protecting their privacy. But your Majesty, they missed a very significant point. You see when Manucher was arrested and was under interrogation, the usual protocol is that the prisoners have to leave their shoes outside. We took this wonderful opportunity and placed a hearing device in the sole of one of his shoes, therefore every syllable of what they said was clearly heard by us and recorded. Up to now, we haven't heard anything that involves any explosives or terrorism. We are waiting and watching."

"All right Rauf, let me know if you find something interesting."

Rauf bowed and left.

CHAPTER 19.

Marzban arrived home in a very distressed state of mind. He had come to Southern Iran for a specific purpose. His mission was to kill the most significant enemy of the Islamic Republic, which he then thought was the Shahnshah. He once really believed that it was his duty as a faithful Muslim and a loyal Iranian to kill this pagan who was a danger both to Islam and Iran. But the more he came in contact with the Shahnshah, the more he liked him and had started to seriously question his former opinion of the Shahnshah and his role in Iran. The idea of murdering this man now appeared to him to be downright evil and deceitful. The kindness and hospitality with which he had been treated made him ashamed of himself. He was seriously considering ways of parting from Manucher, but even this was a very dangerous and scary thought. He was quite sure that if Manucher suspected that he was not interested in continuing with the original plan, he would not have the slightest hesitation in exterminating him.

As he was contemplating the complicated situation he was in, the front door opened and Manucher walked in. Without being greeted he sat down in front of Marzban. "I have found out that tomorrow you are attending an appeal hearing by the Shahnshah. This pagan bastard is going to try a devout Muslim and an infidel Jew who have rightly interfered with the marriage of their children. It is a pregone conclusion as to what the Shahnshah will decide. I've also come to know that once the trial has been concluded, a large number of media representatives from all over the world are coming to interview him. This case is of such significance to the infidels that they want publicity for the Shahnshah's new dictate. The number of press reporters will be in the hundreds. Both, for reasons of space and security, they will not be permitted to enter the courtroom or the Imperial Palace, so per force, this pagan king will have to step out of the courtroom for a few minutes to talk to the reporters. We are all aware that you have been provided with a car and a chauffeur. Therefore, it will not be possible for me to be your chauffeur. Leave from your residence as late as you possibly can. Tonight I will arrange to impair the engine of your car. It will not start and they will try to obtain another one for you. This is when you will calmly suggest that you can use your jeep and hand over the keys to your chauffeur."

"Pretend that you have injured your foot and that you are unable to walk unassisted to the car. If offered, take the assistance of your chauffeur. The expected consequence of this is that your vehicle will be parked as close as possible to the courthouse. I have checked that entrance myself. It is the same one from which the Shahnshah will exit to greet the reporters. Take your cell phone with you, keep it on, but keep it in the vibrator mode. When the Shahnshah leaves to greet the reporters, I will dial your cell number. Don't answer. Immediately apologize to the Shahnshah and say that you have to go to the washroom. Tell him that you will join them outside. Stay in the washroom for at least ten minutes until you hear the explosion. Wait a while until the smoke has cleared. When speaking to the Pagan's followers pretend to be shocked and extremely upset at his untimely demise. Then, with tears in your eyes request that you be escorted to your residence. I will be watching you and will arrange to get you back to the real Iran where we will have the greatest celebration you have ever known, for we will be celebrating the death of the infidel usurper and the freeing of our Iran from pagan rule. Any questions?" Then Manucher left.

Marzban was too stunned to respond immediately. Of course, they both had come to Southern Iran to assassinate the Shahnshah. He had not expected such perfect planning and precision so early in the game. He had not expected to feel the respect and affection he felt for the Shahnshah. Strange he thought, I have come to assassinate a man and now I have developed a fondness for him. No ordinary person could generate such emotions in me. The fact that I feel all this is the very evidence that the Shahnshah is not only a brilliant man but a very kind and decent human being and I'm not going to let him be harmed. He was in a dilemma as to how he should accommodate his lately acquired loyalty to the Shahnshah by betraying his compatriot. How could he possibly stop this massacre without exposing Manucher's schemes to the Shahnshah. He was absolutely certain that the Shahnshah would protect him, reward him and keep him wealthy for the rest of his life, but would he be able to look into the mirror and not want to spit at his own image?

He knelt down to pray to Allah. "Ya Allah, the creator and benefactor of mankind, guide me and deliver me from this horror that I'm facing."

The telephone rang. It was an eerie feeling that he experienced. He had just finished his prayers and here the telephone was ringing as if Allah had heard him and was responding. Reluctantly, he picked up the telephone.

"Salaam alaikum Minister Marzban," said the voice of the other end. There was no mistaking the depth and warmth of the voice. It was the Shahnshah calling.

"Your Majesty, to what do I owe this honor?"

There was a ten second silence at the other end before the Shahnshah spoke. "From your voice and intonation Mr. Marzban, I detect some anguish, are you not well today?"

"I'm fine you're Majesty, just a bit tired."

"I was wondering whether you would accept an invitation for dinner with me at the Palace tonight."

Marzban was now totally befuddled. He did not know what to say. The Shahnshah did not wait for a response. "I will send a vehicle to pick you up. Will you be ready in half an hour?"

"I will be ready Your Majesty and I will look forward to the honor you are bestowing upon me."

In spite of his acumen, Marzban was a very religious man. All religious men are usually contaminated with the idiocy of faith. Faith is always the progenitor of superstition. His intelligence normally would have prevented him from imagining an omen from God, but just now that is exactly what he wished for. He convinced himself that

Allah had responded to his prayers and had sent him that omen. Allah wanted him to confide in the Shahnshah. He had tacitly ordered him to expose the nefarious scheme of Manucher.

Exactly half an hour later, the Shahnshah's limousine arrived and he was taken to the Palace. The Shahnshah was there to greet him at the entrance. "Welcome to my home Minister Marzban. Please treat this as your own abode."

To his shock Marzban noticed that the Shahnshah was drinking an alcoholic beverage without the slightest pretence of hiding it. The Shahnshah noticed a slight discomfiture in Marzban's eyes. He looked straight at him and said, "Oh Mr. Marzban, this is Scotch whiskey I am drinking. I know you are a strict Muslim and do not consume alcohol. That was the only reason I did not offer it to you. Please accept my apology for my lack of hospitality."

"Sit down, Mr. Marzban. Every citizen in this country is free to believe in what he wants to. Every one has to make his own choices. The State has no business to interfere with the private life of citizens. I am not a Muslim and I like my scotch so I consume it. You are a Muslim and you are opposed to the consumption of alcohol and I respect your belief. Would you like to have some orange juice, tea or coffee?"

"Thank you Your Majesty, I will have some coffee."

"Mr. Marzban, you are my guest and as your host it is my duty to mitigate your anguish when I see it. Your eyes do not focus and are constantly moving. Something is bothering you very deeply. Why don't you tell me what it is?"

"Before I tell you anything, Your Majesty, let me make a confession. I think you have already guessed and perhaps I have already told you that I have never agreed with the free thinking pattern you have advocated in Iran. With the utmost respect I believe that this should be kept as an Islamic State and the law and governance of this country should be strictly according to Sharia law. Now comes the most difficult part of my confession. It is quite possible that I may lose my life as a result of this confession, but I have no choice. After hearing me out, I will plead with you to take pity on me and perhaps give me a lenient sentence."

"Mr. Marzban, one does not promise a conviction or a sentence prior to hearing the facts of the case. You make your confession and

I will definitely consider it a mitigating factor. Keep in mind that whatever the crime you're confessing to, consists merely of the intent to commit a crime. Certainly intent to commit a crime is punishable, but in civilized countries people are not sentenced to death because they have an evil intent. Open up and be truthful about everything and perhaps I will forgive you."

There were tears in Marzban's eyes. Alright Your Majesty, I will tell you everything. I am ashamed to break the confidence of a co-conspirator but my guilt is mitigated by the fact that this other person is an evil and wild animal. You have heard of my companion Manucher. We were sent by the Islamic Republic for the sole purpose of assassinating you. I was a willing conspirator. My job was to win your favour and trust. Every one believed that I, as a Minister of the Islamic Republic, who had willingly given up my position to seek refugee status in Southern Iran, would be welcomed by Your Majesty. You would invite me to your palace and sooner or later, I would be able to bring in Manucher, who is an expert in weaponry and explosives, and he would eventually succeed in assassinating Your Majesty. I succeeded in gaining your trust and I admire your brilliance, sophistication, and your unlimited kindness. I see the Iran you have created. I cannot deny the fact that you have basically achieved a miracle. Your ideas are very difficult for me to understand but in spite of my beliefs, I've come to the conclusion that your theories and your governance are the only answers for the future of Iran as a civilized nation. Tomorrow morning, after the trial has been concluded, the vehicle in which I arrive will be detonated by remote control at the exact time that Your Majesty goes out to speak to the reporters. Your Majesty, I plead with you, do not leave this building after you have given your judgement. Please have your experts search the vehicle as soon as I am out of it. Manucher must never suspect that you are on to his schemes. I will go home and go along with his plan to arrive tomorrow morning in his jeep for the court case. Tonight, I have to act normally and continue to agree with his scheme. Do not worry about me being in danger. If I'm injured in any way, I am to blame and I deserve it."

"Are you suggesting that I should allow you to go back to that murderer especially after you have alerted me and possibly saved my life?"

Marzban fell to his knees and placed his head on my feet. "My Shahnshah, I think I realize why millions of Iranians love you and would sacrifice their lives for you. I just confessed to you that I had planned to assassinate you and here you are concerned about my safety. I plead guilty to my abominable crime. Give me whatever punishment you deem fit."

I stood up and beckoned him to his feet. "May I call you Marzban?"

He had tears in his eyes, "Your Majesty, the very thought that you will even speak to me and call my name after what I have confessed to you, is an indication of your greatness. When you call me by my first name, I will consider it an honor bestowed upon me."

"Marzban, you may have wanted to kill me but it takes great courage and integrity to admit such a thing. Especially when your life is in jeopardy for making the confession. I accept your apology and I completely forgive you." He hugged me and I could feel him sobbing silently.

"As you want to take the risk of going home and being in the company of that monster Manucher, I will take the necessary precautions. Your home will be watched so that no harm will come to you. Go home, my friend, and be at peace."

After bowing to me Marzban left the room. I immediately called Rauf and he picked up the phone on the third ring.

"Rauf, come to my office immediately. It is very urgent."

"I will be at Your Majesty's service in exactly three minutes."

When Rauf arrived, I narrated the whole story with details of the plot which Marzban had provided me. Initially he was in total shock but then he smiled at me. I did not think that this was funny and asked him why he was smiling.

"Does Your Majesty not remember that I mentioned the defusing of the explosive devices in Manucher's jeep? We defused the devices and left them there for a specific purpose. We have been watching this man ever since that time. He does not know it, but we have placed a talking device in his cell phone. We know his every move. We want him to attempt to blow up that jeep. When he does that, all that will happen will be a booming sound and a lot of smoke. This will give us the evidence we need to prove that he attempted to assassinate Your

Majesty. We will be able to grab him within seconds, with the remote detonating device in his hands. Once we do that, we will be at Your Majesty's command as to Manucher's fate. What does your Majesty wish?"

"No Rauf, arrest him and bring him before me but be absolutely certain that the attempt to arrest him is after Marzban has left the vehicle and is safely inside the Palace. Under no circumstances should Marzban's life be in jeopardy. Is that clearly understood?"

"Absolutely, Your Majesty. Our monitoring device has clearly indicated to us that the explosion will take place after Marzban has left the jeep and when Your Majesty goes out to meet the reporters. There is no jeopardy to Marzban when we arrest Manucher. I want to assure Your Majesty that there will not be the slightest jeopardy to you. Without sounding frivolous, I can assure you that he will not go to the washroom without our knowledge."

"Major Rauf Irfani, you have done an excellent job and I'm very proud to have a man of your calibre in my service. Accept my gratitude."

"Your Majesty, I am only a Captain and your grateful servant."

"No you're not! As of this moment, you are a Major in the Armed Forces of Democratic Iran." With a smile I added, "And don't argue with the Shahnshah."

Rauf saluted smartly. I could see the pride and joy in his eyes. To be very honest, he did not realize how deeply I felt about such loyal men working for me.

A strange realization came to me. I did know that in spite of all the precautions taken by Rauf and his officers, there was going to be some danger to me the following day. In spite of that, I was not too concerned. The task I had to perform and the anticipated results were of such great importance that the life or death of a man in his seventies was of very little significance. I went home to my quarters with the peace of mind I had not enjoyed in a long while.

CHAPTER 20.

The court opened exactly as scheduled at 10.00 a.m. the following morning. From my office I could clearly see the intense security that was provided by Rauf and his team of officers. I could literally see the tension in the expressions of the officers. In our judicial system in Iran even during the final appeal, the accused or convicted person is permitted to address the judge. The two appellants were Moise Waldman the father of Maleka Waldman and Mohamad Razaak, the father of Abdul Aziz Razaak. Both fathers were very strongly opposed to the union of their children. Mr. Waldman was a Rabbi and Mr. Razaak was a devout Muslim. There was no issue that the opposition was on the grounds of religion and the law was clear that barring certain limited circumstances, parental interference in such a union was forbidden. The law courts had already decided that as both parents had refused to butt out and apologize for their interference, the penalty was death. The only thing I had to determine was whether they had repented, or if there was some other justified non-religious reason why the interference of the inferior generation should be tolerated in these particular circumstances. Basically there were no legal issues. All I had to do was to convince them to change their minds and if they did, they would get a lenient jail sentence, if they did not, the sentence would be their execution.

"Rise and bow to the Shahnshah of Iran, the supreme authority and Judge of free Iran," the bodyguards announced. Every one stood up as I arrived in court to take my seat. I gestured for everyone to sit which they did after bowing to me.

"Your Majesty, I am Shahrukh Husseini, the prosecutor and counsel for Democratic Iran. With Your Majesty's permission I will now present my case on behalf of the State. From the documents already presented to you, you are aware that Maleka Waldman is a university graduate with a degree in economics. Her father, Mr. Waldman, has a grade ten education and has never been to university and does not have any professional qualifications. Abdul Aziz Razaak has exactly the same qualifications as Ms. Waldman. They were students together at the University of Zahidan. Abdul Aziz's father has never attended high school. He has spent most of his teenage years at a madrasa and has no formal education. The state authorities have repeatedly warned both these men that interference in a mixed marriage is a severe offense under our legal system and they have refused to comply. However, they have requested that they be permitted to address Your Majesty prior to their sentences being carried out. We have granted the request and they are now before Your Majesty. We have clearly enunciated to them that once Your Majesty rules against them and they continue their illegal interference with the superior generation, Your Majesty may sentence them to death."

"Mr. Moise Waldman you will now address the court and present your statement."

Mr. Waldman bowed to me," Your Majesty, before I present my statement to you let me first express my gratitude for the incredible progress and civilization you have brought to Iran. Even your worst enemies will agree that every citizen in this country is now prosperous and well looked after. As far as the Jews are concerned, we owe you even a greater debt of gratitude, because your Majesty has given us equality and respect for the first time in decades. However that is not the issue before you Your Majesty. I beseech you, hear me out completely and then express your judgment. For the last forty years we have been oppressed. Our synagogues have been burned to the ground and our daughters and wives have been raped. We have been deprived of education and investment in this country. All this was done by the Iranian Muslims. I have only one daughter. Thanks to your benevolent intervention in this country, I was able to educate her so that she can establish herself. I was also hoping that she would marry one of our young men and have a nice Jewish family. Now Your Majesty, not only has she chosen a Muslim boyfriend but a boy who is the son of a fanatic, who believes in the total annihilation of all non-Muslims from Iran. How can I forget the memory of those decades of torture and accept this boy as my son-in-law?"

"Carefully listen to me, Mr. Waldman. Let me assure you that I'm completely aware and sympathize with the predicament of the Jews under the fanatical regime of the Islamic Republic. Do you not realize that the main reason that they succeeded was because there were segregated groups described as Muslims, Jews, Christians and Zoroastrians? Now let us look at a different scenario. If those same oppressors had a daughter married to a Jew and they had three children, a son married to a Christian with two children, would they have been able to oppress the minorities without hurting themselves? If every one was an Iranian instead of being a Muslim, a Christian or a Jew, would any one be able to oppress his fellow citizens? In the history of mankind no disease has killed more people than religion. This should be left to the individual and not in the hands of ignorant men and women who want to impose their own unproven beliefs on their children. You, Mr. Waldman, are not a Jew in my eyes. You are an Iranian, a productive citizen of our country. To further classify or categorize you is not only degrading to you, but also to Iran. We will make all possible efforts to suppress and crush any attempt by religious organizations to divide the population of Iran into segments and the best way of achieving this is by actively encouraging mixed marriages and forcefully eliminating any interference by the inferior generation. I am requesting you to join us in this endeavour. You must cease being a Jew and consider yourself a full-fledged Iranian with the same rights and privileges as any other citizen. You have complimented me on the progress I have brought to Iran. You have thanked me for bringing equality and giving rights to the Jews. I accept your thanks. Now, let me have the privilege of convincing you that you are a fully fledged Iranian and nothing less than that."

"Your Majesty, my daughter Maleka is the only person in this world who can connect me with posterity. When I'm old and feeble I want to hold my grandchildren against my heart. Tell me your Majesty, how will I feel if I know that my grandchildren are the descendants of the same people who persecuted and killed us for decades? How will I possibly give them the love of a grandfather?"

"Whether the child is fathered by a Muslim or a Jew does not matter at all. They will be your descendants and have your genes. When you hold them against your heart it will not make the slightest difference. We all live under the illusion that we are pure Jews, Christians, Zoroastrians or Muslims. This is a myth perpetuated by ignorant religious fanatics to control the population and to dominate them. You are a kind man. In spite of all the propaganda you have received and heard all your life, ultimately your inherent goodness will prevail and you will love your grandchild exactly as much as you would have, had he been fathered by a Jew. The first time you hold him or her against your heart, you will realize that what I'm telling you today is quite true. Mr. Waldman, each one of us has the blood of other races mixed with our own. There is no such thing as a pure race. As you know, I'm a Zoroastrian. My ancestors were persecuted or killed and a large number of them had to migrate to India. Do you think therefore for a minute I will hold a grudge against a single Iranian who may have descended from those barbarians? Believe me Mr. Waldman, if I were to meet the direct descendent of a man who had butchered my ancestors a few hundred years ago, I would not have the slightest resentment against him, because he's not responsible for the sins of his parents. I have now spoken and have nothing more to say. I'm giving you the opportunity to reach out to your daughter and her chosen mate and hold them against your heart with love. If you can do that, I will forgive the serious crime defined in our penal code as; `interfering with the unity of the nation.' Your death penalty will be commuted to time served and I will allow you to return home to your family as a productive Iranian citizen. Are you ready to do that?"

Mr. Waldman fell to his knees in front of me. "After all, I'm facing a man whose ancestors were mistreated by the same Muslims who are doing the same to my people. You have the strength and kindness to forgive them and have become their Shahnshah. More significantly, you have convinced them that the message and civilization you have brought to Iran is the only way in which we can enter the twenty-first century to become a refined and productive nation. My Shahnshah, I still have grave doubts in my soul, but I will obey your command and I'll accept my daughter's decision and take my future son-in-law to my heart."

I raised my hand and gestured in the direction of Maleka and Abdul Aziz, who were standing at the back of the courtroom. "Come in front, my children. Maleka, hug your father. Abdul Aziz come forward and hug a great man, who at the age of sixty-five has the capacity to forsake his prejudices and to accept you as his son. Abdul Aziz hesitated for a minute and raised his hand to shake that of his future father-in-law. To my satisfaction and joy, Waldman hugged him and called him son. The impact of this on the courtroom was unbelievable. Every one was standing and cheering. I could even hear voices praying in their different religious languages. It was sad I thought that they were thanking God for what a simple mortal like Mr. Waldman had achieved, all on his own.

Suddenly, I heard this incredibly raucous yelling at the back of the courtroom. I looked up and noticed that it was the second prisoner, Mohamed Razaak who was cursing his son in Farsi. "Aren't you ashamed of hugging a pagan and a Jew in the presence of your father? Have you no respect for your family?"

I ordered the guards to bring Mohamed Razaak to the front of the courtroom. "Anything you want to say you must address to me and not to any one else in this courtroom! What is your problem? Have you noticed that I provided an opportunity to the father of the bride to atone for his uncivilized and criminal behaviour? He took that chance and has not only apologized to his daughter, but to your son as well. You do see that he has been totally forgiven. Now it is your opportunity to address this court and if you apologize for your criminal behaviour, I will reduce your sentence. On the other hand if you continue to behave like the sick fanatic you are, your execution will take place tomorrow morning at six a.m. Is that clearly understood?"

"A foreign pagan has come into my country, hypnotized our people with his corrupt and UnIslamic philosophy. He has ruined the culture and faith of my land and then he has the audacity to sit in judgment over me, a true and devout Muslim. Ya Allah, why have you inflicted upon us this curse of Shaitan."

"Have you ever visited a very close friend whose dog continuously barked at you? Naturally that barking gets to be irritating but do you blame your friend for it? Your rantings and ravings fall into that category."

"In the name of Allah, Pagan, are you calling me a dog?"

"No sir, I did not call you a dog. It was just an example to indicate to you that your opinion of me is of no significance. But then, of course, I am talking logically and you would not have a clue as to what that means. I would never call you a dog, because that would be an insult to the canine world."

"Are you trying to confuse me with all these complicated pagan words? I do not understand them, nor do I want to."

"For the first time I completely agree with you. Comprehension of anything logical or scientific is an impossibility for your intellectual faculties. With that brain sir, you should be permitted only two sentences either yes sir, or no sir. However, enough of this nonsense. Are you willing to admit your mistake and apologize to your son and future daughter-in-law, or are you willing to die in the morning? You have committed a very serious and grave offence. You have interfered with the unity of the nation by opposing a mixed marriage which, under our laws, is the greatest unifying factor for the people of Iran. This is your last chance."

Abdul Aziz Razaak, the son of the accused stood up and bowed to me. "You're Majesty, please forgive this interruption. May I speak?"

"Go ahead Abdul Razaak; what do you want to say?"

"Your Majesty, I admit that my father is an ignorant and fanatical man but he is not evil. In that ignorant era when he grew up with the madrasas brainwashing the children, logic and rationality were never taught. The capacity to think for oneself was frowned upon. My Shahnshah, how can we expect him to think scientifically with such a background? I therefore plead before you on my knees to spare his life," he said as he knelt down.

"Oh you admirer of the infidels, I am ashamed that such a son was born to me. You have no respect for your father or your faith. How will you face the wrath of Allah on the Day of Judgment? Do you think this Pagan King and his followers will come to your rescue?"

This shocking demonstration of idiocy did not make me angry at all. As a matter of fact I now completely agreed with the description given by Abdul Aziz. This man was not a criminal. He was an ignorant nonentity who deserved and needed treatment rather than punishment. Before I could speak to him, Malcka stood up and bowed. "My Shahnshah, may I address you?"

"Speak my child, what do you want to say?"

"My Shahnshah, this has been a very sad and difficult year for both me and Abdul Aziz. Our parents have made our lives miserable. Your erudite and brilliant intervention in this matter has brought me back my father with his approval and love for which I will be eternally grateful to Your Majesty. Now Abdul Aziz and I have the opportunity of living a happy and loving life. But if at the commencement of our union, I am responsible for the execution of his father, the rest of the days will always be shadowed by the sad circumstances. This man is the father of my future husband. I do not want his death on any of our consciences. Your Majesty, please spare his life, I beg of you."

"Mr. Mohamed Razaak, did you hear your future daughter-in-law speak for you? The child that you offended and insulted? A young woman, whom you described as a pagan, is pleading for your life. What have you to say for yourself?"

There was pin drop silence in the court room. In the front seat I could see Marzban sitting and watching the proceedings. Amazing I thought, how much this man had changed. Mohamed Razaak was tongue-tied for a few seconds and I thought he was mellowing but then he stood up.

"This pagan woman will bear the child of my son. My heir and all the successors of my family will be contaminated by pagan blood. I do not want the support of such a person. So pagan Shahnshah, do your worst, kill me! I will reach the arms of Allah and on the Day of Judgment do not ask me to intervene on your behalf to ask Allah to forgive you."

"Is that your final word on the subject?" I asked. "Abdul Aziz, do you want to have an opportunity to speak to this demented man?"

"I tried your Majesty, he spat in my face."

"Mohamed Razaak, I have provided you with the opportunity of atoning for your crime and you have rejected it. I now confirm your conviction for the offense described in our legal system as interference with the unity of the nation. You have already been sentenced to death. I have given you the opportunity of begging for the forgiveness that was so willingly offered to you by your intelligent and educated children. You have rejected that as well. I therefore sentence you to death. You will be executed at dawn. As per section 246 of the criminal code, your family and friends will not be permitted to hold a funeral ceremony and no burial will be permitted. Your body will be electrically cremated and your ashes will be disposed off along with the garbage from the city."

For the first time there was abject fear and shock in the eyes of Mohamed Razaak.

"Ya Allah! You cannot do that to a devout Muslim. If my body is burnt, how am I supposed to face Allah on the Day of Judgment?"

"That is precisely what we want to do. We want to eliminate the possibility of Allah having to suffer the indignity of looking at and dealing with a low life like you. Officers take this animal out of my sight. Abdul Aziz and Maleka, you have shown your sophistication by the kindness you offered to him and I do respect that. Remember, it is he who has refused your kindness and support. Tomorrow and for a few months thereafter, you will feel sad, you might even feel guilty but it is not your fault. Don't think of him only as an ignorant man, he is a bigot and his annihilation will help us to cleanse our Iran. If you both feel that you are losing your father, I completely understand your anguish. There is only one thing I can do for you. As of this day, in the presence of every one here, I promise to take his place my children. As of today, I am your father."

As I said these words, I realized that the pain and anguish that Abdul Aziz and Maleka were feeling could not be easily removed by mere words. But what else could I do? Unfortunately, these two young people would have to learn to accept the fact that the reason for the pain, suffering and discrimination that Iranians had suffered for centuries, could be remedied in only one way. This was by harshly eliminating members of the inferior generation who refused to listen to the voice of rationality and insisted on continuing with their fanatical beliefs in spite of the logical solutions provided to them. I was not sorry for Mohamed Razaak. I would not have hesitated to behead him myself with a sword. The sad part of it all was that in punishing the criminal, we were also hurting his innocent children. I prayed that God would give comfort and solace to the two innocent victims, Abdul Aziz and Maleka.

The courtroom was almost empty when Rauf and four of his guards approached and surrounded me. We all knew that I had to go out to address the press.

"Nothing to worry about Your Majesty. Let me quickly explain what steps we have taken to protect you. As previously arranged, the vehicle which is picking Mr. Marzban up broke down at his residence. He offered the use of his jeep, and we agreed to that. He was driven to Your Majesty's palace by our chauffeur and the vehicle is parked a few yards from the spot where you will address the press. I must say that Mr. Marzban performed admirably by limping on his aching foot. The vehicle had to be parked very close to the entrance of the palace. Our hidden cameras indicated that Manucher had taken the detonating devices with him. At this time, Manucher is sitting in the restaurant on the twelfth floor overlooking Your Majesty's courtyard. He has a clear view from this location. We think that he will wait until your interview with the press is half done. He will then attempt to detonate the vehicle. Your Majesty will hear a loud explosion and see a lot of smoke, but do not be worried. The purpose of the smoke is to prevent him from seeing that the explosion did not cause any harm at all. He is being watched by two armed men who will actually see him trigger the device which will provide us with conclusive evidence of his guilt. He will immediately be arrested or shot if necessary. If he survives, we will bring him before Your Majesty for justice. Are you satisfied with these arrangements Your Majesty?"

"Everything is perfect Rauf. But one very important step should be added. Not a word of this incident should be leaked to the press. The Iranian authorities will automatically realize that the information we obtained to arrest Manucher may have come from Mr. Marzban. This will jeopardize the safety of his family in Teheran. I will arrange to get them out of Northern Iran before this information becomes public. Is that completely clear Rauf?"

"Absolutely Your Majesty."

With my four guards I walked out of the courtroom to the courtyard. There were approximately one hundred press reporters waiting for me. They all bowed and I responded by waving to them.

"Your Majesty, you are actively encouraging and supporting mixed marriages between Muslims, Jews, Christians and Zoroastrians. Do you think your majority Muslim population will support you, especially since you are not a Muslim?" A British reporter asked.

"In our Democratic Iran our people have slowly started realizing that a loyal Iranian can be whatever he wants. Religion is the personal privilege of every citizen and the state has no business in interfering with it. My subjects have completely accepted that. By supporting me they have indicated to the world that all religions are acceptable and tolerated as long as they don't interfere with each other. The fact that our people acknowledge me as their Shahnshah even though I'm not a Muslim is the evidence of that statement."

"There have been attempts to assassinate you, Your Majesty, aren't you concerned about your safety?"

"Of course I'm concerned for my life, who wouldn't be? Please keep in mind that my mission is to make Iran a sophisticated, civilized country of the twenty-first century. With education, hospitalization and freedom for all citizens. The success of this mission is more important to me than anything else in the world. My fellow Iranians have cooperated with me and I believe that we are halfway to achieving this dream. At my age the significance of my existence is less important than the important mission I am trying to achieve."

"The Islamic Republic and many other Arab and Muslim countries are violently opposed to you. Do you think they will allow you to establish a sectarian state in Iran?"

"The people of Iran are not blind. The standard of living in our portion of Iran has increased by eight hundred percent. Education of women has shot up by one thousand percent. University graduates have tripled since the formation of the Democratic Republic. Intermarriage between the different religious groups has greatly reduced religious tension in the country. Prosperity and peace are prevailing now. Under these circumstances, why do you think the people of Iran would like to go back to the decrepit era of religious fanaticism?"

Suddenly there was an enormous explosion and the whole courtyard vibrated. I was about to fall but was supported by Rauf and his companions. Smoke billowed and nothing was visible around us. I heard shouts of panic and people were running in every direction. Rauf whispered in my year, "Nothing to worry about, Your Majesty." They hurried me inside the building and closed the windows and the doors. We sat down and waited for the smoke to clear. Then I heard Rauf `s cell phone buzzing. He answered it and smiled at me." My Shahnshah, the monster has been arrested and disarmed."

"Rauf, I hope you remember my very specific instructions. Not a word to the media. Keep telling the press that the matter is under control and we are trying to find out who the perpetrator is."

"Yes, Your Majesty."

"Get Mr. Marzban in here immediately. Do not have any discussions with him on the way here. Say that I want to see him."

"Of course Your Majesty."

When Mr. Marzban was brought in, I saw the shock in his eyes in spite of the fact that he knew the explosion was going to occur.

"Mr. Marzban, that criminal Manucher has been arrested. He was caught red handed with the detonating device. His culpability is therefore established beyond any doubt. I have ordered my officers to withhold his name and details of the charges against him, since this information may lead to the Islamic government realizing that you may have alerted us to his plans. This could jeopardize the security of your wife and children and I do not want to take that risk. I have made some arrangements for your family. Please use the public telephone to call your wife. Tell her to immediately contact a man called Mehemet Suleymani at the Turkish embassy in Teheran. Ask her to speak to him privately and say that Sharuq has sent his greetings to `Azadi'. This is a code he will immediately recognize and understand the reason for her visit. He already knows what he has to do. Your wife and children will be issued Turkish diplomatic passports and safely transported to Ankara, Turkey. With these passports, the Iranian authorities will let them through without checking. Once they are safely in Turkey, they will be able to travel here legally. My only request is you must tell your wife not to mention this to any one, not even to close friends. You are solely responsible for saving my life and the lives of my faithful followers. I will never forget that debt. Mr. Marzban please assure me that you will carefully follow my instructions."

Marzban fell to his knees. "My gracious Shahnshah, I do not have words to express my gratitude for your generosity and kindness. I came to assassinate you. I realized my mistake and have tried to atone for it, but the guilt that I feel for wanting to hurt you has darkened my existence for a very long time. You have graciously forgiven me and now you are trying to protect my family. I cannot tell you how grateful I am. However, I cannot forgive myself. Yes, my Shahnshah, every syllable of what you have told me will be followed to the letter. If my wife and children successfully escape from the Islamic Republic and are reunited with me, I will return to Your Majesty for one more favour. That is that we all be able to visit the Royal Palace and bow our heads in gratitude to the greatest and the noblest human being that I have ever met."

I helped him onto his feet and hugged him. "Hush, my friend, you are not the only one who owes a debt of gratitude. We owe each other and we are now even. May I request that I be permitted to call you by your first name, Behram, is that acceptable?"

Marzban was now in a better frame of mind. "Does the Shahnshah of Iran need my permission to call me by my first name? Majesty, I will be honoured."

"One of the greatest qualities of a sophisticated person is to be able to respect others who are diametrically opposed to their views. Disagreement should never be the basis of disrespect for any one. You are a devout Muslim and I'm a firm believer in the concept of total rationality. Faith to me is the bankruptcy of reason. Our ancestors were ignorant uneducated trivialities. They used dogma and unproven assertions to support their ignorant religious beliefs. When that ignorance interfered with that of others they tried to kill or suppress each other. Behram, since the beginning of time this has been the history of religion and I am hopeful that with the advent of education for all citizens of Iran, we will reduce this ignorance to a tolerable level. All citizens can mumble in their extinct religious languages and obtain some comfort, as long as they do not interfere with other similar mumblers. As a devout Muslim, can you live in this world which I'm trying to establish?"

"I came here with the firm belief that Islam is the only true religion on earth. I also believed that the most destructive enemy of Islam was you and that as a devout Muslim it was my duty to stop you. Living in this part of Iran, seeing the progress, the education, freedom and prosperity, I was compelled to question my own thinking. On top of that, I have the honour and pleasure of your Majesty's friendship. Your logic and rationality have convinced me that Islam is one path to the realm of Allah, but not the only path. I will always remain a devout Muslim, but I must candidly admit that my fanatical beliefs of the past are now shocking to me. I think Your Majesty is quite right. All religions were created to remedy the ills of their times and with evolution, they must either change, or be suppressed."

Marzban, I could see, had actually amended his beliefs out of respect for my position. Years of experience as a chartered accountant and now several years of experience as the ruler of a country to which I had come as a total alien, had taught me to observe and analyze people very carefully when I interacted with them. I have been told that the optic nerve is twenty times thicker than the auditory nerve, so that your initial observation is much better than listening. I was therefore quite convinced that Marzban was totally genuine about his change of heart and mind. He could perhaps fake those expressions from time to time, but I did not believe that he could possibly keep it up. An example of that was a chat I had with him about religion. His strong beliefs clashed drastically with his logic. From childhood, this man had been brainwashed with the idiocy of faith and he could not get rid of that illogical thinking pattern in spite of his wisdom. I came to the following conclusion. That there was not the slightest doubt about his integrity and that he could be of great service to Iran. Sooner or later, his rationality may win over his religious fervour.

"Behram, I have to discuss something extremely important with you. I honestly believe that with your talent and knowledge of economics, you can be of great service to Iran. I trust you completely and I am going to offer you a position as Minister of Industrial affairs in Democratic Iran. You are quite aware of the fact that I have many critics and enemies, but I hope even they will not ever accuse me of deceit. I like to believe that my integrity is beyond question. I will be honest as to my reasons for appointing you a Minister. Two of the reasons are for selfish and self-serving purposes, the third reason is my genuine belief that you will contribute a lot to the growth of our industry. My selfish reasons are for the pure propaganda value. The fact that you were a Minister in the Islamic Republic and voluntarily left that area, espoused our cause and became a Minister in our government, would be a great benefit to Southern Iran. It will deflate our enemies to know that one of their Ministers saw the error of their ways and abandoned them. Many right-thinking Iranians in the North will see this as evidence that Southern Iran is not only prosperous, successful and sophisticated, but is also not against Islam."

My last and most important reason is that I am completely aware of the many contacts and enormous control you have over several governors and officials in the North. This can be useful in convincing them to join us in Southern Iran. Of course our ambition will be to unite Iran. If necessary we will attack the North and annex it. Military action would cause enormous loss of life on both sides and we would like to avoid this. Think about it and make your contacts with the various military personnel, governors and other powerful men and women in Northern Iran, anyone who trusts and respects you. Convey your opinion of us in the South and convince them to join us."

"If there is a need to meet with them, I can make arrangements for you to meet them in Turkey. The Turks are our very close allies, they are willing to help us in any manner possible and they will welcome you with open arms. They're completely in support of our position to establish a secular state in Iran while at the same time, preserving different religions."

"Behram tell me, are you interested in working for us?"

Marzban started laughing and I looked at him with surprise. "Why are you laughing?"

"If I may say so Your Majesty, you're a very strange man. You have befriended me even though I had come to kill you. You completely changed my way of thinking and now you are offering me a job. I now realize why you became the Shahnshah of Iran. How can my colleagues and co-conspirators ever compete with your acumen?"

"Will you accept my offer?"

"Your Majesty, I not only accept your offer without hesitation, but I give you my word of honor that I will faithfully serve you at any cost, including that of my own life."

"There is one very important thing you must always remember Behram. Not a word of this should be mentioned to any one else. Your wife, children and other family members are still in the Islamic Republic. If word gets out that you have been appointed a Minister in our government, their safety and life will be incredibly jeopardized. As we have discussed earlier, let your family go to Turkey first and then come into our territory."

"I understand Your Majesty. Thank you very much for your concern for my family."

The necessary discussion having been completed, Marzban bowed and left my presence.

CHAPTER 21.

Several days had elapsed since my conversation with Marzban. Almost every alternate evening Marzban would visit me and we would have dinner together. As is my principle, I did not amend my habits to accommodate him. I would normally have my glass of scotch before dinner and during our conversations. Initially, I noticed that Marzban was uncomfortable with alcohol on our dining table, but to his credit, he learned to accept it and as a matter of fact started asking me questions as to exactly how I felt as I consumed the scotch. I of course did not hesitate to exaggerate the enormous pleasure I got out of the drink. He realized that I was teasing him and I was impressed by the fact that he was capable of changing his mind about the enormous sin allegedly involved in the consumption of alcohol. Sometimes, I even had the impression that he might have enjoyed a swig, if I could somehow convince Allah to forgive him for that one breach. It was not my concern to change his beliefs and ideals, I just wanted to be sure that when he became a Minister in our government, he was capable of appreciating and accepting the views of others.

Alcohol now was perfectly legal and openly sold in stores and restaurants in our part of Iran. It was also a matter of great concern to me that people who were unaccustomed to the consumption of alcohol may be unable to control their consumption and behaviour, thereby causing accidents and other tragedies. To prevent this, our laws regarding drinking and driving and criminal behaviour after this sinful pleasure were very severe. Any person arrested for such an offense had to undergo counselling and if there was the slightest chance of a possible recurrence, then that person was forbidden the consumption of alcohol, sometimes even for life. Universities and other educational institutions had programs to teach students that this indulgence had to be curtailed, if it became problematic. To my great satisfaction, though there was an increase in some of the illegal activities as a result of this, on the whole a serious deterioration in the attitude of the citizens had not occurred.

Monogamy was now the law in our part of Iran. Marriage and divorce were now completely under civil law and Sharia law was abolished. The wearing of 'pardah' and other face covering materials was forbidden to all civil servants and government employees. Individuals could cover their faces by choice, but enforcement by husbands or fathers was strictly forbidden. If a woman was forced to cover her face, she could lodge a complaint with the 'Unity Commission' and on the first occasion, the perpetrator would receive a severe warning not to interfere with the behaviour of the female. On the second occasion, such intervention would result in one year of compulsory imprisonment without parole.

Initially there were four or five incidents where the inferior generation had interfered with their daughters' choice of garb. Several parents were sent to prison and now there was hardly a single case involving their interference. The freedom and privileges provided in Southern Iran were so popular with women, that thousands of them and particularly the educated ones from the Islamic Republic, would flee to Turkey and some other Arab states in the vicinity and then emigrate into southern Iran. Direct movement from northern Iran to our territory was not prevented by us, but by the Islamic Republic. Young people in our part of Iran now called the sealed border between us and the Islamic Republic, 'The Berlin Wall.'

There was a new joke which was very popular with young people in Southern Iran. The Shahnshah may have forbidden polygamy, but the resultant influx of modern females from the North had provided far more selection to the young men and therefore they loved him for improving their choices.

Our income and standard of living was now approximately two hundred and fifty percent of that in the Islamic Republic. There was a joke currently aired on our television channels that the Shahnshah should be grateful to the Islamic Republic for keeping the border closed, otherwise their whole population would emigrate South and work for a pittance, thereby causing the citizens of Southern Iran to lose their lucrative jobs.

Another common joke was that all those women, whose husbands were terminally ill wanted to emigrate South, because in the South, they could inherit their complete estate, whereas in the North under sharia law, they would get next to nothing. They looked after their husbands very carefully in the Islamic Republic, but once they crossed into the South, they abandoned them to Allah, since now their inheritance was safe. A radio announcer in the Islamic Republic had jokingly referred to these two southern Iranian jokes and was imprisoned for being critical of Islam.

Naturally, the first and most important incentive for emigrating to the South was the money as the income was much higher than in the North. The other important factor was the free education, hospitalization and medical services.

It had been a long and complicated day and I had just finished listening to the news both on our television channel and the one from the Islamic Republic. I was in my pyjamas and was thinking of going to bed, when suddenly I heard a loud discussion emanating from the adjoining room. Two of my guards ran into my living room and bowed. "Your Majesty, Major Rauf Irfani seeks permission to see you immediately. He claims that it is very important. I tried to convince him that it was rather late and that you were relaxing, but he insists that it is very important."

"Please let the Major in."

Rauf walked in and bowed. "I apologize for disturbing Your Majesty at this hour of the evening, but it was absolutely necessary that I see you immediately."

"Your Majesty, that criminal Manucher has escaped from prison. The manipulation and brutality he has shown are incredible. He pretended to have a heart attack and collapsed as if he was in agony. Two guards rushed into the cell to help him. He jumped up and broke the neck of one of the guards killing him instantly. Before the second guard realized what was happening, Manucher did the same thing to him and killed him as well. The incident was so fast that other personnel in the prison did not realize anything was taking place. Equipped with the weapons of the two dead guards this beast quietly walked out of the cell to the front entrance and without warning shot and killed four guards at the entrance of the prison. He then changed into the clothing of one of the dead guards. I do not know exactly what happened thereafter, since there is no one alive to tell me, but it appears that he approached one of the police vehicles. The poor driver must have thought that he was a colleague wanting to discuss something with him. He was shot in the head and killed instantly. Some of the other guards must have noticed the erratic movement of the vehicle, but before they could react, Manucher had already driven away. They found out about the massacre only when they went to the prison. Your Majesty, strict instructions are given to these guards not to enter the cells of dangerous criminals, but I suppose his acting was so good that they were conned into giving him immediate assistance. We have announced an `All Points Bulletin' and all police officers are alerted as to the description and registration number of the vehicle as well as the description of the accused. I hope we can catch the bastard before it is too late. I have also taken the liberty of sealing off your Majesty's palace, so as far as your security is concerned, there is nothing to worry about."

Initially I was in shock and quite concerned as to what this nefarious animal could do to other innocent citizens. Then the shocking possibility dawned on me that his first concern would be revenge. To a man like Manucher his own security was second to his desire to exterminate his enemies. I was now completely obsessed about Marzban's safety. "Rauf, the first thing that bastard will do is to kill Marzban. Take immediate steps to surround and protect my friend."

"Your Majesty, we have already done so. We immediately sent a convoy to Mr. Marzban's residence and not only did we surround it, but we got him out of there and he is now safely in a guarded vehicle downstairs. Would you like me to bring him in?"

"Yes Rauf, I want to see him now. If Manucher is free, he will be able to contact his fellow hoodlums in the Islamic Republic and I would not be surprised if Marzban's whole family is exterminated. Bring him in."

As Marzban had been in protective custody he already knew of Manucher's escape. My great concern was that my friend must have been in fear for his life. When I observed him as he entered my living room, he did not seem to be terrified. He was a bit shocked, but not devastated by the news.

This brilliant and sophisticated friend of mine was as capable of reading my expressions as I was of his.

"My Shahnshah, my closest friend and brother, I know exactly what your concern is. You'll be relieved to know that before all this happened and the beast escaped from prison, I was on my way to Your Majesty's palace to inform Your Majesty that the arrangements for my family to escape from the Islamic Republic are almost completed. My immediate family and sixteen others are already in Turkey. Thanks to your instructions, they are now in protective custody in Turkey and will fly into Zahidan tomorrow morning."

The relief I felt upon hearing this good news was unbelievable. I ordered some refreshments for Rauf and Marzban and a large Scotch for myself. I then decided to call my contact in the Turkish Republic even though it was three o'clock in the morning. The response from the Turkish officer was almost immediate. I asked him about Marzban's relatives and was relieved to hear that they were doing well and were eagerly looking forward to reuniting with him. I requested our Turkish contact to immediately arrange a chartered flight from Istanbul to Zahidan and advised that I would pay the costs. I was concerned about the criminal contacts which Manucher may have in Turkey and who he may use to attack or assassinate Marzban's family. The earlier they got into our territory, the safer they would be. The Turks agreed to do their best and promised that the family would be in Zahidan at the latest by 7.00 a.m. It was already late, so we decided to stay together until the newcomers were picked up and brought to the Royal Palace. Their fatigue was secondary to their safety which was our primary concern. Marzban completely agreed with this and Rauf and his unit were to take him to the airport as soon as our Turkish friend confirmed the arrival time.

We sat and waited anxiously. Our tension was exhibited by the poor quality of jokes and topics we discussed. At 4.30 a.m. we received the first good news. Our contact in Istanbul had successfully chartered a small aircraft which had already left Turkey. I felt a part of my tension relax. A possible assassination attempt in a foreign country where we had no control was now out of the question. Now I just had to protect Marzban's family upon their arrival in Southern Iran, where my faithful subjects were ready to protect them. Rauf and his officers had established radio contact with the pilot of the aircraft and he informed us that the plane was safely in our airspace and was expected to land in Zahidan in approximately thirty minutes. At his request, I allowed Marzban to go with them to the airport to welcome his family. I had some concerns about his safety at the airport, but Rauf assured me that he would be protected. I also made arrangements for Marzban and family to stay with us at the Royal Palace for their protection.

Approximately an hour later, I received a call from Rauf informing me that the family had arrived safely and had retired to their quarters. The relief I felt at this news was indeed refreshing. I felt a sense of exultation that I was successful in protecting the family of my dear friend and that I was able to keep my word that no harm would come to him or his kin.

The next morning at approximately 10.00 a.m. I received a telephone call from Marzban requesting permission to introduce his wife to me. I immediately agreed.

Marzban and his wife bowed to me, "Your Majesty, may I introduce my wife Karima, she is fluent in English, since she was educated in England. Your Majesty will be relieved to find someone with whom you can converse again."

"Welcome to Democratic Iran, Mrs. Marzban. Your husband must have already told you how much we appreciate his cooperation and efforts to bring this country into the twenty-first century. I have great affection and admiration for Behram. I've always admired people who have allowed logic and reasoning to change their way of thinking and their preferences. As his wife you will always be welcome in our residence and in our presence."

"Your Majesty, at this time, I'm trying to recover from the many surprises my husband has sprung on me. He left Iran as your sworn enemy and even though I'm a relatively good Muslim, I did not agree with many of his fanatical beliefs. Because he is a wonderful man, I have made the sacrifice of understanding and accepting these beliefs as trivial compared to what he has given me. I'm honoured that Your Majesty has condescended to welcome us into your royal presence."

For a minute I was totally shocked. Karima not only spoke English, but her accent was completely English. It was surprising that a woman who had lived most of her life in England had for some time at least compromised and accepted Marzban's rather rigid religious beliefs. I immediately concluded that this woman was not going to wear a pardah or play second fiddle to any man. I was therefore convinced that she really respected and loved her husband.

"Your Majesty, my beloved Karima is not only fluent in English but can also be quite vocal in Farsi when she disagrees with me," he said with a smile.

"That my dear friend Behram is a justifiable price one has to pay when one chooses to marry an intelligent and educated woman. With your intelligence you would never have been able to tolerate a passive and obedient wife whose only desire in life would have been the constant recounting of the trivial details of your children's routines."

Both of them started laughing. "I am indeed grateful for Your Majesty's kind words," Karima said. "Do I have your permission to use Your Majesty's approval as an argument when my husband tells me to fast and pray during Ramadan? Those rather tedious chores have been the most difficult part of my settling back in Iran."

The statement clearly indicated to me a loving and respectful relationship between this couple. After all they had come from the Islamic Republic of Iran and such a warm and open discussion would not be feasible in an average family in the North.

I now decided that it was the right time to appoint Marzban a Minister of the government. I had carefully thought and considered the portfolio to be given to him and I came to the conclusion that it would be that of Science and Technology. There was absolutely no question in my mind that he was qualified for the job.

There was another angle that I had considered. I was hoping as I had stated earlier, that contact between the different governors and other politicians in the Islamic Republic and Marzban, would perhaps turn them around and convince them to rebel against the Islamic Republic and join our cause. The portfolio 'Science and Technology' was so benign sounding that the Northerners would not become suspicious of any political motive.

CHAPTER 22.

The news regarding the appointment of Marzban as the Minister of Science and Technology in Democratic Iran seemed to have greatly shocked the sensibilities of the leaders and people of the Islamic Republic. The television news from the North described Marzban as a traitor who had sold Islam for dollars. Our informants had also told us that as soon as the Northern authorities found out about his appointment, they had raided the home in which he formerly resided. Instructions had been given to take members of Marzban's family into custody, presumably as hostages until Marzban surrendered. However, when they tried to execute this plan, they were unhappily surprised to find that everyone had moved away. I had reached a stage when I enjoyed the irrational statements made by their media.

When they found out that Marzban's family had moved south via Turkey, they labelled it a traitorous Muslim country which had abandoned Islam to please the infidel Shahnshah. The funniest part of this announcement was their description of me. They stated that I, the infidel Shahnshah, had demonic powers to remove the faith out of decent individuals and used these powers to convert law-abiding and pious Muslims like Marzban into a pagan like myself. They predicted that Allah was not going to sit quietly and let this happen and that my passage to hell was now guaranteed.

I normally listened to their nonsense in both Farsi and English and it was fascinating to note that the majority of the most absurd statements were only in Farsi. I concluded that they did not want their nonsense aired in English, as this would make them a laughing stock in the eyes of the rest of the world. This convinced me that the people who were in charge of controlling these programs were a lot more intelligent than they appeared to be.

The news bulletin had ended and as I was about to turn off my T.V. to go to bed, I heard and felt an enormous explosion. Articles and debris were strewed everywhere in the room. My first concern was Zainab's safety but I was relieved when she came running into my office.

"Oh my God! What was that?"

"I don't know!" Before I could say or do anything Rauf and three of his officers charged into the room.

"Are you all right Shahnshah? It looks like a bomb went off in the basement. Our first concern is to see that you are safe and we will start investigating!"

Zainab and I were both in shock and could not respond immediately. She was also dressed for bed and was embarrassed to be in the presence of so many military officers. They on the other hand were too preoccupied to notice her appearance. They bowed and left to investigate the bombing.

An hour later Rauf returned to my chamber and presented me with what appeared to be a plastic container. "Your Majesty, we found this in the debris. It appears to be plastic but it isn't. It is made of a fire resistant material and we are quite certain that it was left in the package on purpose. We opened it up and found a message addressed to you."

The contents looked like a folded letter without an envelope. I opened and read it. "Hey, pagan Shahnshah, if you're already dead as a result of our bomb this letter has no value. However, if you have escaped death, consider this a warning. Remove your sinful pagan carcass from my country. Go back to your pagan Canada and leave all Iran to us Shi'ites. If you have escaped death this time, you will not escape it the second time."

"I'm sure Your Majesty knows who wrote this. It has to be that evil bastard Manucher. His arrest and extermination are our top priority and I've already ordered my officers to concentrate on his arrest or extermination. As a matter of fact, I have given instructions, subject to your approval, that if he is found he should not be arrested but instantly shot."

"Yes Rauf, I completely approve. Several of our faithful employees have been killed by this monster. We should not give him a second chance."

"Your Majesty, this is not the only bomb that has exploded today. He has blown up a synagogue approximately twenty kilometres from here. Three other bombs were placed in three military installations. One of them was successfully disarmed but the other two detonated. Seventeen faithful officers of our Armed Forces have been killed. All the bombs contained a similar fireproof case and the message delivered was, `if you serve the pagan, you will die the death of a traitor.' The message at the synagogue read, `Empty my nation of all Jewish infidels or go to your Satan in little pieces.'

This news was very devastating to me. We had made so much progress. Thousands of Iranian citizens who had once been fanatics, had realized the error of their ways and most Muslims, Christians, Jews and Zoroastrians lived in harmony in our territory. What could I possibly do to stop this monster from killing innocent citizens? Our radio and television announcers had already been informed to broadcast the nature of these heinous deeds and we had requested the citizens to immediately inform us if the suspect whose description and photograph were televised, was seen anywhere in our territory.

It was interesting to note that not a word of these atrocities was mentioned by the media of the Islamic Republic. I was not certain whether they were ashamed of what one of their citizens had done or even worse, this atrocity was committed by him at their behest.

No point in worrying, I told myself. I had a highly qualified and perfectly trained investigating unit and sooner or later, this monster would be exterminated. In the meantime, I had several other important tasks to perform. Marzban had successfully contacted many governors, elected leaders and politicians in the Islamic Republic. He was concentrating only on those individuals for whom we had respect and who were well educated and enlightened. Several of these men had rudely called him a traitor and asked him to get lost. Others had tried to convince him that he should abandon his evil choice and come back to face the consequences in the Islamic Republic. A majority of his friends had not supported him but those who had a lot of influence in Iran, had the intelligence to realize that their own security was in danger. This was the reason they would communicate with him through third parties in our territory. It was therefore a situation where his logical arguments were winning him their support tacitly. One has to understand that open support for a man who was considered to be a traitor by the regime, would be extremely detrimental to them.

There were two Provincial Governors and two Generals of the Islamic Republic of Iran, who seemed to be converted to Marzban's point of view. Naturally there was no question of them coming to Southern Iran or Marzban going in that direction as that would mean certain death. Therefore once again, I requested the help of my Turkish friends without specifically telling them what the purpose of this meeting was. The Iranian officials from the north would travel to Turkey and their passports would be stamped indicating their entry into Turkey. Thereafter at our request, the Turks would let these individuals travel to Southern Iran without an exit stamp on their passports. At the end of the meeting they would fly back into Turkey and from there back to Iran. If they were questioned, they would say that they had spent all their vacation at a resort in Turkey.

It was a complete surprise to us when Marzban approached me to mention that General Raza Rahmani had indirectly contacted him and wanted to secretly visit us in Southern Iran. General Rahmani was no ordinary military officer of the Islamic Republic. He was one of the most brilliant generals the Regime ever had. He had been decorated for valor as well as brilliant strategy during the Iran-Iraq war. The most important point was that he was the General in charge of the nuclear weapons of Iran. Iran of course did not confess to possessing them but the rest of the world knew that they existed. The technical knowledge and skill which was required to man the missiles and to control and maintain them, were not possessed by any other officer in the service of the Islamic Republic. Above all, the General's integrity and loyalty to his country were totally beyond question. Therefore such a man seeking an audience with us was indeed a surprise and a very pleasant one.

We made the necessary arrangements for the General to fly into Turkey and then into Southern Iran and to secretly reside with Minister Behram. They came to my Palace in a civilian car and were taken into my private garage from where an elevator brought them directly to my office. As a necessary precaution, both visitors were passed through a weapons detection monitor. For the General's protection, none of my employees were present during the interview. I was extremely curious to meet this man about whom I had heard so much. I wanted to find out why he was so interested in meeting with us.

They both arrived and bowed to me. "Your Majesty, I have the privilege of introducing to you one of the greatest military officers of Iran. This is General Raza Rahmani". The General saluted me very crisply and even the salute indicated the smartness and discipline embodied in this officer. I got up and shook his hand.

"Welcome to Democratic Iran, General, please take a seat." The General did not sit down.

"Your Majesty, unfortunately I am totally unqualified in the nuances of diplomacy and behaviour before royalty. I seek your permission to come to the point immediately and to indicate to you the purpose of my visit."

"Your Majesty, as a General of the Iranian forces, I would have had no hesitation in fighting your armies and destroying your facilities where necessary. I do not agree with the fanatical thinking pattern of our regime, yet Your Majesty, as a loyal servant of the Islamic Republic, I have complied with every order issued by our government. As a military officer it is not my privilege to question the morality or ideals of my government. Needless to say, I would lay down my life for the Islamic Republic of Iran to protect it from attack or invasion. To be honest, Sir, I have not come to visit you because of a disagreement with the Iranian government or for any specific admiration for you or the democracy that you have created in the South. My reason for this visit is something that makes me ashamed of myself. I freely admit that I should be now labelled a traitor."

His words were so emotionally charged and he seemed to be so ashamed of himself that I did not know what to say. I was totally uncertain of his reasons for visiting me. I merely nodded for the General to continue.

"Your Majesty, I'm going to give you some information which definitely makes me a traitor. I humbly request that this information should not leave this room under any circumstances. I am not interested in my own personal security, but in that of thousands of innocent soldiers of the Islamic Republic." I nodded my assent.

"There is something even more important than the security of the Islamic Republic and that is the preservation of my fellow Iranians, whether they be in the South or in the North. We all know that slowly Southern Iran is occupying more and more of our territory. You have won the hearts and minds of a majority of Iranians and you have occupied more than forty percent of the territory of Iran. The government and leaders of the Islamic Republic have made a decision, which to my mind is totally unacceptable and criminal."

"They have ordered me to deploy our nuclear facilities. I am to fire a nuclear missile and completely annihilate Zahidan, your capital. For me, an Iranian officer, to shoot a nuclear device at Iranians whether they agree or disagree with us, is worse than a criminal offense. I will not comply with that order. I will not kill innocent fellow Iranians. I initially debated discussing this matter with the Prime Minister of the Islamic Republic and expressing my opposition. However, I soon realized that if I did so, I would be removed from my post and some other officer would take over and use the nuclear devices. Therefore, I kept my mouth shut and I've come here to prevent such a catastrophe."

Marzban and I both stood up in shock. We had anticipated any kind of violence from the North, but the thought that they would use a nuclear weapon against their own people never seemed a possibility. Every time we took a portion of the North, we were extremely careful to avoid any civilian casualties. What kind of sick moron would kill hundreds of thousands of his own people for political gain? I suddenly realized that I was tongue-tied and had no solutions to offer. Marzban was dumbfounded as well.

"Well, General, I. don't know what to say. We profusely thank you for bringing this to our attention. You are the military officer! You guide us as to what should be done!"

"Yes, Your Majesty. This is the most shameful part of what I have to do. The military unit in charge of the nuclear facilities is completely under my control and loyal to me. Under no circumstances will they disobey my orders. I've already talked to several of the senior officers in my regiment and they have agreed to comply with my orders. I would request Your Majesty to send two military units to a specific area of

Iran. I will inform you as soon as I've communicated with my army units and have coordinated the arrival of your forces to that location. Your troops can then cross the border and they will be welcomed by my units which will surrender the area to your forces. As a matter of fact, our forces will help you occupy the whole region and territory where our nuclear facilities are located. It will then become part of Your Majesty's territory. I have calculated that after the occupation of this area, Your Majesty will be the Shahnshah of sixty percent of Iran. For being a traitor, I do not want money or power. I want your word of honor that the soldiers of my unit will be treated with respect and not as prisoners of war. After the necessary evaluations are completed and they are found to be loyal, let them join the Shahnshah's forces. Then Your Majesty, with your permission, let me retire from the Army and spend the rest of my life in shame as a defector and a traitor."

"I, as the Shahnshah of Iran, give you my word of honor that my troops will never attack your soldiers, unless it is in self-defence. I also give you my word that after the necessary inquiries, they will be permitted to freely settle in Democratic Iran. We will do our utmost to bring their families into Southern Iran through other countries. Our investigators will check each soldier and if we are satisfied that they will faithfully serve Southern Iran, they will be accepted as soldiers of our country. They can also retain their military ranks. The only area, General, where I will not comply with your request is to let you resign and die in shame as you put it."

Let me explain something to you. A man follows his conscience, sacrifices all his principles, abandons all his beliefs. He relinquishes his career to protect the people of his nation. Should I allow a man of such integrity to wither away in solitude when he has saved the lives of hundreds of thousands of our countrymen? No General, your request is not granted. I am requesting you for something. Do not deprive Iran of such an able officer of integrity. Join our forces as a General."

"I'm very grateful for your Majesty's kind words but, a traitor is not a good officer. Even if you trust and respect me, I cannot trust and respect myself."

"You are approximately twenty years younger than me. You are brilliant and disciplined, but once in your life concede to the wisdom of an older man who has seen life as you would never have and hopefully never will. You are wrong in condemning yourself. No one should be ashamed of himself for saving the lives of hundreds of thousands of innocent people. You are in our territory and can become my subject. As the Shahnshah of Iran, I demand that you be my friend," I said with a smile.

The General turned away. I thought that he had tears in his eyes, which he was ashamed to show. I allowed him his privacy and changed the subject.

Behram got up and hugged the General. "From this day, you are not just my brother, you are my respected brother. A man whose friendship makes me proud. Do not despair. You have a brilliant future in a free country, I give you my word of honor."

The General kept his word. My troops entered the district where he was the commanding officer. His troops surrendered, all the nuclear weapons were confiscated and the whole area was annexed to Democratic Iran.

I received this happy news and sent a message to the General to visit me the following morning as I wanted to thank and reward him.

I was awakened at midnight by a call from Marzban. "Your Majesty, General Raza Rahmani is dead. He committed suicide. He shot himself!"

Time has not mitigated my sorrow at the loss of such a wonderful, brave man and to this day, I still feel the anguish I felt that night.

CHAPTER 23.

The diminishing rhetoric from the leaders of the Islamic Republic was indeed noticeable. The daily news broadcasts which condemned us as infidels who were ruining Iran and Islam had greatly reduced. I had anticipated this change and was not surprised. All the nuclear facilities with its weaponry were now under my control. The Islamic Republic was quite concerned that we might use their own weapons against them. My media experts had not hesitated to tell the people of Iran that the Islamic Republic had initially planned to use these nuclear weapons against their own people. In support of this statement we had used the evidence provided by the late General Raza Rahmani. My experts believed that the Iranian people on both sides of the border had accepted this evidence and were disgusted at the thought that the Islamic Republic would even consider such a barbarous act. There was no doubt in my mind that with our enhanced industrial capacity and with the newly acquired nuclear weapons, the Islamic Republic was now quite concerned about its own existence and was perhaps ready to make a deal with us.

There was another interesting development. The United States of America, the European Union and many other countries, who had insisted that Iran discontinue the manufacture of nuclear weapons, had suddenly become quite silent in their opposition. I now realized why. The Islamic Republic, with its religious fanaticism was a danger to the non-Muslim world. We on the other hand, were a developing peaceful nation, which had strictly controlled the involvement of religion in our governance. We would have no reason to attack any other nation. In the past, Iran was considered the greatest threat to the existence of Israel, but now they were our allies. As a matter-of-fact, our nuclear weapons were now a threat to the Islamic Republic. This was considered a plus by the Europeans and Americans. All talk of nuclear disarmament on the part of Iran had ceased.

Lately, the Islamic Republic had been hinting at a possible concord between our two nations. My reaction to this so-called peace offer was very simple. There was going to be only one Iran and that would be Democratic Iran. The Islamic Republic had the option of completely surrendering its territory to us and becoming part of our nation. I had made it very clear to them that under no circumstances would we use the nuclear weapons on our citizens but, every step would be taken to crush the Islamic Republic and annex it. We had no place for a fanatical, theological regime in the twenty-first century. This would be an insult to the sophisticated and highly cultured traditions of our ancient Iran.

In spite of this harsh response, the Islamic Republic continued to make several overtures to negotiate with us, but at no time was there an offer to surrender its territory to us.

Manucher was now depicted by the Islamic Republic as a great hero fighting for the preservation of Islam and the culture of Iran. It was my policy not to just listen to their propaganda, but to investigate the effect it had on the common people. My experts told me that the average Iranian even in the Islamic Republic was disgusted with this brute and his activities. He had recently succeeded in blowing up one of our railway trains that was supposed to transport troops to the border. Luckily, it was empty at the time it was blown up. Knowing the psychology and vanity of this uneducated man, our propaganda experts had decided to ridicule Manucher as an inept terrorist. I was quite amused by the description they had given him. They labelled him `the brainless brute.'

Statistics indicated to us that if there was a free vote in the Islamic Republic, seventy to eighty percent of the citizens were in favour of joining us to form a united Iran.

It had been a very eventful day. A number of European nations and the United States, which had initially ignored our existence, were suddenly offering to protect us from the Islamic Republic, at a time when we did not need any protection.

I tiptoed into my bedroom to avoid disturbing Zainab. I gently laid down beside her and turned to look at her. Each time I looked at her I was amazed at her beauty and could not imagine what this lovely woman was doing in the bed of an old man like me. She seemed to be fast asleep.

"Even the Shahnshah of Iran must realize politics is not his only duty. He also owes a duty to his woman." She hugged me, pressing every inch of her delicious body against me. I kissed and she responded passionately. "Take me my Shahnshah, you have been too busy and have ignored your woman for too long. I want my man inside me!"

I did not need persuasion. My seventy one year old frame was twenty again. In a flash she had undressed and we were making love. When we were done, I held her in my arms and against my heart.

"See Shahnshah, even powerful monarchs like you are in need of women like me to reduce you to your proper size."

CHAPTER 24.

Manucher had now become the single greatest curse my country faced. He was solely responsible for blowing up two synagogues, four military hospital locations, one Sunni mosque and a railway train. He had also successfully detonated devices aimed at military camps causing considerable loss of life. His picture and a description of his voice pattern, was announced on television both in the South and North. We had requested all our citizens and also those of the Islamic Republic, to help us track down this manic terrorist. Our investigators had almost arrested him on several occasions, but somehow, he was smart enough to anticipate their moves and managed to escape. Our experts had told us that one of the reasons that it was so difficult to trace him was the fact that he always acted alone and had no accomplices.

In the early stages of his activities we were absolutely certain that he was funded by the government of the Islamic Republic, but since our taking over of their nuclear facilities, they were anxious not to rile us, hence the funding that he received had ceased. The evidence of this was that Manucher had recently taken to robbing banks. It was rumoured that he had succeeded in obtaining approximately six million US dollars by robbing our financial institutions. Several citizens had given us information with which we were trying to track him down. A very large reward had been offered to anyone who facilitated his arrest.

I was having a discussion with our police officers when my bodyguard came and whispered in my ear that my chief investigator,

Rauf, wanted to immediately see me in private. I left the assembly room for my office and Rauf was ushered in.

"I apologize for the inconvenience, Your Majesty. This is urgent and I thought it is imperative for you to meet with this person."

"Who is this person and what is it about?"

"A citizen claims that she has some very pertinent information regarding the habits and whereabouts of Manucher. She absolutely refuses to talk to anyone and insists that this information is for Your Majesty's ears only."

"Who is this woman?"

Rauf had a mischievous leer on his face. "Does Your Majesty wish for a description of this woman or that of her occupation?"

Rauf noticed the confusion in my expression and smiled. "Your Majesty, she is Fatima Abbasi. Sir, to put it politely, she is a very famous courtesan from the city of Isfahan."

"Rauf, don't you think I'm a little old for such company?" He responded with a laugh.

"Your Majesty, as she insists that the information will be provided to you in private, I will never know of Your Majesty's response to her charms. I will say one thing sir. We have checked her very thoroughly for weapons and she is safe. As a matter-of-fact, the body search conducted by our officers was more than thorough. Once you see her, Your Majesty will understand why our officers were so enthusiastic." We both laughed.

Rauf left my office, ushered the woman in and closed the door. "Your Majesty, this is Fatima Abbasi. She wants to provide some significant information to Your Majesty in private. May I be excused sir?"

He bowed and left the room closing the door behind him.

Fatima bowed deeply to me. To put it mildly, she was absolutely gorgeous. She was about five feet six inches tall, with a very fair complexion. Her figure would have made Marilyn Monroe jealous. She had blue eyes with long eyelashes. The combined effect of which would have been disastrous to me had I been twenty years younger. When she looked at me, I realized that she knew exactly how beautiful she was and was accustomed to the effect her looks had on men. I decided to fool myself by thinking of her as some one who was young enough to be my daughter. All but one part of my anatomy accepted this obfuscation.

"Please sit down Madam, what can I do for you?"

She sat down and looked straight into my eyes with a smile.

"My Shahnshah, how does a poor courtesan thank Your Majesty for giving an audience to my unworthy self?" I observed that apart from her physical beauty, she also had a beautiful voice.

Madam, let us cut out the formalities and get to the point. I have been informed that you have some pertinent information regarding a very vicious and violent criminal by the name of Manucher. Am I correct?"

I could see a flash of anger in her eyes. She must have realized that I had seen through her coquetry. However she immediately recovered and gave me an enchanting smile, bowing to me as if she was submitting to my command.

"Your Majesty is absolutely right. From the news reports I've obtained, the description of this criminal Manucher completely matches one of my generous customers. During my dealings with him, he has been extremely generous in rewarding me for my services; however, I can sense a certain viciousness in this man and have to remain constantly on guard not to offend him because I believe he's capable of incredible violence, if provoked. Your Majesty, if my information helps you arrest this man, then I hope you will compensate me adequately so that I may use those funds to protect myself."

I clearly understood her intent from those convoluted words. She was basically telling me that she would provide that information only if she was adequately rewarded.

"Madam, this man Manucher is a very dangerous and violent criminal. If your information is correct and we are able to arrest him, we will reward you with one hundred thousand American dollars."

She gave me a lascivious smile and bowed. "Your Majesty's generosity has no limits. Your humble servant will provide you with any service that you may require."

I pretended that I did not understand what she was saying. "Madam, let us now proceed with the details of what you have to say. Be assured that your name or the source of this information will never leave this room. Your security will be looked after. You will have nothing to fear from Manucher."

"Your Majesty, he visits with me every Wednesday or Thursday night and stays until the morning. He is rather aggressive and demanding and sometimes hurts me. However, if I ask him to be gentle, he complies. He pays me a very large sum of money which amply compensates for his roughness."

"Have you by any chance found out where he resides or do you have any other pertinent information of his activities?"

"Your Majesty, every time he goes to the bathroom, I go through his pockets to find out anything about him. I have never found any photographs or addresses, but I've found credit cards in the name of Abbas Malik, so I presume that that is his alias. One credit card had an address on it which was 47 Raza Boulevard in Zahidan. I tried to find that address and was surprised that there is no such address in the city of Zahidan. Before this happened, I was not certain that this man was Manucher, but after the discovery of false documents in his wallet, I am quite certain that he is the man Your Majesty's police are after."

"All right, Madam, this is what I suggest we do. I will give you a little device which looks like a wristwatch. You will wear it from now on. It has some other attractive features and no one will know what it is. When Manucher visits you, just press this button and we will immediately know that he is at your place. Our officers will then surround the building and arrest him. You will pretend that you do not know what is going on."

"Your Majesty, with the utmost respect, I do not think you understand this man you call Manucher. If he suspects that I am involved, he will not need evidence to kill me. Another great concern to me is that if he realizes that my residence is surrounded by the police, he will not hesitate to take me hostage to use as a bargaining tool to escape custody. I'm trying to do my duty as your loyal subject, but Your Majesty, my life is more important to me than any patriotism."

I could sense two very significant qualities in this woman. There was a streak of incredible harshness camouflaged by her incredible beauty, but there was also significant evidence of intelligence.. This woman was here to make her hundred thousand dollars. She had considered every angle and had decided exactly how much risk she was willing to take. Frankly, I admired her and at the same time, I pitied any man who would be foolish enough to take her as a life partner. How could you blame a prostitute for doing the utmost to protect herself? I realized that the two concerns she had mentioned were absolutely legitimate.

"Madam, I think you have made a good point. Manucher is quite capable of doing what you say he might do. I will do even more to protect you. As soon as you press that button on your wrist watch, the police will be dispatched to your residence. Before they surround your residence, you will receive a telephone call telling you that the new furniture you had ordered will be delivered in the morning. When you receive this call, tell Manucher that you have to go to the washroom and lock the door. Early tomorrow morning, your bathroom door will be changed to a bullet and explosion resistant one. When locked, no one will be able to open it from the outside.

Once you are safely locked in, press the button on your wrist watch again and our troops will move in to arrest Manucher. This way, he will not be able of either hurt you or take you hostage."

She nodded, but I could see her shiver inadvertently. Fear under these circumstances was quite natural and expected. At the same time her strength and determination were equally visible. I felt sorry for a girl with so many excellent qualities who had to live her life as a common prostitute.

I decided to give her an opportunity to live a civilized life by obtaining education and perhaps to settling down as a decent citizen of Democratic Iran.

There was no news for several days. I had left strict instructions with Rauf that I should be informed of any new developments as soon as they occurred. We did not expect Manucher to get caught over night but, at the same time, he had not visited Fatima in a while and this concerned me since it could be an indication that he had learned of our contact with her. If that was the case, she was in great jeopardy in spite of the continuing surveillance of her house.

It was about 10:30 p.m. when I received an emergency call from Rauf. "Your Majesty, Fatima has just given us the alarm signal indicating the arrival of Manucher at her residence. Our forces have covertly surrounded her property. Would Your Majesty like me to keep you fully informed on developments?"

"Yes Rauf, I do. I want you to update me on the proceedings throughout the night."

"I will do that, Your Majesty."

It was difficult for me to go to sleep as I felt guilty we may have put a young woman's life in jeopardy in order to arrest a brutal murderer. However, I consoled myself that she had voluntarily done this for financial reasons. I also had full confidence in Rauf's ability and was quite certain that he would protect her in every way possible. After all, the danger to our policemen was possibly greater than to Fatima. Why was I worried about her more? Was the fear coming from my head or another part of my anatomy?

Rauf's second telephone call came at approximately three o'clock in the morning. "Your Majesty, there was the second alarm. As you remember that indicates that Fatima is safely locked in her bathroom. We will now enter her house to arrest the criminal."

"We have identified the vehicle in which he drove to Fatima's house and we have successfully tampered with the engine so there is no fear of him escaping. Our equipment has indicated to us that there are no explosive devices in the vehicle. However, we cannot be certain that he has not taken any such devices into her house. We have taken all precautions to protect her Your Majesty, but I cannot help saying that with a man like Manucher, there is always the possibility of something which we may not have anticipated. Are there any other commands or questions that Your Majesty has?"

"No Rauf, I have full faith in you and your ability to successfully conduct this operation. However, if there is a choice between arresting this culprit and endangering Fatima's life, let him escape."

"As you command, Your Majesty."

I tried to sleep after the telephone call but remained awake, constantly hoping that the telephone would ring.

It was about 6 a.m. when the telephone did ring. I quickly grabbed it and was about to ask Rauf what had happened when I heard the caller laughing uproariously in my ear. I was totally surprised when I realized that this was not Rauf. My number was private and available only to Rauf. Who could this be?

"Good morning you pagan bastard. You have outdone yourself this time by working in cahoots with a whore and sacrificing the lives of innocent young Iranian men. But then, what can one expect from a pagan and an enemy of Islam? I wish you a good night's sleep tonight. I hope you have pleasant dreams of your achievement and the deaths of eight young Iranian boys. By the way pagan, from my healthy voice you must have realized that I am alive and kicking. Eagerly awaiting the opportunity to slit your filthy throat!"

He hung up before I could respond. Needless to say I did not have any doubts who the caller was. One does not easily forget the voice of a monster like Manucher.

Zainab saw my anguish and asked what had happened. I summarized the situation. She hugged and consoled me and went off to make some coffee. The telephone rang again. It was Rauf. I had never heard a voice so dejected and sad. "Your Majesty, I'm making this call to admit to you that I have been a failure. That bastard anticipated every single step we intended to take. As I mentioned, he had taken some explosive devices into Fatima's house. Fatima did successfully lock herself in her bathroom and he did attempt to break down the door. Our first sign of trouble was when he disconnected the fuse in the house and it became dark. He must have had night vision glasses, because he fired at my officers from various windows of the house killing four of them. As we had surrounded the house and were about to enter the officers were totally exposed. Before we even knew what was happening, there was a tremendous explosion and the whole house, except for a small portion of it, was demolished. The debris injured two of my men but that is minor. Before we could arm ourselves, the culprit disappeared into the blackness of the night. One other reason for us not immediately tracking him down was our concern to save Fatima."

"After he escaped we combed the whole area using tracking devices and equipment, but to no avail. He had vanished into thin air."

"Is Fatima dead?" I asked.

"Your Majesty, the only consolation and good news I have for you is that she is safe and uninjured. That armoured door withstood the explosion itself even though the whole house collapsed around the bath room. She is in shock and very nervous, but she is alive and well. I thought I had done everything in my power to prevent this from happening Your Majesty, I have failed."

I was consoled by the thought that the woman who tried to help us was safe. My concern was also for Rauf. "My son, you have done your best. You have saved our informer. Do not worry, we will ultimately catch this beast."

I was also quite impressed with the fact that Fatima had not contacted us to collect the reward. Conceded that the agreement was that if we arrested the accused because of her help, we would pay her and as we were unable to arrest him we could renege on the offer. In reality, the arrest was not completed, not from any lack of cooperation on her part, but because our officers had not anticipated all his moves. I had decided that she would receive her reward to compensate her for the anguish and fear she must have suffered and the human decency of not immediately coming to claim the money. I also felt that it was my duty as the Shahnshah of Iran to somehow convince this talented young woman to abandon her dubious profession and qualify herself for something more useful in life. I summoned her into my presence.

The next morning she was escorted into my office by two police officers. She was now on round-the-clock security protection and was not allowed to travel anywhere by herself. Anyone visiting her was carefully checked before being allowed on her premises.

She approached me and bowed. "Shahnshah-e-Iran, I am here, pursuant to your command."

I was watching her very carefully. A certain very noticeable change was visible in this girl. The beauty and charm were still present, but there was a certain nervousness in her expressions. Moreover, the seductive coquetry was missing. Over the years, as a chartered accountant, and particularly when dealing with my extremely polite but not expressive Japanese clients, I had learned to read the expressions of people and not just listen to them talk. People can lie, only geniuses can lie with their expressions. I was therefore extremely curious as to what transformation had occurred in this girl and what had caused the change in her personality.

"Fatima, how come you did not approach us for your reward?"

For a few seconds she seemed confused and silent, which indicated to me a significant change in her personality.

Very hesitantly, she said. "Your Majesty, your officers were unable to arrest Manucher so why would I be entitled to a reward?"

"You did what you were expected to do, if my officers were unable to arrest the criminal that is not your fault."

Again, there was that pregnant silence, an expression of embarrassment and the incapacity to articulate. These qualities in this woman were completely alien. Very softly she whispered something which I did not hear, since it seemed to be for her own ears only.

This is when I finally decided that as the Shahnshah of Iran, it was my duty to remove this woman from her present environment and place her into the productive world we were trying to create.

"Sit down Fatima and listen to me very carefully. As the Shahnshah of Iran, my job is not only to rule the country but to improve the life and well-being of every citizen. I can possibly help. Let me enumerate the qualities I see in you. I know that you are completely aware of your beauty and that you are a very intelligent woman. I have absolutely no idea how good-natured you are, but in your occupation there is very little place to be good-natured. From the way you have handled the traumatic experience you just had, I'm satisfied that you're a very strong woman. The transformation of your personality after the traumatic experience indicates to me that whatever good nature you initially had, was forced deeper into you. Let us look at what things are lacking in your life."

"You are living the life of a courtesan, are constantly on guard and do not have the time to be kind and loving to the people you are associating with. This is not an indication of harshness, only the evidence of not having enough opportunity to demonstrate inherent kindness. Naturally, with the right opportunity, those qualities will automatically develop. You probably have very little formal education, which can be easily remedied, because you have the brains to study. Tell me, with all these hidden talents which one have you used in making your life? Only one, your beauty to seduce your clients to make a living. I am going to provide you with the opportunity to develop your talents. Are you interested?"

There was absolute shock on her face. Then, without any warning, she was crying. I placed my hand on her shoulder. "Fatima, I am like your father. As a matter of fact, I would be very surprised if you ever had a father who loved and cared for you. Stop crying and tell me all about your background. I will see to it that your future is bright. You will succeed if you follow my instructions."

"My Shahnshah, my background was very evil and painful. My father was an evil brutal man. He used to constantly beat my mother and his two mistresses. My mother died when I was four years old. No one knows what caused her death. My suspicion is that she died of injuries he had inflicted on her. He was very closely connected with the religious hierarchy of the village and it is my belief that they did not investigate the cause of my mother's death, since they wanted to protect him. He used to physically assault me until I was twelve, then he started assaulting me sexually. I attempted to tell my teachers at school, they just scolded me for imagining things to hurt my poor decent religious father. I had no help and no mother to go to. There was no family left on my mother's side. I had noticed in school, that most of the boys were interested in me and found me attractive. One day, a teacher at my religious madrasa befriended me, he appeared to be very sympathetic and kind, I told him my story. He sympathized and offered me an escape; by this time I was sixteen. He offered to marry me. Certainly he was not the most intelligent or handsome man I had seen or met, but he appeared to be kind, so out of desperation, I accepted his offer, basically to get away from my brutal father. He told me that my father would never accept him as a son-in-law and therefore we should elope, to which I agreed. He drove me to Teheran, took me to a hotel room and basically raped me. The agreement was for us to get married but all he wanted was a mistress. In those days I was a religious girl and did not want to live in what I considered sin. Where could I go? Every evening he would come back to rape me. If I objected, he would beat me mercilessly. Even if I did not object, he used to hurt me on purpose because he was a sadist. I had to do his cooking, cleaning, house work and provide him with sex and for my reward, I was constantly beaten."

"One day I was shopping for groceries and was short of money at the counter. A very decent looking well-dressed man offered to make up the difference. I initially refused to accept the offer, but he seemed kind and I accepted. Every few days, I would see him at the supermarket and we would talk. One day he suggested that I should meet his wife and family and I agreed to accompany him to his house.

The drive was taking too long and I was a bit concerned about not getting home in time for my brutal keeper. When I objected to the long drive, an incredible transformation occurred in this man. He stopped the car, punched me in the face, handcuffed me and threw me into the backseat. He drove me all the way from Teheran to Zahidan . He stopped for a couple of bathroom visits and for meals, which I had to eat in the car. After arriving in Zahidan, he took me to a house where he lived alone and continually raped me. When he left home, I was handcuffed and left in the basement. This went on for approximately a month, before he brought a second woman, whom he treated exactly like me. As a matter of fact, he seemed to enjoy raping each of us in the presence of the other. If we cried, he exulted. I presume he liked the other girl more than me, because about a month later, he tied me up, put me in his car and drove me to a house in a seedy part of town where he sold me to the head pimp, thereby making me a prostitute. This continued for approximately a year and that pimp died. Interestingly enough, the pimp sold me to men but never assaulted me. Strange as it may seem, that man was less cruel to me than my father or the one who was supposed to become my husband. After the pimp died, I saw my opportunity and I escaped. By this time, several policemen and military men were my customers. They promised to protect me if I set up my own establishment. The men who had bought me were threatened with death if they touched me, so they left me alone. That is when I learnt that the only weapon with which I could protect myself was my beauty and my capacity to control the men in my life. Your Majesty, you now have the complete confession of a whore."

Talking of transformations, at one time I had found this girl sexually provoking and attractive, now, I felt that she was like my daughter, who needed my protection. That protection, I decided to give her for life. I stood up, asked her to stand up and hugged her. "Fatima, the confession you have made to me must have hurt you tremendously. I am thankful to you for your trust in me. I give you my word of honor that as the Shahnshah of Iran, from this moment on, you are my daughter and I will be your father. I promise you, I will be a better father than your real one.

She was now crying uncontrollably. "Thank you my Shahnshah, I will be grateful to you for the rest of my life and I will be your slave."

"That is a ridiculous statement. I do not want a slave. I want a daughter. As of today, you will not call me Shahnshah in private. You can either call me Sharuq or you can call me Dad.

She had a benign sweet smile on her face, something I had never seen before. She looked deep into my eyes.

"Thank you, my dad, I love you, at last I have a father."

I handed her the envelope with a cheque for one hundred thousand dollars.

"This is your reward and compensation for the anguish you have suffered."

"I do not really deserve this. Especially since today, for the first time in my life, I feel like a normal human being with a real family."

With a teasing smile I said, "You will feel even better with a hundred thousand dollars in your bank account."

Later that day, upon my specific instructions, Fatima was admitted to the Faculty of Business and Accounting at the University of Zahidan which had now become the most significant educational institution in Iran.

CHAPTER 25,

Ayatollah Tabrizi and I had not met for a considerable period of time. Tabrizi was busy convincing the opponents of our State that fanatical Islam was not the answer or solution to Iran's problems. All over Southern Iran, he had attended religious and other seminars attempting to convince Iranians that one's belief in one's religion was a personal affair and not something which should be imposed on others, or their children. He lectured on the need to completely accept the Jews, Christians and Zoroastrians as citizens of Iran and give them equal rights. This transformation into a civilized thinker, especially since he grew up as a religious fanatic, was indeed a compliment to his intelligent and receptive mind. An Ayatollah, speaking on behalf of all the minorities and supporting their rights, had tremendous benefits for the people of Iran. His reputation as a scholar convinced them that if he believed in the equality of all people, then that must be the correct interpretation of the teachings of the Koran.

I was delighted to hear that Ayatollah Tabrizi had come to Zahidan and wanted to meet with me. I immediately invited him over for dinner.

After the usual formalities and exchange of news, the Ayatollah sat down in front of me and I noticed that he seemed to be very seriously considering something.

"Shahnshah-e-Iran, I have a rather serious matter to discuss with you. You are quite aware of the fact that I am a complete supporter of your views, policies and government. I do not claim any credit for this, it is your Majesty's brilliant mind and logical thinking that has converted me into a rational human being without the need to abandon my faith. There are many like me now in Southern Iran. As far as the religious hierarchy is concerned, a majority of religious leaders, imams and ayatollahs grudgingly accept our concept of equal rights for all citizens of every religion and creed. I was therefore absolutely amazed when nine mullahs, who are known for being extremely traditional, approached me to inform me about a plot to assassinate or remove Your Majesty from the throne of Iran. Your Majesty, a couple of years ago, these very men would have willingly participated in the effort to oust you. They do not believe in the total equality of non Shi'ite Iranians. They still crave for an Iran that is completely Shi'ite Muslim, but your Majesty, you have performed a miracle. You have convinced them of your wisdom and nobility and surprisingly, not only have they become your loyal subjects, but would happily sacrifice their lives to protect you and your government. You see, your Majesty, these men may be slightly bigoted, but they are not totally stupid. They have seen the enormous progress you have brought to Southern Iran. They now enjoy security and peace and they are without any doubt, your loyal subjects. It is they who brought this matter to my attention and assured me that under no circumstances would they countenance a revolt of any kind against their beloved Shahnshah."

Tabrizi must have seen by the expression on my face that I was very touched by these words but would prefer if he came to the point right away. He smiled.

"We all know about that monster Manucher. Even the most bigoted Iranians were disgusted when they heard of the death of those innocent young soldiers who were doing their duty. This Manucher is now approaching all the ayatollahs and imams and asking for their support to overthrow Your Majesty's Government. He is seeking funds and volunteers and has requested them to convince young Iranians to join him in this nefarious endeavour. These religious leaders were smarter than I thought they were. They did not refuse him but instead, they said they needed time to arrange for what he had requested. That way they would keep contact with him and would know exactly which way he was proceeding. They called me with information of the conspiracy.

If that is not loyalty for your Majesty, what is?."

"What do you suggest we do Ayatollah?"

"Your Majesty, I may have some ideas of the strategy on dealing with these people but I have no qualifications to advise you on the handling of this matter by the police or the military."

"I think I know what we should do. I will summon my most efficient police and military officer Rauf, who will deal with the physical aspect of this operation. I am requesting you to cooperate with him and advise him on dealing with those imams and mullahs."

Tabrizi nodded in assent. I immediately called Rauf to the palace and suggested that it was quite important. Within thirty minutes, Rauf was in my office.

The Ayatollah and I both explained the situation to him. Rauf was also very impressed that these religious men had sided with us and not the religious fanatic, Manucher. With his agile mind, he had a basic idea within minutes. I noticed grim determination on his face. "Your Majesty, I have two ambitions in my life. The first is to serve you at any cost and in any way I can. My second ambition is to kill this monster. I feel personally responsible for the loss of my men and the only way that I will recover from this anguish is to see Manucher in his grave."

The three of us discussed the steps and all the nuances with the possible results. Then Rauf came up with a final plan. Approximately one hundred perfectly trained military officers will independently go to meet the religious heads whom Manucher had approached. They will take weapons with them. The mullahs will see to it that these men are dressed like very devout Muslims and they will be introduced as such to Manucher. The weapons they take with them will be the genuine ones. They will be demonstrated to Manucher so that he's convinced of their efficacy. This is only a token demonstration, as the remaining weapons to be provided later will be the fake ones. These men will conspire with Manucher on how they will secretly install an explosive device in the Royal Palace or blow my vehicle up as I was traveling from the palace to another destination.

As these negotiations are proceeding, they will carefully investigate Manucher's contacts and their locations and most significantly, his hiding place. A fake plan will then be completed and he will be lured into joining them. Knowing Manucher, he will never miss the opportunity to participate in assassinating or capturing me. After all, a fanatic like Manucher cannot survive without engaging in the overthrow of the pagan's regime, as he calls our State.

I left strict instructions with Rauf that no person involved in the previous attempt to arrest Manucher be a part of this endeavour. A familiar face will make him suspicious causing him to escape once again. Rauf indicated to me that Ismail Farzana, an extremely intelligent and well-trained military officer, will be the leader of this new group. His first priority will be to meet with Manucher and to convince him of his own dedication to Islam, hatred for the pagan Shahnshah and his deep-seated ambition to rid his beloved Iran of all non-Shi'ite elements.

Our meeting ended that night after this discussion. I specifically instructed him to inform me of every single development.

A couple of weeks later, Rauf returned to my office. "Your Majesty, the basic plan has now been completed. Some of the mullahs introduced Ismail Farzana to Manucher. Ismail seems to have been able to convince Manucher of his authenticity. Initially, Manucher refused to meet with him or to let him know where he was. All communication was completed by e-mail. As they became better acquainted, Manucher agreed to meet with Ismail and drive him to a remote area where they were to discuss the plan. Every time they met, Manucher decided on the location and arranged the transportation. After a few meetings, he seemed to have been convinced that Ismail was a genuine enemy of the Shahnshah and a willing participant in an effort to oust Your Majesty. We have allowed Ismail some leeway in becoming more intimate with Manucher."

"Excellent work Rauf! Do not forget to keep me continuously informed."

CHAPTER 26.

"My beloved brother and leader, salaam alaikum. It has been several days since I had the pleasure of your company and the privilege to learn the wisdom and faith that you always provide me with. I've generated what I consider to be a very good plan for our future activities. Naturally, it is subject to your guidance and approval," Ismail said.

"Manucher looked him in the eye and nodded, "Tell me about it."

"Brother Manucher, I think the first thing that all of us should do is go on a pilgrimage to the grave of Ayatollah Siddiqui. A serious and dangerous endeavour like ours should not be commenced without the blessings of Allah and his Holy Imam. I will make a public announcement that a number of us devout Muslims are going on this pilgrimage. The moment they hear the word `pilgrimage,' their interest in checking us out will be reduced. However, since the police are on full alert at this time, they will definitely check our buses which will be good since there will be no weapons on any bus. Approximately three kilometres from the place of the pilgrimage, there is an abandoned factory which is private. This is where we will load the weapons and explosives. We will then return to Zahidan taking the same route which we had taken to go on the pilgrimage. Hopefully the same guards will be present. The chances are that since we are returning from a pilgrimage, we won't be searched and if they do search us, our bus has specially built compartments under the seats. It is highly unlikely that the police will be looking for weapons. In any event, we will be one hundred armed men who can without any difficulty, exterminate the search team and any others."

Manucher nodded in agreement.

"There is one thing that I will insist upon Ismail. Before we load the bus with these weapons, I would like to personally check every corner of the factory for its safety. I will also personally install some explosive devices in both vehicles just in case we are ever in a situation of being discovered. I want to be sure that the enemy is blown to bits. Every single policeman and army officer serving the pagan King is an enemy of Allah and his extermination is the religious duty of every devout Muslim. Do you agree?"

In spite of all his preparations, Ismail was stunned with the innate brutality of that statement. He realized that in spite of all his prior preparations, his shock was observed by Manucher, whose only reaction was to stare straight into his eyes without any change of expression.

"Brother Manucher, is there not a danger of the bus accidentally blowing up in case of any defects in these explosives?"

"Trust me Ismail, I know exactly what I'm doing. I will not endanger any of our lives!"

"Brother Manucher, we will comply with your decision."

"Have you determined the location and manner in which we are going to blow up that pagan bastard?"

"I have studied every aspect of it. Our first choice is to blow up the limousine in which the Shahnshah will be traveling to Parliament building. This is far easier than planting hundreds of explosive devices and then trying to simultaneously trigger them next to the palace. On Wednesday, the 17th of August, the Shahnshah is expected to go to the legislature building to address Parliament. Thousands of people line the streets to watch him pass by. We will all be dressed as Muslim pilgrims returning from a pilgrimage and well in advance of his trip we will park our buses and join these masses. When the time is right, we will detonate the devices. The buses will blow up and so will the Shahnshah and his limousine."

"Aren't you concerned about hundreds of innocent Muslims being killed in that same explosion?" Manucher asked with a twinkle in his eye.

"Those who stand in line to watch the pagan bastard pass by are not devout Muslims. They are admirers of the pagan, their extermination is our duty!" As he uttered these words, Ismail realized that he was being carefully observed by Manucher. He said those words with fanatical emphasis, but did not fail to notice that their impact on Manucher was less than what he had desired.

In response, Manucher merely nodded.

As agreed, they all went on the pilgrimage and after their seemingly devout praying; they went to the abandoned factory. As per Manucher's wishes, he was allowed to install his explosive devices in the buses by himself without the presence of any of the military officers.

On the way out to the shrine, the police checked their buses and found them clean. After the buses were loaded with the explosives, Manucher insisted that they not travel on the main highway to Zahidan, but take smaller inner roads into the city as a precaution. Every one thought this was a sensible thing to do and complied.

Ismail was always extremely uncomfortable in his relationship with Manucher. Of course he was completely aware of the violence and perfidy of the man. He had also become keenly aware of the extreme intelligence and acumen that this vicious being exhibited. There was a certain ruthlessness which actually scared him. He was very unhappy that his superiors had ordered him not to kill this man at the first opportunity but to arrest him and bring him to justice.

Presumably they wanted to interrogate him to find the involvement of the Iranian government in this criminal activity. Perhaps they also wanted to find out if he had other colleagues in Southern Iran who were collaborating and assisting him in his crimes. This necessitated the avoidance of the fifty men on the bus just grabbing him and taking him over to headquarters. After all, they were going to be travelling together in the same vehicle and it would be a cinch to arrest him and ignore the restriction which exposed him and his men to traveling on this bus loaded with explosives, not the fake ones that they had placed there, but the loaded ones that Manucher himself had installed. This was a crazy man, who if necessary, was willing to blow himself up, as long as he was doing this in the company of the supporters of the Shahnshah. Under these circumstances, every single step would have to be carefully watched. Of course his own life was precious to Ismail but he also had to protect the lives of the other officers under his command. Another very scary matter was that he had an instinctive feeling that Manucher was suspicious of him and did not feel comfortable with the respectful way in which Ismail treated him.

As the bus was driving along, Ismail was engrossed in his thoughts when Manucher came and tapped him on his shoulder. "I have something extremely important to discuss with you. If we do not take care of it immediately, the whole mission may be jeopardized. We should discuss this privately. Ask the driver to stop the bus and come with me."

Ismail did what he was told and they both left the bus and walked out into the bush.

"Tell me brother Manucher, what is all this secrecy about?" They had now moved a hundred yards or so from the bus and were completely invisible to the passengers. Suddenly Ismail felt a metallic object against the back of his head.

"Don't even think of calling for help. One sound and you will be a dead man. Manucher reached over and took Ismail's revolver from its holster.

"Now sit down quietly and look at me. Do not speak, just listen." Ismail nodded, trying to hide his panic.

"Let us look at all the facts before us. You claim to be a devout Muslim whose goal is to eliminate the pagan Shahnshah. I carefully watched you at prayer at the shrine as well as at several evening prayers. You did not recite them reverently, just pushed through them. You have never indicated to me that you were a trained military officer and yet you have excellent mastery of weapons. You could not have obtained that training during the days when the Islamic Republic ruled this part of Iran, you were too young then. You must have obtained your training under the pagan Shahnshah's forces. You and your men never once asked me for financial assistance in the purchase of weapons, so the money has to have come from the pagan's coffers. When you and your colleagues curse the pagan, it sounds like a rehearsal and not genuine hatred. Every man in your group claims to be fighting for Islam as an ordinary civilian Muslim, yet each one is completely conversant with guns and ammunition. I have observed the manner in which you all walk. This stance could not have been achieved without military training. You are their leader and I have seen them stand to attention, almost ready to salute you when you address them. Last but not least is the fact that they obey you implicitly. They do not question any aspect of this mission. Civilians do not behave in this way, only the military. So what have I concluded from all this? Simple. You are all military personnel in the pagan's forces who have been sent to exterminate me. A little additional piece of information for your benefit. Do you realize that I can see fear in your eyes and not surprise? This clearly indicates to me that you're not surprised by my revelations but are terrified that I may hurt you. This proves your guilt beyond any doubt."

"Manucher my brother, your imagination is running away with you. You are so wrong in what you believe. I am your faithful friend and follower. Trust me."

"Ismail, the time for talk is now over. It is time for your justified punishment for all your treachery. You are going to see each one of your colleagues blown to bits, knowing that you are solely responsibility for their brutal demise."

Ismail raised his hand in protest and noticed that Manucher had transferred his revolver to his left hand without stopping to aim at him. He then put his right hand into his own pocket and seemed to press something. Two earth shattering detonations followed each other, just a second apart. There were distant screams and a gust of heat flowed over them and then silence.

"That takes care of your one hundred infidel traitors, Ismail. The world is slightly cleansed of infidel lovers. Allah has given me the privilege of sending one hundred sinners to hell. Now it is your turn to join them. Don't you think it would improve your lot in hell if you admitted your guilt to me before leaving this earth?"

"You have killed one hundred innocent Iranians who were devoted to Islam and you are asking me to repent? I thought you were my brother, not a monster and a murderer."

Manucher let out a cynical laugh. "For an alleged fighter for Islam you have quite a talent for lying, Ismail. It does not matter anymore. Goodbye traitor!"

Manucher raised the revolver and fired. Ismail felt an explosion in his head but there was no pain. Then he felt as if he was a third party slowly rising from the scene to watch. Then there was darkness.

CHAPTER 27.

The explosion in the news media on both sides of the border was phenomenal. Initially, the Islamic Republic's media portrayed the killing of our troops as the rightful punishment for the supporters of the infidel. However, the brutality of the act and the previous record of the perpetrators were well known to all Iranians and even the most fanatical ones in the Islamic Republic were appalled at this barbarity. My most fervent critics felt that killing one hundred innocent young men could not be justified. Some of the most devout and despotic religious leaders in the Islamic Republic proclaimed their abhorrence. Surprisingly some fanatics in the North had requested their regime to prove to them that the monster Manucher was not acting on their behalf.

My pain and anguish at this horror was inconsolable. Somehow I felt responsible indirectly for their deaths. Rauf was so heartbroken that I ordered him to seek counselling. I did not want to lose the most devout of my officers as well.

I had realized over the years that organization and effort to remedy a problem were the only ways to eliminate them. When problems were not under our control, we needed love and support to trivialize them or to at least make them seem solvable in the future. For me that source of comfort was my Zainab. Her boundless and unselfish love was my tranquilizer. She did not offer advice or recrimination, just unlimited love. I went to my private quarters to be with her.

She just took one look at me and her green eyes were oozing with care and concern for me.

"My man, my Shahnshah, what is the cause of your anguish? You don't have to say a word, I feel your pain by just looking into your eyes." I took her into my arms and just held her. I then told her of the murder of the one hundred officers and the nervous breakdown of Rauf. She had tears in her eyes and held me tight.

"My darling the most difficult thing when you are the Shahnshah of a country is not the exercise of the power invested in you, but the capacity to accept the pain when the consequences are tragic and unacceptable. You cannot be responsible for every failure. You did the best you could have done, this failure is not your responsibility."

She then kissed me passionately on my mouth, her warm body against me. I could feel the tension draining out of me. She undressed me before stripping herself. She took me into her mouth until I was hard. "Take me my love and my Shahnshah, your woman's love will eliminate all your pain and anguish."

I entered her and made love to her. Her passionate moans were the sweetest music I have ever heard. After we had finished making love, I still held her against my heart. Her warmth and love were soothing to my anguished soul.

As I was grudgingly dressing to go to my office, I received an urgent telephone call from Rauf who was taking counselling after the unfortunate experience of the murder of his comrades. I gathered that he must have been feeling better if he wanted to contact me regarding a military issue. This was the first good thing that could happen since the massacre of our innocent soldiers. I immediately asked him to come to my office.

"Salaam alaikum, my Shahnshah," he said bowing.

"Are you feeling any better Rauf?"

"Your Majesty, I have succeeded in convincing myself that the only way I will be able to forgive myself is by dedicating my life and services to you, my Shahnshah. Secondly, to perfectly plan and achieve what is now my greatest ambition in life, which is to accost this monster Manucher and kill him. I want to witness the anguish and fear in his eyes as he stops breathing and realizes that he is dying."

"It is imperative that you keep one thing in mind, Rauf. The annihilation of Manucher is definitely necessary for the protection and well being of Iran but you, my dear son, are more important to me than the death of a monster, so do not take any unnecessary risks. We should have a watertight scheme to trap that bastard, otherwise he will escape and cause us more grief."

"Understood, Your Majesty and that is the main reason I have come here today. Has Your Majesty ever heard of a man called Lateef Al Mehri?"

"Is that not the Arab religious fanatic who once proclaimed that he had settled in Northern Iran for the sole purpose of helping real good Muslims kill me and destroy Democratic Iran?"

"Precisely, Your Majesty, after the murder of our troops, Mr. Al Mehri seems to have changed his mind. Normally, I would not even consider talking to him but he went on television and openly admitted his folly by criticising Northern Iran for using the services of a convicted murderer. He also claims that your achievements have convinced him that he was wrong about you. He wants to visit Your Majesty and plead for forgiveness and offers to support Democratic Iran in the future"

"I am sorry Rauf, but that sounds a little too glib to be believed."

"Quite right Your Majesty, but he was convicted by the Islamic Republic and spent three months in prison for his comments. Then he left for Dubai and now seeks asylum in our Iran."

"I have met him Your Majesty and at my insistence, he took a lie detector test and successfully passed it. He had not received any prior notice of such a test being contemplated by us and could not have prepared for it."

"So what does he want from me?"

"He claims he has some very significant information regarding Manucher's whereabouts and future plans but will communicate that information only to Your Majesty. He has also obtained a promise from me that no one except the two of us should ever know that he has entered Democratic Iran. I am completely aware of any possible danger to Your Majesty so, every millimetre of his body will be searched before he is brought here. Secondly, he will not be informed in advance that you have agreed to meet with him. This will eliminate any sinister plan, if one exists."

"And you suggest that I see him?"

"Yes I do but I request that I be present throughout the interview just to be totally certain that Your Majesty is not in any jeopardy."

"All right Rauf, arrange this meeting immediately. Go and bring him in right away. This will eliminate any possibility of a devious plot."

Rauf bowed and left my office.

CHAPTER 28.

"Salaam Alaikum, Shahnshah," the man accompanying Rauf said, bowing. I noticed that he was about six feet tall, had a long beard and a turban. My impression was that he was definitely an Islamic fundamentalist and a devout Muslim.

"I have been searched from head to foot, every crevice in my body has been fingered and your troops did not find any explosives anywhere. Even my fountain pen was taken away from me, so Your Majesty, I'm sure officer Rauf and your other military personnel are now satisfied that I'm not a terrorist, nor have I come to assault or attack you. I have come here voluntarily, Your Majesty, because I believe the information I have to give to you is of the utmost significance. That information will be of no value to you if any one else finds out that I have communicated with you. I'm therefore requesting you to speak to me privately, in the absence of these officers."

"Mr. Lateef Al Mehri, I have heard about the noble intentions you have expressed about our Democratic Iran. My trusted officer Rauf informs me that he trusts you and that is why I'm welcoming you as the Shahnshah of Iran. I will concede to your request that all other officers leave our presence but, I will insist that officer Rauf be present during our conversation. I give you my word of honor that not one syllable of what you have told us will leave this room."

"Well Shahnshah, with that guarantee I have no objection to Mr. Rauf Irfani's presence during our discussions."

"Please sit down Mr. Al Mehri, may I offer you a coffee or tea or any other beverage?"

"Thank you Your Majesty, but I'm fine."

"You appear to be extremely agitated Mr. Al Mehri, please relax and take your time and let me know when you're ready."

"Forgive me Your Majesty, recently I've had great difficulty compromising my principles and my integrity. I've come to one simple conclusion. If my beliefs and ideals ever conflict with human decency and my integrity, then human decency shall prevail. Now please Your Majesty, do not take offense at my blunt manners. I do not mean to be rude. I just have to get it off my chest before I can be candid with you. When you took over as the Shahnshah of Iran, at first I felt the utmost hatred for you. I was one of the individuals in the Islamic Republic who actually helped in plotting your assassination. I genuinely and honestly believed that you were the enemy of Islam and that you were destroying our faith. The authorities in the Islamic Republic completely agreed with me. This monster Manucher was instructed to come to your area of Iran at the behest of the Prime Minister of the Islamic Republic. I was the one to instruct him as to what steps we should take to overthrow your government. Then certain unbelievable things happened. Broken down mosques, churches and synagogues in Iran were repaired by a man I considered the enemy of Islam. Education was introduced for women and they started taking active part in the government as well as in all walks of life. The education level shot up and today almost ninety-nine percent of people under the age of forty are literate in Southern Iran. In Northern Iran, about eight percent of the population has gone to University, whereas in your area of Iran seventy-eight percent of people under the age of twenty-five are attending universities. Conceded that you have eliminated Islam as the sole religion of Iran, but in a true sense you have actually followed the dictates of our prophet Mohamed by giving rights and privileges to the `Kitabis', or the followers of the holy books that preceded the birth of Islam. This was the mission of the Prophet himself. Then comes the massacre of one hundred faithful soldiers, instigated by my Prime Minister and that criminal, who performed that task for him, was a convicted murderer awaiting execution in our own prisons. That was the turning point at which I decided that even though I might disagree with your views about the supremacy of Islam, I cannot support an administration and government that deliberately deceived the people of Iran and participated in the massacre of innocent Iranians. I've therefore come to you with humility and shame to plead for your forgiveness and offer my services as and when you may require them, as well as to help you catch this monster Manucher and exterminate him. That is all I have to say, Your Majesty."

"Mr Al Mehri, I am very happy to hear that you are so impressed by our progress and so supportive of it. You are absolutely correct that this Manucher is a beast and a criminal and for sure we want to exterminate him before he kills any other innocent civilians. Any help that you can give us will be greatly appreciated. Just let me know what kind of protection you and your family will need and we will provide it to you."

"Alright Your Majesty, I will now expose the whole situation completely to you and to officer Rauf. Let me reiterate though that if the Islamic government finds out that I'm involved, not only will they kill me but they will eliminate my whole family including my children and grandchildren. Let me give you the facts as I have already indicated. I was one of the instructors of Manucher and was part of the scheme to assassinate you. You already know that. There is more to it. Because I was an Arab and had come to Iran from Dubai to live in a totally Islamic state, my credentials as an Islamic fundamentalist appealed to the Prime Minister Mr. Sharukh Mukhtiar of the Islamic Republic. Both of us organized Manucher's trip to Southern Iran. Thanks to your devoted officers, Manucher failed. The second attempt and the massacre of those young Iranian soldiers was his idea. After that massacre, Manucher came back to the Islamic Republic and met with us. To my utter shock the Prime Minister complimented and congratulated him. By this time I'd already decided that I was going to expose this monster to you and would do anything in my power to get him arrested by your forces. However, the slightest change of expression would have alerted the Prime Minister and Manucher so I vociferously joined in the compliments and then took a summer holiday to Turkey and got into Southern Iran to meet you. At that last meeting with the Prime Minister and Manucher, a new plan was created. Manucher will now don the attire of a Westerner. He will obtain a false Omani passport and clandestinely enter Southern Iran. He will be accompanied by approximately twenty explosives experts equipped with materials that can be fired from a distance of approximately twenty kilometres. They will first ascertain that Your Majesty is in your Palace and then fire the device. As you are well aware, by this time I had decided to come to Southern Iran and become a part of this progressive country. I therefore informed the Prime Minister that the introduction of the explosives into Southern Iran without detection will be an impossibly difficult task. The statement was made by me not because I really believed what I said, but because I wanted to find out how they were going to smuggle the material into your area. I was then informed that a perfectly camouflaged fishing boat will land in a town in the south of Iran where there are no particular security concerns as this is so far away from the Northern Iranian border. I therefore made a suggestion. I informed them that I was constantly in contact with certain devout Muslim leaders who had publicly sided with Your Majesty for political reasons but, in fact had been aiming to destroy you and your government. To my utter surprise, the Prime Minister looked at me extremely suspiciously and demanded that I provide the names and locations of these individuals to him. I argued that I had given my oath to these men never to reveal their identity and secondly, several of these individuals were not personally known to me and that I was merely informed of their participation and interest in our scheme. He then wanted to know how I could assist Manucher and I grabbed the opportunity. I stated that approximately forty kilometres south of Khorramshahr there is a little village called Samura where some of my trusted men reside. Your Majesty knows that Samura is located in an inlet, so the entrance inlet is only approximately one kilometre wide. If we could lure this fishing boat into that inlet and close off the entrance there can be no possible escape for the culprits. I pretended to provide them with geographical data. I also pretended that I had information on the location of your troops in the area and then informed them that as this was an area far distant from the Islamic Republic, the security precautions were lax."

"Do you think the Prime Minister believed you? Also, do you believe that Manucher was not suspicious of what you were saying?"

"Your Majesty, when I was giving this information I was totally petrified. You do realize that I had no previous notice of this discussion so I created all this hypothesis right on the spur of the moment. The only information of which I was certain of was the inlet surrounding Samura and that information I remembered from my school days. To be very honest with you Sir, for days thereafter, I was extremely scared that the Prime Minister and his officers would investigate and ask questions about the so-called companions in your part of Iran and that I would not have a believable response to such queries. I was very fortunate. They took my word for it and I later informed them that I will sneak into Southern Iran through Turkey, make contact with my compatriots and inform them of the time when the boat could come into Samura. Now Your Majesty, you have got all the facts and I'm ready to give them the time when they can bring their boat in. Thereafter, whatever action you decide to take is your decision and responsibility. Before you do that, please help me get my wife and children into your portion of Iran. I do not want any rewards or honors conferred upon me. All I want is that my family should be safely resettled in Southern Iran. After that has been completed, I am at your service and we can proceed with the plan which I have revealed to you."

"Immediately inform your family to take a trip to Dubai where you can say that they're going to meet your Arab relatives. Do not come in through Turkey, the Iranian government will become suspicious. Come in via Dubai!"

We were successful in removing Al Mehri's family from Iran into Dubai and then into our own state. I was extremely relieved that they were safely united. Rauf, in the meantime, had been planning for the arrival of the boat loaded with ammunition and its destruction as well as the possible arrest and elimination of Manucher.

Al Mehri in the meanwhile contacted the gang of saboteurs in Iran and once again confirmed with them, the date, location and approximate time of their arrival. He himself had spoken to Manucher and reported to me that he seemed to be convinced that everything was going as planned.

Rauf arranged for fifty trained Iranian soldiers to be dressed as devout religious Muslims. They were to be located in strategic areas surrounding the inlet and some of them would pretend to be the welcoming committee awaiting their arrival. The sixteenth of September was selected as the date of arrival of the boat at six a.m. A completely separate contingent would be concealed at the entrance of the inlet to prevent the boat from escaping into the open sea. As a secondary precaution, our air force was on alert to blow the boat to smithereens if it did manage to escape into the open sea. We had also set up highly sophisticated tracking devices along our coastline going all the way up to the Islamic Republic. This would make it easy for us to track the boat as it came along our coastline on its way to the inlet.

Each day of waiting was excruciating torture. On the night of September fifteenth, Rauf came to my office to inform me that everything was ready. I shook his hand and wished him well. He was regretful that he could not personally participate in the impending action. This was because he was known to Manucher and could not risk the possibility that he would be recognized even though disguised as a religious Muslim. However, he was going to direct the activity concealed behind the frontline. He was looking forward to the joy of a dead or arrested Manucher being brought to him. I wished him well and he left the Palace.

The following morning I eagerly awaited the news from our troops. When the first message arrived I could not believe what they told me. As per schedule, the fishing boat had entered the inlet and gradually moved in the direction of Samura. Our troops successfully closed the inlet so that there was no escape. To the surprise of Rauf and our soldiers there was absolutely no resistance. The sailors surrendered. They were not armed. There was no objection to our soldiers boarding the boat. They loudly admitted their guilt stating that they were trying to smuggle fish into Southern Iran even though they were Northerners. They said they were poor fishermen and the price they got in Northern Iran for their fish was far lower than in the South. Their motive for coming into the inlet was to sell the fish in prosperous Southern Iran, make a quick buck and return to the Islamic Republic. They fell to their knees and apologized for not seeking prior permission to enter into Democratic Iran. They said that they were afraid they would not be given permission because they lived in the Islamic Republic. The boat was thoroughly searched and no explosives were found. This was a total shock to Rauf. He asked why they had decided to enter the inlet at Samura. The response was that they had met a very reputed military officer in Northern Iran who had laughed at them for their efforts to make money fishing. He was the one who suggested that a quick way to make a few bucks would be to smuggle the fish into Southern Iran. They informed Rauf that even the location of Samura was provided to them by that officer. He had told them that this was a safe area as there were no customs or other presence in the inlet.

Rauf asked them for the description of the man. He brought in identity experts and with the description provided by the sailors, a sketch of the military officer was created. The sketch exactly and entirely represented Manucher. Rauf felt that in his whole life he had never felt so frustrated and angry. This was the second failure against the monster Manucher. He had been outsmarted and out manoeuvred once again by Manucher. As he was recovering from this affront, his cell phone rang and he answered it. All he heard at the other end was uproarious laughter. "You dirty filthy lackey bastard, do you think you and your pagan Shahnshah can con me that easily? Do you genuinely and honestly believe that I was totally taken in by that traitor Al Mehri? That bastard tells us that he has friends in Southern Iran who will help us enter and blow up the pagan Shahnshah. What he did not realize was that I knew every single person he was in contact with in Southern Iran. He even fooled our Prime Minister but I suspected him. Suddenly his whole family takes a trip to Dubai, sixteen relatives, at the same time. I try to track his cell phone and realize that a device has been installed to make his calls untraceable. You tell me why would an ordinary civilian be so concerned about his outgoing calls? The answer is simple. He did not want us to find out he was communicating with the enemies of the Islamic Republic. Well, you have caught the fishermen. Have a good fish dinner." The line went dead.

Rauf initially felt extremely disappointed and humiliated. Once again that criminal had outwitted him. But Rauf was not an ordinary man who would allow his disappointment and shock to interfere with his analysis of the situation. He questioned himself. If Manucher had stumbled on their scheme to nab the terrorists, why would he not avoid sending the ship to the inlet and instead send it to another destination. What was the reason for this complicated plan of sending the fishing boat into the inlet where it will be caught? There had to be an ulterior motive for all this complicated manipulation. Suddenly Rauf smiled. With all his brilliance and acumen Manucher had not thought of the possibility that all ships coming from the Islamic Republic and going in the direction of Southern Iran were being traced. He concluded that Manucher must have done all this to misguide the Southern Iranian forces, send them to a wrong destination and sneak the real ship into another location of Southern Iran where no one would be wise to their arrival. He immediately picked up his cell phone and contacted the naval authorities in charge of the tracking devices. He was told that a suspicious looking boat was proceeding in the direction of an uninhabited coastal area. Ships would normally move South at a considerable distance from the coastline if they were aiming for an Iranian port or a harbour in the Emirates. The movement of this boat towards an uninhabited portion of the Iranian coastline was rather suspicious. Rauf immediately instructed the naval authorities not to take any overt action to stop or investigate it. He requested them to have the area completely surrounded by Southern Iran's navy and to keep aircraft and helicopters ready for immediate action if necessary. He also ordered them to provide him with helicopters to transport them to the location where the ship was going to dock. Rauf was also concerned that if Manucher and his men failed to land safely and continue with their nefarious activities, they were fanatical enough to blow themselves up together with the Southern Iranian forces, considering that action martyrdom. It was imperative that none of his forces were in the vicinity where they could be blown up.

The helicopters arrived and Rauf and his troops were flown to the coastline and landed in an area not visible from the sea. Rauf was informed by the Navy that the incoming ship was completely surrounded and there was no possibility of any escape or retreat.

Rauf had installed loudspeakers and they were watching every move the boat made. It was obvious that the individuals on the boat had no idea that they were under surveillance. Rauf's suspicions were confirmed by the fact that the boat was moving in the direction of the shore where there was no landing or residents. They observed the boat until it reached the shoreline and laid anchor. At this moment Rauf announced on the loudspeakers. "You are totally surrounded and cannot escape from this location. There are naval ships outside of this coastal area which will not permit you to go back to the sea. Do not try to land or we will blow you to smithereens. Your only option is to obey our commands or perish if you are disobedient!"

After a few minutes, there was a response from the boat. "Officers, we are Iranian citizens escaping from the tyranny of the Islamic Republic. We have come to seek safety and security in the land of the Shahnshah. Why do you want to shoot at us? We have no weapons. Please let us in."

Rauf carefully listened to the voice pattern of the speaker. There was no question in his mind that this was an Iranian speaking Farsi. This voice did not belong to a humble man from Northern Iran. Instead it sounded like the voice of a man who was either with the military or police forces. Rauf did not miss the harsh commanding accent behind the apparent plea for protection.

"You will leave the boat one by one with your arms raised. If there is the slightest indication that you are armed, you will be immediately shot."

"Why are you doing this to us? We are peaceful fishermen only interested in selling our catch to the local people. We have no weapons or equipment in our possession," some one answered from the boat.

"Interesting isn't it, that a fishing boat has its own microphone system. All right, you claim to be fishermen. Let us see what fish you have caught!" Rauf demanded.

For several minutes absolutely nothing happened, then a very hesitant voice announced over their microphone system. "We have run out of fish."

"I thought you just told me that you were trying to sell fish in this area. How are you hoping to do that with no fish? Stop all this crap and surrender peacefully or we will blow you to smithereens!"

Their arms upraised, one by one the alleged sailors came out of the boat, walking in the direction they were ordered to.

With the help of our new allied American friends, we had obtained equipment and technology which could be remotely aimed in any direction and we would be able to determine whether there were any explosive devices in the possession of these individuals or in their immediate vicinity. This device was aimed at every individual who left the boat and no weapons were found. When the last man had come out, our experts aimed this device at the boat. To their utter shock, the instrument revealed that the boat was filled to the brim with explosives and weapons. Rauf ordered each individual from the boat to walk alone in the direction of our troops. As each one approached our soldiers, he was handcuffed, thoroughly searched and arrested. One by one it was confirmed that no individual had any weapons or explosives on his body. Rauf then started questioning them about their permanent addresses, occupations and other pertinent information to help identify them. He also instructed his soldiers to check for any tattoos on their left arms. This was done because a large number of Iranian soldiers had tattoos depicting certain Islamic symbols on their forearms. Sixteen of the individuals searched were found to have those military tattoos.

"Sixteen fishermen coincidentally have military tattoos on their forearms? You expect me to believe this nonsense? You better confess exactly what you're doing here or you will be severely punished. What is your answer?"

There was an uncomfortable silence in the group. Each man was looking at the other and not responding.

"Who is your leader? Let him speak up!"

Again, no one answered and they kept looking at each other uncomfortably.

"We know that your ship is laden with weapons and explosives. Can you explain this to me?"

Again no one answered. At this point Rauf ordered his technicians to check for any remaining occupants on the boat. The equipment was capable of tracing the slightest movement and if there was anyone remaining on the boat, he would be immediately detected. The technicians quietly whispered in Rauf's ear that there was indeed one person remaining on the boat. Rauf approached the last man he had spoken to. "You will tell me who is on the boat. I demand a truthful answer. We know there is someone. I'm going to take each one of you away from the group and ask that same question. If you do not identify this man, you will be shot on the spot!"

Rauf had carefully orchestrated a method of questioning these men. Each one was taken from the group to a secluded area which was invisible to the remaining prisoners. He was then handcuffed and a muzzle was placed over his mouth. Before this was done he was asked to tell the investigators who was on the boat. If he refused to answer or provided an answer that the investigators did not believe, a bullet was fired into the air and one of the men investigating imitated a yell or scream that would emanate from a man being shot. The remaining prisoners on the beach naturally thought that the individual being investigated had been shot. This resulted in enormous anguish and fear in the minds of the remaining prisoners. One by one the prisoners were escorted away and a similar pretence and sound were fabricated to indicate to the remaining, that this man had also been shot. The fourth prisoner taken from the group had decided to come clean and tell the investigators who was on the boat. He admitted that they had all come as a group from the Islamic Republic with the intention of blowing up the Parliament of Southern Iran and as many institutions as they could manage, which had been created by the Shahnshah. Their most significant job was to assassinate the Shahnshah together with many of his ministers and followers. The investigator specifically asked who the leader of the group was and the prisoner indicated that he was an eminent officer of the Islamic Republic who had been honored and decorated for his valor and bravery. After some more prodding, very grudgingly the prisoner gave the name of their leader as Manucher.

His handcuffs were replaced but the investigator whispered in his ear that henceforth he would be treated kindly. The prisoner begged of the investigators that his name should not be released to the rest of his crew as he did not want to be considered a traitor to their cause. The investigators agreed that nobody would find out who had given out the actual information about the presence of Manucher.

Rauf's next task was to determine what should be done to the boat and the terrorist still on it. It would have been easy to blow the boat up, but that was not acceptable to Rauf as he was looking forward to the pleasure of arresting Manucher and taking him before the Shahnshah. It would be such a moral victory both for himself and for Southern Iran if this animal was tried, convicted and executed. The publicity generated by this trial, especially when the citizens of Northern Iran became aware of the involvement of their own government, along with their efforts to brutally kill other Iranians, would be priceless propaganda for Southern Iran. Rauf ordered his naval personnel to surround the boat, just in case Manucher tried to escape or to swim ashore.

Before all the naval vessels could surround the boat in the inlet, a strange occurrence was visible. Smoke started billowing from the vessel. It was so dense that nothing in the vicinity was visible. Then, a huge explosion blew the boat to smithereens. By the time the smoke cleared, Rauf was unable to determine whether Manucher had been killed in the explosion or had somehow escaped.

The area was now completely surrounded and with the help of sonar equipment, they were trying to determine whether any one was in the vicinity. Suddenly Rauf received a call on his cell phone from a naval officer. Apparently the equipment had tracked someone wearing scuba equipment attempting to swim away and he had almost reached the shore on the other side. Military personnel on the opposite shore were asked to immediately arrest him but not injure him unless it was absolutely necessary for their own preservation. The waiting was indeed very tense for Rauf. Approximately twenty minutes later, the officer called back. Rauf sensed the joy and victory in the officer's voice.

"Officer Rauf, we have caught the bastard. He had reached land and was trying to remove his equipment when we arrested him. Believe it or not he was carrying explosives on his body and was attempting to blow himself up when we arrested him. The explosives have been removed and deactivated and the prisoner is in our possession ready to be delivered to you."

"Sergeant. Major, this is the best news I've had in several months. Be assured that your excellent work will be reported to the Shahnshah. I also personally thank you for giving me the greatest gift I have ever wanted. Would you kindly bring this animal to me."

Twenty minutes later a tall shackled male was brought into Rauf's presence. Rauf looked at him to be absolutely certain that it was Manucher. To his great satisfaction it was the monster Manucher. There was no fear in his eyes only sheer hatred. "So, you pagan loving infidel, you think you have won don't you? It won't last very long. I would like to see you facing the wrath of Allah."

In spite of his determination not to be perturbed by the behavior of this criminal, Rauf could not control his temper. With his right fist he hit Manucher in the mouth. Though he was a civilized man, Rauf was thrilled to see that he had dislodged one of his front teeth and that he was bleeding from his mouth. Strangely enough, Manucher started laughing. "Do you think that you can scare me with that fist of yours, you imbecile. All you can do is kill me. But on the Day of Judgment, when I stand before the Prophet and Allah, where will you be? Washing the toilets of your pagan Shahnshah!"

Rauf had regained back his composure. With a very even voice he responded. "Your presence before Allah on the Day of Judgment is not going to be likely and I will tell you why. First of all I'm going to have you hung on a post. Your beard will be shaved off, then I'm going to personally enjoy the pleasure of slowly cutting your testicles off with a blunt knife, savouring the musical joy of your screams of agony. We will bring the excreta of a pig to fill and seal your mouth. We will burn you alive and your ashes will be spewed onto a pig farm so that pigs can defecate on your ashes till eternity. Day of Judgment or no Day of Judgment, I do not believe Allah will welcome you under those circumstances!"

In spite of all his bravado, Manucher was now visibly scared. The sight of fear in his eyes was the most beautiful thing Rauf had seen. His first impulse was to tell Manucher that he would never do such a barbaric thing, but then he enjoyed the pleasure of letting Manucher stew for a few hours. No civilized officer in the service of the Shahnshah of Iran could have done such a thing. A law-abiding and religious Muslim or any other civilized human being could not commit such an act of barbarity. The pleasure of causing anguish to a monster like Manucher was something that Rauf could not resist.

The remaining prisoners were reunited and escorted away. The shock in their expressions to see the ones who had been supposedly shot was incredible. They could not comprehend such humanity coming from the people they had come to butcher. A number of them bowed to Rauf and apologized profusely. One prisoner went to the extent of telling Rauf that he had been misguided and misinformed about the character of the Shahnshah's army and police. They had been specifically warned that they should never get caught or surrender, because that would mean certain torture and death.

Manucher was securely handcuffed and leg irons were placed on him. Rauf made absolutely certain that there was not even a remote possibility of this animal ever escaping.

CHAPTER 29.

The news of Manucher's arrest and the admission by all his collaborators of the brutal mission they were entrusted with by the Islamic Republic of Iran, became headline news in newspapers around the world. News reporters had infiltrated and obtained the opinions of several citizens of Northern Iran and there was total consensus that the average person was appalled at the disgraceful behavior of their government. They were particularly angry that the government had planned to kill so many Iranians just to spite the regime of the Shahnshah. The interesting thing was their shock at the fact that all the conspirators were safe in custody and that a proper legal trial was expected where defence counsel would be provided to each one of the accused persons, even that monster Manucher. This legal process was unknown and unexpected in Northern Iran. Naturally that increased interest in what was happening to these culprits in Democratic Iran and had enhanced their curiosity about the standards of life and freedom which were prevailing in the Shahnshah's regime. The time had now come when Southern Iran was not just a place with a better standard of living, higher education, freedom and equality for women and non-Muslims. Even the most bigoted fanatics in the North had come to the conclusion that their religion was not in jeopardy and in fact the genuine principles of Islam were better protected in the Shahnshah's regime compared to the Islamic Republic.

The leaders of the Islamic Republic initially denied any involvement with Manucher and his gang but our media had placed the prisoners on TV and their admissions and abject pleas for forgiveness were broadcast to all Iranians. The authorities in the Islamic Republic had now reached a point where they could not categorically deny their involvement, so grudgingly and slowly they admitted, to the extent that no massacre was ever contemplated. They only wanted the removal of the pagan Shahnshah as the ruler of a devout Muslim state. There was one thing very wrong in their thinking pattern. In spite of the religious fanaticism imbibed and forced upon them since childhood, the education system had not totally collapsed. There were a huge number of educated people who could see through the malicious, lies propagated by their leaders.

A shocking new development was the fact that several devout Muslim imams in the North had condemned the Islamic Republic. A few of them even went to the extent of suggesting that Northern Iran should quietly join the Shahnshah's regime and the country should be reunited under a brilliant and illustrious leader who had once again brought Islam to the level of greatness which it had enjoyed in the thirteenth century. A strange new wine of change was coming out of Northern Iran. Several leaders of religion and education were agreeing that though the Shahnshah maybe a foreigner by birth, his ancestry was Iranian. The Zoroastrians were the original Iranians and there was absolutely no reason to persecute them as they were not detrimental to Islam, nor had they ever attacked or insulted Islamic beliefs. The Shahnshah's successful efforts in refurbishing dilapidated mosques for their architectural value and the protection given to Sunni Muslims against Shiite fanatics, was now greatly lauded by intellectual Iranians.

I was watching the TV broadcast from Teheran where the usual clichés of the Islamic Republic were being broadcast. To my utter shock and disbelief the TV station went blank for a few seconds before the broadcast commenced again. The speaker was a completely different person. The Iranian TV announcers normally wore jackets without ties and now I was looking at a bearded Muslim in a long robe and a religious hat. Before I could consider the reason for this sudden change, the speaker announced his name. In northern Iran this particular imam was considered one of the most devout Muslim leaders and one of the most fanatical critics of my regime.

"Fellow Iranians, I suppose you are totally shocked that the announcer has been removed from this broadcast. My companions and I have taken over this state television station. I think it is high time that the people of Iran be told the truth. Every evening, I listen to the fabrications of the Islamic government of Northern Iran. I myself initially believed what they said but now I have independent evidence that most of the information they broadcast is insidious propaganda. Look at me, my fellow Iranians. I am Imam Mahmoodi. I'm sure that most of you have heard my speeches and my criticism of the Shahnshah of Iran for what I considered un-Islamic activities. I have now studied the Shahnshah's achievements, the progress he has brought to our people and to my shock, the protection he has provided to our beloved Islam. It is now time for me to stand in front of the universe, bow my head to this great and beneficent leader and apologize for my ignorance, past malicious behavior and pronouncements. If you are watching me oh Shahnshah of Iran, please accept my humble apology. Now, the rest of you Iranians, please listen to me carefully. We have just captured the staff of this TV station. The Islamic regime is not going to tolerate that. They will send the army to remove us from the station. They may also kill us after condemning us as traitors. It does not matter anymore. It may be the last chance I have to tell you all the truth. Oppose with all your might the Islamic regime of Northern Iran. Move in masses towards the border of Southern Iran and plead with the Shahnshah to incorporate you and your provinces into Democratic Iran. It is your last opportunity to wake up in the twenty-first century. Before I can……"

Suddenly the broadcast ended. A lot of shouting in the background could be heard. I thought I heard some bullets being fired and the TV station went dead.

This was such a shocking situation and yet there was no information about Iran at that time from the station. Zainab had come running into the TV room. "Oh my Shahnshah did you hear that? Have they killed that Imam?"

I was in shock. I did not know whether to be elated or sad. A man who was supporting me was butchered before my eyes and I couldn't do a thing to save him.

The television station did not resume broadcast that night. I tried CNN and also the Turkish broadcasting stations but there was no news available about what had happened at that Tehran station. I was fiddling with my TV monitor when Zainab suggested that I try BBC. They seem to get international news much quicker than all the other channels. I tuned in to the BBC.

A deep voice in a perfect English accent was speaking, "Shocking information today from the Islamic Republic of Iran. One of the greatest supporters of the regime and one of the most virile and vocal critics of the Shahnshah, together with his compatriots attacked the national television station in Tehran and after arresting the announcer and the staff, openly proclaimed his disenchantment with the Islamic Republic and his realization that indeed the Shahnshah was the only salvation for Iran. At this point in time we do not know exactly what happened after the announcement was completed, but it is believed that the militia of the Islamic Republic attacked and shot the imam and eight of his followers. The sudden change on the part of the Imam from being one of the greatest supporters of the Islamic Republic to becoming such a vocal critic has caused shockwaves in Iran. The government of the Islamic Republic has not yet announced what steps will be taken against the remaining prisoners taken at the television station."

"It is also rumoured that four separate military battalions of the Islamic Republic have indicated to the government that they now completely and absolutely disagree and will not obey orders from the Prime Minister if they are ever asked to attack the Shahnshah's regime. The other perturbing fact is that there is no announcement from the Islamic Republic's regime and no reaction to these events. Tom Richards, BBC news, London."

Under our new constitution, if there was a trial involving the security of Democratic Iran, apart from the regularly appointed judges, the court administration could request me, the Shahnshah of Iran to preside over the case. Of course I had the right to decline if I so wished. The trial of the compatriots of Manucher was not a problem as all of them had admitted their guilt and even provided evidence that they were misguided by the Government of the Islamic Republic. By showing their repentance and as no actual physical injury was caused to any one, their only crime was the conspiracy itself. They were all sentenced to three years imprisonment with the possibility of earlier release on probation for good behavior. There was a motive for the leniency of the sentence. Their help and admissions were televised all over the world and that was the main reason why so many Iranians in the North had decided to join our side. I decided that they deserved this leniency. The final and most significant criminal of course was Manucher and I had been requested to preside over his trial. I did not want it to be the typical Middle Eastern procedure where, if an accused was not in good standing with the government, he would get the pretence of a trial and then be executed. I had no desire whatsoever to let this animal live but it was essential that he had a fair trial and was represented by properly qualified and able counsel.

Names of several counsels were presented to him and he was asked to choose. Without hesitation and very vehemently he stated that no supporter or subject of the pagan would be allowed to represent him. He also stated that since he did not believe in the legal system introduced by the pagan, he was not subject to the laws of Southern Iran. Ultimately he had decided that he would defend himself. Of course that was his right and we had no objection.

The trial date was fixed and names of qualified counsel were provided to Manucher should he require any guidance in the law of the land.

On the specified date, I sat as the judge and Manucher was marched into the courtroom in shackles and chains. Charges of the murder of our officers and the conspiracy to attack our country were read out in court. He was then asked how he wanted to plead. I was fascinated at the incredibly violent expression in his eyes as he looked at me. He then stood up and spat in my direction. "This is my plea you pagan bastard!" he yelled at me. The guard standing next to him was so appalled and shocked that he lifted his gun and hit Manucher in the face. With the impact of the blow Manucher fell to the ground and appeared to be stunned for a second or two before he stood up again and continued staring at me. There was blood oozing from his mouth but the contemptuous sneer still remained on his face.

"Do not use physical violence against this man. Pay no heed to his empty words or behaviour. Officer, we do not have to reduce ourselves to his level. This man is uneducated filth. His rantings are not significant to us. This person's opinions and existence are trivial. The next time, just ignore him. Exhibit your contempt, not your anger"

"You pagan bastard, are you calling me, a devout Muslim, a dog?"

"No Sir, I would never call you a dog because that would be an insult to the canine world. What has a poor dog done to me that I would want to insult him by comparing him to you."

In spite of the seriousness of the occasion, the spectators in the courtroom including the attorneys started laughing. I must say I was fascinated with the expression in Manucher's eyes. I think at that moment in time, he would have very gladly given up his life if he could kill me or severely injure me.

As the witnesses started presenting the case in court, Manucher constantly interrupted and cursed them. The prosecutor requested that a muzzle be placed on him to silence him. As I felt this was totally necessary, I ordered that this be done. The evidence took approximately four days. After the crown's case was concluded the muzzle was removed from Manucher's face and he was asked how he wanted to respond.

"Do you have anything to say in defence of these charges?" I asked.

"Yes, you pagan bastard. You now have the power to take my life but you do not have the power to take the faith that has kept me alive for so many years. What is life? Every one loses it sooner or later and so will you. Someday we will both be standing before Allah. Only I will be wearing my religious garb and hat and you will be in chains looking like a castrated pig waiting for the door to open so that you can be transported into the custody of Satan. Then, pagan Shahnshah, I will be laughing and you will be pleading for mercy from Allah. I am waiting for that hour. So end this mockery of a trial and expedite my execution."

The prosecutor stood up and bowed. "Your Majesty, this convicted murderer was responsible for the lives of almost one hundred innocent Iranians soldiers. Naturally the crown is going to ask for the death sentence. My only concern Your Majesty is that shooting him like any other criminal would bring the administration of justice into disrepute. This man cannot be compared to any ordinary murderer. This man needs to be beheaded in the market square. It is respectfully submitted that we should set an example, so that all future mass murderers are clearly warned that in Southern Iran this kind of behavior will not just be punished, but will be eliminated, if necessary, with the utmost violence. One other thing Your Majesty, I heard this criminal talking about standing in front of Allah and the other derogatory comments he made about you and your position before Allah. Perhaps Mr. Manucher is not aware of the new legislation that we have passed. As Your Majesty knows, a convicted murderer, who is executed, is not buried in a grave. His corpse is cremated and the ashes are discarded. I think Mr. Manucher would have a slight problem appearing in front of Allah, whether it is to receive a warm welcome or the deserved censure."

It was amazing to me how religion perverts the mentality of every human being. Manucher, a man who was not afraid of dying and who actually requested that I expedite the process, was absolutely stunned. I could even see an inadvertent shiver. The thought of being cremated and not having a grave from which he dreamt of rising to meet Allah, was more terrifying to him than death itself.

"Aren't you satisfied with killing me pagan Shahnshah? Do not forget you still rule an Islamic country. Whether you like it or not, Islamic law will ultimately prevail here. You cannot cremate a Muslim. That is against Islam!"

The prosecutor once again bowed. "Mr. Manucher, in case you have forgotten, it is against Islam to murder innocent people. It is also against Islam to enter a country illegally and attempt to subvert and destroy its government. Your cremation is a triviality compared to the horrors you have inflicted on innocent people. Your Majesty, once again I am requesting the death penalty. As a matter-of-fact I am requesting that, to set an example, this man's arms and legs should be cut off and he should be allowed to die in the agony he deserves."

"Mr. Prosecutor, we have now created a civilized, democratic country. Our aim is to punish criminals who come before us, but it is also to civilize animals like Manucher. A barbarity such as cutting off his arms and legs in public and letting him die in agony does not help our cause. If we behave in that fashion, then we have perpetuated the evil that existed in this society before we took charge and hopefully brought some civilization to."

"Mr. Manucher, for the barbaric crimes that you have committed against so many innocent individuals, I am hereby sentencing you to death. You will be taken from this courthouse and shot immediately. However the prosecutor is totally accurate in one aspect. Your body will be cremated and the ashes will be discarded. It is imperative that we do not provide the opportunity for fanatics like you to have a spot where they can come and bow to you as their martyr. Most of Southern Iran is now civilized and educated but we have no doubt that there are still a lot of fanatical criminals like you, who must not be given an opportunity to create an altar."

"You have convicted me and sentenced me to death and I did not plead for mercy. This cremation of my body is totally unacceptable to me. I hate to do this because I consider you an enemy of Islam and Iran but please do not cremate my body. Let me die like a Muslim."

"In order to die like a Muslim you must behave like a decent Muslim. Being a good Muslim is not a right, it is an earned privilege. Your brutality, malice and crimes have completely disentitled you to ask for the privileges of a good Muslim. Take this beast out of my sight and execute him immediately. As I previously stated, throw his ashes into the first garbage container you can find. This court is now adjourned."

"May you rot in hell you bastard," were the last words I heard from Manucher.

The following morning I was informed by the jail guards that he tried to bribe them to have his body removed and secretly buried. They rejected the offer and my sentence was carried out. Rauf had requested the privilege of witnessing the execution and cremation and came to provide me with the details. I was watching him very carefully because he was the one man who hated Manucher more than any one else, yet there was no satisfaction in his eyes. There was no pain and no pleasure either. I then realized that Rauf was indeed an honorable man.

After the court proceedings were completed I went back to my office and turned on the television channel from Tehran. It was approximately five hours since the execution and cremation of Manucher. Both CNN and the BBC had detailed broadcasts of the event but not a single syllable was mentioned on the TV channel from Tehran! Such was the loyalty of religious fanatics towards their fallen compatriots.

CHAPTER 30.

One of the things that I resented most about any Asiatic culture was their respect for age. It was claimed that age brought experience and following the thinking of an experienced person would prevent the young person from making serious mistakes. But experience was like a weapon, it was useless in the hands of an untrained person. An uneducated person learned the wrong lessons from experience. The pleasure of controlling the lives of other people was so great to an ignorant person, that he never hesitated to give advice even when he did not know what he was talking about. If a highly qualified and experienced individual gave advice in his field to young and inexperienced persons, that was acceptable; however in ninety percent of the situations involving so-called parental guidance, the views of the uneducated parent were totally useless and in many situations, actually quite harmful. I also had come to the conclusion that a parent's insistence that the child follow his or her advice had the more sinister motive behind it, control. Every human being since the beginning of time has had the desire to control others. This is acceptable only in situations where the controlling person is educated sophisticated and experienced and the person being controlled is receptive and in need of such guidance.

It was imperative that one of the most deleterious elements of Asiatic societies should be crushed or at least greatly reduced, namely, respect for parents and elders. For this very reason I had established universities and colleges which consistently downplayed respect for tradition and customs. This originally met with a lot of resistance from the older generation, but the young were absolutely thrilled and totally supportive of my concepts. Universities were actually teaching them about all the pain, anguish and suffering that respect for religion, traditions and age had brought to the world.

The only concept which was actively encouraged was total unmitigated rationality. One example of this was the Ten Commandments in Christianity. How could one possibly disagree with something that says that one should not commit any kind of injury to another. Forget the Bible and respect the inference of those Ten Commandments. One does not have to be a Christian to believe in them.

Coming to Islam, the ban on pork at the time when Mohamed preached was absolutely necessary, as the consumption of pork which was so badly contaminated in the Middle East, would have caused enormous health problems. The difference in the situation was that even today, rationality does not disprove the tenets of the Ten Commandments, whereas the ban on the consumption of pork is totally unnecessary. In conclusion, I decided that one of the most fundamental changes to be introduced into a developing society was disrespect for the golden agers. In my personal life, I have never tried to interfere with the personal issues of my children. They are all educated and responsible adults and I sought partnership, not patronage over them.

This is the reason I always wanted to maintain close contact with the younger generation. Whenever there were awards or scholarships given out for merit, I always made it a point to attend and honor these recipients.

One of our top universities was having such a celebration so I decided to attend. Rauf heard about this and requested that he be permitted to come with me for my security. I liked Rauf very much and I enjoyed his company so I welcomed him. A military escort accompanied us to the University. There was a huge hall filled with students both male and female and of course the professors. When I arrived, they stood up and bowed. I heard the chants of "Long live the Shahnshah". Their next sentence was a great delight to me. "Our Shahnshah, liberated us from our parents' ideals."

A list of sixteen brilliant students and prizewinners was presented to me. As I was reading the names, I recognized one of them and looked up at a face I knew. It was Fatima Abbasi, the prostitute who tried to help us track down Manucher. I remembered that I felt so much affection for her that I had arranged the scholarship and had promised that I was going to be her father in the future. Her presence in this line of students was a matter of incredible joy to me. She looked at me, smiled and bowed. I was amazed at the change in her personality. Gone was the coy smile and flirtatious twinkle in her eyes and in its place was poise and dignity.

I continued with the speeches and awards, meanwhile observing everyone's expressions. I could not mistake that look in Rauf's eyes. For a man who was here to defend me, Rauf could not take his eyes off of Fatima. This look of devotion and his sudden desire to accompany me, I realized, were not independent of each other!

When the ceremony was completed, I told Fatima that I wanted to speak to her privately. I asked Rauf to accompany me to the private room which was reserved for us.

"All right Officer Rauf, tell me, what was your motive for coming here with me?"

"Your Majesty, first your protection, of course. That is my duty".

I started laughing. "Rauf, you are like a son to me. Let me tell you where you made your mistake. You just said that the first reason you are here with me was for my protection. At the ceremony I was looking at you and realized that you had other reasons. I recognize that love filled, drooling admiration you have for Fatima, was not for my protection. My son let me enlighten you on my analysis. I think you have fallen for this girl and you want my opinion on the propriety of your plight. Am I correct?"

Rauf was smiling."My Shahnshah, do you ever miss anything? Yes, Your Majesty, I have fallen in love with Fatima. We worked together when we were trying to arrest Manucher and that is when I realized that she is a treasure and that I would like to share my life with her. Her past has been a matter of grave concern to me and I want to know if you will approve a union between us."

"Rauf, if you love this girl you are insulting her by considering my opinion. You must decide, together with her of course, whether you want to become one. I am the Shahnshah of Iran but I have no business in your private lives or of any citizen of Iran. Having said that, I am very proud that my opinion matters to you. You have my blessings and support for this union. I already call her my daughter. She's a brilliant, beautiful and kind girl and will make you a wonderful wife. Her past life may actually be an advantage to you. In a traditional country like Iran, you are brave and strong enough to marry her in spite of that past. My congratulations."

Rauf bowed to me and I could see the hesitation in his demeanour. "What is bothering you Rauf?" I asked.

"My Shahnshah, there are very few people of your calibre and intelligence in your Majesty's generation. My father is a very decent and loving man and has brought me up with kindness and love. He is also very prejudiced in several areas. Unfortunately Fatima's past was very much in the news so every one knows about her, including my father. I took her home to meet my parents and when they found out that it was Fatima, they refused to meet her. I was very offended and asked the reason for such rudeness. Their response was they did not want to either welcome or tolerate their son being in the company of a prostitute. However much I explained to them that she had completely changed and was educating herself to become a sophisticated woman, they refused to talk to her. I love Fatima more than any one else on this Earth and I do love my parents too and I want to amicably settle this with them."

"Rauf, let me list your qualifications. You are a University graduate in economics and throughout your University career you earned merit scholarships. You decided to join the armed forces because of your beliefs and became a Major at a very young age. Your valor and achievements with the forces have earned you several medals. You are a handsome man who is very well read and extremely well liked by your companions. I have noticed several women `giving you the eye' at parties."

"Now please do not be offended. You have asked for my advice and I'm going to be blunt with you."

"Your father appears to be a good man but let us look at his qualifications. He never finished his grade eight education. He is a manual labourer. He is a religious man and in his whole life he has probably not earned the amount of money you make in a year. Then of course there is the despicable quality of the inferior generation. They believe it is their right to advise their children on all matters irrespective of their lack of intelligence and qualifications. A man must never forget his limitations. I am the Shahnshah of Iran but I know absolutely nothing about engineering and medicine."

"Suppose I were to give you advice on a medical condition from which you are suffering, what would you think of me? That is the biggest defect in all Asiatic cultures. Parents have the illusion that they know more than their children then the children themselves! The idiocy of faith has perpetuated this myth and today, in our civilized new Iran we are trying to crush that myth."

"You are a brilliant military officer, who has been given the respect and power that you deserve and are actively involved in the elimination of that myth. You should never take advice from any ignorant human being even if that person is your parent. Do you want me to continue? If you're offended, I will stop right here."

"No, my Shahnshah, I asked for your advice."

"Then my son, an intelligent, educated man who has decided to love and unite with a woman, does not need the consent of his parents. Your position should be, my father, I have decided to marry Fatima. Kindly understand I'm not asking for your permission, I am informing you of my decision. I would love to have a united family with you as a part of it."

"Your Majesty, if I speak that way to him he will throw me out of the house and never look at my face again."

"Yes my son, but you must never forget that if you abide by his decision and discard this beautiful woman whom you love so much, there is something much more powerful which you will have to live with. Do you know what that is? Your reflection in the mirror. Every time you look in the mirror, you will be ashamed of your weakness in not following your heart. What can be worse? Again, the inferior generation may kick their son out of the house because he does not obey them, but surprisingly, they will never be able to do this to a grandchild. Once you have children, they will quickly make up with you and your wife. Ultimately you will have total victory and the same marital happiness. The alternative is lifelong sadness for losing the woman of your dreams combined with the shame of abandoning someone who truly loved you. The choice is yours."

"There is something else I can do for you. Remember my son, unlike you, the inferior generation is very much impressed with the wealth and position of the person they are associating with. If you have carefully observed your parents, you will notice something very interesting. A very wealthy friend is invariably described as intelligent and attractive. When you initially look at this person you are amazed at how any one can refer to them as either intelligent or attractive. The same applies to their position in life. If the older generation thinks that he is an important man they will attribute qualities which he does not deserve. A completely objective analysis of his qualifications is never possible with their small minds."

"You, my son, must use their limitations to your advantage. I will help you in that regard. I will invite your parents, you and Fatima to my Palace. Don't tell them that Fatima is coming. At dinner, I will pay a lot of attention to Fatima and praise her achievements. I will say that if I had a son who was unmarried, I would have been honored to accept her as my daughter-in-law. They will only take two things into account. First, the Shahnshah of Iran with all this power likes this girl and second, the Shahnshah has enormous wealth and with his admiration for this girl some of that wealth may be passed on to her, thereby making their son wealthy. It is your decision, whether I should get involved. I have a very strong suspicion that once I support your cause, Fatima's past will cease to be objectionable to your parents and as a matter-of-fact they will bend over backwards to accommodate her. They may even pretend to love her. Do you want me to try this?"

"Your Majesty, how can I thank you for your kindness, generosity and total acumen. I still find it difficult to believe that the older generation is as ignorant and bigoted as you have described them. I must admit that every time we have had a discussion and I've disagreed with you in my heart, I have been proven wrong. Those occasions did not matter to me because I was doing my job as a military officer. My job is to obey your orders, but this time you are doing this for me. I sincerely hope that on this occasion, you are wrong. If you are right, and they capitulate because of your input and involvement, then two things will happen to me. I will be eternally obliged to you and in the future I will never disagree with you."

I picked up the phone and asked my secretary to contact Rauf's parents and invite them to the Palace for dinner. The reason for the invitation was the great military service performed by their son and the Shahnshah's desire to meet with the family of such a valiant man. No mention was made of an invitation to Fatima. Except for Zainab, no one else would be invited to that dinner. She was going to see to it that alcohol was freely served at the party. If Rauf's father did not want to consume alcohol, that was his right. He should never be allowed to have the illusion that he could exert any influence on what we should consume. Rauf quite enjoyed his Scotch and I advised him not to desist from drinking because his father was present.

All the details were properly arranged. Rauf's parents would arrive first after which Rauf and Fatima. Rauf would apologise for being late. I would act as if I was totally surprised at the arrival of Fatima. I would introduce Fatima to Rauf's parents as my adopted daughter and warmly laud her achievements at the University as well as her brilliance. Let us see whether the inferior generation has the audacity to disrespect the Shahnshah's protégé.

My personal assistant brought Rauf's parents into the drawing room. "Your Majesty, let me have the pleasure of introducing you to Mr. and Mrs. Irfani, parents of your illustrious officer Rauf Irfani."

Both the Irfani's bowed to me. "Shahnshah-e-Iran, how can we express our gratitude at the honor you have bestowed upon us by inviting us to your Palace."

"Mr. and Mrs. Irfani, your son is a rising star of Iran. He is not only the most loyal officer, but also one of the most brilliant and successful law enforcers in Democratic Iran. I am honored to meet both of you. Please sit down. Rauf has just informed me that he is running a little late. Can I offer you some refreshments?"

"Let me introduce you to my secretary and my most reliable and trustworthy employee, Zainab." Both the parents and Zainab exchanged bows.

Rauf's parents requested coffee which they sipped. A few minutes later Rauf and Fatima arrived. "Fatima, my daughter to what do I owe this pleasure? It is good to see you my child. I had no idea that you know Rauf. Come and hug your father."

Fatima hugged me. "My Shahnshah and my beloved father, it is such an honor to be in your presence. Rauf assured me that I would be welcome at the Palace if I came with him."

"My child, you are welcome in my home at any time with or without Rauf. Let me introduce you to Rauf's parents. "Mr. and Mrs. Irfani let me introduce you to my adopted daughter Fatima. She is no different to me than my naturally born children. She is a brilliant University student who has won several gold medals. Over and above that, she is one of the kindest young women I have met."

"Your Majesty, I have already been to Mr. and Mrs. Irfani's home. However, on that day they were otherwise engaged and unable to meet me."

I pretended that I didn't have a clue as to what she was talking about. I very carefully looked at the expressions of the Irfanis. Rauf's mother seemed to be indifferent to the whole situation, but Rauf's father appeared to be shocked at my respect and admiration for Fatima, a woman he had refused to speak to, or welcome in his home.

"Help yourself to drinks Fatima and Rauf." As per our earlier agreement, Rauf poured himself a glass of Scotch and without hesitation a glass of wine for Fatima. The elder Irfani's expressions indicated despair and disbelief. Rauf looked straight at him and I could see the challenge in his eyes. The elder Irfani did not say a word. I think he realized that Rauf was doing this in my presence to put him in his place.

"Your Majesty, I have come to seek your approval about a very important matter. Fatima and I are in love with each other and would like to get married. I'm asking for your approval."

All this had been rehearsed before, so I looked into his eyes and said "I am disappointed with you Rauf! The decision to marry should be made by only two people, the man and the woman. If you two have decided, then who am I to give you my approval?"

"Thank you, Your Majesty, that means you approve of our union. You are the only person on this planet whose approval matters to me."

"The decision is yours, but as the two young people I admire the most are going to be united in wedlock, my congratulations my children." I hugged them both.

"My daughter Fatima, hug your future in-laws and accept their congratulations."

Rauf's mother quietly hugged her and Rauf and then kissed him on his cheek. Rauf's father was stunned for a little while but then slowly walked over to Rauf and very coldly offered his congratulations. He then returned to take his seat.

"When are you planning the wedding? Let me have the pleasure of hosting that lovely event at this Palace".

"Oh my God, your Majesty, do you really mean that? There is no greater honor than what you're offering us today." Rauf said.

"Then that is settled. Mr. and Mrs. Irfani, I will be honored if you would be my guests on this great occasion and accompany the bridegroom to the ceremony. If Fatima approves, I will give her hand to the groom as a father should."

"My Shahnshah, how can I express my gratitude to you? You have taken me out of the hell in which I was born and raised and have put me in the Royal Palace to wed a man who is my prince." Rauf kissed her on the cheek. "Thank you my princess."

I felt this incredible triumph. For the first time in my life I had succeeded in exterminating the control of the inferior generation by putting an uneducated father in his place and preventing him from interfering with his intelligent and educated son. My greatest joy was that it was all done without any bickering, arguments or recriminations. I do not think that Mr. Irfani even realized that today's events were all rehearsed and organized. As a matter-of-fact, I suspected that after going home he would probably tell his wife of the great sacrifice he had made for his son, all because he did not want him to be heartbroken. Of course he would never admit to himself or his wife that he had no choice in the matter because any opposition to the union would be an opposition to the Shahnshah of Iran, which was a real impossibility.

Rauf and I had also prearranged the little act of asking for my approval and not the father's before announcing the engagement. This would be excellent training for both the parents and would serve as a good warning to them not to interfere with their children in the future.

I felt an ecstasy. The inferior generation had been crushed. In a way I was a little jealous of Rauf. I wish I had this power when I was young.

Zainab was the most organized person to arrange for any celebration. She and Fatima had become friends and they jointly arranged the festivities. Hundreds of important Iranians and foreign dignitaries present in Iran were invited to the wedding. I had left the choice of the ceremony to the couple but they decided to have a civil ceremony before a judge. I knew that this was done to please me and I was very grateful.

For several years one of my close friends and associates was the Prime Minister of Turkey who had always supported us. Being an Islamic country which had reformed itself into a secular state, I not only considered Turkey our best ally, but also an excellent guide as to how we should proceed in the future. Our situation was now very stable as several provinces of Iran had rebelled against the Islamic Republic and had voluntarily joined Democratic Iran. A military attack from the North was no longer feasible and our security was excellent. Within the last year and a half the proportion of Iran controlled by us had risen from forty-two to sixty-eight percent. Inviting a foreign guest did not pose any danger to him. I took this opportunity to invite the Prime Minister of Turkey to the wedding. In the invitation he was told that it was the wedding of my adopted daughter. He responded the next day directly by telephone. The warmth he exuded made my heart glow with pleasure.

"Your Majesty, my beloved friend and Shahnshah of Iran, I am extremely honored to be invited to your daughter's wedding. I have conversed and communicated with you for years but never had the pleasure of meeting with you. This is my opportunity and Your Majesty, I will definitely attend with my wife to pay homage to a friend."

"Mr. Prime Minister, it is I who will pay homage to you. During those years when our existence was in jeopardy, you Mr. Prime Minister, were our only ally and supporter. I do not forget these things".

"Then Shahnshah, I don't think you would object to doing me a favor. My name is Osman. It would give me great pleasure if you would call me Osman."

"Well Mr. President, I will grant you that favor on one condition. My name is Sharuq. Please call me by my name."

"I will be honored Sharuq. I eagerly look forward to meeting you."

Television and radio on both sides of the border had announced the upcoming festivities at the Royal Palace. Naturally, there was concern of terrorist activity so my experts had taken all possible security precautions. There was another factor they had also considered. Recently the population of the Islamic Republic had become completely disillusioned with their own government. I think if a plebiscite had been taken in Northern Iran they would have definitely joined us without reservation. My spies and secret agents had informed me that the Prime Minister of the Islamic Republic and his cabinet were very concerned for their own safety. Lately they had even criticized some of the most vocal opponents of Democratic Iran. I gathered from all this information that they would have liked to sign a treaty with us agreeing not to attack Democratic Iran as long as we did the same for them. I had no intention of signing such a treaty. My dream was to unite Iran as one Democratic nation. However, this information made it highly unlikely that they would try something during the wedding celebrations.

Everything went perfectly well. The pomp and ceremony of the occasion was televised throughout the world. The couple looked extremely happy and handsome which was the only important thing as far as I was concerned.

My contact with the Turkish Prime Minister was very fruitful. As soon as we met, we clicked and became excellent friends. Turkey had been a secular state for almost a century. Fortunately for them, it was a relatively powerful military nation in the Middle East. Yet, they were always worried about being attacked by other Islamic fundamentalist nations and before my advent, Iran was the most powerful fundamentalist nation in the area and therefore a matter of concern to Turkey. Democratic Iran was something that Turkey was very happy to have as a neighbour. Our democracy therefore was a significant advantage for the security of Turkey. Before I came here, Iran was a nuclear power. All the areas where nuclear weapons were created and stored were now under our control and as we were the best allies of Turkey, our possession of these weapons was not a threat to them but reinforced their security. Apart from the Prime Minister and I becoming friends, we also signed a treaty of mutual protection. If either of our nations was attacked, the other would automatically be there for military support.

CHAPTER 31.

For the first time in several years there was a sense of peace and prosperity in Democratic Iran. Most of the people who were opposed to our regime, even some fanatical fundamentalists had either been converted to our rational view of life and governance, or had left Iran. The remaining fanatics were not scared of us but of other Iranians. The public opinion now was so favorable, that any overt act of violence or terrorism against Democratic Iran would probably be avenged by the people themselves even without any government intervention. In the history of Iran in the last three centuries, such peace and prosperity was never experienced. Women who had lived under oppression for centuries were our greatest allies. I normally check statistics about the migration patterns of people and was happily surprised to note that almost one million Iranians had emigrated to our territory within the last six months. This was not only because of our democracy, but due to a higher standard of living, freedom and better education for their children, especially their daughters. Only eight individuals had moved North and two of them because of strictly family-oriented reasons.

I was now seventy-four years old and I thought it was time for me to relax a little and to contemplate the future for my country of choice. Naturally the best part of that relaxation was provided to me by Zainab a woman whom I considered to be the most beautiful in Iran. She did enjoy the wealth of being a king's mistress, but she was not a queen and therefore did not have the honor and dignity that would have been provided to an empress. This did not matter to her. To me, a man who had lived most of my life in the West, this was totally incomprehensible. When she took me into her arms at night and we made love, the warmth and passion in her eyes were absolutely genuine. I knew she loved me deeply, for whatever reasons.

Zainab and I were watching television as usual in the evening, when there was a call on my private line. This access was only provided to my senior ministers and military officers. The fact that the call came at ten-thirty in the night was a bit surprising. I had made arrangements that anyone who wanted to contact me must do so through Rauf. This was for my protection as Rauf was provided with a device to trace my calls. I answered the phone and it was Rauf. "Greetings, your Majesty, I know you must be watching television but the most significant event of the day is still not on the news. There is a military coup in the Islamic Republic. A majority of the Generals and Commanding Officers have rebelled against the regime in the North. It appears that they will depose the present government and take over the regime, but we are not clear what they will do thereafter."

"Is there any indication that they might infringe on our territory?"

"It is my feeling Your Majesty that there is no such intention. The military situation at the moment in the Islamic Republic is very confused and inefficient. As a military officer, I can assure you that if they attacked us they would not have a hope in hell of succeeding. Before calling you, I contacted our navy, air force and army and have obtained information and statistics which indicate to me that all three forces of Democratic Iran are at least three times superior in men and equipment compared to the Islamic Republic. As your Majesty is aware, all the nuclear facilities originally created by the Islamic Republic are now totally under our control. It would be insane for them to attack us as we could exterminate them immediately. The General who is leading the rebellion is Brig. Gen. Abbas Mahmoodi. I do not know the man personally, but I have carefully studied his career and can assure you that he is a very experienced and talented military officer. Such a man will not be dumb enough to attack Democratic Iran fully knowing that his country could be exterminated and there would not be the slightest chance of victory. My conclusion therefore is that the military in Northern Iran are fed up of the regime of the Islamic Republic and have decided to take power as a military regime. Whether they want to join us or remain an independent State is not still clear. Does Your Majesty want me to arrange a meeting with all the relevant officers of our country?"

"Rauf, immediately contact the following individuals. Minister Behram Marzban, General Yazdegard Malek, Minister Feruz Kermani and General Hashmat Osmani. Tell them to come directly to the Palace for an emergency meeting. I don't care how late it is, this is very important.".

"As Your Majesty commands."

Zainab seemed to be very concerned. "Is there any danger to you my love?"

"Nothing to worry about my darling. They cannot touch us militarily or politically. We have won the hearts of the Iranians. Our Armed Forces are at least three times as strong as theirs. This revolution in the Islamic Republic may be the event we have always wanted and waited for. We are mentally morally and spiritually superior to them. Annihilation of the inferior generation, religious bigotry and fanaticism are close at hand. I am hoping that this is a sign of the dream I've always had since I became the Shahnshah. A united, free Iran cured of the disease called faith."

I mixed myself a drink and waited for the team to arrive at the Palace. I then realized that this grave political situation did not scare me at all. As a matter-of-fact, it appeared to be the first step to a final victory.

Rauf's telephone call came at 3.00 a.m. "Your Majesty, everyone you summoned is here and we seek your permission to enter the Palace."

I called my guards and told them to let the men in.

When my Ministers and generals arrived they bowed to me and in spite of the fact that all these men were highly qualified, I could see the tension in their faces.

"My beloved Ministers and Generals, it appears to be the most significant day in the history of Democratic Iran. You all know exactly what is happening in the Islamic Republic and I will not reiterate those facts. My main reason for requesting a meeting is to get the opinion of each one of you as to what actions we should take and which officers in the Islamic Republic should be contacted or supported by us. Our respected Minister Behram Marzban was a Minister in the Islamic Republic at one time, I'm requesting that he be the first one to let me know his views on some of the individuals involved in this rebellion. Behram, do you happen to know this officer in Northern Iran called Brig. Gen. Abbas Mahmoodi?"

"Indeed I do, Your Majesty. When I was a minister in the Islamic Republic, which was several years ago, he was a Major. There are a few characteristics of this man which I am familiar with. He is probably one of the most efficient and disciplined officers in the Army of the Islamic Republic. His integrity and loyalty cannot be questioned. One other aspect of his character will be very much appreciated by you my Shahnshah. He is not a religious man. He respects all religions but is not a fanatic. I've personally seen him reprimand some of the officers for being unduly harsh with a few Sunni and Christian military personnel in the Northern Iranian Armed Forces. I also know that he was severely criticized and reprimanded for being so tolerant towards the minorities. His disagreement with the fundamentalist regime is not in doubt. What surprises me is that he would revolt against that country's government. He is the kind of man who may disagree with you in every way but his loyalty remains with the regime he serves. I would therefore suggest very strongly that we try to find the motivation behind his revolt and his ultimate aim."

"General Yazdegard Malek, do you know this man or do you have any opinions of him?"

"My Shahnshah, several years ago I met Gen. Mahmoodi when I was an officer in the Army of the Islamic Republic. I completely support and agree with the views expressed by the Hon. Minister Behram Marzban. I cannot go any further since I do not know the officer personally. As a military officer I can say two things. He is too intelligent and organized to believe that a victory against Democratic Iran is possible with our present military strength. If that is his belief, then there are only two plausible reasons for the revolt. He may have decided to join us and become part of Democratic Iran, or he has decided to eliminate the present government of the Islamic Republic and become a military dictator. I have no idea in which direction he wants to go."

"General Hashmat Osmani, what is your opinion?"

"My Shahnshah, I have never met or known this man but I know of his reputation. I tend to agree with the views expressed by General Malek"

"Minister Feruz Kermani, what is your opinion?"

"Your Majesty, this is a military matter and our respected military officers know much more than I do. I believe it is necessary to look at the history and character of a man before coming to a conclusion on how he would react. Throughout his career, Gen. Mahmoodi has remained faithful to his country's leaders. I do not believe this man is interested in becoming a political leader or a dictator. Somehow that does not fit with his character. A man of his intelligence and military power would not have waited this long to take over the government. I believe the loyalty that he commands from his troops was such that he could have tried to oust the government several years ago. Gen. Mahmoodi is almost sixty years old. It is highly unlikely that he would risk his life at this stage. He has no idea how we would react to this revolt. It is my guess that he is not motivated by personal ambition. My suggestion Your Majesty is to somehow contact this man, meet with him and discuss this issue on a personal level."

"Minister Kermani how do you suggest we go about doing that?"

"Your Majesty, I've already carefully considered this. The first thing in our favor is that he is no longer under the control of the Government of the Islamic Republic or the Prime Minister. Your Majesty's reputation as a man of honor is now international. If Your Majesty were to contact him to arrange a meeting and assure him that he is safe when he visits you, and would be permitted to leave whenever he wishes, irrespective of whether you agree or disagree, I think he may decide to take the opportunity to meet with Your Majesty. I further recommend that this offer should go directly through General Yazdegard Malek who knows him and I have a strong belief that Army officers trust each other much more than they trust civilians."

Minister Marzban stood up. "Your Majesty, if you permit me, I will contact Gen. Mahmoodi, visit him and persuade him to come and visit you."

"Behram, you are too precious a friend and supporter to take such a risk. What if this Mahmoodi is not who we think he is and harms you? I cannot take that risk! I think Minister Kermani's idea is the most feasible. General Malek, are you willing to set up a contact with Gen. Mahmoodi?"

"I will do that right away Your Majesty."

At 11.00 a.m. the following morning Gen. Abbas Mahmoodi arrived at my Palace. He was a very imposing man approximately six feet four inches tall, extremely well-built and exuding a kind of strength and confidence that one does not normally notice in an average person. He bowed to me when he was introduced. I noticed that it was not a humble bow of submission but a respectful bow indicating his appreciation of my position at the same time tactfully demanding the same from me. That gesture impressed me. I do not like servile people who grovel before you and when the opportunity arises, stab you in the back without batting an eyelid. I was convinced that this was a man of honor and strength, the kind of man I admired.

I stood up to meet him and shook his hand as an equal. "Brig. Gen. Abbas Mahmoodi, I am honored to meet a man of your reputation. Please sit down."

"I am honored by the kindness and respect with which you have received me Your Majesty. A compliment coming from a man of your integrity is indeed an honor."

"General, when speaking to a man with a busy schedule like yours, I think it is improper to go into a long discussion about trivialities. I will come to the point right away. I am totally satisfied with the information I've received about you. Our countries have been at war for a long time and that does not mean that I do not respect a military officer of your repute. Your revolt against the Islamic Republic must have a very significant reason. I am not going to ask you to reveal any secrets which you do not want to, however a discussion of your future ambitions in this area will be greatly appreciated by all of us if you condescend to do so. Needless to say, every syllable of this conversation will remain in this room. Can you tell me General, what are your goals?"

"Thank you very much for your courtesy, Your Majesty. Please realize the fact I'm here and have without hesitation accepted your word of honor on my safety is my respectful way of thanking you and my confidence that your word is sacrosanct. I would however once again reiterate my request that my presence here before you and any discussion which takes place today, must remain absolutely secret. I've already arranged for my wife and children to be out of the Islamic Republic and will seek your permission to allow them to settle here in the South. The rest of my family are still in the North and I do not want to jeopardize their safety. You have given me your word of secrecy and I accept it with thanks. Yes, your Majesty, I'm ready to give you all the facts on the motivation for my revolt."

For a long period of time, I have been saddened by the lack of a judicial system which provides justice. As you're probably aware I'm not a religious man but I respect every person's right to believe in religion. However, I do not accept religion when it is forced down my gullet. The oppression of women in the North and the deliberate effort to keep them out of schools and universities is totally unacceptable to me. The treatment of minorities such as the Sunnis, Jews and Christians is also not acceptable to me. The economic situation has deteriorated to such an extent that there are more poor people today in the Islamic Republic than there were ten years ago. Your Majesty is aware that the standard of living today in Northern Iran is approximately one third of what it is here in your realm. I accepted all this for years because I was a military officer sworn to protect the Islamic Republic. I genuinely believed that the decision to change the governance of the country was not in my hands. The military has no business in politics. Having said that, the constant deterioration and corruption was however not acceptable to me and then Your Majesty, an incident occurred that made me totally ashamed of myself for being a part of the army. The information I'm about to reveal is totally unknown to anyone except four other ministers and the Prime Minister of the Islamic Republic and I hope it will stay that way."

"For a long time the incredible enhancement in the quality, strength and capacity of your Armed Forces in Southern Iran has been a matter of grave concern and anger in the North. Continuing information about the incredible prosperity here has not only made the Government in the North jealous, but totally paranoid. Approximately a month ago I was invited by our Prime Minister, Sharukh Mukhtiar. I am not particularly fond of him since I believe that his fanatical thinking is responsible for the deterioration both economically and politically in the North. However I attended as I was ordered to and then I was told something that completely shocked me. The Prime Minister went into a long tirade calling you the pagan Emperor and stating that you were ruining Iranian culture. He then said that drastic measures had to be taken to destroy Southern Iran as it was very close to taking over the Islamic Republic."

"I told him that a military assault on the Shahnshah's state would be totally insane, that you would crush us in a week. I also reminded him that all the nuclear weapons were now in your possession and they could be used against our cities and military installations."

"Mr. Mukhtiar had a sinister smile and agreed with everything I had said. Then he stated that the Shahnshah of Iran has given a pledge to all the nations of the world that these nuclear weapons would never be used. They are not even in the hands of the military in Southern Iran. The idea is to defuse them sooner or later. For this reason, though the weapons are guarded, there is an excellent possibility of raiding the area, taking charge of those weapons and exterminating Zahidan, Khurramshahr and, Abadan. This would completely eliminate the government of Southern Iran and also the possibility of them receiving naval assistance from any other friendly power."

"I asked Mr. Mukhtiar about the loss of Iranian lives as millions of our own people would be exterminated. His response Your Majesty still gives me nightmares. He looked straight into my eyes and said. "Those Iranian's have supported a pagan and have become rich with the pagan's help. They are destroying Islam and the culture of Iran. Their total annihilation is a religious duty." Believe me, Your Majesty, my first impulse was to hit this maniac in the face with my fist. Never mind the consequences. Then I thought that would be a grave error. He could very easily eliminate me and put another military officer to do his nefarious job. Indirectly, I would be responsible for the deaths of at least two to three million Iranians. I swallowed my anguish, asked for time to plan the action and left the Prime Minister's residence. I then went back to my army base and discussed this whole matter with my trusted officers. I am happy to report that there was not one officer in my group who was not totally appalled at the Prime Minister's scheme."

"Within a week, I arranged the revolt against the Islamic Republic and without any difficulty eliminated the small element that was still supportive of the government. As your Majesty is aware, approximately sixty-four percent of Iran is under your control. I have taken over a portion of Northern Iran which I estimate to be about twenty-eight percent of the total area of both Irans. The only area which is not under either your control or mine is about seven percent. Three other rebel groups are involved there and of course the Government of the Islamic Republic."

"General Mahmoodi. Let us be totally frank. I think you are very close to success and then you will gain total control over the whole thirty-six percent which is not in our jurisdiction. What do you propose to do with that territory?"

"Your Majesty, I have absolutely no interest in forming a state of my own. As a matter-of-fact, my intention is to immediately surrender the territory to Democratic Iran. Before I can do that, I urge you not to intervene in any way. As you're very well aware there is still a portion of Iran which is controlled by the Islamic Republic and some of the rebels who are all traditional fundamentalists. If Democratic Iran attempts to attack these people, it would be immediately perceived as an attack on Islam. If I attack and crush this rebellion, the fundamentalists will not be able to argue that it is an anti-Islamic attempt to crush their beliefs. Once we have gained control of the remaining portion of Iran, we will voluntarily surrender the territory to your democracy and that way Iran once again, will become a united nation."

"Your Majesty, I have another personal problem on my conscience. I can tell you very honestly that there are very few people in the world I dislike more than Mr. Sharukh Mukhtiar, the Prime Minister of the Islamic Republic. There is no doubt whatsoever in my mind that he is a devious unscrupulous fanatic. Having said that, I took an oath to serve him and his government, if necessary, at the cost of my life. My heart aches at the thought that I have broken my oath of loyalty and have rebelled against his regime. I've tried to justify this by telling myself that I'm doing this for Iran. To be honest Your Majesty, I sometimes feel that is only an excuse. The injustice and economic distress he has caused to Iran partially justifies my behavior and revolt. However, if I succeed in ousting this man, I do not want his death on my conscience. If I succeed in bringing the rest of Iran under your control, I would request and plead for only one thing. If we arrest him and either I or your own troops bring him before you as a prisoner, grant my one wish Your Majesty, please do not execute him. Let him go and live somewhere in exile."

"General, a man who has ruined the economy of our country and who has brought the benevolent dicta of Islam into disrepute, who has insulted the religion that your prophet created, who has killed thousands of innocent people, you want me to let him go free?"

"Your Majesty, all the reasons that you have just provided are responsible for my decision to oppose the government of the Islamic Republic and the Prime Minister. As I already mentioned, this was not an easy decision for me. I cannot forget the fact that when I took my oath of allegiance, it was not only to the Islamic Republic but also to the Prime Minister himself. Conceded that I did not know at that time what a monster this man was, however, I still have to live with my conscience. After he has been removed from his position he will not be able to do any more harm. If you could let this man live I will be able to sleep at night and my conscience will be free. In return Your Majesty, I promise that I will bring the remaining portion of Iran under your control."

I suddenly realized that this was too important a decision to be made without consultation. I asked Minister Marzban for his opinion.

Behram, you are a very careful and rational man. Consider the situation for a while and then give me your opinion."

Behram considered my question for a few seconds and then slowly stood up. "Your Majesty, I will answer your question from two different points of view. From a purely political one, there would be no better person to have in our camp as this respected General. It may make a tremendous difference in the time required to completely annex the rest of Iran to Your Majesty's existing domain. There is also a second and very significant issue. The loyalty of a man such as General Abbas Mahmoodi is something I greatly respect. It not only enhances my opinion of his character but, I also believe that any person, who supports the loyalty of this man, will himself be enhanced. My suggestion therefore is that we grant the request General Abbas Mahmoodi has made. We must also safeguard the future of Iran, so we will tell the Prime Minister that he will have to live the rest of his life in exile and the charges against him will remain intact but not proceeded with. If he tries anything contrary to the interests of Iran, then we will retain the right to prosecute him."

I noticed that Behram said all these things with that certain gleam in his eyes. Behram was a very cautious and conscientious man. The enthusiasm I saw on his face when he said all this was normally only seen when somebody offered to take him to a movie or a game of golf. I therefore concluded that he had absolutely no doubt in his mind that cooperating with the General was the best choice for us.

I stood up and faced the General. "General Mahmoodi, my learned adviser and I have concluded that under these specific circumstances your request will be granted. Naturally, you will have concerns about my keeping my word and sparing the life of the Prime Minister. Do not be concerned. You have my word of honor that he will be exiled from Iran and if he does not do anything detrimental to the interests of Iran, we will not prosecute or harm him in any way."

The General bowed. "For the first time I'm seeking your permission to address you as my Shahnshah. As of today, I am your humble servant. As to trusting your word, there is no other person on this planet whom I trust more than you. My Shahnshah the rest of Iran will become part of your domain in less than three months."

I felt this amazing sense of warmth for this man and instinctively felt the same coming from him. We formally shook hands and the deal was done.

The meeting was now concluded and everyone left after bowing. Enthusiastically, I returned to my quarters looking for Zainab.

"Oh, I've never seen my Shahnshah so happy in months. I hope you have not found yourself a new mistress?" She said with a smile. "I have a suspicion that my Shahnshah has some non-regal intentions and desires towards me. Am I right?"

"One does not go looking for a new mistress when the good Lord has very kindly provided him with a goddess and you're absolutely right about my desires but the fault is all yours." I kissed her passionately on her cheeks, mouth and neck.

With mischief in her green eyes she said to me, "Take me to the bedroom my man." When we reached the bedroom she gently pushed me into the armchair near my bed. She pulled my zipper down and took me into her mouth. The ecstasy I experienced was far more than

I felt when I became the Shahnshah of Iran. After a few seconds I got up and asked her to undress. With a leer in her eyes she undressed and lay down on the bed. I kissed her from head to toe. Her skin was like satin. Christian Dior could not compete with her aroma. I entered her and we made love passionately. She moaned at every move I made and the music of her moans would put any orchestra to shame. When we were finished I tried to get up and she said "Just stay on me for a while, I want to feel the weight of your flesh on mine." I got up, washed and came back to bed. She said, "My man, I have not seen such a satisfied smile on your face in several months." I nodded with a smile.

CHAPTER 32.

The performance and achievements of Gen. Mahmoodi were indeed amazing. Approximately three weeks after our last contact, the three minor revolting groups were completely surrounded and annihilated by him. These groups consisted mainly of religious fanatics and their support from the Iranian population had dwindled considerably in the last year. There was no support or protection granted to them by the people. The only remaining military force in the Islamic Republic was the Army of the Republic which was under the control of the Prime Minister. The majority of the officers and soldiers of this Army were great admirers of Gen. Mahmoodi, not just his military acumen but also his integrity and loyalty. This strong belief prevented them from accepting the propaganda generated by the government of the Islamic Republic. The typical military thinking pattern was that if such a loyal and brilliant soldier was opposing the Islamic Republic, there had to be something wrong with the Republic and its politicians.

According to our latest information, the Islamic Republic still retained thirty-seven regiments. At the behest of the General, sixteen regiments had surrendered, leaving twenty-one under the control of the Prime Minister and his henchmen. Mahmoodi had given them several warnings to surrender but when they failed to comply, he used his Forces and our Air Force to completely annihilate the Iranian Navy and Air Force. Aerial bombardment by them now, was completely out of the question, leaving their Army completely exposed to our attack.

Sixteen districts of Northern Iran had been captured by Gen. Mahmoodi. The portion of Iran still under the control of the Islamic Republic was now disconnected from any other foreign border and supply of weapons from supporting nations was impossible for them.

Iran's greatest supplier of nuclear and other weapons was North Korea. Mahmoodi had diplomatically contacted the president of North Korea and offered his friendship on condition, that he did not support the collapsing regime of the Islamic Republic. Very reluctantly, Kim Jong-Il had acceded to his request and promised not to intervene.

The Western powers, including the United States, naturally were favoring our government and ideals. Russia and China both had difficulties with their Muslim fanatical elements and therefore sided with the Democratic Republic of Iran.

Israel was overjoyed at the expected annihilation of its most powerful Middle Eastern foe. A majority of the moderate Arab states were indifferent to what was happening in Iran, as they did not expect any threats. More significantly, there was not one single Arab state which could have successfully attacked Iran and they realized that a consequence of their defeat would be catastrophical.

We ourselves had contacted and established a very amiable relationship with the Republic of India, a nuclear power and they in turn had tactfully informed Pakistan that any interference in our affairs by them would be greatly detrimental to their existence. Pakistan would have been the most potent military power against us, but India's help in this area had forced them to grudgingly become neutral.

Gen. Mahmoodi had so beautifully organized and manipulated the military situation, that the Iranian forces were transformed from an attacking mode into a defensive posture. They were totally surrounded and had prepared themselves to be attacked from all sides. The location in which they were trapped was not one from where an attack could be successfully launched.

It was rumored that before Mahmoodi forced the Army of the Islamic Republic into its present position, he had considered two or three different locations for them and ultimately came to the conclusion that this was the best one. Was it a coincidence that one of the most esteemed religious sites of Iran was located only half a kilometre from the area where Northern Iran's Army was forced to take cover? Or was

Mahmoodi completely aware that the devout Muslims of the Islamic Republic's Army would not imperil the mosque and burial site of one of the most respected leaders of Islam. If the actions of the Northern army were in any way impeded because of the fear of destroying the sanctuary, then from the military point of view, Mahmoodi had scored. He himself was a decent religious Muslim but like all intelligent men, he was not a fanatic.

Conceded that such a religious site should be protected as far as possible but if one soldier's life was saved because of fear of the Islamic Army, then it was worth destroying. Islam has never permitted its followers to attach much significance to man-made structures. Under these circumstances, I came to the conclusion this was an excellent piece of military acumen.

I had noticed that over a prolonged period of time, our television and media were rather slow in obtaining the current information about what was happening on the battlefields. The media of the Islamic Republic of course would underplay our victories and overplay our defeats. The news media from the United States and Europe obtained information rather slowly so that when I wanted authentic current information, my first choice was always the BBC.

I turned on the BBC channel and waited for the news to begin. Roy Hawkins was currently the most famous BBC announcer. Mr. Hawkins did not report the news everyday; he was only on for significant events. When they announced that Hawkins was going to report the news today, I knew it had to be important.

"This is the BBC evening news, London. Roy Hawkins reporting. The Islamic Republic of Iran has suffered perhaps the most significant military defeat in its history. The government of the Islamic Republic does not permit any of our reporters to be at the front but the Army of the Shahnshah of Iran does not have any restrictions, hence our reporters were present at what appears to be the greatest defeat of the Northern forces"

The rebel commander, General Mahmoodi, attacked the remaining twenty-one battalions of the Iranian forces in their entrenched position approximately forty kilometres south of Teheran. The loss of life on the side of the Iranian Army is reported to be in the thousands. The defeat was absolutely final as approximately three battalions consisting of about thirteen thousand men have surrendered to General Mahmoodi. The General, who has now voluntarily joined the forces of the Shahnshah of Iran and has been assisted by them, indicated to our reporters that on the specific orders of the Shahnshah, the captured troops were not to be harshly treated. He related to us the statement made by the Shahnshah. "Whatever be their political affiliations, they are still faithful soldiers of Iran. We are willing to overlook their allegiance in the past to the despotic and brutal government of the Islamic Republic. They are now welcome into our fold as our long-lost Iranian brothers."

I could not control my laughter at these alleged instructions that I was supposed to have given to Gen. Mahmoodi. I had told him that all prisoners should be treated with kindness and fairness but the specific words he had used and the nobility of the expression that he had attributed to me, were his own creation. I was convinced that Gen. Mahmoodi was not only a brilliant military officer but would also be an excellent diplomat and politician.

The BBC news bulletin further added that Gen. Mahmoodi had informed the politicians and administrators of the city of Tehran to surrender immediately. Any resistance to the Armed Forces would not only be futile but would cause a lot of unnecessary loss of life and destruction and annihilation of the city of Teheran. He also assured the authorities of Tehran that no one would be treated in a cruel, brutal manner and those who were taken prisoners, would be treated kindly at the express orders of the Shahnshah of Iran. On the other hand if there was resistance, no sympathy would be forthcoming.

Gen. Mahmoodi was quoted as follows, "Our brothers and sisters in Tehran do not consider us your enemies. We are not entering your city to oppress you. We are entering Teheran to unite the great and historic land of Iran under the Shahnshah who respects every religion race and culture and gives them total equality in the ancient land of Persepolis. Oh my sisters of Iran, at last the day has arrived when you will have equality. All oppression against you will cease as soon as we enter our beloved capital city. I want you all to come and welcome not just us, but the final and irrevocable union of Iran under a benevolent Shahnshah."

The newscast ended at this point. Later news reports indicated that Mahmoodi's forces were on their way into Teheran. I thought it would be politically wise to add some of our own forces to Mahmoodi's troops and at my request Mahmoodi immediately agreed to take ten thousand of our troops into Teheran with him. We did not want to leave the impression with the people of Teheran and Northern Iran that the final conquest was by a rebel general. Occupation of Tehran by the forces of Mahmoodi as well as Democratic Iran would remove all possible future propaganda that a rebel general had ousted the legitimate government of the Islamic Republic. This way it would appear that at last Iran was united.

It was difficult for me to sleep that night. The final and total victory over fundamentalist Iran was so close to achievement that at any moment during the night the war could be over. This was not a good time to sleep, so I tried to stay awake. At the same time, if the final victory was going to occur the next day, then it was necessary to remain alert and active for the incredible responsibility I would have to immediately shoulder.

CHAPTER 33.

I had spent two nights and days in restless anguish, waiting for some coherent information regarding the progress of the war. All the news media kept repeating was that Mahmoodi's forces were entering Tehran and that until now they had been received with warmth and welcome. They indicated that in fact, Mahmoodi had not entered Teheran but had completely surrounded it. Initially this was a bit of an enigma to me as to why he would surround the city when he was welcomed by the citizens, then it dawned on me that Mahmoodi did not want any of the ministers and other government officials to escape to other parts of Iran where they could hide or go into exile.

I was very happily surprised when I received a telephone call on my private line and it was from Gen. Mahmoodi. "My Shahnshah, I have the great pleasure of informing you that Tehran has now completely surrendered to our forces. There is absolutely no resistance and in fact incredible warmth and welcome. Thousands of Iranians are waving placards with your photograph. Please accept my heartfelt congratulations on Your Majesty now becoming the Shahnshah of all of Iran!"

"Gen. Mahmoodi, thank you very much for your congratulations and please accept my heartfelt thanks for the miraculous victory you have achieved. You and I will die and disintegrate in time, but history will record for ever that you have brought Iran back into the civilized world. Is there anything you want me to do at this end to help our cause?"

"My Shahnshah, you must have noticed that I initially surrounded Teheran to prevent any of the political criminals from escaping. Your Majesty, it has worked. Many of them surrendered peacefully and others who have been in hiding were exposed to us by other Iranians. The Prime Minister tried to escape. When he failed to do so, he went into hiding, but our forces located and arrested him. I am at your command as to whether I should bring them all to Zahidan to be tried or do you want me to keep them here until you arrive in Teheran to deal with them. The next and most important issue, Your Majesty, is your arrival in the capital of our Iran. I want to be absolutely certain of your security, so I request a few days to organize your welcome."

"There is no urgency my dear friend. I will await your invitation. When I arrive in Teheran, I will express my appreciation before the Iranian people and reward you for your noble achievement."

"I've already received my reward Your Majesty. Your warmth towards me is all the thanks and gratitude I need."

After our brief conversation, I went to my private quarters to tell Zainab of our victory. She hugged and congratulated me. "I had absolutely no doubt from the beginning that my man and Shahnshah would ultimately rule the whole of Iran." She kissed and held me in her arms.

I received a call from my secretary that a large number of my ministers and officers were waiting for me in the assembly room. They all stood up as I arrived. All the formality had disappeared. There was this feeling of total ecstasy. No formal salutation or clichés were mentioned. Behram hugged me. "Now I can say with a clear conscience that I'm hugging the Shahnshah of Iran, not the Shahnshah of a sector of Iran."

An abundance of alcoholic beverages was laid out on the table together with other refreshments. I did not miss the fact that some of the more traditional Muslim ministers and officers selected coffee mugs. However, I noticed that they did not go to the coffee machine. They looked around them and very cagily filled their mugs with non-Islamic beverages, such as scotch, rum, brandy and gin.

Rauf came up to me and bowed . "My Shahnshah, this is the happiest day of my life. The man, whom I respect more than anyone else in my life, is now not only the most significant man in Iran but the Shahnshah of all Iran. My heartfelt congratulations Your Majesty!"

Behram's wife Karima came and congratulated me. "My Shahnshah, my husband and I both congratulate you from our hearts. Single-handedly, Your Majesty, you have at last brought civilization to Iran." She was the only person amongst my associates, who spoke perfect English. I always believed that she was an extremely intelligent woman and sometimes felt that she was wasting her talents being a housewife.

I was seriously considering her for the position of Minister of Women's rights. We definitely needed a westernized woman to end the bondage that Iranian women had suffered over the centuries. I was thinking about all this as I greeted her and she looked up and smiled at me again. "Your Majesty, my husband Behram is usually not very fond of going to dinners and celebrations. Any mention of a movie or a golf game and he comes alive. I am totally convinced that he really cares for Your Majesty, because today he was scheduled to play golf and cancelled to be before you."

Behram overheard the conversation and with a guilty smile he was shaking his head, thereby suggesting to his wife that the conversation should be changed. He then looked at me and bowed. "I would not have missed this occasion to congratulate my Shahnshah under any circumstances." We all started laughing.

"Mrs. Marzban, have you ever thought of joining the government of Iran as a Minister?"

With a playful smile she responded, "Your Majesty, when my husband goes to golf with his friends, he needs at least two cakes to take with him. His friends love my baking. I have to take care of his clothes and golf equipment too. Who will do all this if I'm a Minister in the government? Last time I was occupied and could not pack his clothing, he called me in panic from a golf resort, claiming that he had forgotten to take his underwear with him." She was giggling as she said this and Behram did not seem too impressed with this line of conversation. Iranian women normally did not joke in the presence of other people so the laughter and communication between the two of them relaxed me and made me feel as if I was back in Canada again.

"Think about it carefully Mrs. Marzban. If you agree to join the government, the necessary arrangements will be made."

"I. will carefully consider it, Your Majesty."

After the celebration and socializing had been completed, the spouses and others left my Palace. I had requested all my Ministers and Generals to stay behind. I told them that there was a very serious matter to be discussed. After so much feasting and drinking it took a little while for them to settle down around the Cabinet table.

"My loyal Ministers and Generals, I have an important matter to discuss with you. Now that Iran is a United and Democratic nation, we should do whatever is necessary to perpetuate that situation and create alliances so that no one will ever be in a position to take away our democracy from us. I have thought of a plan and I want your opinion. Let us first go to Teheran to establish our headquarters there. Once they are firmly set and securely ensconced, let us tell all world leaders that Iran wants to celebrate its escape from religious fundamentalism. All religions will be protected and the rights of citizens to practice their faith will be protected. To celebrate this newly attained freedom, we want to invite these world leaders to come and celebrate our joy with us. I was thinking of inviting the President of the United States, the Queen of Britain and the Prime Ministers of all European countries as well as Japan, China, India and Pakistan. Our most honored guest will be the President of Turkey. They stood behind us when we had no friends and were surrounded by enemies. We will make sure that every one is made aware how educated, sophisticated and industrialized Iran has become."

"Rauf will be in charge of security and will see to it that the security of our guests is never jeopardized. From the warmth or coolness shown by these world leaders, I will be able to conclude who our real friends are and who are merely making political gestures. It is at that point that we should make the necessary treaties with some of these nations, forever protecting our future from any attacks or political interference from fundamentalist nations. What are your opinions on my suggestions?"

All the Ministers and Generals were in deep thought. I could see that this was too sudden for them to express a cogent opinion. After a few minutes of contemplation Behram looked up at me. "The concept you are proposing Your Majesty, is absolutely excellent, but I have two concerns. If such a large number of foreign potentates and leaders are to come to Iran at the same time, the security issues will be incredibly difficult. Just in case an attempt is made on the life of one of these men, the repercussions will be terrible. Secondly, in my humble opinion, close relationships can be established if we invited these leaders one at a time and Your Majesty communicated with them on a personal level."

Most of the assembly agreed with Behram's suggestion and our next detailed discussion was our move to Teheran as the new capital of Democratic Iran.

CHAPTER 34.

The entry into Tehran was a phenomenal success. Gen. Mahmoodi had completely surrounded the airport with his troops. When our jets landed, we were escorted into the airport building which was again heavily guarded. Eleven armoured vehicles had been obtained by Gen. Mahmoodi to safely convey us to the Royal Palace in Tehran.

This palace originally belonged to the deposed Iranian monarch Reza Shah. It had been completely refurbished and modernized. Since there was always the possibility of terrorist activity, highly specialized devices had been installed throughout the building, so that not even a mouse could enter without detection.

As our convoy moved towards the Palace, thousands of people welcomed us. " Long live the Shahnshah of Iran! Long live Democratic Iran!" they shouted. For our protection, the military had intermittently positioned men with machine guns en route to the Palace.

There was no question in my mind that the people of Tehran were welcoming us but that did not mean that there would not be some terrorists or fundamentalists who still wanted to get rid of us.

It was a wonderful feeling to be so warmly welcomed by the citizens of a nation which had adopted me as their Shahnshah. At the same time I realized that there was no possibility of my friends and myself ever walking freely in a public area without security. It was wonderful to be the Shahnshah. It was wonderful to have enormous wealth and power. The feeling that I had brought a country back to its original glory was great, but still, the thought occurred to me that I was after all a glorified prisoner. With this morbid thought on my mind, we arrived at the Royal Palace.

Approximately twenty immaculately dressed senior military officers were on guard. They crisply saluted our convoy. For the first time I was entering the actual Palace of the monarchs of Iran.

Several experts from Germany and the United States had been commissioned to supervise the hiring of reliable staff. Latest available technology was used to ascertain that the employees were telling the truth about themselves and were not involved with any terrorist groups.

The first two days after arriving at the Royal Palace I just rested. The tension and all the preparations I had to make regarding the move to Tehran had completely exhausted me.

On the third day I decided that the first and the most significant task was to open the congratulatory messages from various world leaders and to respond. The first message I opened was from the new President of the United States, Barak Obama. I had always admired Mr. Obama and believed that he was a brilliant and authentic statesman. He is one of the rare leaders of the world whose word could be relied upon. I was greatly touched by the fact that Mr. Obama had not sent me the usual typed message with his signature but had written a letter personally addressed to me. I opened the letter.

"Your Majesty, Shahnshah of Iran. On behalf of the people of the United States I want to congratulate you on your incredible achievement in becoming the Shahnshah of Iran. I have never met or known you personally but I know one thing. Any man, who has origins in Africa just as I do, settled in Canada, was invited by the Iranians to rule their country and has succeeded in doing so, must be an exceptional person. My heartfelt congratulations to you Shahnshah for what you have achieved. Not only for Iran but, for the whole of the Middle East. I will hope and pray that what has been achieved in Iran will pervade throughout the Middle East. Your Majesty, in a period of less than five years you have pulled your country out of the decadent Middle Ages into the twenty-first century, giving all your citizens equal rights. This should make Iran an example for the other Middle Eastern and Asian countries."

"If your Majesty ever decides to visit me in the United States, you will be welcomed and I will consider it a personal honor."

To put it mildly, the warmth and acumen of those words touched me deeply. Leaders are quite accustomed to meting out clichés and compliments, but it is very easy to distinguish between genuine warmth and political niceties. I decided to respond to the President and extend a personal invitation for him to visit Iran.

"Dear Mr. President, to say that I was touched by your warm message would be an understatement of my emotions. You, the most powerful man on earth, has taken the time to write a personal letter to me!

I am extremely grateful for your genuine warmth and sincerity. Yes Sir, we have liberated Iran from the religious oppression and outdated concepts of life. Remember Mr. President that whatever I achieved was not invented by me. It is the great democracies like the United States, Britain and Canada where I lived and was educated, that have taught me the concepts I am trying to introduce into Iran. By the same token, Mr. President, I honestly feel that a visit from you to celebrate with us the unification of Iran would not only enchant the Iranian people but would be perceived by them and the rest of the world as a seal of approval by the most powerful democracy on earth.

Mr. President, I am completely aware of the enormous load you carry on your shoulders and the commitments you have. If you condescend to spare us some of your time, we will postpone the celebration date to accommodate your schedule. Once again, allow me to express my gratitude for your warmth and sincerity."

I did not sign my name as the Shahnshah of Iran but signed with my actual name, Sharuq Damania. The letter was then personally delivered to President Obama the next day.

To be perfectly honest, I did not expect an immediate visit from President Obama for several reasons. First of all, he was an extremely busy man with enormous commitments and could not just take off for a holiday to Iran. I also thought that the President's advisers would strongly deter a visit to Iran for security reasons.

We had created a security system in Tehran which was the envy of several Middle Eastern countries, but the Americans did not realize this and I do not blame them. When one thinks of security, the Middle

East is probably considered the most dangerous and insecure part of the world. That situation had now been completely rectified and I was sure that sooner or later we would be able to convince the Americans that the President would be as safe in Iran and probably even safer, than he would be in parts of the United States. I am sure that time will tell.

I was also in touch with our most sincere and closest ally, Turkey. The Turkish President had been contacted and agreed to pay us a visit much earlier than the arranged date of the celebrations.

I was busy scheduling all the arrangements in my office a couple of days later when my secretary entered in a panic and whispered. "Your Majesty, there is a long distance call for you and the person on the line claims that he is the President of the United States. He wants to speak to you personally."

I immediately answered the phone.

"Good morning Shahnshah of Iran, this is Barack Obama. I hope I have not disturbed you?"

"Mr. President, a call from you is an honor that I cannot easily forgo. Nothing is as important as the pleasure of speaking to a man like you."

The President laughed loudly. "My Shahnshah, your command of the English language convinces me beyond a doubt that you grew up in an English-speaking country. How can you be sure that this call is from me and not some imposter?"

Now it was my turn to be complimentary. "Mr. President, very often a voice pattern can portray a person's intelligence. There are few people I've ever met who could compete with yours. Secondly, who can imitate your voice with such perfection that your call would be transmitted to my personal line by our security personnel?" We were both enjoying this conversation and had started liking each other. My experience has taught me that sometimes you can chat with a person on just one occasion and know for certain that you can become good friends.

"However, I do have a request Mr. President. Please do not call me Shahnshah. My first name is Sharuq and I would request you to grant me the favor of addressing me by my first name."

I could hear him laughing again. "Well Shahnshah, that depends upon you. If I am to call you Sharuq, you will have to renounce your Asiatic politeness and call me Barack! Is that agreed?"

"I will be honored to call you Barack, Mr. President."

"Your kind invitation for me to visit you in Iran is one visit I eagerly look forward to. For decades Iran has been extremely antagonistic to the United States. Both parties have been responsible in part for the situation. You Sharuq, have single-handedly converted Iran into a possible ally of the United States. I have always wanted to visit the historical sites of Iran, especially Persepolis, but it was never possible in the past. I do not want you to change your celebration date for my benefit. How does March twenty-first suit you? I realize that it is already the fourth today and that does not give you much time."

"Barack, if I was a superstitious man or a religious man, I would consider your suggestion an omen, a good omen. The twenty-first of March in Iran is Nauruz Jamshedi, the traditional New Year of pre-Islamic days. It is considered a very auspicious day in the year. Your visit on this date is particularly welcome. Coincidentally, we were thinking of scheduling our celebrations for that day. It is perfect. "Then with a chuckle I added."Maybe Allah, or the good Lord, or whoever is in charge, is sending you to us as his messenger."

Barack Obama laughed uproariously. "I've represented many organizations and businesses, but have never had the pleasure of representing the Gentleman or Lady above. You seem to have direct contact with Allah or God, so you better be sure that he provides me with the proper credentials."

"Barack Obama does not need any credentials to be welcomed in Iran by a person who is extremely keen to gain his friendship. Are there any special needs or arrangements that I can look after for your visit?"

"Nothing at all. I request you not to be offended if I bring my own security personnel with me. It is not because we distrust your security, but my advisers will have tantrums if I travel without my own officials and security."

"You're all absolutely welcome. Just let me know your plans and we will be honored to escort you to the Royal Palace."

When this conversation was completed, I contacted Minister Marzban and told him of the pending visit of the President of the United States. Behram as usual, pondered this information for a while and then assured me that he would look after all the arrangements. Knowing Behram and his organized mind, I knew I had nothing to worry about.

Public buildings had been repainted and refurbished. All roads leading from the airport were repaved. A huge auditorium and a stadium had been quickly constructed for the celebrations and the visit. My Palace was refurbished. A suite was newly constructed for the President and his wife with every conceivable luxury included. Within the grounds of the Palace, there were several residences and many of these were refurbished for the President's entourage. This was an extremely busy time for all of us, yet the excitement of the pending visit was felt by all.

A special honor guard was created to welcome the President. Our experts had thoroughly checked each person. Their history, their opinions of the United States, their background and records, lie detector tests were taken, every possible precaution was being taken to protect the President.

In spite of all this, I was extremely anxious when March twenty-first rolled in. I had arrived with my own entourage at the airport at least a half hour before the expected arrival of Air Force One. The jet landed smoothly and Barack and Michelle Obama stepped out of the aircraft. We had originally considered firing cannons in celebration but came to the conclusion that misunderstandings could occur if the Presidential guards did not realize what was happening. As soon as they stepped out of the aircraft, the national anthem of the United States was played by a well-trained band.

I walked over to the President "Well, Sharuq, at last we meet, "The President said with a very warm smile as he shook my hand."Let me introduce you to my wife Michelle."

"It is a pleasure to meet Your Majesty, I have heard so much about you and Barack seems to think so very highly of you." Michelle said, as we shook hands..

"Mrs. Obama, I am very grateful to you and the President for your warmth. Talking of warmth, there are very few people who have the power and prestige of your husband and yet possess so much kindness and exuberance. Welcome to Iran, your new ally."

The President and his wife walked through the honor guard battalion, after which I escorted them to the limousine which was taking us to my Palace.

There were several historical structures we passed on the way to my Palace and I was amazed that Obama knew that they existed, and enthusiastically related the history and origin of each building. This man was not just the most powerful man in the world but also an extremely enlightened scholar of history.

When we arrived at my Palace, I escorted the couple to their quarters. They were both very impressed with the luxurious decor of the furnishings. Our expert designers had combined modern and ancient Iranian decor to furnish the President's suite. Michelle in particular was very impressed and did not hesitate to show her appreciation.

For the first two days and nights, including the night of March twenty-first, we attended many balls and watched several parades. Music and ballroom dancing had been brought back to Iran by me. World class orchestras had been commissioned from Europe to perform all over Tehran

When the celebrations were all completed, the President and I decided to meet with our Ministers to discuss the future relationship between the United States and Iran. In the company of other individuals, both Barack and I were formal with each other but behind the words we had a bond which our astute ministers did not fail to notice.

The following day, our first official meeting began at approximately eleven a.m. in my conference room. Minister Marzban, several of the Ministers and military officials respectfully greeted President Obama. Before meeting with Obama we had agreed on the topics we were going to raise for discussion. It was arranged that I would start the meeting.

"Mr. President, since I have had the good fortune to meet with you, I've come to the conclusion that you are a very rational individual who does not mince his words and comes to his conclusions with quick deliberation. I realize that you are under extreme pressure and therefore I will come straight to the point."

"Mr. President, as you have very kindly remarked in the past, we have brought Iran into the twenty-first century. We have introduced modern education and a thinking process to make Iran a successful, industrialized nation. I am not the only person responsible for this success. There are millions of Iranians who have joined and supported me. There are also millions who were originally antagonistic to our cause but later on realized the error of their ways and joined us. The fundamentalists and fanatics have been defeated and removed from power but they are not dead. Many of them are still plotting to destroy Democratic Iran so that they can once again establish a fanatical regime. I am an old man and my life or what remains of it, is of no consequence. It is however my duty to protect Iran from the resurgence of fanaticism."

"For this reason Mr. President, we have carefully considered several proposals and would like to present them to you."

"The Middle East consists of some very civilized nations. They may all be devoted Muslims but they are not fanatics and are actually supportive of us. The King of Jordan and some of the Emirates are in that category. Turkey of course is the epitome of what I consider a civilized Middle Eastern nation. Unfortunately some of the militarily powerful Middle Eastern nations are fundamentalist and in their opinion we are the enemy."

"We have considered a plan to place before you. We request that you create a new political body similar to NATO. Suppose we were to call it the Middle East and American Cooperation Union or MEACU. Your question of course is going to be, what good does this do for America and I will answer that right away."

"By creating and joining this union, America will be assured that their investments in oil and other commodities in the Middle East will be protected by the already existent Treaty organization of Iran and Turkey." A recurrence of the situation like the attack on Kuwait by Iraq and Saddam Hussein would be a physical impossibility."

"We guarantee that our American allies will be protected in the Middle East. From a trade or dollars point of view, we will agree to trade with the United States with very few tariff barriers. If we have a choice of importing certain necessary materials, whether it's industrial machinery or other products, naturally our first concern will be the cost, but if US manufacturers match the best available price, then we will import products from the United States."

"We will also guarantee the United States that our oil will be sold first to them in preference to any other nation. Mr. President, you and I are both aware that the United States is very concerned that some day the Middle East, particularly the Arab world, may close down its supply of oil because of some fanatical regime, thereby causing enormous difficulties for America. I am absolutely certain that America will not accept this which could lead to a war, occupation, loss of life which no one wants."

"With our new treaty, you will be assured the necessary supply of oil for a prolonged period of time. This will give you the opportunity to create and manufacture an alternate fuel source."

"Your next question I'm sure will be, why would Iran want the Americans to find a new source of energy thereby depleting the value of Iranian oil."

" My answer is very simple. Sooner or later such a source will be created either by America or some other industrialized nation. If we sell you our oil in preference to all other oil suppliers, we will make enormous amounts of money to industrialize this nation to the standard of any western country."

"Thus when our oil resources are depleted, we will be able to exist without any problems. You on the other hand will never have to worry about being deprived of a regular oil supply."

"Mr. President, let us look at our recent history. The war in Afghanistan and Iraq led to enormous loss of life on both sides and let us not forget the loss of life in the Iran/Iraq war. The reason for America's intervention in the Middle East is not our concern. Its success or failure is a debatable issue. One thing is absolutely certain. If the treaty I'm suggesting had been in existence, there would not have been any Iran/ Iraq war. There would not have been a Saddam Hussein attacking Kuwait. There would not have been any Taliban in Afghanistan to cause the twin towers disaster."

"Our alliance will keep a continuous and well-informed surveillance on any fanatical elements capable of destroying any advanced nation. From your point of view Mr. President, imagine the number of American lives which can be saved by the creation of this Treaty."

"That is all I have to say and now let us have some idea as to whether you agree with this and to what extent."

President Obama looked at me for a long time and. I was not sure whether it was curiosity, disbelief or doubt.

"Your Majesty, the treaty organization that you have suggested has occurred to me in the past, but such an exquisitely described and focused plan was not conceived by us. I agree that this would be beneficial to us all. However, as you will understand, I am unable to make any commitment without consulting my advisers and the military. However I have one question. Apart from the United States, Turkey and Iran, will there be any other members invited to join this organization? One of the nations which is our close ally is Israel and we would of course want them to be part of this Treaty. What is your view on this membership?"

"Mr. President, my concept of this Treaty is to start a union of states. As time advances and other nations in the area begin to agree with our concepts, we can add new members from time to time. But at this time, Israel's admission will be perceived by other Arab nations as a danger to their existence. At the same time I do see your point that if someone shares in protecting Israel from its enemies, that will greatly relieve the burden upon the shoulders of the United States."

"So here is what I'm suggesting. Once the Treaty organization is formed, we will start acting as arbitrators in Middle Eastern disputes. If necessary, military force will be used against any aggressor. As you and I both know, Israel has no territorial ambitions against its neighbours. Their dream is to live peacefully in harmony with its neighbours. This dream of Israel can be protected by our Treaty organization. To all appearances, it would seem like a guarantee to the Arab nations that Israel will not be permitted to attack them militarily, and by the same token, Israelis will have the assurance that they will not be attacked by any of their neighbours. In the long run this will ensure political stability and peace in the Middle East."

"Initially the Emirates were also part of the fundamentalist group in the Middle East. Prosperity and the attack on Kuwait by Saddam Hussein, have both contributed to making them slightly disgruntled with fundamentalism. They too want their independence guaranteed. Sooner or later, they will also want to join our Treaty organization. Mr. President, you must have realized that the Emirates have never actively joined the Arab nations in attacking Israel."

"Mr. President, let me raise a point which may be considered a criticism of the United States. It is not meant as such. I do not doubt the desire of the United States to bring democracy to the world. I do not doubt the integrity of Americans in what they want to achieve."

"However, there is one aspect of American foreign policy which unfortunately, has a serious defect. That is the ignorance on the part of Americans of the thinking pattern and behavior of Asian nations. An innocent joke or gesture may be considered extremely offensive in the Arab world. I remember an incident in Iraq where there was some rioting and breach of peace near a shrine in Karbala. The Americans wanted to ease the tension, so they started playing Western music. The playing of such music in front of the religious shrine was considered an affront and an insult. I'm quite certain that this was innocently done but this clearly demonstrated serious lack of knowledge on the part of the American occupation forces. That situation will not occur when a Middle Eastern nation such as Iran, intervenes in the area. Iranians and Arabs have the same religion. Conceded that there is some animosity between the Shiites and the Sunnis, however the cultural pattern is similar. It will be very easy for us to guide American troops as to what is expected of them in the Middle East. Thousands of American lives will be saved in this manner."

"Your Majesty, what you have suggested to me is totally logical and I sincerely believe that it will work. Let me go back to the United States, consult my advisers and get back to you on this point. I want to also add that your analysis of the situation is absolutely brilliant. I now understand why a chartered accountant from Toronto, Canada, at the threshold of old age, could successfully come into Iran and convert it into a civilized nation."

"Are you calling me a fuddy-duddy Mr. President?" I asked with a smile.

He bent his head close to me and whispered in my ear. "Sharuq, when I get to your age I would wish to be a fuddy-duddy like you."

"Alright Mr. President, my Ministers and Generals, I believe we have successfully completed the business we wished to discuss. Our guest needs some rest and relaxation and this meeting is adjourned."

All the participants of the meeting stood up, bowed to both of us and left. After the door had been closed I looked at Obama. "Barack let's have a party, just you, Michelle, myself and a lady I want you to meet."

"Sharuq, is this lady who you are going to introduce to me your private secretary, but who in your private life is a whole lot more?" Obama asked with a mischievous smile.

"You wily American. You must have investigated my private life before coming to Iran. Am I not correct?"

Barack Obama laughed uproariously. "Well, I was informed that there was an extremely beautiful woman in the service of the Shahnshah of Iran. She is so beautiful that the press wants to get her pictures every time they have an opportunity. She shuns those contacts completely. She lives in the Royal palace. Nobody has ever seen her performing any secretarial duties. At all private functions in the Palace, she acts as the hostess."

"It is also reputed that when the Shahnshah looks at her, his admiration for her seems to exude from him. Under these circumstances, do you blame the advisers of the American President when they asked me to meet this lady and then express my appreciation to the Shahnshah for his good taste?"

"Barack, you're a very sly man and thank God for it. This will enable you to protect the United States. Come on, Michelle has already met Zainab and they are awaiting our arrival."

We both walked into our quarters where Zainab had already prepared a reception for the President and his wife. Michelle and Zainab seemed to hit it off very well. Each had a drink in her hand and seemed to be busy chatting about something rather funny. I hoped it was not me.

"Zainab, let me introduce you to the most illustrious man you and I have ever met. President Barack Obama of the United States."

"Mr. President, this is my very close friend and personal secretary, Zainab."

Obama walked over to Zainab took her right-hand and gently kissed it. "Madam, I'm delighted to meet you. The Shahnshah speaks so well of you and now I know why. I'm delighted to meet the most beautiful woman in Iran."

Michelle smiled. "Didn't I tell you Zainab that my husband has very clear vision when it comes to beautiful women?"

Zainab bowed and with a smile she responded. "If the First Lady attributes such clarity of vision on the part of the President, then I am indeed flattered by his kind remarks."

I must say I was really impressed with my Zainab's astute and charming response to the President. Especially as it was so well worded in the English language.

I remember that evening and the party with a sense of nostalgia. There were no further political discussions or unnecessary protocol. It was amazing to realize that such informality and friendship between two individuals could come into existence in such a short period of time. At my age and with my experience, I do not accept or believe anything without evidence. It was not only a beautiful friendship we had formed, but I felt much honored that the most powerful man on earth could show such warmth and consideration towards me and my household. Some music had been provided in the form of CDs and we even danced a little before the evening was concluded.

The following morning, President Obama left for the United States. Zainab and I escorted them to the airport and wished them a happy flight. True to his word, a draft of the treaty arrived at my office within a week of his departure. The terms of the treaty were as follows. The United States, Iran and Turkey had all agreed to form an alliance whereby an attack on any one of these three nations would be considered an attack on all three. In particular the United States categorically agreed to protect Iran from not only an attack by a neighbouring nation, but even from any internal revolt against my regime, if we requested their intervention. Barack Obama had kept his word and now we were safe from any resurgence of fundamentalism.

All three nations also agreed that they would maintain peace in the Middle East and use necessary military force against any aggressor. This was an indirect and diplomatic way of protecting Israel from attack. Israel had no intention or desire to occupy other Arab countries. It only commenced military activity when attacked.

The constant rocket fire from neighbouring countries, particularly the Gaza Strip was a chronic problem for Israel. We therefore introduced the system whereby any such attack was now unacceptable and instead of Israel taking unilateral action, the treaty organization would take the necessary steps against the aggressor.

Theoretically speaking, this would equally apply to Israel if she herself attacked any Arab nation. Of course this was only a cliché, because Israel had no desire or intention to take any land from her Arab neighbours. We were acting like a police force by keeping peace in the area.

After that day's chores were completed I went up to my quarters. I complimented Zainab on the sophistication she had displayed during the Presidential visit. I also told her how impressed I was at the way she had mastered the English language. As usual she gave me that tantalizing warm smile. "Perhaps living with my Shahnshah has made me absorb his royal acumen.

I was looking at this lovely woman who was mine. I had never met anyone so amazing and so perfect. She was the most beautiful woman I had ever known. She was kind, generous and extremely intelligent. Even though she did not have much formal education, she was in effect an extremely educated and enlightened woman. She had mastered the protocol of the Royal Palace, as if she was born to it. She controlled the staff without difficulty and without being bossy or obnoxious. She was totally loyal to me and had never shown the slightest interest in any other man in spite of so very many handsome young men in my employ.

We had an abundance of money and she had an extremely generous allowance, which she hardly spent. She donated large sums of that money to charity.

The only issue which baffled me was the fact that she loved me, an old man, old enough to be her father. When she became mine, she said she really started loving me. Now I was not the Shahnshah of Iran to her, I was her man. I'm sure this thinking pattern was a characteristic of her Asiatic background. Centuries of oppression against women could have made them conducive to the total acceptance of the shortcomings of their men. Perhaps, I was her man and psychologically, she was prepared to accept me with all my faults and shortcomings. However I did not want to completely believe this. I wanted to feel that she really loved me for myself and that thought made me divinely happy. I kissed her and suggested that we go to sleep. She did not reply, just nodded her head, came into my arms and fell asleep. Her soft breathing against my chest was, as always, soothing to me.

CHAPTER 35,

Mansur Ghaznavi was a man of great personal charm. He was approximately six feet five inches tall and extremely well built and had bright shiny eyes. He spoke Dari, Pashtu, Farsi and English almost fluently. His accent and cadence in all of these languages was excellent. He was educated in England, had graduated from Oxford University and throughout his studies had obtained merit scholarships. He attempted to enlist in the British Army and had hoped for a posting in Afghanistan. He had gone to Britain as a refugee, allegedly to avoid Taliban persecution. Unfortunately he was not permitted to join the British Army since he was still not a citizen of that country. Because of his physical and mental skills and charming personality, the British military officers who had interviewed him were keen to take him into the armed forces. They had him investigated thoroughly. Their first concern was to ascertain whether he was an Afghan sympathizer or terrorist trying to sneak into the British forces. He had been carefully monitored and one of the most revealing pieces of information obtained about him was that he was extremely fond of Scotch whiskey hence not a devout Muslim. He had several sexual relations with English girls. He was extremely critical of Islam and Muslim fundamentalism. The officers concluded that he would have been an ideal man in the British forces in Afghanistan. Unfortunately for him, British law did not permit foreigners to join the British Army, especially if they were to be posted in the country of their origin. Reluctantly, his application had been rejected.

The officers still had hopes of convincing the British government to make an exception of this man and were a little disappointed when one fine morning Mr. Ghaznavi disappeared. He had left no forwarding address. His immediate family were not aware of his whereabouts. It was an enigma.

The circumstances of his disappearance were so suspicious that they were initially concerned that he may have been abducted by some Afghan extremists and taken to Afghanistan. This did not make any sense at all as he had never exhibited any disrespect or dislike for the Taliban. The British then started an investigation in Afghanistan to find out what had become of him. To their utter surprise their contacts informed them that Ghaznavi was now living in a small town close to Kandahar and was reputed to be an active participant in several terrorist activities started by the Taliban. This information was not cogent complicity and uncharacteristic of the man they had known. Since he was highly qualified and intelligent, he could be dangerous so they had decided to keep a constant eye on him.

Mansur Ghaznavi had just completed his Friday prayers. The mosque he was praying at was approximately forty-five kilometres from the city of Kandahar. This was an area of Afghanistan which was totally controlled by the Taliban. There were no British or American troops in the vicinity. They would not dare to come into this area as they would be blown to pieces.

Mansur was picked up by five men armed with machine guns and taken away in a Jeep.

The inhabitants of the area were in awe of Mansur Ghaznavi and his followers and kept a respectful distance from him even during prayers at the mosque. If he was even approached or greeted by some one, Mansur had the horrible habit of glaring at that person without responding. There were rumors that a few individuals had challenged him in the past and had disappeared without any trace. It is for this reason that all the local citizens of Kandahar left him alone.

The Jeep in which he was traveling arrived at his residence. There were no paved roads or neighbours in the area. The area was heavily guarded by his militia and no one dared to approach within miles of his compound. Mansur invited the occupants of the Jeep inside. He took them to the dining room and without further ceremony asked them to sit down.

"My brothers, as you are aware, the most powerful Islamic country has now fallen into the hands of the infidels. You do know that there are only two Muslim countries which have nuclear weapons, Iran and Pakistan. Pakistan is still on our side, but is constantly afraid of a military encounter with India which is far more powerful. Expecting any military aid from Pakistan to defend our Islam and to bring Iran out of the hands of the infidel, is a dream. The present government of Pakistan is corrupt and weak. As a matter-of-fact, at the insistence of the United States they are crushing our Taliban brothers in the Northwest Frontier province. The Saudis are lackeys of the Americans. The rest of the Arab world is totally powerless, but that is not the worst part of it.

This new treaty between the United States, Iran and the semi-infidel land of Turkey is a disaster for us. Don't believe the cliché that they circulate. They are not here to maintain peace in the Middle East, they are here to crush Islam and steal our oil.

The pagan Shahnshah has joined them so that we cannot kick him out to bring Iran back into the fold of holy Islam. We have to take action now, otherwise we will sink back to the life we led in the eighteenth century when Britain, France, Turkey and Russia controlled the Islamic world and treated us like servants and slaves."

Mansur's followers nodded very respectfully. It was customary for them to nod when he made a statement since in his world there was no place for disagreement. He had enormous wealth, the source of which was unknown to any one. The Taliban leaders were quite scared of him. There were two incidents which his followers could not easily forget. One of Mansur's well-respected companions had disagreed with him on an occasion and had walked out. Mansur said nothing at the time but a few days later, the man's body was found in the bushes. His testicles had been cut off, his eyes had been gouged out, his tongue was cut off and in his mouth was a note which read "Arrogance leads to death."

The Taliban leader who had disagreed with him met a similar fate. His body was later found with both arms and legs cut off. Investigation into the cause of death revealed that the man was not killed instantly but after the amputations he was allowed to bleed to death. A cassette tape of his pleas for forgiveness, the screams of agony and the slow fading of his life, was found next to his body.

Whoever joined Mansur's organization was automatically a rich and powerful man in the area. He could commit just about any crime and get away with it since no police officer had the nerve to arrest him. Many of Mansur's followers had abducted young girls, raped and abandoned them. and the parents were helpless in having them arrested.

Farmers, businessmen, even government officers were ordered to contribute funds to his organization. The purpose of this collection was allegedly for the preservation of Islam, but in reality it was distributed to Mansur's followers as long as they obeyed him.

He told his followers that he was the representative and guardian of Islam in Afghanistan and that Allah had endowed him with the right to take any action for its preservation. Hence if any one disagreed or disobeyed him, it was Mansur's duty to exterminate the offender and sometimes even the whole family, so that such blasphemy could not recur.

Originally his followers used to think this was a threat to keep them in shape but actual extermination of his opponents had convinced them that Mansur meant exactly what he said. There had been instances where a follower did not show adequate enthusiasm for Mansur's plans or speeches. On the first such travesty, the man and his family were deprived of their homes and property and on the second occasion, he perished. There was no third chance.

"Now listen carefully, "Mansur continued. "This treaty between Iran, Turkey and the United States is extremely detrimental to the interests of the Taliban and the Lashkar-e Taiyaba. In the Kandahar area we actually had started winning against the Americans and the other pagan forces. Our resistance and strength were growing, particularly because we were receiving sophisticated weapons from Iran. The pagan Shahnshah was powerless in stopping us until the whole of Iran had fallen under his control. Even then we successfully continued our resistance, because of the ignorance of our American occupiers. Now, that has changed."

"The supplier of our weapons and our most powerful ally has become our most potent enemy. Iranians know our culture, thinking pattern and our geography. It will be very difficult to resist their intrusion into Afghanistan. Physically, to go to war with Iran is impossible. Our only recourse is to make the Shahnshah look like a traitor to his own people. He must be shown as a man who is purely antagonistic and is a real enemy of Islam who has conspired with the American pagans to eliminate our noble faith from the Middle East."

I have created a scenario which will convince even moderately religious Iranians that their king is an American agent placed in Iran for that specific purpose. My brothers, we Afghans and Sunnis have fought against the Shiites for centuries. We hate them and they hate us. At last the time has come to use those Shiites to bring down the Shahnshah and at the same time kill thousands of these semi-pagans so that once again the true faith of Sunni Islam is re-established in the Middle East."

"Brother Mansur, how are we going to achieve this goal without sophisticated equipment? It is bad enough to fight with the Iranians and their sophisticated weaponry but now we have the Americans to deal with and we have no aircraft," one of his companions said.

"Let me answer that. The Shahnshah has a very complicated system of communicating with his Generals and Ministers. The equipment he uses makes it impossible for any one to ascertain what is being said. The Iranians have successfully defeated the Islamic Republic and one of the reasons for their final victory was an incredibly sophisticated communications system which was used by the military and its agents to locate pockets of enemy resistance and then exterminate the enemy by leading the Shahnshah's armies to their locations. The Islamic Republic did not have a chance when it came to tracing the methodology of this equipment and my endeavour is to find that source. Obviously, Iranian scientists do not have the qualifications or expertise to create such software. Lo and behold I found out that the equipment was originally imported from England."

"When I was a resident of Britain and was attempting to join their Army, I developed certain significant contacts with military scientists and the manufacturer of this equipment. As you are all aware, the British Army actually wanted me to join them. Unfortunately their pleas to the British government were ignored by the authorities. This however did not stop me from getting closely acquainted with this computer manufacturer."

"When the economic depression of 2008 occurred, a large number of manufacturers were in serious financial difficulties. Mr. Robert MacIsaac, the president of Transcom, was one of them. Before coming to Afghanistan, I purchased the formula for the equipment for seven million pounds. The money was provided to me by our Taliban supporters in Afghanistan. As I was so strongly supported by the military hierarchy of Britain, it was easy for me to convince Mr. MacIsaac that I was secretly acting on their behalf."

"The seven million pounds were not paid into the accounts of the company but paid in cash to Mr. MacIsaac in part and a major portion was deposited in an account in a Swiss bank. Mr. MacIsaac had some doubts about my integrity, but he looked the other way when he saw the seven million pounds."

"This had a double advantage for us. Mr. MacIsaac was not too keen to know where the equipment was going and as a matter-of-fact made every possible effort not to find out, as that would be considered treason in Britain, if he had knowledge or suspicion about our activities and had still made the deal."

"Gentlemen, I have that equipment and now I can successfully trace every message from the Shahnshah and his officers to other Iranian authorities. They are so certain of the perfection of their equipment that they would never for a single minute doubt that the orders are not coming from the authentic source when it is used."

"We will select approximately fourteen famous religious Shiite sites and install bombs with remote controls so that we can detonate them without being anywhere close to the sites."

"We will then create fictitious orders from the Shahnshah, telling his Army personnel that the time has now come to rid Iran of Shiite Islam. He has introduced many so-called reforms which have completely eliminated Sharia law and has put restrictions on religious intervention in schools and government activities. The people of Iran will not doubt the authenticity of these messages since the Shahnshah is extremely popular with Iranians. They will have suspicions about the integrity of the messages. There will be a significant doubt in their minds about the Shahnshah wanting to destroy these religious sites."

"We now come to the most devious part of our plan. We will not send these messages to the Army of Iran, we will leak them to the public. Some of them will be sent to respected Islamic leaders in Iran from Saudi Arabia, which is basically not antagonistic to the Shahnshah. Others will be leaked to the Army which will be so surprised at such orders coming from the Shahnshah, that they will immediately send senior officers to him for confirmation of the orders. I do not have the slightest doubt that the leaked information will be disbelieved, but at least it will stir up some suspicion."

"Exactly at that moment of slight suspicion, every single Iranian Shiite religious site that we have earlier targeted, will be blown to bits. The specific date of these explosions will coincide with one of the most significant religious days of Shiite Islam. The institutions and sites will be full of pilgrims and all of them will be killed."

"My brothers, this will greatly reduce the number of semi-pagan Shiite Muslims. With the combined effect of the false messages and the enormous destruction of religious sites and loss of innocent Shiite lives, doubts in the minds of Iranians about the Shahnshah's perfidy will be cemented."

"We will keep some of the false messages with us for future use at other locations to be targeted. When the shock of the Iranians is at its peak, we will use some of these messages to create the impression that the Shahnshah is planning to blow up some more Shiite religious sites."

"I'm sincerely hoping for pandemonium in the Iranian government structure. At this time, we will make an effort to assassinate the Shahnshah. The man chosen for this purpose will be a native of the Iran/Afghanistan border region and will be trained to pose as an Iranian. We do not have to worry much about his communicating with the Iranian authorities, because he will be a suicide bomber and will be dead with the pagan Shahnshah."

"The explosive devices are ready and I will delegate some or all of you to install them right away. We have one great advantage. The Shahnshah has made Iran safe and no one is guarding these religious sites, since they are not expecting any terrorist activities. Allahu Akbar, what can be better! We are using the safety and security established by the Shahnshah to destroy him."

"We are destroying Shiite religious sites, killing thousands of Shiites, and using those Shiites to destroy the pagan Shahnshah."

"The Americans will not know about this. Their ignorance of our culture is an excellent weapon. As a matter-of-fact, they will be so shocked that they will start believing that the Shahnshah has taken an active part in this tragedy."

There was pin-drop silence in the room. One could actually hear the breathing. The shock on their faces was so incredible that even the sour expression of Mansur Ghaznavi had changed to what resembled a smile.

"Well gentlemen, do you have any questions?"

"What happens if any of this information reaches the Shahnshah?" One of his accomplices asked.

"Listen Rahim, you are the only five people who have been told this. I am entrusting each one of you with the additional responsibility of watching each other. If the information gets out, it must be from one of you. If that happens, all five of you will be brutally tortured and executed. So you should be absolutely sure that nothing is revealed by this group. Each part of the outlined plan will be executed in Iran or Saudi Arabia. There should be no connection perceivable with Afghanistan."

Each one of you will be in charge of five operatives. These individuals will set up the bombs but they will not know the purpose of their entry into Iran or the location to which they will be sent until you are actually there. If at any time you have the slightest doubt about the reliability or courage of any of the operatives, kill him instantly. We are doing this for Islam. The life of an individual is trivial and insignificant. Are my orders completely understood? Any questions?"

They all nodded in assent but the fear they felt was visible in their eyes.

"Brother, how are we going to transport these explosives from Afghanistan to Iran without being discovered?" Rahim asked.

"Those plans have already been completed. Have you heard of the bus company called Kabul Transport? They are the most significant transportation company connecting Afghanistan with Iran. Every day at least thirty to forty buses cross the border. The Iranian authorities have believed for a very long time that this is the major link between the two countries and for this reason, these buses are not checked. The Iranians have absolutely no fear of any kind of explosives entering from Afghanistan, especially on buses used by common civilians."

"Every step of our plan has to be kept secret. If a bus is blown up, the Iranians will not find any evidence to connect us to the explosives. As far as dead Afghans are concerned, think of them as martyrs who have died for the protection of Islam."

"The first bus leaving Kandahar departs at 7:50 AM tomorrow morning. It is a direct bus to Teheran but you will not be traveling all the way. You will be informed when to get off the bus. Any more questions?"

No one had any.

Rahim and three of the organizers, each in charge of five operatives, boarded the bus in Kandahar the following morning. They had absolutely no idea which location they were going to. Rahim knew that the remaining two leaders with their operatives would board other buses bound for other destinations.

The drive was long and slow and the anguish which they suffered made the journey even longer to endure. After approximately five hours, Rahim received a call on his cell phone. He was asked to get off the bus with his five operatives in the city of Mashad. The others were to continue further on into the interior of Iran. At this point in time he had absolutely no idea where he was going or what he was going to do. They had been instructed to wait for another call.

They all sat in a little cafe sipping coffee. An hour after their arrival, Rahim received his call. He noticed that the voice of the caller was distorted so he could not recognize who was on the other end of the line. It had to be Mansur but there was no way of being certain..

"Today is the Iranian holy day of Id-ul-fitr. Approximately two to three thousand people will be attending the prayers at the Mohinuddin mosque. The prayers are not scheduled to begin for another four hours. You all should walk in like devoted pilgrims and set up the bomb as per my instructions. At this time the mosque is not guarded, the only people you may see there will be the cleaning staff. Do not speak with them as they will recognize your Afghan accent. Pretend that you are praying and then affix the bomb behind the podium where the mullah gives his sermon. I've already given you a list of four of the mosques in Mashad. Give identical instructions to your remaining four operatives regarding the placement of bombs in these mosques.

After the explosives have been planted, do not remain in the vicinity of any of the mosques. Return to the bus terminal and remain there until you hear the prayer call. At this time wait for exactly twelve minutes and then use your remote control to detonate the bombs simultaneously. If possible, wait for the azan call, and board the bus before detonating the bombs. The explosions will be so fierce and loud that most probably the bus drivers will not be in a hurry to start their vehicles, since they will be curious to find out what has happened. Even if they do start the bus, every passenger who leaves Mashad without finding out the reason for the explosions would become suspect. If you're already on the bus, no one will suspect you. God be with you my brothers!"

Rahim obediently conveyed the orders about the setting up of the explosive devices to all his operatives. One single remote control device would explode all the bombs and that device would always remain in his possession.

When his instructions had been completed, one of his operatives, Osman, approached him. "Brother Rahim, did I understand your instructions correctly? Are we supposed to blow up five mosques in Mashad alone? Thousands of Muslims will die. This religious festival is not for Shiites alone, Sunnis may be praying at some of these mosques. Is it fair to kill all these innocent people? I will not comply with such barbarity."

"You are to obey orders, not question them. Come with me. I do not want to explain everything to you before the others. Let us talk privately."

Rahim took him a few hundred yards away from the others into a secluded area.

Osman followed him expecting a friendly explanation of the situation. Suddenly Rahim turned around and Osman noticed a gun pointed in his direction. "You have committed the one sin that a mujaheddin is not permitted to commit. You questioned our authority." Rahim may have been his leader, but Osman was a much better trained Taliban militant. Without drawing his weapon from his pocket Osman fired his gun directly at Rahim's right elbow. Rahim's elbow was totally shattered. He screamed in agony and fell to the ground. The gun had fallen from his hand.

"You bastard, you believe that you can sneak in and kill a Taliban warrior as if he was a boar in the bush?"

Osman realized that very soon Rahim's supporters would come and kill him, so he decided to leave the scene very quickly. "You cowardly pig. I could have easily killed you but that would force Allah to receive you. I would rather you suffer, living without your right arm for the rest of your life."

Osman bolted into the bushy area and disappeared from view. There was a huge commotion from the followers of Rahim when they saw that his arm had been totally shattered. They made some cursory attempts to catch Osman but were unsuccessful. They patched up Rahim's arm as best as they could and one of his followers accompanied him to the bus terminal where he was asked to rest.

Other passengers at the terminal surrounded them, curious to know how the injury had occurred. Rahim's accomplices told them that a robber had attacked him and taken his money. In spite of his tremendous agony, Rahim called for the most senior operative in his group and handed him the remote control and advised him as to how it should be operated. A bus was leaving for Afghanistan and Rahim was taken by his accomplice into that bus. The man who had been given the remote control waited for approximately fifteen minutes before pressing the button.

Five huge explosions rocked the area of the bus terminal. Men and women were yelling and screaming in total fear. No one was sure where the explosions had taken place. The remaining operatives joined the other passengers in expressing their shock and fear as if they did not have a clue as to what had happened. Most of the passengers at the bus terminal were local residents and being concerned about their family's safety and the safety of their property, returned to the city of Mashad to see what had happened. Rahim's gang joined them initially but after some loud lamentations, expressed concern for their own families further up in western Iran. During this conversation they kept away and pretended not to know each other. After exhibiting sufficient grief for the innocent citizens of Mashad, they finally arranged for several taxicabs and moved to the next town where they could catch a bus.

The devastation of life and property in Mashad was mind boggling. Five mosques had been totally destroyed. Thirty five thousand pilgrims and local worshippers had been blown to bits and their bodies could not be identified. During such festivities thousands of people prayed outside the mosques, hence whole neighbouring areas of each mosque had been destroyed.

The news media, the Iranian Army and several police forces were finding it difficult to comprehend the tragedy and take steps to mitigate the anguish caused to the remaining people. Troops had already been dispatched in the direction of Mashad when the Iranian authorities were informed that several mosques were similarly destroyed in the cities of Birjand, Yezd, Qum, Hamadan and Emamshahar. Total loss of life was estimated to be approximately two hundred and twenty thousand people. The people of Iran were totally stunned by this calamity.

As police investigated the devastated areas of Mashad, Yezd, Qum and Hamadan, they discovered a very strange object in each case. A memo on the private and specialized stationery of the Shahnshah of Iran allegedly addressed to specific operatives in the Iranian Secret Service with the following instructions. "Officers of Democratic Iran, this private communiqué is for your information only. As discussed in the past, the Shahnshah of Iran has concluded that in order to continue the progress achieved in Iran, the total annihilation of Islam is requisite and necessary. The details of our plan have been communicated to you. You must now proceed to complete this mission." The signature of the Shahnshah was on the document, partially destroyed by fire. Identical documents were found in the vicinity of several mosques in other cities of Iran, including Tehran, but the mosques had remained completely intact. To an ordinary observer, it looked as if the perpetrators who were going to destroy the intact mosques, had panicked after hearing about the other explosions and were afraid of being discovered and in their haste to abandon the area, they had forgotten these documents.

Interestingly enough, the impact on the Iranian public was not as strong as was anticipated by Mansur Ghaznavi. The Iranians had experienced the prosperity and kindness doled out to every one by the Shahnshah and his regime and such brutality on his part was inconceivable. However, there were still several fanatics and fundamentalists residing in Iran and they immediately used this information to spread rumors all over the country that the Shahnshah was an enemy of Islam.

When I first heard this news of the disaster in Iran, I was totally shocked and heartbroken. Not only had they killed more than two hundred thousand people in my country, but it appeared that this was a well conceived plot to put the blame on my shoulders. It was therefore imperative to find the culprits, try them and exterminate them. Those were police and military actions which the authorized officers would manage by themselves. My main task was to completely convince the Iranian people that this barbarity was not promulgated by me.

I immediately summoned all my military and political advisers to an emergency conference. Jahanbaksh Mirza, our Minister of Religious Affairs, Gen. Hashmat Osmani and Ayatollah Maliki were the Ministers more closely associated with Islamic practices. If they trusted me and this trust was then indicated to the Iranian people, they would be very easily believed. So all of them were summoned to my palace. My closest associate, Behram Marzban was of course my best advisor and he was also present at the meeting. Rauf, my best military asset and Brig. Gen. Abbas Mahmoodi were also present at the meeting. I could see total shock in the expressions of all my ministers and officers. I then decided that they should be asked straight questions and permitted to give me straightforward answers.

"Sit down gentlemen and without hesitation answer my questions truthfully. I give you my word of honor that if your answers are derogatory or critical, there would be absolutely no adverse consequences to you. Before I approach the Iranian people and ask for their trust, I must be sure that my own ministers and officers trust me completely. Now gentlemen, how many of you believe that I had anything to do with this barbarity. Please raise your hands."

Not one single member of the committee raised his hand.

"Gentlemen, how many of you believe that my administration or the steps I took to develop Iran, was at least partially responsible for this calamity."

Again not one single hand was raised.

"Am I to understand that you totally and absolute trust me?"

Without consultation with each other or any hesitation, they all stood up and Behram Marzban addressed me. "Your Majesty, you are looking at a man who came to assassinate you and who then became your close associate, friend and servant. You forgave my crime, you made me a Minister and now you're asking me if a man such as you could possibly have committed a heinous crime killing two hundred thousand Iranian citizens? My Shahnshah, the question is absurd. Not one of us has ever suspected you, but then, we have the advantage of knowing you. The Iranian people have great respect and regard for you but they do not know you. Your integrity and honesty will show when you speak to them and you must tell them how pained and shocked you are."

All the other Ministers and officers nodded in agreement.

"I was thinking of going on national television today to address the people of Iran."

"Certainly, your Majesty, I will order the television authorities to bring their equipment to the Palace and you can make your broadcast from here where you're properly guarded. It does not take a genius to realize that the Shahnshah, under these circumstances will address the people of Iran and will go to the television station to do so. If these assassins have any brains, they would have considered this possibility and will take this opportunity to assassinate you. Your life, my King, is as precious to me as the lives of my family. With the utmost respect, I will not let you go to the television station."

I was touched to know that Behram cared so deeply for me.

Behram, my friend, you're absolutely right. Please arrange for the television equipment to be brought to the Palace."

Within two hours the equipment was set up at the Palace. I did not want to prepare myself for the speech. I did not want any artificial emotion to contaminate my grief. I walked up to the microphone and addressed the people of Iran.

"My Iranian brothers and sisters, I'm here to share your grief with you. I wish you could see the agony that my heart is suffering. Some monsters have killed two hundred thousand of my sisters and brothers or more accurately my sons and daughters. In the name of Allah, the holy prophet Mohamed and Zarathustra, I swear to you that I had absolutely nothing to do with this brutality."

"Muslim mosques are structures from where you can pray to Allah. They are structures that pay respect to the prophet Mohamed, the man who first introduced women's rights, the man whose philosophy basically civilized Christianity in Europe and whose philosophy eliminated the inquisitions in Spain and Portugal. His follower Akbar created the most civilized empire where Hindus and Muslims lived in peace and harmony. Which civilized human being would want to destroy such a heritage? Conceded that Muslims and Muslim governments have committed unpardonable atrocities, but they were not committed by the prophet Mohamed, they were committed by uncivilized barbarians who only pretended to be Muslims."

"I am not a Muslim. I came to Iran, to the land of my ancestors, not to persecute the religion of the people but to enhance its kindness and at the same time eliminate those who have misrepresented your prophet's philosophy and noble teachings. I thought we had achieved this and now I'm faced with this calamity."

There are two points I would like to make and I would like you to carefully listen. One of the mosques which was destroyed was the one in Zahidan. My children, do you not remember that very early in my reign, that mosque was damaged by some fanatics and I had it rebuilt? Why would I destroy that mosque?"

"I would also like to draw your attention to something very interesting. All the mosques which have been destroyed were in Birjand, Yezd, Qum, Hamadan, and Emanshahr. Notice fellow Iranians, all of those cities are in close proximity to Afghanistan. Do you think that is a coincidence? I don't! No Iranian, whether Shiite, Sunni, Zoroastrian, Christian or Jew, would ever destroy a building belonging to another religion. Our Iran is now a cosmopolitan land where all religions are respected and when necessary, prevented from inflicting injury or pain to others."

" I refuse to believe that there is one single Iranian who would perpetrate such a tragedy."

"I've come to the conclusion that there are three factors to consider. The proximity of all these cities to Afghanistan. The fact that all mosques where Shiite and the fact that the documents had my forged signature. Falsely attributing this barbarity to me is a clear indication that their main purpose was to discredit me and hurt our Shiite citizens. Think about it my fellow Iranians, even if I was the monster they've depicted me as, am I so stupid that I would write several memos to my officers with my signature telling them to destroy mosques? If you have the slightest doubt about my integrity, do you not agree that such stupid behavior on my part is illogical and impossible?"

"Inshallah, we will catch these barbarians and we will punish them. In the meantime my brothers and sisters, if you have the slightest information regarding the whereabouts of the culprits, contact us. Be assured that your names and locations will never be revealed to any one. As a matter-of-fact you can even provide information to us anonymously. Allahu Akbar. May Allah protect you. But keep one thought in mind. No atrocities or violence against our Afghan brothers or our Sunni brothers will be tolerated. The price for this atrocity would be paid by the criminals, not by innocent Afghans or Sunnis!"

At the completion of my speech I realized that I was exhausted, both physically and emotionally. There was a sense of great pain and anguish in my soul that I had tried so hard to develop Iran into a nation of the twenty-first century and I was being accused of one of the most heinous crimes ever perpetrated. It was Behram, who, with his warmth and sincerity relieved that tension.

"My Shahnshah, the words which you spoke were from the heart, so sincere and warm that no one in his right mind can ever believe that it was you who perpetrated this crime. My dearest friend, it is my duty to support and advise you and also to look after your health. Please go to your quarters and rest comfortably. This kind of tension at your age may be detrimental to your health."

I hugged him and then went to my quarters. I lay down to sleep but sleep eluded me. Finally I fell into a disturbed slumber and was awakened by uproar. I jumped out of bed and looked out of the window. To my surprise thousands of people were gathered in front of the Palace. It took me a while to figure out what they were yelling. I had learned to speak Farsi pretty fluently, yet sometimes it was difficult for me to understand the accent. Then Zainab came and stood beside me, putting her arm around my waist. I tried to concentrate on hearing what the crowd was saying.

"Shahnshah, Shahnshah, do not fret with the words of the criminals. Your loyal subjects will support you!" They repeated that slogan from time to time. My heart jumped for joy. My people still believed in me. There was a microphone always kept in my bedroom and living room. I waved to the masses and addressed them. "Thank you, my Iranian brothers and sisters. Thank you for your trust in me. I will make a promise to you. These barbarians will pay for their crime."

CHAPTER 36.

In spite of the pandemonium prevailing at the bus stop, some kind locals came to Rahim's rescue after he told them that a robber had shot him in his arm and taken his money. They bandaged his arm and gave him some pain killers and at his request put him on a bus leaving for Kandahar.

The return journey for Rahim was torture. When he was taking the pain killers, he was partially conscious and when the effect of the painkillers ended, he was in agony. Upon reaching Kandahar, Rahim took a taxi to his home. His wife and children were very concerned and looked after him for approximately two days without an incident.

On the third day a vehicle arrived at his gate. Two men came inside his house and greeted him. They said they were sent by Mansur Ghaznavi who had heard about his unfortunate accident and was very concerned about his health. They had been sent to escort him to meet with Mr. Ghaznavi. They said they were all very proud of him and Mr. Ghaznavi wanted to personally reward him for his valor. They also added that Mr. Ghaznavi had made arrangements to track down the treacherous swine Osman who would be brutally punished for his crime.

Rahim may have had some doubts about their authenticity but he also realized that this was not a request, it was a command and he quietly accompanied them to Ghaznavi's residence. He was directly taken into the living room of the mansion and noticed that Ghaznavi was sitting in his usual office chair from where he could see every person approaching him. Ghaznavi asked him to sit down and asked the guards to leave the room closing the door behind them.

After the guards left and their footsteps could no longer be heard, Ghaznavi looked at Rahim who did not miss the abject anger in his eyes. "I had given you specific and strict instructions that if any one of the operatives did not completely obey our commands, he should be instantly exterminated. I have been informed that you took Osman into a secluded area and had a chat with him. Then like a gutless pig, you let him shoot you in the elbow. That traitor escaped because of your weakness and inefficiency. That man could surrender to the Iranian authorities and our secret plan to destroy the Shahnshah's regime could be exposed. The Iranians and the Americans may attack us and thousands of innocent Afghan lives would be lost, all because of a gutless wonder like you. Have you no balls? Could you not have shot him with the other arm?"

Rahim was too shocked to respond immediately. Ghaznavi did not wait for a response. "Guess I was right. You may have balls but you do not deserve them, so I'm going to get rid of them. He pulled out his pistol aimed carefully and shot Rahim in his testicles. The agony was unbearable. His head was spinning. For the first time in his life Rahim was praying for unconsciousness or death. A huge patch of blood and skin tissue had plastered the wall behind Rahim. Even with this pain and anguish, Raheem realized that the patch was the remains of his genitalia.

"You have a brilliant future, you cowardly pig. No right arm and no balls."

Rahim looked pleadingly at Mansur. "Please kill me. I beg of you."

Mansur pointed the pistol at Rahim's head and pulled the trigger. The calibre of the bullet was large and Rahim's head exploded, his brains splattering the wall behind him. Mansur rang his bell and four attendants arrived with drawn guns.

"Take this filthy pig's carcass and discard it."

Even though they were totally shocked at what they saw, the guards immediately obeyed. The body was removed and the room cleaned up without protest.

Ghaznavi rang the bell again. An employee responded. "Bring four of the operatives in immediately." The employee nodded and left and soon four operatives were standing in front of Ghaznavi. "Gentlemen, this cowardly pig has been defeated by the more dangerous and villainous traitor, Osman, who is still alive and kicking. We must stop him but there is a greater priority. We must set an example so that no operative will ever dare to disobey our commands in the future. Osman has a wife and four children. I want you all to go to his home in camouflage, and kill the whole family. If anyone of you hesitates, your fate will be the same. Is that understood?" They nodded obediently. The fear in their eyes was clearly visible and that assured Ghaznavi that he would be obeyed implicitly.

All four operatives went to Osman's house. Osman's wife opened the door for them.

"Madam, Osman has returned from his mission. He believes that it would be very dangerous for you and the children to remain in the house because there are terrorists trying to attack his family. We have been instructed to take you and the children to a safe haven. Are all your children in the house?"

"Who are you? Why did Osman not come here himself to take us out?"

"He's being watched by the enemies of Islam and his arrival here would be very detrimental to him, to you and your children. Would you please get the children here, madam."

Osman's wife called the children out. They came running out and surrounded their mother. Suddenly four guns were fired at the children. There were screams and all four children collapsed to the floor as their heads exploded.

Osman's wife screamed in terror but that was the last sound she would ever make. The leader of the group aimed his gun at her head and fired. The note which they left on her body read. "Our message to all traitors of Islam, Taliban and the Lashkar-e-Taiyaba. You will not be permitted to survive and live in Afghanistan."

CHAPTER 37.

Osman had constantly remained in touch with his wife. After the incident involving Rahim, he was always concerned about possible repercussions from Ghaznavi. When there was no response by his wife to his calls he was very concerned and contacted some other relatives in Kandahar.

The news of the annihilation of his whole family totally devastated him. He sat in the little motel room in which he now resided and cried for the first day and night all the while hitting his head against the wall. "Allah, I have remained a devout Muslim all my life. I did not miss my prayers. I served you with all my might, all my life and this is your reward to me? You have exterminated me. The only reason I did not blow up the mosque was to prevent other innocent Muslims from dying. You did not save my own family when I left them in your protection."

"From this day, I'm saying to you loud and clear. Go to hell. You do not exist, you do not count, you do not matter to me anymore. How can I worry about going to hell when I'm already there? I have only one desire and that is to exterminate that bastard Ghaznavi, his family and friends and every member of the group who were my colleagues and allies and who have betrayed me. I do not need your help Allah. You cannot help me, since you do not exist in my world."

When tragedy strikes, a person's first reaction sometimes tends to be self flagellation. This state of emotions is inconsolable. It cannot be remedied, and the alternative is anger and hatred which leads to the desire for revenge and the hope of causing excruciating pain to the enemy. In itself that emotion is also harmful, but it mitigates the pain of misfortune and calamity.

Osman took this option. He was going to get even with the monsters who had taken his family from him.

Osman traveled to Tehran, walked into the first police station that he saw and insisted on talking to the Police Commissioner himself. When he was told that the Commissioner was busy with important matters, he told the attending officer that there was not a single matter in Iran which was more important than what he wanted to discuss. He told them that he had pertinent information to provide regarding the mosques which had been blown up.

He was immediately introduced to the Commissioner after he was thoroughly searched for weapons. "I have been told that you have some information pertaining to the mosques which were blown up. Is this correct?"

"It is absolutely correct, Commissioner, but this matter is of such magnitude that the information can only be imparted to the Shahnshah and no one else."

"Let me get this straight. You expect me to take you to the Shahnshah only on the strength of your word that you have some important information to convey? My dear man, the Shahnshah is a very busy person and does not have time to listen to every little detail about the crimes committed in the country. Why don't you tell me what it is and then we will see what action is to be taken."

"Commissioner, let me explain something to you. I am not here to provide you with information relevant to the crime committed. I am able to provide you with every single detail regarding the perpetrators, their motives, their names and addresses, their descriptions and last but not least, their future plans. After providing this information, my life is worth nothing, they will kill me but I do not care. One thing I do care about. If the information I provide becomes public, these monsters will never be caught, they will escape and death to me is not half as significant and important as their annihilation."

He took out a Koran from his pocket and placed it before the Commissioner. "I want you to swear on the Koran that this little bit of information which I have provided to you will never be disclosed to any person except the Shahnshah of Iran. Please take the oath." The Commissioner took the oath.

"You have no reason to be concerned about my causing any injury or danger to the Shahnshah. Search me to your heart's content. I have no weapons of any kind on my person. I'm putting my hand on the Koran and I swear that I do not mean any harm to the Shahnshah. More importantly, any harm to the Shahnshah would deprive me of the chance to take revenge against these monsters. One thing is absolutely certain. The information I have will only be revealed personally by me to the Shahnshah of Iran." Osman reclined in his chair indicating that the matter was over and there was nothing more to discuss.

The Commissioner was in a quandary. He did not know what to do. After all he could not contact the Royal Palace and tell them that a man who claims to have information about the bombed mosques wanted to speak to the Shahnshah without revealing what he had to say. Osman had refused to give his name or any personal details. No amount of persuasion could change Osman's determination.

Ultimately the Commissioner decided that he should contact the head of the Shahnshah's personal security, Major Rauf. Rauf was not at his headquarters at that time. The Commissioner had left a message that the matter was very urgent yet the response only came the next day.

When Rauf called, the Commissioner explained the situation to him including the reticence of the so-called informer. Rauf agreed to come immediately to the police station and talk to the man himself. Rauf tried very hard to convince the informer to give all the details which would be conveyed by him to the Shahnshah, but Osman would not budge. At this point in time Rauf felt that the Shahnshah had to be informed.

Rauf requested an immediate appointment with me and when I called him, he gave a description of the informer and the type of information he claimed he had. After the short discussion, we both agreed that I should meet with this man and Rauf was very concerned about my sitting alone with the informer.

Osman was searched both physically and electronically for weapons and explosives and then brought in to me. He bowed just slightly to me. I do not miss these signs. That bow indicated to me that he did not feel any specific loyalty to me and that he was not afraid of me. I politely asked him to sit down.

"Obviously I do not know your name so I cannot address you by your name. I have been told that you will only provide this information to me personally. I do understand your concern. Now let me provide you with the concern my most trusted officer Rauf has. We do not know your name. We do not know who you are or where you come from. When an officer like Rauf is in charge of my security, do you blame him for being concerned to leave a seventy-two-year-old man alone in your company?"

The man before me had a strange look in his eyes as if my politeness and courtesy were totally unexpected. Then he looked straight into my eyes. "I presume that you want this officer to be present when I convey this information to you?"

"I consider it very rude to talk to a man without using his name. Would you at least give me your first name?"

"My name is Osman".

"Listen to me carefully Osman. You understand the concern officer Rauf has about my security. I also realize that you have some serious concerns about the repercussions of this information leaking to outsiders. I will do the following for you. I will put my hand on the Koran or a copy of the Avesta, which is the religious book of the Zoroastrians and swear that your name, description or source of your information will never be revealed to any person either by myself or by officer Rauf. Naturally we have to use this information to apprehend the criminals who have caused the massacre of our innocent countrymen, but the informant's name need not be mentioned. Officer Rauf is a Muslim. He will put his hand on the Koran and take the same oath. Is that agreeable?"

Osman nodded his head in assent and we took the oath.

"Shahnshah-e-Iran, I have never been your supporter or admirer. My life now is worth nothing to me. My death would be a relief to me, so I'm not afraid of you. Let me tell you this honestly. Two weeks ago, if I had the opportunity, I would have killed you myself. My motivation for coming here is not because I regret what I've done or to apologize for my beliefs. It is just one simple thing, revenge. The main architect of these explosions and massacres is Mansur Ghaznavi. Mansur was my leader and patron. I believed in him. He convinced all of us that you are the enemy of Islam and that you are trying to eradicate Islam from our world. The truth or falsehood of that allegation is now totally irrelevant to me."

"Five leaders were appointed by Mansur. Each leader had individuals under his control. We were provided with training and explosives and we came into Iran from Afghanistan to blow up these mosques and to destroy and kill as many Shiites as possible. Our plan was to place the blame on your shoulders and therefore those false documents with your forged signatures, were distributed all over Iran. To be honest with you, I completely agreed and cooperated with the plan."

There was only one single area where my conscience would not let me proceed with the scheme as planned. The mosque in Mashad was often visited by Sunnis. Even if they were not in the mosque they could be praying in the surrounding area. Their annihilation was contrary to my principles. I was also a little concerned about the unnecessary destruction and massacre of innocent children. I therefore approached my leader and objected to the mosque being blown up under these circumstances. You must remember Shahnshah, that when we left Kandahar, we were only informed that our purpose was to destroy you. No details were given to us. My objection was taken relatively lightly by my leader who took me to a secluded area because he said he wanted to discuss the matter with me. Suddenly he pulled a gun on me but I was faster than him so I shot him in his elbow. I could have easily killed him thereafter, but I'm not a coward and I do not kill injured men, so I let him go."

"Well, the cowardly bastard goes back to Afghanistan and tells Ghaznavi the whole story without revealing the fact that I spared his life. I am glad to say that Ghaznavi shot him dead, calling him a coward for not killing me instantly."

"Ghaznavi sent his men to my home and killed my wife and my four children in cold blood. Allah didn't protect them. I don't believe in Allah or destiny anymore. I only want one thing, I want to see each one of those rats brutally killed, if possible, slowly tortured to death. I will be happy to do it myself if you bring them over and permit me to do so."

"I have already admitted to you that I came to Iran to destroy your regime and to kill you. Once you have killed these bastards, kill me without hesitation, any way you wish. My only wish is that you keep me in prison. Do not kill me until my enemies have been exterminated and I can enjoy the pleasure and satisfaction of knowing that I was instrumental in their annihilation."

"Osman, in a civilized country like our present day Iran, we do kill people who are traitors or enemies of the realm. Under our law the conspiracy in which you participated is an offense for which you would normally go to jail. There is one problem. Your crime was only your intent to participate in the conspiracy, you were not a participant. Your offense basically is a rather minor one."

"You have provided us with significant information which may enable us to apprehend these criminals. That must also be credited to your account. Under these circumstances, a death penalty in your case would be a total travesty of justice under our legal system. We will never kill you for what you intended to do. We leave such barbarity to regimes that operate like your leader Ghaznavi does. There will be charges against you for the intended conspiracy, but even they may be withdrawn upon evidence that you have cooperated with us."

There was total shock in Osman's expressions.

"Are you telling me that you are going to let me live after all this is over?"

"That is exactly what I have been telling you."

"Shahnshah, life or death to me is of no significance. All I want is revenge. If you decide not to imprison me, then why don't you give me the opportunity to assist your troops in the capture and annihilation of our mutual enemies."

"Let me understand your proposition. You traveled all the way to Iran to destroy my administration. Your ambition was to kill and maim thousands of Iranians and it was only circumstances that prevented you from achieving your ambition. Now you do not regret your actions and have not changed your views of our government or philosophy. Why should I believe you when you say that you want to help us eliminate our enemies?"

"Shahnshah, I do not believe in your philosophy or agree with your beliefs. Allah, in whom I had total faith has also ceased to exist for me.

Why should I propagate a philosophy or belief about an entity that did not prevent my innocent wife and children from being massacred? Shahnshah, all I want to do is to eliminate these animals. All I ask of you is to give me that opportunity. After I'm, done you can kill me in any way you wish. I don't care!"

I realized that I was talking to a vicious religious fanatic. There were tears in the man's eyes and normally vicious, violent men do not condescend to exhibiting their emotions.

"All right tell me what you can do for us?"

"I will provide you with information regarding the whereabouts, hideouts, appearances and behaviour patterns of Ghaznavi and all his companions. You have police artists to whom I will provide exact descriptions of these men so that your officers can identify them. I will accompany your operatives into Kandahar as their guide. Please give me this opportunity."

"My dear fellow, if one of them identifies you, you will be dead and the lives of my operatives will be in grave danger so why should I trust you? You are an enemy of our State. What if you are working for both sides? You destroy your enemies first and then deliver my operatives to the Taleban or other terrorist groups? Where is our guarantee?"

Yes Shahnshah, you are justified in your concern. My word of honour is of no value to you. I have already considered all these things and want to present a solution to you. I hope that this will guarantee the success of the mission, as well as prevent me from betraying your men."

"You are absolutely right that I cannot be seen by any of my colleagues. Keep me as your prisoner so you are sure that I will not be able betray any of your men. I am willing to be completely under constraint during this whole operation. Let me be in a location where I will be able to guide them on tracking down Ghaznavi and his men"

"Shahnshah, it is extremely difficult for a man to disguise himself as being of another race or religion. With all the makeup in the world, I cannot pass as a white man or a black man. But there is one community whose expressions and complexion match mine. The appearance and style of dressing of the Sikhs will provide the anonymity that we need. All practicing Sikhs have long beards, wear turbans and have a metallic wrist band. In my respectful opinion unless you're incredibly fair complexioned or totally dark, the best disguise for an infiltrator is to take on the appearance of a Sikh. An additional precaution will be to refrain from communicating with any one and that can be easily done since a Sikh does not speak Pashtu."

"Your men can provide me with a passport and a Sikh identity and I can cross into Afghanistan without difficulty as an Indian tour operator."

"All right. Tell us what is the best way to go about this operation."

"Shahnshah, in this operation which is organized by Ghaznavi, there are exactly one hundred and twenty-eight operatives. He very strongly believes that in order to preserve the safety of the group, new members are enlisted when their loyalty has been determined and they have become vulnerable"

"When a new person wants to join the group his first assignment is to execute a member who has disputed an order. This disagreement may be quite trivial, but to Ghaznavi, it is a death warrant. Evidence of this initiation is kept by Ghaznavi and if there is ever a doubt about the reliability of the newcomer, this evidence is anonymously sent to the authorities in Afghanistan."

"Everyone is aware of the severe consequences if they lose the favor of Ghaznavi. Also, brutal and cruel punishment is meted out to the family of the offender."

"Shahnshah, my dream is to bring every one of these one hundred and twenty-eight operatives to justice. I have no noble motives for doing this. It is just pure revenge!"

Rauf, who was attending the meeting, addressed us. "Shahnshah, I have been very carefully listening to what Osman has been saying about bringing these culprits to justice. I have carefully analyzed each and every venue of our operation and have come up with a plan that I would like to present to Your Majesty."

"First of all I have consulted my experts to get some information on a new device which can duplicate voices. This instrument will be made available to us. Let's say I want to send a message to some one in Osman's voice. The equipment has to be trained to duplicate his voice. All I have to do is speak in the microphone which will convert it to Osman's. It is almost identical, very few people are able to distinguish a difference."

"The second new discovery on which I have obtained is some information from our technical experts on a special gaseous drug which is odourless. When this drug is introduced into an area, within minutes every one goes into a stupor. There are no injuries or repercussions as a consequence of the inhalation of this drug. This gives us an opportunity to arrest them without the need of the police. With the right vehicle to transport them and provided that the location is sufficiently secluded, only two individuals will be needed to handle the prisoners. As a secondary precaution, we have a similar spray which is poisonous. This I will use only if it is absolutely necessary."

"For additional security, it is imperative that our operatives entering Afghanistan do not travel as Iranians or Shiites. The animosity towards Shiites, especially from Ghaznavi and his cohorts, may be quite dangerous to our position. I'm presenting to Your Majesty the following proposal. I will choose two of my best trained and intelligent operatives. They will be dressed as Arab visitors with Saudi passports and will enter Afghanistan. Both of them, Your Majesty, are fluent in Arabic and so am I. As discussed earlier, Osman, whose identity has to be carefully protected, will don the attire of a Sikh."

"Now wait a minute Rauf, there are a couple of points which you have made that are of great concern to me. First and foremost, what makes you think I will allow you to endanger your life by going into Afghanistan to expose yourself to those animals? Son, you are one of my most efficient and devoted officers. I cannot allow you to risk your life, especially when we are dealing with such a dangerous bunch of terrorists. Secondly, if you succeed in capturing all one hundred and twenty-eight terrorists and load them onto your vehicle, how on earth will you be able to cross into Iran at the Afghan/ Iran border?"

"Your Majesty, I am honored and very grateful for your kind description of my services to Iran and to you. Please forgive my arrogance. I believe that my operatives and I can easily manage a situation created by a bunch of sick, religious bigots. We earnestly believe that we are superior to them."

"Rauf, there is a second problem. What about crossing the border which I mentioned earlier?"

"Your Majesty, that is indeed a serious problem. Here is where I need Your Majesty's consent and approval. I do not think bringing any of these one hundred and twenty-eight culprits to Iran after their capture would be of value. We should exterminate them and let their bodies rot."

I was totally amazed at the strength of his emotions. I always thought of Rauf as a very brilliant and qualified officer and operative, but I had never realized the depth of his hatred for bigots and fanatics. I was actually very happy that such a strong, efficient man was devotedly working for me. I nodded my head to indicate to him that he could deal with these animals in any manner he wished.

"When you return from this expedition, you will be knighted and rewarded and you can look upon me in the future as your father."

I made several attempts to convince Rauf not to take this inordinate risk but he was absolutely firm in his resolve. However, I was able to persuade him to conceal a tracking mechanism in his clothing which would enable our technicians to know exactly where he was at all times. We wanted to be able to monitor this mission from our headquarters in Tehran. From where, if necessary, help could be immediately dispatched. I suddenly realized the enormous responsibility on my shoulders in risking the lives of my most loyal and intelligent subjects. This was the most unpleasant part of being the Shahnshah of Iran.

CHAPTER 38.

Rauf returned home and discussed the details of his plan with Fatima. To his utter shock Fatima suggested that she accompany him to provide a certain anonymity. A husband and wife travelling together with relatives would appear less suspicious she said. Initially, Rauf was totally appalled and refused but then she said. "Rauf, I'm not doing this for you. I'm doing this for my Shahnshah, the man who from his exalted position was able to look at a common prostitute and make her into an honourable woman. He gave me the support I needed to find a wonderful husband like you."

Tell me Rauf, how many kings, prime ministers or world leaders have you met who would protect a prostitute and make her into a respectable woman? For that man, even my life is not enough. I insist on accompanying you to serve my Emperor and to protect my beloved husband."

When Rauf told me this I was touched by these kind words and had to turn away so that no one could see the tears welling up in my eyes.

"Are you willing to risk both your lives for this dangerous mission?"

Without a moment's hesitation Rauf replied, "Absolutely, Your Majesty".

Rauf, Fatima and two very trusted lieutenants Zahir and Aksum left a week later for Afghanistan. The Jeep in which they were travelling was equipped with all the necessary equipment we had agreed on. There were special compartments built inside the vehicle where explosives and other detecting devices could be hidden. There were special coatings applied to prevent these weapons from being detected either by x-rays or other scanning apparatus. Osman was dressed as an Indian Sikh. He was strictly instructed that under no circumstances should he speak in Farsi or Pashtu. All of them had perfectly fabricated Saudi passports with Saudi names. The vehicle had been marked with the name "India-Middle East Tour Company" and in smaller print, the locations of its offices. The head office was in New Delhi with branches in Riyadh, Dhahran, Beirut and Damascus. There was an accompanying map high-lighting all the tour destinations which could be organized by this company. They reached the Afghan border near Herat, without any difficulty.

"Salaam alaikum, where are you people from?" asked the border guard. Osman pointed in the direction of Rauf and Fatima and shook both his hands indicating his inability to speak Pashtu. In a perfect Saudi Arabian accent Rauf told the guard that he, his wife and her two brothers were going on a pilgrimage to several Afghan Islamic centers including Mazar-e-Sharif. He explained that they wanted to visit as many Islamic centers in the Middle East and Pakistan as was possible. They were told that this Indian travel company was the safest way for them to travel across international borders.

Rauf then requested that the officer delay the completion of the entrance requirements until they had finished the evening prayers, just as the call for prayers was announced from the minarets of the local mosques.

"Allahu Akbar, it is nice to see and welcome our devout Arab brothers and sister. Of course, go and take your time with your prayers. As far as the entry formalities are concerned, I'm going to immediately stamp your passports. Finish your prayers and welcome to Afghanistan!" He stamped their passports as well as the fake Indian passport Osman was travelling with. "Just one question. If you are on a pilgrimage in Afghanistan, why do you use the services of a pagan like this Sikh infidel?" As per his training, Osman again pretended he did not understand a syllable. Rauf smiled and told the officer that this was the cheapest travel company he could find. The guard smiled and let them pass.

After they finished praying, they got back into the Jeep and travelled in the direction of Herat without any problems.

The journey of Herat and Kandahar was uneventful. They were able to secure modest accommodations in Kandahar City. On a detailed map of Kandahar, Osman had marked the locations of each one of the one hundred and twenty-eight terrorists who were working for Ghaznavi. He had mentioned that all the conferences and meetings were conducted at that remote villa approximately fourteen kilometres north of Kandahar city where he himself had attended on several occasions to obtain instructions from Ghaznavi.

No one resided at this property. It was strictly for meetings and because of its remoteness from the city centre, the Afghan authorities were not aware of the activities here. This provided the privacy and security to Ghaznavi and his followers.

On the second night, after their arrival in Kandahar, Osman, Rauf and his two lieutenants drove out to the cottage after midnight. Since it was dark they used their radar equipment to ascertain that there was no one on the premises.

Osman had indicated that there was a sophisticated alarm system which had to be disarmed. Zahir, who was an expert with this was able to disarm the system within seconds of entering the villa. They then installed two containers of different gases in the central air system. One of the gases would cause loss of consciousness and the other was more lethal, as it would cause instant death. Each cylinder could be activated from a distance of up to ten kilometres.

They left the villa after carefully securing the alarm system and the door. They drove away without any incident. The relief they all felt was visible by their comfortable breathing. Rauf jokingly told Zahir that he was in the wrong occupation and perhaps should change his vocation to become a bank robber. The expert manner and speed with which he had handled this whole operation had not gone unnoticed by his companions.

The next important task was to obtain a recording of Ghaznavi's voice. The difficulty was how to call him and have a normal conversation without alerting his suspicion. The team discussed this matter but could not come up with a plausible solution. Ultimately, it was Fatima who came up with a viable plan.

"Listen to my idea. I will call Ghaznavi, cursing and yelling at him for being responsible for the death of my husband who was a devout Muslim attending his prayers in Mashad. I will ask him how he could even allow a good Sunni Muslim to be butchered with the other Shiite pagans. I will ask him whether it was not his absolute responsibility to be certain that no faithful Sunnis were killed."

"From my comprehension of Ghaznavi's temperament, if the criticism is associated with the massacres which he organized, he may use one rude word and hang up the phone. On the other hand if I mention the loss of life of an innocent Sunni, who was a law-abiding Muslim, my impression is that he would immediately respond."

Maybe it will be something to the effect that in doing Allah's work some innocent lives had to be lost and that they would definitely be welcomed by Allah into heaven. Hopefully, it will be enough to trigger your device into duplicating Ghaznavi's voice. What do you think?"

There was surprise and admiration from the team. The fact that a soft female voice filled with grief could almost compel Ghaznavi to make at least some conciliatory remarks was a brilliant idea and they all nodded in agreement.

Osman had prepared a list of the names of all the operatives and their telephone numbers. This did not need any great effort because Osman already had all this information available to him.

Rauf's assistant Zahir was an expert in handling telecommunications equipment. He had worked all morning on a device which would ring all the telephone numbers of the hundred and twenty-six operatives simultaneously and leave one taped message from Ghaznavi, ordering them to immediately come to the villa for an emergency meeting. The possibility of telephone contacts between each other would be considerably reduced, as the message would forbid this because of possible danger.

The next difficult part of the plan was getting Ghaznavi to the cottage. The answer to this was provided by Osman. He stated that almost every day, Ghaznavi went to the villa to organize his several schemes. It was his absolute rule that no one should call him on his home telephone. Contact was restricted to a specific line at the villa.

The cell phone was in the name of a nonexistent party and there was no possible way that the Afghan authorities could connect him to that cell phone. This limited communication with him was only permitted when he was at the villa. Zahir planned to have this connection with Ghaznavi disconnected. He was absolutely certain that he could do this with the equipment in his possession.

How could one be sure that all the operatives were in the vicinity of Kandahar. What if some of them were travelling outside of the area and did not receive the summons that Ghaznavi had called an emergency meeting.

After some detailed discussions they concluded that a member of the team would go to each address and ascertain that the resident was in town on that particular day. However, this did not guarantee his receipt of the message or that he would be able to attend the meeting. There was one advantage to be derived from Ghaznavi's regulations. Failure to comply had very serious repercussions. The team was going to use these rigid rules to undermine Ghaznavi and his followers.

It took approximately two days for Rauf and Osman to covertly travel in the area of all the operatives to make sure that they were in town. After a thorough check it was determined that one hundred and twenty-five of these men were in Kandahar at this time. It was hoped that the last one would get the message to attend and in the alternative, he would have to be dealt with separately.

After the final details were discussed by the team, Fatima was ready to make the call to Ghaznavi. Everyone was quite nervous and a bit amused at the same time. They noticed that she was deep breathing to calm her nerves before making the call.

She dialed Ghaznavi's telephone number and he picked it up after the fourth ring. "May I speak to Mr. Ghaznavi please," pretending to cry as she said this.

"Who is this?" The voice at the other end of the line enquired.

"I always thought that you were a protector of Sunni Muslims. My husband and I had no disagreement with you about destroying these Shiites, but how could you be so brutal that you would destroy a mosque where Sunnis were praying? What will you say to Allah when he asks you why you killed my innocent husband and made my four children fatherless?" After these words, she gave an excellent rendition of a woman sobbing uncontrollably.

There was a pause at the other end. "First of all, I completely deny that we were involved in any such activity. Even if we had been involved, we would never touch a Sunni brother. I give you my word of honor that I was not involved in any activity which could have hurt a Sunni Muslim."

At this point in time Zahir jumped up, enthusiastically doing the `thumbs up' signal, gleefully indicating that the voice recording had been successfully completed. Fatima had a victorious smile on her face as she concluded her telephone chat by saying to Ghaznavi, "May you rot in hell!" They all knew that the call could not be traced.

Rauf had a new issue. The equipment was ready to make simultaneous calls to all the one hundred and twenty-six operatives, summoning them in Ghaznavi's voice. Ghaznavi should not be at the villa before the others arrived as this would make him suspicious. Therefore, it was essential that the operatives arrive at the cottage before Ghaznavi did.

Osman very quickly came up with a solution for this problem. Ghaznavi usually worked very late at night and normally slept in during the mornings. From his own experience, Osman had noticed that Ghaznavi did not arrive at the villa before noon, so they decided that the emergency call to the operatives would be made early in the morning asking them to arrive immediately. They could all be dealt with before Ghaznavi arrived. Then he would be the only person left to be arrested.

The team now had to decide on the dialog that they should use. A final handwritten script was created and Rauf was going to be the announcer. He rehearsed the exact words several times since his accent in Pashtu had to be modified. The instrument was only going to imitate Ghaznavi's voice but not his accent. After the rehearsal had been completed to perfection, they all went to bed, agreeing to be up and ready at 7.00 a.m. sharp.

One could feel the tension in the room when Rauf sat at his desk. All the telephone numbers of the operatives had already been digitally entered into the system. The first thing for him now to do was to record the message and transmit it.

After gaining his composure for a minute, Rauf started speaking. "Salaam alaikum, my brothers. A serious emergency has arisen and I need your immediate attendance at our usual meeting place. You must be there at 8.30 a.m. I cannot give you any details and for security reasons do not contact me. Also, do not try to contact each other as your phones may have already been tapped. May Allah protect you all."

After the recording had been completed, there was a serious discussion on the pronunciation of certain words in the Afghan accent. Those words were amended until every one was totally satisfied that a listener would not be able to tell that this was not an Afghan speaking. Osman listened to the recording and could not hide his shock when he realized that the voice in the recording appeared to be exactly that of Ghaznavi.

The cassette was placed into the telephone messaging equipment and they all got into their Jeep and drove to Ghaznavi's villa. An area approximately half a kilometre away had been selected as a good location where they would be completely out of sight. Zahir pressed the call button on his telephone system and the messages were sent out.

With the help of binoculars, they were able to watch the operatives as they arrived at the villa. The first four vehicles arrived within fifteen minutes of the call and then a few more within half an hour. Osman had a list of all one hundred and twenty-eight operatives and he marked the names off as they arrived.

The tension in the jeep was increasing by the minute. They still had not decided what they would do if some of the operatives did not show up at the villa.

By 9:30 a.m. one hundred and twenty-two of Ghaznavi's men were already at the villa. Zahir and Osman were very nervous. "Rauf, only six men are missing. Shall we start the operation? It is already 9:30 a.m. and things can go wrong if Ghaznavi turns up earlier than expected," Osman said.

"Let us wait for fifteen more minutes," Rauf said.

Waiting was rather tense. The smokers in the group were dying for a cigarette but that was dangerous under the circumstances. After about twelve minutes, four more of the men arrived, followed by another two.

Now all the operatives were finally here. Rauf looked at the others for agreement. "I think it is now time to use our remote control." They all nodded vigorously in agreement. Rauf pressed the button to release the gas which was going to make every one unconscious. They heard a loud whoosh, a few rapid movements and then pin drop silence.

Armed with guns equipped with silencers Rauf and his men ran towards the villa. A section of the path leading to the cottage was visible from where they were parked so there was no danger of them being seen should Ghaznavi arrive.

"We have a few things to do before we complete our task in the villa." Rauf said. "It is quite possible that Ghaznavi may arrive before we are done. If he sees all the vehicles parked here, he will become suspicious since he does not know what is going on. It is essential that one of us stay outside to arrest him if he shows up while we are inside. Osman, can you manage this by yourself?"

Osman nodded his assent.

"Don't kill him. We need him for interrogation."

Again Osman nodded his assent.

All of them approached the building from four different sides, with their guns drawn. Rauf kicked the door down and the sight they saw inside was like a movie. One hundred and twenty-eight men lying on the floor in different rooms of the villa, all unconscious.

Rauf said to his two companions, "Pull these bastards into the room at the end of the building and shoot them in their heads. Leave the bodies in that room and lock the door so that Ghaznavi will not know what has happened to his companions. Start now."

All three of them started pulling the men into the other room. Once in there, they were shot in the head and then checked to see that they were actually dead. Within twenty minutes one hundred and twenty-eight terrorists had been executed.

Now Rauf had the task of being absolutely certain that when Ghaznavi arrived on the scene, he would not become suspicious and take off or try anything which would jeopardize his arrest. Approximately half a kilometre away from the villa they sawed down a lamp post and laid it across the track, so that an approaching vehicle would have to stop. The location where the lamppost was laid was surrounded by a number of trees and other bushes so Rauf and his team could safely hide until Ghaznavi's vehicle arrived. Osman was sent in another direction away from the villa, where he stood with his gun ready, in case Ghaznavi tried to escape.

The most difficult and tedious part of their project was the uncertainty and the waiting. Unfortunately, they had been unable to go to Ghaznavi's home and plant a homing device to track his movements. They had considered the possibility of doing this but had come to the conclusion that if they were discovered in the vicinity of his home they may have severely jeopardized their progress.

This was not a busy road since it was a mud track. Hardly a car passed this way while they were waiting. After about forty minutes of waiting they heard the sound of a motor vehicle approaching. As soon as it passed the bend, Rauf was able to identify the black Mercedes-Benz. He looked in the direction of Osman who immediately nodded indicating that he had recognized Ghaznavi's car. The latter was driving at comparatively high-speed for the condition of the road and had to sharply apply his brakes to avoid hitting the lamp post. Instantly, he seemed alerted and tried to make a U-turn. This was not feasible as the road was too narrow and a three point turn was essential. Suddenly two bullets were fired and both his front tires were deflated. Three of the team members had now surrounded the car and pointed their guns at Ghaznavi. He tried to reach into his glove compartment but before he could do so Rauf fired a single bullet at his elbow. The agonizing pain slowed Ghaznavi's reflexes and in a second Rauf and Osman jumped in and handcuffed him before putting leg irons on. Ghaznavi had not yet realized that one of his assailants was Osman but when he saw his face, he was shocked. He was taken into the villa and his car hidden in the bushes.

Once they were securely inside the villa, Osman slowly approached him as two of the men were bandaging his shattered elbow. He said, "To call a Muslim a swine is a very serious insult and I would normally not do it to my worst enemy. But in your case, to call you a swine is equally improper, because it is a greater insult to the swine. You filthy, dirty bastard! I served you with absolute loyalty for years and you murdered my innocent wife and children."

"You were a traitor to our cause and you deserved the punishment. I guess you're going to kill me, so go ahead and finish your job,." Ghaznavi said.

In spite of his hatred for a man like Ghaznavi, Rauf could not help being impressed by Ghaznavi's courage in the face of imminent death.

Osman turned to face Rauf. "May I speak to you privately for a minute. You have heard the Shahnshah offer me a pardon, wealth and position if I succeed in nabbing this bastard. I do not want any of those gifts from you or the Shahnshah. Both of us know that we are going to kill Ghaznavi. I want you to grant me the privilege of leaving me with him so I can kill him. You two just leave and stay out. When I'm done I will join you."

Rauf was a bit concerned. "What are you going to do to him? Remember I have to report every detail of our actions to the Shahnshah."

"Exactly. That is why I want you to leave me alone with him. When a man who has lost his wife and children requests the pleasure of being the executioner of a man who is already condemned to die, the Shahnshah will not be upset that you conceded to my wishes. It is therefore imperative that you know as little as possible about what I will be doing."

"Osman I just want to be absolutely certain that you do not do something for which the Shahnshah and Iran will be ashamed."

"You and the Shahnshah cannot possibly be ashamed if you did not know what I was going to do. Just go, leave me alone with him!"

Very reluctantly Rauf and the others walked away to their vehicle.

"You think after killing me you will get away with it? Each one of my hundred and twenty-eight operatives will consider it his religious duty to take revenge on you and your accomplices." Ghaznavi said.

"Highly unlikely Ghaznavi. All your accomplices are right here at this moment. Do you want to meet them?"

In spite of all his bravado, Ghaznavi was shocked by this statement.

"Well you better meet your loyal friends." Osman grabbed Ghaznavi by his hair and roughly pushed him in the direction of the room where the dead bodies were.

He opened the door. "Here you bastard, enjoy the company of all your colleagues."

In spite of the pretence of composure that Ghaznavi had so successfully maintained up to now, his shock at the sight of the hundred and twenty-eight dead bodies was now completely obvious. "Oh my God, you killed all of them, you animal!" Ghaznavi said.

"They were very lucky. They did not feel any pain as they died. You are going to. You remember you asked me to kill you when we first met today? That is not good enough for me. By the time I'm done with you, you will beg me to kill you. That is a promise!"

Now Ghaznavi appeared to be in a daze avoiding eye contact. Slowly Osman approached and with a knife ripped off the front of his trousers.

"What the hell are you doing, you bastard?" Ghaznavi asked.

"I'm making sure that brutal beasts like you are not allowed to create a new generation. Your DNA must die with you. Don't worry, you will not die of blood loss. I have bandages to prevent that. This is only the beginning and there is much more to look forward to." Osman continued.

With three or four very harsh swipes of the knife, Ghaznavi's assets were detached from his body. The screams and yells of his agony reverberated through the cottage. Very calmly Osman applied bandages to the area to prevent severe blood loss. The agony was so great that Ghaznavi was just partially conscious now.

"Keep awake you bastard, this is only the beginning. When you talk, you normally use your hands. You're very fond of making gestures. Isn't that correct? Tell me, what gestures did you make when you ordered your accomplices to go and kill my wife and children? Did you use your right hand or both hands? You are not answering. I take that to mean that you were using both your hands!" Osman drew his sword and hacked off Ghaznavi's right arm right from the shoulder, then he did the same to his left arm. Ghaznavi had now collapsed. Osman once again applied bandages to both the shoulder stubs. He then poured water over Ghaznavi's face. It took approximately fifteen minutes for Ghaznavi to recover, but when he did, he was in incredible agony.

"Tell me Ghaznavi, when you're giving your directives, do you normally pace back and forth to impress your followers? Did you do that when you were giving your orders to your underlings to kill my family? I think you must have been. Which one of your legs should I cut off first, your choice."

" Please, please, kill me. Don't do this to me." Ghaznavi pleaded.

"Did my children have that option, you bastard?"

Osman hacked off both of his legs with his sword, applied the bandages and waited for him to regain consciousness. He patiently waited for approximately forty minutes before Ghaznavi became conscious again. He tried to look in Osman's direction but could not focus. The agony and anguish in his expressions made Osman feel pity for him.

"Listen, you filthy bastard. When you ordered the execution of my wife and children you must have looked at the animals who complied with your wishes. You must have heard their responses with your ears. I am going to gouge out your eyes and your ear drums. What do you have to say about that?"

"In the name of Allah, please kill me. I can't bear any more pain. I humbly ask for your forgiveness and seek death at your hands. Please, please kill me."

"Unlike you, Ghaznavi, I am a weak man. I do not have your determination or will to commit atrocities without batting an eyelid. You have suffered enough pain. May Satan and Allah both take pity on you when you reach hell. I won't torture you anymore."

Osman waked over to Ghaznavi and fired a bullet at close range into his head, literally blowing his head apart. Without looking back Osman walked out of the villa towards Rauf and his companions. "My job is done. Go and have a look and do whatever else you want to do!" he said

Rauf and his companions ran into the villa. They were shocked at the condition of Ghaznavi's body. "Oh my God, how will I explain this barbarity to the Shahnshah?" Rauf asked. "What could I possibly say to him in your defence?" Rauf continued, as he realized that Osman had followed him into the villa.

"You can tell him that you left me inside to discuss the tragedy which was inflicted upon me. Tell the Shahnshah that it was the only request I made. Explain to him that you did not know what I was going to do. As for the Shahnshah punishing me for my barbarity, do not worry about it. No punishment can be inflicted. I have avenged my family's deaths." Without further ado Osman placed his gun to his head and pulled the trigger.

The men all felt ill from what they had just witnessed.

"Brother Rauf, our mission has been accomplished. It is time to go back to Iran."

"Not until we have properly buried our companion Osman," and they all agreed.

They dug a hole at the back of Ghaznavi's villa and buried Osman's body.

Rauf was quite surprised at his own emotions for this man. He was an avowed terrorist who had come to destroy the civilization in which he lived and who had changed his principles not because of conviction but because of the cruelty inflicted upon him. He had become their ally and friend and had helped them destroy one of the worst enemies of Iran. Suddenly, life seemed to be mystifying and irrational.

He suddenly remembered the words that Shahnshah had once said, "Faith is an idiocy, adopted by uneducated people to believe in things which they could not interpret. They used these ancient principles for their own purposes of controlling others. Rationality should be the only true religion, whereby discarding all primeval dogma."

They slowly drove back to their hotel. All of them felt a sense of victory, but with heavy hearts. Strange, Rauf thought, that the death of a man whose original intention was to kill them, was the cause of their depression.

When they arrived at their hotel, Fatima was eagerly waiting for them. Her quizzical expression was clear to Rauf, that she wanted to know where Osman was. Rauf quickly explained to her what had happened, their success in the mission and Osman's suicide. He did not give her any details of Osman's torture of Ghaznavi or of his suicide. No one was surprised when Fatima started to cry.

"Do not cry for Osman, my love, he died a hero. He may have started out on the wrong foot, but he was ultimately responsible for the annihilation of perhaps the most brutal group of terrorists."

Fatima nodded in agreement, only partially convinced.

They decided to immediately go back to Iran. Sooner or later, the annihilation of the terrorists would come to the knowledge of both the Afghan government and other Afghan sympathizers. It could prove dangerous for Iranians and Arabs to be travelling in Afghanistan.

The drive to the border was uneventful and fortunately for them the same border guard was on duty. He asked about their pilgrimage and Fatima was exuberant in relating the sense of satisfaction which she felt. He nodded respectfully but then asked what had happened to their Sikh driver. Fatima was faster and smarter than the others in her response. She explained to the officer that they had seen the wisdom of his words which was the impropriety of going to a Muslim holy site in the company of a pagan. She continued that with a substantial tip they had let the driver go at the first pilgrimage destination. This somehow had a positive effect on the guard and they were immediately allowed to cross into Iran.

Once safely over the border back into Iran, they were no longer as tense as in the previous days. They had started to joke and laugh. "How wonderful it is to be back home where there are no terrorists or religious fanatics," Rauf said.

"Can you imagine that we spent our childhood and youth in this country which was governed solely by fanaticism and hatred for all non-Muslims? We accepted that as the norm and did not question the arrogance and ignorance of the religious fanatics who taught us in schools. One man turns up from a foreign land and enlightens us to our ancient culture and civilization and awakens us to the error of our ways. May God preserve our Shahnshah."

Fatima looked at him with deep affection as she did not want to talk about her past to the others, but wanted to express her feelings to her husband about the Shahnshah and his regime.

"He has brought civilization to Iran and been a guide in the lives of devastated citizens to help them become happily married couples. Iran is indeed indebted to our Shahnshah!"

As they were driving through the countryside, they noticed some other aspects of their beloved land. They had newly paved highways with speed limits of one hundred and twenty kilometres per hour, posted on cement columns. Beautiful new cities, clean and prosperous. Education was free for all citizens from nursery school through to university. There was protection for the retired and elderly citizens. Medical care was free for every one and above all, the total annihilation of religious oppression from any sector upon another.

The approach to Tehran was a sight to behold. Shiny new skyscrapers, bright lights, beautiful hotels and restaurants. Most women were in western attire and quite a few now did not cover their heads or faces. The Shahnshah had taken Iran from a hole in the heart of Asia and placed it into the heart of Europe.

CHAPTER 39.

The news of the total annihilation of Ghaznavi and his group of terrorists was a hit all over the Middle East and Europe. No one could prove that we were responsible for the extermination of the Afghan terrorists, but it was suspected that we were the only ones who would be interested in doing so. Thereafter a very interesting phenomenon developed. The opposition from the fanatical elements in Iran dwindled considerably. The terrorist groups in the Arab states and Pakistan had come to the conclusion that we were too strong to be dealt with and as a result we were left alone. They concentrated their activities in other parts of the Middle East.

I learnt a brand-new lesson in the thinking pattern of the uneducated classes. As long as it was feasible, they would perpetuate oppression and violence against anyone who disagreed with them. However, if you retaliate in kind and they felt threatened, they were fickle enough to start admiring all the features of your policy and government.

The uncultured mind did not work on logic but, on emotions which had no connection to logical facts. Some of the biggest fanatics, who had opposed our regime and were willing to die as long as they were the ones to perpetuate this, were now loudly proclaiming that they had been misinformed or they misinterpreted our motives and beliefs. I suppose this amounted to what is generally described as `join them if you cannot beat them'. Basically it is the militant's way of hiding his defeat and pretending that they had befriended us and were instrumental in changing our concepts and ideals.

Resistance against my government and administration in Iran had almost disappeared. The most fervent religious elements were convinced that my purpose was not to crush Islam but in fact to protect and enhance its noble concepts originally enunciated by the great prophet, Mohamed. I came to the conclusion that it was the proper time and environment to institute a written constitution for Iran, which would outlive my existence and perpetuate the reforms we had brought about for centuries to come.

The following philosophy and dicta now became the law of Democratic Iran:

The wealth that oil had brought to Iran was a temporary feature for two reasons. All oil resources anywhere in the world were of limited duration. They would be exhausted sooner or later. For this reason I passed a law that sixty percent of the income from oil resources must be utilized to develop other industries in Iran.

A good portion of our national revenue was now used to educate the citizens. All education including University was totally free. Men and women were treated equally and were to be educated in the same manner. Any interference with the education of women was a criminal offense with very serious consequences. The `Unity Commission,' which I established would severely punish the parents of a girl, who interfered with her education. In the last five years almost eighty four percent of all young people were in University. Forty percent of people over the age of thirty had been encouraged to join universities and had obtained degrees. Education in practical fields such as engineering, medicine and business, were distinctly encouraged and as a result, business and industry were now booming in Iran.

Women's' rights were now part of the legal system. Monogamy was the law and Sharia law was abolished. Marriage and divorce could not be conducted by any religious institution or authorities. They had to be completed by the judiciary. Pardah attire for Muslim women was abolished. If a woman wanted to cover her face, that was her privilege and right but enforcement by the inferior generation, such as parents and even husbands was illegal. A woman had the right to complain to the Unity Commission, which would summon the offenders and warn them to desist. If this warning was ignored, the person was imprisoned for five years for the first offence and life on the second occasion.

After reflecting on my past, I came to the conclusion that respect for the inferior generation which were parents and grandparents, was a kind and benevolent thought but it had a detrimental effect on the growth of civilization and progress. The inferiors, since the beginning of history, had enjoyed controlling their children. A majority of these people were either uneducated or less educated than their off-spring, therefore the control over their more sophisticated and educated progeny led to disaster and had to be terminated. Their arguments had always been that age and experience brought wisdom. All it brought was idiocy and prejudice. Elimination of their control was essential in creating a developed and sophisticated population. People did not become wise because they were older. Wisdom and experience were significant only when they came from an educated mind.

The last and most significant change in the law was the total annihilation and removal of religion from the legal field. Every single law in Iran governed all individuals of all religions and so a secular law was passed by Parliament.

A special edict and law was introduced into the legal system to encourage mixed marriages. We wanted to create a population of Iranians which was not Muslim Iranians, Jewish Iranians, Christian Iranians or Zoroastrian Iranians. Intermarriage between these religions was common these days and the State encouraged it by giving a twenty-five percent income tax exemption for life to both parties who intermarried. There had been tremendous animosity between Muslims and Jews prior to my taking charge of Iran and intermarriage between these two communities was absolutely essential for our unity. The income tax exemption granted to these couples was fifty percent for life.

Interference in a mixed marriage by any parent or relative was defined as the crime of "Interference with the Unity of the Nation." Any person who was involved in this activity would be summoned by the Unity Commission, which would do its utmost to advise the person that this was a crime. He would be permitted one week to approach the intended couple to retract his objections. Failure to do so was followed by a trial and if they were found guilty they were summarily executed.

CHAPTER 40.

President Obama and I had become very close friends. We had established a computer line where we could discuss political issues without any one ever being able to retrieve that information. It was common for us to just to contact each other by e-mail to discuss current political issues of the world and seek each others opinion.

I was surprised when I received a formal invitation from President Obama for an international conference. He had come to the conclusion that my suggestion for a union of specific states as guardians of the Middle East was not a bad idea. He had arranged with the British Prime Minister and the Prime Ministers of Canada, Germany, France, Turkey and Russia to hold a meeting in London. I was surprised that my idea was so easily accepted by these Western powers.

The Turkish president and I had already discussed all these matters in great detail and had agreed on the issues which we were going to suggest to the Western powers. The only significant power to convince was Russia. The President very strongly felt that this issue should be raised by me rather than the Western powers, since Russia did not trust the West, but they considered us as a second grade power which could not do them any serious harm.

Russia was also seriously concerned about Islamic fundamentalism slowly creeping into the ex Soviet Asian republics, which were now independent and any intervention by them would be looked upon as interference in their domestic matters. That whole issue could be so easily avoided if an Islamic state like Iran was discouraging any kind of fanaticism. One thing about the Russians had to be admired. They were always very well-informed of the political situation in the ex-Soviet States.

They knew that Iran had now become an ideal nation in the eyes of the so-called Soviet `States'. If that ideal nation was using its influence to keep Islam at the personal level, while propagating the true and sophisticated philosophy of the Prophet Mohamed and actively discouraging any kind of violence and terrorism, the possibility of Iran's philosophy being accepted was far greater than any propaganda presented by Russia. Particularly as the brutal oppression of the Soviet government against these people was still remembered by the residents of Soviet Central Asia. I anticipated that there would be no difficulty in convincing Russia to support our scheme of a protective union in the Middle East. It was however necessary to convince them that we were not the underlings of the Americans or of the British.

My private jet arrived at London's Heathrow airport on schedule at 10.00 a.m. From the window of the aircraft I had noticed a contingent of the British army surrounding the building and the area of the airport. As the door opened up I noticed approximately ten British officers on either side of the staircase and in front of me, stood Prime Minister Gordon Brown with an extended hand and a warm smile.

"Your Majesty, on behalf of her Majesty the Queen and the British people I welcome you to Britain."

I shook his hand warmly. "Mr. Prime Minister, as you know I became a chartered accountant and finished my education in your lovely country. That was such a long time ago and yet, there are memories of my life in Britain which I still cherish."

He quickly walked me to a waiting Rolls-Royce and beckoned me to take a seat. As soon as he got in, the luxurious car pulled out from the airport at high speed. He looked at me with a smile, "Your Majesty, you are an honored guest of our Queen and we want to be absolutely sure that you are well protected. Please forgive the haste and speed at which we are moving. On a personal note Sir, as a Prime Minister, I can sincerely state that of all the dignitaries I have received in this country, there is not a single person whom I've admired and respected more than you."

"That is very kind of you Mr. Prime Minister. I am equally delighted to meet you and to express my gratitude for the warm welcome I have received from you and Britain."

Mr. Brown was silent for quite a while as the vehicle was driven in the direction of one of the royal residences which was reserved for me.

"As the necessary formalities have now been completed, Your Majesty, I would like to express my respect for what you have achieved. There are Prime Ministers and Presidents who come and go. Their impact on their own countries is minimal. Britain and America progress from year-to-year and will continue to do so. The contribution of the Prime Minister or the President in our countries is of minimal significance, but, Sir, today I'm sitting next to a man who at the age of seventy, has settled in an alien country and has mastered its language, culture and traditions. He has made himself acceptable as the Emperor and sole ruler of the nation, has succeeded in changing the fanatical beliefs of the majority of its citizens and transformed it from a backward Asiatic nation into a sophisticated and modern democratic state." He smiled, "don't you think Shahnshah, that there is a slight difference between your achievements and mine?"

I returned his smile and the exuberant warmth he had exhibited towards me. "They claim that the British have a stiff upper lip." I said with a smile. "Perhaps brilliant men like you are responsible for creating such warmth in the British people."

We both smiled at each other and I suddenly realized that warmth and friendship with this man was a clear possibility.

CHAPTER 41.

The international conference was officially hosted by Prime Minister Brown of Great Britain. The concept and arrangements were at the behest of President Obama of the United States. The Prime Ministers and Chancellors of France, Germany, Italy and Russia had been invited to the meeting. From the Middle East, the Turkish President the Israeli Prime Minister and I were all part of this meeting.

Upon arrival at the conference center which was very close to the House of Commons in London, I was greeted very warmly by Prime Minister Brown and then ushered to my seat. President Obama went over to the podium to introduce me to the other delegates.

"Warm greetings from the United States of America to all my acquaintances. I have a unique duty to perform today and I promise you that I am going to immensely enjoy this conference. I would like to introduce you all to one of the most remarkable people I have ever met, Sharuq Damania, the Shahnshah of Iran. I will not go into details about his qualifications and experience as a chartered accountant but, in that career his greatest achievement was to create an economic bond between Canada and Japan that is unparalleled. Business contacts established by him are still prevalent even though his Majesty the Shahnshah has not resided in Canada for over seven years. Let me list his achievements in Iran. He was a total foreigner to Iran when he was invited by the Iranians to become their Shahnshah. He had never visited the land nor spoke one single word of Farsi. Today, his political discourses and speeches in Farsi to the Iranian people have become classics and are read by all intellectuals. That is evidence of his intellectual calibre. Let us look at his achievements as a world class statesman."

"The Shahnshah took Iran out of the control of religious fanatics and developed industry, education and hospitalization. Today, total equality for all religious groups, equal rights for women and total annihilation of religious persecution have been established by him. Oil revenues were used to develop industry so that today the most prosperous nation on the continent of Asia is Iran."

"Apart from all that, I believe the most significant thing achieved by his Majesty, is that even the most fanatical elements of the Iranian population are now his firm supporters. He has convinced them that he is not antagonistic to Islam or trying to destroy their religion, but in fact has espoused the noble concepts originally introduced by the Prophet Mohamed and developed them to fit in with the thinking and economic patterns of the twenty-first century."

"Economic and political successes are both laudable achievements but the capacity to change the thinking pattern of a whole population and to convert your antagonists and attackers into faithful followers, is tantamount to a supernatural event. That, ladies and gentlemen, is what the Shahnshah has achieved."

"I therefore have the great pleasure and honor to introduce his Imperial Majesty, Sharuq Damania, the Shahnshah of Iran. Lastly, I will add with pride and joy, also my close and dear friend."

I was almost embarrassed at the description given of me, but I would be lying if I said I was not tickled pink. As I walked to the podium all delegates gave me a standing ovation of welcome.

"Greetings, my allies and friends. I have the privilege of being introduced to you by one of the most brilliant and powerful men in the world. I do not have to convince you of those facts but it gives me great pleasure that a man of his calibre has described me as a friend. Let us not talk of brilliance, intellect and power for a few minutes. Let us just talk of charm. When President Obama was in Iran, we took great care to protect him. However, there was one other area which while causing us concern did not require much effort to protect him. Every single female between the ages of fifteen and sixty was enamoured by his charm. Our troops had to intervene to keep them away from him. That, in spite of the fact that he was always in the company of his beautiful wife, the First Lady of the United States. I must add that as far as I was concerned, if given the choice, the President would have avoided the protection provided by our Armed Forces and mingled freely with the ladies, because some of them were indeed extremely beautiful." There was laughter and clapping from the audience.

"Jokes apart ladies and gentlemen I'm not here to tell you about the power of the President of the United States. Every man in this position has power. I'm here to tell you of the kindness and warmth that exuberates from him. This proves two things to me. I have been fortunate in obtaining the friendship of such an intelligent and kind man and the United States has finally proved to the world that the only qualifications needed for a President are his capacity and kindness. I would therefore like to congratulate the United States on their choice."

"Now that the introductions have been made and all formalities have been completed, let me take you to my own modest analysis of Iran and Islam. Can anyone of you tell me who was the first human being on this earth who brought a certain degree of protection and financial independence and rights to women? Was he a European? Was he an American? Was he Japanese? No, ladies and gentlemen, the first human being who brought financial security and protection for women was the Prophet Mohamed of Islam. I am not talking about the equality that we presently have in the Western world. I am not suggesting for a moment that the reforms he brought about are sufficient or can be compared to what we have in today's world. That is not the issue. In a world which was basically barbaric, this great man brought protection and support for women. It is the seventh century A.D. we are referring to, when we talk about Prophet Mohamed. Let us not forget that as late as the first few years of the twentieth century, women had no property rights in the civilized countries of Europe and America. So the conclusion I'm presenting to you is, we must judge a person's achievement from the point of view of the era in which he or she lived. My conclusion therefore is that Prophet Mohamed's achievement for his era was absolutely magnificent. I would also like you to note something. I am not a Muslim but a Zoroastrian, a person whose ancestors were so oppressed by fanatical Arab conquerors, that they were forced to emigrate to India."

The culture and civilization that Prophet Mohamed generated continued to develop. Algebra, geometry, geography, astronomy were developed and in fact brought to Europe by the Moors who were Muslims. The brutality of the Spanish Inquisitions did not exist when the Moors ruled Spain and Portugal. Then what happened? The civilized countries of the Islamic world collapsed one after the other. Was that the result of the Mongol conquests? I do not know the answer to that but one of the most peaceful eras in India was the period of the Mogul empire and the Moguls were Muslims."

Today, once again, the Middle East has fallen prey to fanatics and fundamentalists. Let us destroy these people and their beliefs, not the civilizing influence of Islam. Fanaticism is the degeneration of their faith. Let us not throw the baby out with the bath water . I have attempted to do this in my Iran and hopefully, I've succeeded to some extent. It is my wish that neighboring nations will join us in propagating the good side of Islam and eliminating fanaticism and bigotry. With the utmost respect, ladies and gentlemen, the world's greatest sickness is not cancer or AIDS, it is faith. Faith without rationality and evidence is used by uneducated bigots to control the world. To act rationally is very difficult, if not impossible, so they loudly proclaim their faith to control the masses. It is this disease that we must eliminate. Let us not tolerate any belief or faith without scientific evidence to support it. This is what I'm hoping to achieve in my Iran."

"The epitome of ignorance and fanaticism is the Taliban. Their destruction of the twin Towers in New York City was not just a tragedy suffered by America but was the main cause of the destruction and enormous loss of life in Afghanistan. Who was the biggest loser in this dispute? The people of Afghanistan. The United States and her allies are completely justified in trying to exterminate the Taliban and Al Qaeda. The difficulty is that the culture of Afghanistan and the Middle East is so alien to the Americans and the Europeans that after occupying these lands, several mistakes were made by the occupying powers. I will give you an example. Apparently there was some sort of unrest near the famous Iraqi mosque in Karbala. Without intending to offend, American troops surrounded the area, gained complete control and then tried to ease the situation by playing Western music. In your eyes that would be a very normal behavior pattern, but from the point of view of the religious Arabs that was considered an insult. It is therefore absolutely essential that the cultural aspects of the Middle East and Afghanistan be completely understood and appreciated by the American and Allied forces. This alone can lead to success in achieving peace in the area".

I must compliment the British on their achievements during their rule in India. The significant military and political officers were very well-versed in Indian culture and traditions. After their near defeat in the Indian mutiny of 1857, Lord Roberts, the representative of the British government, demanded the surrender from the last Mogul Emperor of India in perfect Urdu. That sounds rather trivial but consider the situation where the ruling Indian families consider the British outsiders who were taking over their land and suddenly the commander-in-chief, or chief political officer, speaks to them in their own language. Let us not forget that the people of the Middle East and India are very sentimental and temperamentally exuberant. Such a gesture to them is tantamount to evidence that even though they may be dealing with an antagonist, the individual had taken the trouble and effort to absorb their culture by learning their language."

"The President of the United States and I have discussed this matter in great detail. We have both come to the conclusion that we Iranians are far better qualified to understand and deal with the people of the Middle East, since we are a part of the same culture. It was President Obama who suggested that we make Turkey and Iran the military and political guardians of the Middle East. You have seen for yourselves that I have succeeded to a very great extent in eliminating fundamentalist fanaticism in Iran, which as you know, is the most powerful military nation in the Middle East."

Our closest ally, Turkey, is an equally powerful military state with one further qualification over us. Turkey was once blessed with one of the most brilliant reformers of history, Mustafa Kemal Attaturk, the man who single-handedly separated religion from politics and created the first civilized republic in the Middle East. I am happy that my friend and colleague, President Ata Khan of Turkey, is here today. I will not hesitate to tell you that a large number of decisions I made to bring Iran into the twenty-first century, were decisions that had already been made by the great Mustafa Kemal Ataturk more than a hundred years ago."

"Thank you ladies and gentleman for giving me the opportunity to address you and for listening to me so carefully. All further decisions are in your hands and I have complete faith in your acumen and appreciation of the problems of the Middle East."

I bowed and took my seat. All the leaders stood up and clapped but that had no effect on me. I had to control my emotions not because of my speech, but because of the intense love I felt for my Iran.

Prime Minister Brown of Great Britain and several of the other dignitaries present, spoke for a few minutes each and then the conference ended and we moved to an adjoining hall for discussions. There were a lot of questions about Iran and its future and I noticed that almost all of the leaders were very positive about our contribution to the peace in the Middle East. It was approximately 5:00 p.m. when the conference ended and we were free to return to our residences.

Prime Minister Brown approached me with a warm smile. "Your Majesty, as I've already told you I have admired you for several years, but that was for your achievements in Iran. I had no idea that you were such a brilliant speaker."

I bowed to thank him.

"Her Majesty the Queen has asked that I invite you to Buckingham Palace for dinner tonight if you are available. Needless to say I will accompany you to the royal residence.

"I will be honored to visit and pay my respects to the Queen."

The visit to Buckingham Palace was interesting and enlightening to me in several ways. The Queen greeted me as a monarch from one country welcoming a monarch from another country. I still remembered the days when I was a student in England, most of them being happy days. I had no difficulty living and studying in England and I asked myself the question, how would I have reacted if at that time some one had told me that I would one day be invited to Buckingham Palace to meet the Queen and Prince Philip as their equal. My impression that Royalty would be snobbish and distant was totally incorrect. Her Majesty was very kind, warm and surprisingly, extremely well informed on the history of Iran and my contribution to its development.

One very significant aspect of the meeting was my feelings that Her Majesty indicated that I was a friend and ally of Britain and the one who was responsible for bringing Iran into a close relationship with Western Europe and America. This was particularly gratifying, because I had always held Her Majesty in great regard. I think the most enjoyable part of the evening was the fact that Prime Minister Brown and I were treated with extreme warmth.

We left Buckingham Palace at approximately 11:30 p.m. and Prime Minister Brown accompanied me to my residence. As he and I had developed a good working relationship, I commented on the warmth which her Majesty had exhibited towards us. He once again brought up the subject of the so-called British reserve and laughingly told me that that had disappeared with the British Empire.

Mr. Brown joined me for a cognac at my residence and we chatted into the wee hours about several other topics in the history of both Britain and Iran.

How many presumptions we make of people, cultures, civilizations and their anticipated reactions. So many of these are based on our own opinions or thinking patterns and attitudes and how wrong we are when we come to conclusions without any evidence based on facts. I, a seventy-two-year-old man, had still to learn a lot about people but, more importantly, about the inaccuracy of preconceived notions.

CHAPTER 42.

After several discussions and meetings over a period of one week the final document for the treaty now described as MEDU,(Middle East Defence Union), was finalized. Basically the concept involved making Turkey and Iran the guardians of the Middle East. Any Middle Eastern country was free to join the Union but in order to do so, they had to agree that no military action would be taken against a neighboring nation under any circumstances without the approval of the Union itself.

One of the major concerns in the Middle East was the creation of an independent Palestine. The second most important issue was the Jewish settlements constantly on the increase in the territory described as Palestine. The State of Israel had other concerns, mainly the continuous rockets launched from Gaza and Palestine and the necessary retaliations and loss of life on both sides. If Palestine and Israel could join MEDU, then both would be forced to cease firing.

Israel had already agreed to join MEDU and was willing to let the Union determine the exact territory which would be ceded over to Palestine. On the other hand Israel wanted the guarantee that its territory would be completely safe from aggression and bombardment of any kind. They were not satisfied with any commitment made by the Arab states or Palestine. They wanted MEDU to make that commitment and enforce it. The governments of Syria, Jordan, Lebanon and the existing Palestinian Authority, had been contacted and the matter was discussed. Syria, Jordan and Lebanon all realized that once the Union was established, any military opposition on their part would become a physical impossibility because under no circumstances could they militarily succeed against a Union consisting of Iran and Turkey which were militarily equipped and supported by the United States and Western European powers and again not opposed by Russia.

They agreed that if an independent Palestinian state was established and Israel ceded that portion of the territory to Palestine, the Arab states would see to it that no aggression would be permitted from any of the Arab states including Palestine and Gaza against Israel.

The only issue which was very difficult to negotiate and which was vehemently opposed by Israel was ceding East Jerusalem to Palestine. I personally had discussed this matter with Arab leaders and the Palestinian Authority and suggested to them that East Jerusalem should be allowed to remain in Israeli territory and in return some other area of Israel could be ceded over to Palestine. The Palestinians very vehemently opposed this but as they were not supported by the other Arab nations, they were seriously considering acceptance of the offer.

The most significant thing that we expected to achieve with the creation of MEDU was to eliminate any battles between the nations of the Middle East starting from Turkey and ending in Afghanistan. Whether these nations agreed to join MEDU or not, they would be compelled to bring their dispute to us and we would settle it with or without their cooperation, but by free and democratic vote of all the member nations. If the two antagonistic states did not comply with our decision, then military force would be used if necessary against both of them. This would have two advantages. War in the Middle East would basically be banned and all the Middle Eastern nations would grudgingly join MEDU to have a voice in Middle Eastern affairs.

In return for these arrangements, the U.S.A. and Western Europe accepted Iran as a nuclear nation. As to exports from the Middle East, the first preference would be given to Iranian exports, which would be admitted duty free. Industrial supplies would be provided to Iran duty free as well. Enormous quantities of the most sophisticated military equipment would be provided to MEDU by the U.S.A. and Western Europe, though in reality it would all be handed over to Iran only.

Western Europe and the U.S.A. would wash their hands of the Middle East, thereby saving billions of dollars and thousands of lives.

The death knells of Al Qaeda, Hamas, Hezbollah and other fanatical groups could now be anticipated.

CHAPTER 43.

The night before my departure for Iran there was a farewell party for all visiting dignitaries from Europe and the United States. Prime Minister Brown and President Obama treated me with the utmost warmth and affection. I felt that I was a colleague and a friend rather than a politician from another country.

President Obama sat next to me smiling as he said and handed me a glass, "Sharuq, you fellas from the Middle East always thought that only the Russians knew how to spy. We Americans also do a good job. Taste your scotch and tell me how you like it." I took a sip and gave him a beaming smile.

"A drink fit for the President of the United States." I said. "Johnnie Walker blue label. The only pity is that it is given to me by a man who doesn't have a clue what a good scotch tastes like." I laughed.

"That comment comes from a man who is the leader and Shahnshah of a nation that forbade the consumption of alcohol." We both laughed.

The party lasted beyond midnight, after which I was driven back to my residence. I went to bed because I had to take a flight in the morning back to Iran.

As I lay down in bed trying to sleep I once again realized how many beliefs and expectations were illusions. I had recently dealt with three or four of the most powerful men on earth. Needless to say most of them were brilliant. Some were kind, some not so kind, but a majority of them were capable of warmth, friendship and loyalty. Everything was dependant upon the circumstances in which you met them.

The next morning my plane took off from London's Heathrow Airport at approximately 10.00a.m.. bound for Iran. For security purposes, the Royal Air Force escorted our plane until we had flown over Southern Europe and onto North Eastern Africa. I still had approximately four hours to get to Tehran and I decided to relax and think of what I had to do when I got home. No amount of concentration on my work and responsibilities could take my mind off the delightful expectation of taking Zainab into my arms and making love to her. I chided myself that a man of seventy-two and the Shahnshah of Iran had no business to think of sex and love when he had so many important things to think about. Most of my brain and body agreed with my conclusions, but there was one portion of my anatomy which refused to settle down.

Upon our arrival into Tehran I was received by my Ministers and Military personnel. They greeted me with exuberant joy and pride by telling me that in their opinion I had converted Iran from a backward Middle Eastern nation into a world power. Literally hundreds of news reporters tried to get a statement from me, but my welcoming committee shooed them away because they knew that I needed rest and relaxation after my arduous journey. I kept smiling at the reporters but was quite happy that I did not have to answer their usual redundant questions. My Rolls-Royce was escorted by the military security to the Royal residence and after I entered my palace and the doors were closed, I once again saw the most beautiful sight that I have ever seen in the world.

My Zainab was standing there in the light blue full length skirt which I had purchased for her. The skirt had a slit on the side and when she was walking, the slit made her wiggle seem extremely attractive. She was blushing and her green eyes were looking devotedly at me. There was a secret understanding between the two of us. I would very often call her on our private line from my office and would tell her that I was dying to make love to her and that she should be ready. It was understood that if I called she would wear that light blue skirt. Normally, she was quite shy about approaching the subject of making love and for that reason we had a second understanding, that if she wore that skirt without my asking her to do so, it was tantamount to making a suggestion that she desired me.

Of course I had just returned from England and had had no communication with her for at least two days, so therefore that skirt was my invitation to make love. Our relationship had been so sweet and tender that the actual lovemaking was secondary to the tender discussion and communication between us about the act itself.

After we had finished making love, I held her in my arms until she fell asleep. I asked myself the question. What was my greatest achievement in life, was it becoming the Shahnshah of Iran and making a modern sophisticated nation out of Iran, or was it winning the love and totally possessing and being possessed by my Zainab. The answer was clear to me. Becoming the Shahnshah of Iran was the proud achievement of my life, Zainab was life itself.

I fell asleep and there were no dreams for my dream was in my arms.